"You can't blame me," Millie argued.

No, he couldn't, Sam admitted to himself. This was all his fault. If he hadn't gotten the fool notion about Millie's dress into his head, he could have gone on thinking about her as a...well, a troublesome hostage. But now he was going to be hard pressed to look at her again without thinking of her as she appeared at this moment, that camisole sticking to her collarbone and cleavage, her petticoats outlining her tiny waist, hips and shapely legs.

Damn. He trained his eyes away, toward the spot where they'd left the horses. "All right. It's my fault. Now hurry up and get your clothes on."

She shot him an exasperated look. "First you want them off, now you want them on! And all the while you keep pointing that gun at me—how do you expect me to act efficiently under these circumstances?"

Patience! Sam told himself....

Dear Reader,

Liz Ireland's first book, *Man Trap*, won her the *RT* Award for Best Silhouette Romance of the Year in 1993. Now this talented young author has turned her hand to historical novels and we are delighted to be able to bring you her newest title, *Millie and the Fugitive*. This wonderful story is about an innocent man running from the law who is forced to take along a spoiled rich girl, only to discover that she is the best thing that's ever happened to him. We hope you'll enjoy it.

Pearl is part of *Romantic Times* Lifetime Achievement Award winner Ruth Langan's new THE JEWELS OF TEXAS series featuring four sisters, brought together by the death of their father. It's the story of an Eastern-bred schoolteacher and the rough-and-tumble ranch foreman who wants her sent back home where she belongs. Don't miss any of this terrific series.

Badlands Bride, by Cheryl St.John, is about a newspaper reporter who goes west pretending to be a mail-order bride, only to find herself stranded in the Dakotas for a long cold winter. While Margaret Moore's new Medieval novel, *The Baron's Quest*, is the story of a rough-edged Saxon who falls in love with the refined gentlewoman whom he has inherited along with his new holdings.

We hope you'll keep a lookout for all four titles wherever Harlequin Historicals are sold.

Sincerely,

Tracy Farrell
Senior Editor

Please address questions and book requests to:
Harlequin Reader Service
U.S.: 3010 Walden Ave., P.O. Box 1325, Buffalo, NY 14269
Canadian: P.O. Box 609, Fort Erie, Ont. L2A 5X3

Millie
AND THE
FUGITIVE

LIZ IRELAND

Harlequin Books

TORONTO • NEW YORK • LONDON
AMSTERDAM • PARIS • SYDNEY • HAMBURG
STOCKHOLM • ATHENS • TOKYO • MILAN
MADRID • WARSAW • BUDAPEST • AUCKLAND

ISBN 0-373-28930-8

MILLIE AND THE FUGITIVE

Printed in U.S.A.

Books by Liz Ireland

Harlequin Historicals

Cecilia and the Stranger #286
Millie and the Fugitive #330

Silhouette Romance

Man Trap #963
The Birds and the Bees #988
Mom for a Week #1058

LIZ IRELAND

lives in her native state of Texas, a place she feels gives her a never-ending supply of colorful characters. Aside from writing romance novels and tending to two very demanding cats and a guard dachshund, she enjoys spending time reading history or cozying up with an old movie.

Chapter One

Texas, 1880

"It'll be slow going to Huntsville, boys, with me trussed up like last year's Christmas goose," Sam Houston Winter said, lifting his shackled wrists as evidence of his hindered movement.

Toby Jenkins and Ed Herman, the two deputies riding to his left and to his right respectively, exchanged quick glances and chuckles. The two had loosened their demeanor since they'd left Chariton and their boss, Sheriff Tom McMillan, behind a mile ago. Now Sam had to see whether he could convince the pair to loosen *him*.

"You sure take it on the chin, Sam," Toby said, shaking his head. "Two years in the state prison ahead of you, and you still got a sense of humor."

Ed laughed his wheezy laugh again in agreement with Toby. "Can't say I'd be the same, if'n I was in your boots."

"No, sir," Toby said. "Though I think I would have done the same as you, Sam, if my brother was about to be hanged as a murderer."

"You don't have a brother, Toby," Ed argued. He had to lean forward a little to see his sparring partner across Sam's chest.

"No, but if'n I did, and if they was gonna hang him, then I'd do just what Sam did, and try to hide him."

"Sure you would. I would, too," Ed said. "But what I was just sayin' was that I wouldn't be laughin' when the judge threw me in the clink for aidin' a criminal."

"I know that, Ed," Toby said with irritation. "Wasn't you listening? I was only sayin' I'd do the same thing. Except for the sense-of-humor part," he clarified. "Like you, I wouldn't have no sense of humor about it, neither, like Sam here has."

"No?" Ed asked, a wry smile on his tobacco stained lips. "Maybe that's 'cause you never had one to begin with!"

The two threw back their heads in riotous, whooping laughter.

It was going to be an even longer ride than he'd imagined, Sam thought dismally. Yet the annoying duo steeled his determination to make a break for it.

"Anyway, it's a shame we have to poke along like turtles on account of me," Sam said, lifting his shoulders in a shrug after the two had tamped down their guffaws.

Ed's face was sober for a blessed moment. "Sorry it has to be this way, Sam."

"Me, too," Toby said.

"Stupid rules. Me and Toby both know you wouldn't swat a fly. You only did what you did—which wasn't much, really—'cause Jesse was your brother."

"Same as we would have done."

Sam held his breath, dreading a repeat of their prior interchange, but the two seemed lost in thought. Serious thought, if the way Ed's yellowed teeth sawed on his lower lip was any indication.

"You know, Toby," Ed asked after a moment, "how is it that Sam's all trussed up like so? It's not like *he* was a murderer."

"But he's a prisoner, just the same."

Ed nodded, as if he had forgotten this minor point. "That's right, Sam. You *are* a prisoner. Much as I hate to say it."

"Me, too," Toby agreed.

"You sure play a hell of a game of poker, though," Ed added as an afterthought.

Toby shook his head wistfully. During Sam's weeks in Chariton's tiny jail, the three of them had whiled away many a tedious hour over a worn deck.

Sometimes they'd even convinced Jesse to join in on a hand, but he'd never taken any pleasure in the game. Jesse was in mourning for Salina, his wife, the woman he'd been convicted of killing. For weeks, nothing had been able to keep him from brooding over his loss, not even his flight from the law, or his capture at Sam's farm, or the hurried, hopeless trial that followed.

Sheriff McMillan, fueled by resentment toward Jesse after he'd testified against the sheriff's son in a trial a year earlier, had seized on just enough evidence to convict Jesse. And he hadn't been interested in any information that might contradict his desire to get his revenge, either. As for the rest of the town, most folks considered the crime so heinous, so shocking, they were eager for especially swift justice.

Sam frowned. Now Jesse was all alone in that cell, with no one to even attempt to take his mind off his troubles. He was sure Jesse didn't even care that he faced the gallows in two weeks' time. Jesse didn't think he had much to live for, now that Salina was gone. But Sam wasn't giving up so easily. In his pocket he had possible evidence of another man's guilt—scant evidence that Tom McMillan, who only wanted a man to hang, wasn't interested in pursuing.

Meanwhile, he waited patiently for Ed and Toby's reasoning to progress to the next step.

"'Course, it's not like Sam's a *violent* criminal, Ed," Toby said. "Hidin' somebody isn't the same as killin' somebody."

Ed shook his head. "Nope. Fact, it's practically the exact opposite."

"Practically," Toby agreed. "Sam here ain't never even said a word against anybody. Not that I've heard."

"Me neither."

"He just done what anybody would have done."

On this much, at least, the two seemed clear. Sam decided to give them a little mental shove. God knew, they needed it.

"Well, I suppose that's just the way with the law," he said nonchalantly. "If you start making exceptions . . ."

"Where would it end?" Toby finished for him.

"Why, sure." Sam was silent a moment, then mused absently, "I wonder whether counterfeiters have to wear handcuffs."

Toby and Ed suddenly looked at each other, their eyes wide and almost alarmed, as if the unexpected question had mentally flummoxed them.

"I don't know," Toby said, his voice filled with wonder. "Do you know, Ed?"

"No, I sure don't."

"Counterfeiter. I ain't never run across one of those." Toby bit his lip and squinted in thought as he stared across the horizon. It was morning still, and the sun was just now beginning to beat down upon them. "I bet they do."

"Bet so." Ed frowned. "But then again, maybe they don't."

"Funny thing is," Toby said, "Sam here is even less dangerous than a counterfeiter, when you think about it."

"He's not even a thief or anything like that."

"Hell no. He's just a brother-hider."

"I mean, who's he hurt?"

"Nobody I know of."

The two looked at each other again, communicating silently over Sam's shoulders.

"And if somebody like a counterfeiter doesn't have to be tied up, then why should Sam?"

"You got me stumped," Ed declared.

"Whoa there, boys," Sam said graciously, hoping the triumphant surge he felt didn't show in his face. They weren't even three miles out of town yet. This was too easy. "I don't want to get you in trouble with your boss man."

"With Sheriff Tom?" Ed asked incredulously.

"Why, Tom trusts us!" Toby protested, as if the idea itself were plumb crazy.

"Would he have let us take you all the way to Huntsville by our lonesome if he didn't trust us to use our, you know..."

"Discretion?" Sam prompted.

"Sure, that's it," Toby said. "We'd just be using our discretion. It's not like you would try to escape."

"You certain of that?" Sam asked, darting his eyebrows up.

"Ha! That's a laugh!" Ed said with another wheezing chuckle. "Hold up there, Toby, let's let old poker face here out of these iron traps. He's right, it'll make for faster travelin'."

Easy, it was too easy, Sam thought, proffering his wrists with an admirable show of reluctance.

Toby tossed a large ring of keys over Sam's horse to Ed. "Here, take care of it, will you? I've got to water a bush."

"Already? Hell, it's gonna be slow goin' anyway, even without Sam cuffed." Ed laughed heartily as Toby disappeared to the other side of a scrubby little elm.

After only minimal fumbling, the bonds fell away in a noisy clatter to Sam's saddle. Far too easy. Providence couldn't have sent him two more gullible jailers.

"Now we just have to wait for old leaky-drawers," Ed mused, shifting in his saddle and looking off in the direction where Toby had disappeared. "I swear, the man's as bad as—"

The sound of the cuffs hitting the back of Ed's head made a dull *clump* sound, and then the deputy slumped over and listed to the side, falling from his horse. Sam jumped down and eased the man's way to the ground. He wasn't a violent man, normally; ordinarily he would have felt a sting of guilt for taking advantage of the two men's kindness this way. But these weren't ordinary circumstances he was in. He grabbed the rifle off Ed's saddle and held it up toward the tree Toby just then appeared from behind.

"Hey! What's goin' on here?" Toby demanded.

"Ed had a fainting spell," Sam said, keeping his voice raw and cool, his muscles tense. The time for friendly patter had passed. "Drop your gun, Toby."

"Sure thing, Sam," the second deputy said, scooting forward obligingly with one hand stiffly in the air while the other pulled a derringer from its holster and lowered the gun to the earth. "Heck, you know I don't blame you none. I'd do the same if'n I was you."

"Maybe so," Sam said, picking up Toby's derringer and tucking it into his belt. "I don't have time for making excuses. Now get over here and drag Ed back to that tree."

"Whatever you say, Sam," Toby said, grabbing Ed by the armpits and dragging him backward. His frightened eyes never left the barrel of Sam's rifle. Sam grabbed a coil of rope from Ed's saddle and joined Toby by the tree. "I hate to do this to you, friend...."

"You ain't gonna—?" Toby winced and fell to his knees in supplication. "Please, Sam—I've got a widowed mother."

"You'll see your mother again," Sam assured the man, moments before his rifle butt came down on his head. Soon Mama Jenkins would be treating her boy for a nasty bump on the head.

Quickly Sam cuffed the two men together, then propped them up against the tree and bound them tightly to its trunk. He had enough rope for the job and then a good length left over—yet another sign that the Fates were with him this day.

Feeling magnanimous, he trotted back to the horses and retrieved a canteen of water from one of the saddles. He returned to the two men and propped the water between them.

He didn't want them to die—he just didn't want them to be found for at least a day or two. After a final whack on the head for each of them, he turned and drove two of the horses away, saving the gamest one for his own flight.

The black would have to ride hard in the days ahead. It was nearly four days to the south and west to Little Bend, the town where he had business. Dead-serious business. And Jesse's date with the hangman in two weeks left him precious little time.

He mounted the black and kicked him into an easy lope, due west. In spite of the tension that ate at his insides, a wide smile broke out across his lips. At least he was off to a good start. Yes, sir. Things couldn't have gone much better if he'd planned it step by step.

Then he heard a noise. A horse's whinny, high and shrill.

He sawed the reins of the black and brought him to a stop, turning in his saddle. The other two horses had galloped off in the opposite direction from where the sound had come from. Tense, alert, he surveyed the landscape around him. There wasn't much to it. Just a sloping, grass-covered hill, dotted with elms and other unremarkable trees. Except one...

His eyes caught sight of what he'd been looking for. On the other side of the tree stood a horse, a pretty little dappled gray mare. Raising his rifle with one arm, he rode slowly toward the tree where the horse was tethered. A pear tree. Its branches sagged with fruit.

Sam stopped. He didn't like this at all. A riderless horse practically within spitting distance of where he'd clunked two deputies over the head... Maybe his luck wasn't so good today after all.

"Who's there?" he asked, his finger tense on the trigger. Having come this far, he was ready to shoot his way out of trouble if he had to.

But as his eyes scanned the area once again, he noted something interesting. The mare was outfitted with a side-saddle, polished to a high gloss. Sam had seen few of those ridiculous-looking things in his twenty-eight years. Yet the sight of it made him relax a little. It was only a woman.

He hoped she was alone.

Where the hell could she be?

Just then, his gaze alit on precisely what he'd been looking for—a dainty tan boot peeking out from beneath a limb of the pear tree. The woman was treed...but she'd also been in a perfect position to witness him clobbering two deputies.

"All right, lady. Come on out."

A branch rustled nervously, sending a brown pear dropping to the hard ground below. But fruit was all that appeared.

"I know you heard me," he said, riding forward a few more steps. He doubted the person who belonged to those kid-leather boots rode armed.

The closer he came, the more that tree shook, until, as Sam sat directly beneath a bright yellow dress covering a host of frilly starched white petticoats and a tantalizing peek of shapely, pantalet-clad legs, every branch on the tree was quivering. Looking up, he discovered a pair of the darkest, most frightened eyes he'd ever seen staring down at him. She'd heard him, all right. She just wished she hadn't.

"All, right, little lady," he said in the same gruff voice, "come on down now."

In a split second, even though her gaze never left his face, the young woman's entire demeanor changed. A bright, fetching smile broke out across her rosy-red lips, even if the fear remained in her eyes as she hugged even more tightly to the tree trunk.

"Well, my goodness!" she cried, in an overly friendly tone that was betrayed only by a slight anxious crack in her voice. "I *thought* I heard someone!"

"Right," Sam said, lacking the leisure to be amused by her little show of innocence. "You might also have *thought* you saw a man tying two deputies to a tree."

"Deputies?" she asked. "What deputies?"

"Come on, lady," he said, raising the rifle another notch.

Her expression turned deadly earnest, and she shook her head fervently. "Oh, no, I swear. I didn't see a thing. My— my lips are forever sealed."

"If you didn't see anything, what are they sealed against?"

"That's just it," she insisted. "They won't be able to get a single solitary word out of me, Mr.— I'm sorry, what is your name?"

"Not a chance," he told her.

Desperation crossed her face. "You've got to believe me," she pleaded. "I wouldn't tell a soul I saw anything, even if I did. Which I didn't. Ask anyone. I'm honest to a fault. I never break my word. Never, never, never, never— Ooooh!"

He grabbed her booted foot and tugged. "Are you coming down, or am I going to have to drag you?"

"No!" It took her a moment to regain her composure, not to mention her equilibrium, as her right foot struggled for balance on a narrow limb. "I mean, of course I'll come down," she said, trying the pleasant tactic again. "I'm most eager to make your acquaintance."

"I'll bet."

He leaned against the saddle horn for a moment as the young woman fussed and fidgeted, alternately shooting nervous glances at him and studying with some confusion her position in the tree. "My goodness..." she mumbled absently. "I got up here so fast, I never considered how to get down...."

Sam sighed. He didn't have time for this. "Do you want some help?"

"No, no— Oooh!"

Before she could waste any more precious moments, Sam reached up with both hands, grabbed her about the knees and pulled firmly. It didn't take much effort. In a cascade of starched cotton and pears, the young woman landed across the saddle in front of him, her keen dark eyes rounded in shock. Both Sam and the girl sucked in surprised gulps of air in reaction to his bold maneuver.

She had to be the lightest woman he'd ever held in his arms—not that he made a habit of lifting females. As he looked into her pretty face close up for the first time, he felt a stab of disappointment. This was hardly time for a leisurely getting-acquainted chat with an attractive girl. Seeing the momentary curiosity in the young woman's expression return quickly to fear as she stared back at him reminded him of his purpose.

"Sorry, miss, I'm in a hurry," Sam drawled.

His words, even spoken as casually as they were, sent the young lady over the edge. Tears spilled down her pale cheeks, and she recoiled from him, grabbing behind her at the black mane of his horse. "Please don't kill me," she pleaded frantically as she attempted to squirm away.

"I won't," Sam said.

"Please! I won't say a word—on my honor!"

"I don't believe you, but I'm not going to kill you."

She ran a hand through her tangled black hair, her gaze darting frantically across the horizon all the while, no doubt hoping for rescue. "My daddy will pay you any amount of money for me, if you'll only let me live."

"Lady, haven't you listened to a word I've said?" Sam asked. "I'm not going to kill you."

"What?" She stared at him dubiously.

"I'm not a murderer."

"Yes, you are!" she cried vehemently. "I saw—"

"You saw what?"

Her voice was suddenly meek. "Nothing." But she didn't have to say a word for him to imagine exactly what she'd seen, or what she thought she'd seen.

Sam couldn't help it. He laughed bitterly. Had he really thought the Fates were with him? No such luck! He had a witness who had been close enough to watch him tie up two deputies and club them on the head, but too far away to notice that he hadn't killed them. Now he had to figure out what to do with her.

"Daddy can walk into the bank and take out thousands of dollars for you, just as soon as I'm returned. Believe me, I won't fail to mention how you rescued me from that tree."

"Money's not what I'm after," Sam replied.

"Then how about dry goods?" she asked hopefully. "My father owns a store. There's all sorts of things there you might want. Fabric, food, guns... Well, he naturally might not want to give you guns—"

"Quiet!" He couldn't think, with her frantic babbling in his ear.

What could he do with her? Hitting two men on the head was one thing, but a woman . . . He had never hit a woman before. Besides, a woman was more delicate. He couldn't risk causing her serious harm, or, worse, accidentally killing her. That *would* make him a murderer. He looked down at the rope in his hands. Same if he tied her up. He didn't know when someone would find the two deputies. Could be today, could be a few days.

This woman was just a skinny little thing. Wiry. Despite her dark hair and eyes, she had pale skin that looked soft and pampered. He doubted she'd last two hours out here if he gagged her and tied her up.

What in the Sam Hill was he going to do?

"Why are you looking at me like that?" she blurted out fearfully. "If you don't believe me about my father, just ask anyone. My name's Millie—"

"I don't want to know your name."

"But if you'd just listen—"

"Shut up!"

Tension caused beads of sweat to gather at the back of his neck, and as he reached back to wipe them off, the girl named Millie drew back anxiously. He had her good and scared, all right.

Maybe that fear could work to his advantage. If he could just get her far enough away, where nobody had ever heard of Jesse Winter, maybe find a safe place to dump her... He needed to get moving.

He glanced at the gray mare. She looked like a game little horse, but he wasn't so certain about the silly gear she was decked out in. "Can you ride that thing?" he asked, nodding toward the side saddle.

"Mrs. Darwimple!" she cried indignantly.

In his panic, Sam heard a woman's name and feared the young woman had a companion. He pivoted anxiously in the saddle. "Who?"

Millie recoiled from the barrel of his gun as it swung around her way. "Mrs. Darwimple is my horse," she clarified, boldly shooing the barrel away from her person. "I don't like you calling her a 'thing.'"

"Oh." The tension gushed out of him in one breath as he looked again at the little mare. *Mrs. Darwimple?* What kind of nut named a horse something like that? He glanced back at the black-haired young lady. She was staring back, a slightly indignant, prissy purse to her rosy lips. For a crazy moment, he wondered what would happen if he kissed the pout right off of those lips of hers.

Maybe taking her wasn't such a good idea. Maybe...

He shook his head. He just didn't have time for maybes. "I don't care what her name is. Can you ride her?"

"Can I!" Millie bridled proudly in front of him. "Daddy says riding is the one thing I do exceptionally well," she boasted. Just as quickly, an idea apparently struck her. "If you want, I could ride into town for you and get whatever you need for—"

"Forget it," Sam said, cutting her off. "I hope you're telling the truth, because—"

"I told you, I'm very honest," Millie said, annoyed.

"Fine. Then get up on that horse." He grabbed her by the arm, eased her down, and followed right after her.

"I can mount by myself."

"Good for you," Sam said, watching as she swung up to her preposterous perch. As soon as she'd crooked her leg into position, he took the leftover rope and reached beneath her knee.

"What are you doing?" she cried in shocked outrage.

"Tying you to the saddle and the saddle to me," he answered, looping the rope around her knee and pulling it into a snug knot.

"But that's dangerous!" She shot him an angry glare. "If my daddy hears about this—"

His eyebrows raised in disbelief. "Listen, Princess. Two minutes ago you were telling me 'daddy' was going to shower me in riches."

The reminder failed to calm her. "My daddy will see to it that you're strung up from the highest gallows, you filthy murderer! And don't think he won't. My daddy has influence!"

With a heavy sigh, Sam mounted his horse again, feeling less optimistic now that he was saddled with a mouthy woman. He would have to figure out a way to get rid of her, fast. There was so little time. Two weeks.

"Kick that horse into a gallop and keep your lip buttoned," he instructed her.

In answer, she jutted out her chin belligerently.

Fine. Sam spurred his own horse and watched in solemn amusement as the little princess was yanked into movement. Her starchy white ruffled pinafore and yellow skirt flipped into her face momentarily, until she sputtered and waved them away, tucking both underneath her firmly. She threw him a last angry glance before setting her jaw and concentrating finally on the landscape ahead of them.

Sam was at least grateful to note that she hadn't been lying about her riding skill. Which meant that if he couldn't travel light, he could at least travel fleetly. But then, he had to.

His brother's life depended on it.

"When my father hears about this, you'll be done for."

And her father *would* hear about it, once someone found

the bonnet Millie had dropped as she and the desperado galloped away. Naturally, the man hadn't noticed it was missing—probably hadn't even noticed its dangling chin ties looped around her saddle to begin with. It was her very best bonnet, too, festooned with grape clusters and even a little redbird. But men of this man's ilk probably didn't pay any attention to hats unless they were the type measured by how much fluid could fit inside them.

Once her jaunty bonnet was found so near the deputies, Sheriff Tom McMillan was bound to put two and two together. *If* her bonnet was found. She had to keep up hope. "You'll never get away with this," she said menacingly.

The desperado rolled his eyes toward the star-drenched heavens. "Shut up and eat."

Shut up? Never in her life had anyone ordered Millicent Lively around so brutishly! Just why did he feel it necessary to be so rude, anyway? She was apparently going to spend her night tied to a tree. Wasn't that punishment enough?

This had to be the worst day of her whole entire life, Millie thought, giving in to her sulky mood. First she had had a dreadful argument with her father, who had forbidden her to break off her engagement. He thought she was getting a reputation for being fickle, and needed to settle down. Millie would admit, eleven fiancés was quite a number to have gone through—but that didn't mean she was wrong to *not* want to marry Lloyd Boyd, one of the clerks at her father's bank. And not even a very good bank clerk, as she'd reminded her father. Lloyd, daydreaming about more romantic jobs, was forever counting out the wrong change.

But he was also one of her oldest friends. The only reason she'd agreed to be engaged to him was simply that the supply of men to affiance herself to was running very low. And it was terrible not to have a fiancé at this time of year, with Christmas coming. And her birthday was in December, too. But a girl just didn't marry a *friend*. That would be too boring! For a husband, a girl wanted someone different, mysterious. . . .

She looked over at that outlaw and shivered. Maybe not too mysterious!

But at any rate, she certainly wouldn't marry anyone against her will. So she'd decided to run away. Well, naturally, she wasn't *really* going to run away. She'd simply intended to stay out long enough for her father to begin to worry, then to repent his outrageous ultimatum, and then to feel so terribly guilty that he would never cross her wishes again. Three hours would have done it. He knew she never missed the noon meal.

And she was certain this would have all worked according to plan—except that some ruffian *would* have to come along and kidnap her!

She couldn't be certain, but she was afraid this man was that wife-murderer who'd just been sentenced to hang. There weren't too many murderers in Chariton, after all. Just her luck that she would be out when one of the few managed to escape!

Despair threatened to overwhelm her, but she held her head high. She couldn't give in. Couldn't let this barbarian see her fear. She looked upon him imperiously, turning up her nose at the cold biscuit that he held. "Eat? I'd rather die!" she said, never taking her eyes off him.

Not that she could forget what he looked like. Ever. His deeply tanned skin, dusty brown hair and gray eyes would haunt her forever now. As would the shock of landing in the desperado's fearfully powerful embrace when she tumbled out of that pear tree. The odd thing was, she would have found the man handsome, if it weren't for the fact that he was a murderer and a kidnapper and God only knew what else. He also had strong hands and an impressive build—the better to maim and abduct with, she supposed.

"It seems to me that after going to all the trouble of taking a hostage," she lectured primly, "you could at least provide me with a hot meal."

"Sure," the man drawled. "I guess I should build up a big snuggly fire to warm your dainty feet by, too."

She tossed the black hair that she had braided after her captor finally stopped for the night. For a few hours' rest, he said. As if she could get any rest roped to a tree trunk, out in the chilly night air! "As a matter of fact, I would appreciate a fire very much. And if my daddy ever learned that you had extended that kindness, I am certain he would ask the authorities to be lenient."

"I'll bet," he said flatly. "The last thing I need is you sending smoke signals to daddy."

"I wouldn't know the first thing about that," she assured him, in a voice that let him know precisely how preposterous that idea was. "The only Indian blood in my family is a distant cousin on my great-great-grand-mother's—"

"Forget it," he snapped, apparently not interested in her family's fascinating history. "Fires attract attention."

She folded her arms crossly. "You should have at least let me bring along some of the pears I had collected."

She thought she detected a hint of regret in those gray eyes of his over the crunchy pears they'd left behind. Maybe she was just imagining it. "Stop thinking about the hunger, and it won't bother you so much," he said.

"Well I've *got* to eat something!" she cried.

He laughed gently, his eyes glinting at her with wicked humor. As though he enjoyed her discomfort! But then, why wouldn't he? He was a vicious criminal.

"I thought you'd rather die than eat," he said.

"Oh, give me a piece of that horrible stuff," she snapped, swiping a hunk from his hand. She took a bite of the dry, tasteless biscuit and winced as she chewed. And chewed. Finally, she gathered up the necessary resources to swallow. "How terrible! Daddy probably ate better during the war!"

"Don't blame me, Princess. I got it off my law friends."

"The men you killed, you mean."

"Once and for all, I *did not* kill anybody."

"Ha! I witnessed the crime with my own eyes," she said, not bothering to lie. "I saw that man begging for his life before you pummeled him."

"You saw wrong," he said. "I didn't kill anybody. Think about it. If I were a murderer, why would I be wasting my time hauling you around?"

For a moment, Millie was stumped. But a common criminal couldn't fool a mind like hers for long. "That's simple," she said proudly. "You obviously know how valuable I am."

His mouth fell open. *"Valuable!"*

"Of course. I told you right away that my daddy would pay a high price for my return."

"And I'm supposed to believe that fairy story?"

"It's the truth!" she yelped in frustration.

"Well, I don't believe it, any more than you believe I'm not a murderer."

Millie frowned. "But I can *prove* Daddy's an important person."

The gray eyes glinted in challenge. "How?"

It was so obvious! "Take me back to Chariton. If you ask anyone there, they'll tell you."

This suggestion was greeted with a full-throated cackle. "Princess, you've got to think of something better than that."

"Or any town in these parts. My daddy's well-known. Haven't you ever heard of Sam Houston?"

That name finally got his attention. The man sat up a little straighter. "Heard of him? I'm named after him!" He frowned. "But he's dead. You can't be..."

Her lips lifted in a smug smile. She couldn't help it. It was about time the man started taking her seriously. "No, I'm not. But my daddy used to work for Mr. Houston, before the war."

He tilted his head skeptically. "I thought you said your father was a storekeeper."

"He is. He owns a store, and a bank."

The man frowned thoughtfully. "So...that's how he can get his hands on all those armloads of dollars you keep promising me."

"That's right. Daddy is quite wealthy." She smiled in relief. Now that the man knew she was rich, her situation would surely improve. "So now that you believe me, won't you let me go? It would be better for you in the end. After all, they're bound to catch up with you."

"Don't be so sure," he said. She couldn't see his face too well in the darkness. Just enough to take note of the hard cast to his expression. Its intensity made her shiver. "Don't think I'm swallowing every word you feed me, either."

"Why not?"

"Because I know you'd say anything to free yourself."

"You're a fine one to call *me* a liar, you—" All at once, something about what he'd said seemed odd to her. He'd said he was named after Sam Houston. But the man who'd murdered his wife had been named Winter. Jesse Winter.

"You're not him," she said.

He looked up from the ground. "Who?"

"The murderer," she said, adding quickly. "At least, you're not the one I thought you were. His name was Jesse Winter."

"That's my brother. I'm Sam Winter."

The knowledge didn't comfort her. There was obviously a strain of exceptionally bad blood running in the Winter family, if they could create two such vicious characters in one generation. Her father hadn't allowed her anywhere near the courtroom during the Winter trial, but she suddenly remembered. "You hid your brother, didn't you?"

"That's right."

"They were sending you to jail for that?" she asked.

He nodded curtly. "For two years."

That seemed a bit severe to Millie, but the law was the law. "If everyone aided criminals," she said, "we'd never be able to catch them."

"What if some of these so-called criminals are actually innocent?" he asked challengingly.

"But your brother was guilty. A jury convicted him."

"You think juries are always right, Miss...what did you say your name was?"

"Lively," she told him. "Millicent Lively."

"Don't you think people are capable of making mistakes, Miss Lively? After all—" His words were cut off, and for a moment, Millie wondered if perhaps he wasn't choking. He sat with his mouth open, the strangest expression on his face. "Your name is Lively?"

She nodded. "Yes, that's what I said."

"Your father..." Sam swallowed. "He's not Horace Lively, by any chance, is he? Colonel Horace P. Lively?"

Her face lit up. "That's Daddy!"

"Oh, God." The man swallowed slowly. "This is fine. Just fine!" he said, his voice rising petulantly.

"I told you all along he was important."

The man's searing gray eyes glistened in the darkness, fastening on her with growing anger. "Why didn't you just say it flat out? 'My father is Colonel Horace P. Lively.' I thought maybe he just owned a big store. You didn't tell me he was a man with a statewide reputation. A war hero!"

She smirked in satisfaction. "Well, now you know."

He picked up a rock and tossed it into the darkness. The sound of it hitting a tree echoed back to them. "Now is too late," Sam said. "If I'd known, I could have left you there. Even if you had a big mouth and would have blabbered lies all over the place and told the authorities where I'd ridden off. At least I wouldn't be charged with kidnapping Old Lightfooted Lively's daughter!"

She rolled her eyes. "That's just what I've been telling you all along," she insisted. "If you only would have listened!"

He sighed in despair. Good, Millie thought. Let *him* worry for a while! "This is a helluva fix I'm in," he muttered.

"Why don't you let me go now?" she suggested. "You've seen me ride. You know I can get back to Chariton all right. And I'll tell Daddy that you were a perfect gentleman and released me as soon as you knew who I was."

"I'm in too deep now," he said. "I've got to think of a way to get rid of you."

"You mean—" Instinctively, she touched her neck, as if the ominous words had choked the breath out of her.

"Don't worry," he snapped. "Believe it or not, I'm more concerned about someone else's liberty than yours."

"A murderer's, you mean."

"My brother is innocent," Sam said, his voice suddenly more menacing than she'd ever heard it. "I won't have you talk against him."

She was silent for a moment, watching him. She could just make out his intent expression in the darkness. Finally, she gathered the courage to ask, "What are you going to do with me? Leave me here, tied up?"

"I'll have to think about it," Sam said. "I'll have to decide in the morning."

Millie frowned. Morning. She couldn't believe it would ever come. It seemed a lifetime of darkness away.

"Get some shut-eye," Sam instructed her. He sat back down where he'd been, then stretched himself out to his full length across the ground. "More than likely, tomorrow will be harder than today."

Harder? After a day with no food or rest? Millie had no idea how she was supposed to sleep propped up and bound to an oak tree, but that didn't appear to concern Mr. Sam Winter. "This is no bed of roses, you know," she said tightly.

He looked over at her, frowning. He then stood, picked up one of the horse blankets and spread it across her feet and outstretched legs. "That'll have to do, Princess. Sorry I couldn't provide better accommodations."

Her lips turned down, and she watched with envy as he stretched out across the grass again. Oh, well. At least she was alive. For someone taken hostage by a cold-blooded killer, a man who'd murdered two lawmen, that was quite a bit to be thankful for. But what would morning bring?

She sank against the rough bark and closed her eyes. She *was* tired. And sore! Good rider though she was, she'd never ridden so vigorously for so long before. She'd never needed to—until Sam Winter pointed a gun at her.

Odd, she thought, yawning sleepily. He must be an awfully insightful criminal. "Sam?"

There was a short pause before he answered her. "Yeah?"

It was a deep voice. Soft, husky. Again, she would have liked it, had it belonged to another man. A nice man. "How did you know my nickname?"

"Huh?"

"The one my daddy calls me by," she clarified, her voice tired and heavy.

"What's that?"

"Princess."

His deep-throated chuckle was the only reply Millie received before she drifted off to sleep.

Chapter Two

Even before he opened his eyes, Sam could feel something beating down on him. Not the sun; he could tell by the cool, damp air against his skin that it wasn't yet light. But something equal to the sun's intensity. He allowed himself to take a tentative peek—and was immediately confronted by a pair of angry brown eyes peering at him through the waning darkness.

His hostage's arms were crossed over her chest. "I smell like a horse!" she snapped in an imperious tone Sam wasn't as yet prepared to contend with. Not at this hour, at least.

He closed his eyes again. In his dreams, Salina's murder had never happened. He'd been back at his farm, confronting nothing more than another early fall day of harvesting the fruits of his labors. Honest work. Work that made a man feel satisfied with himself at the end of the day. Unlike kidnapping.

He forced himself to sit upright and face the day ahead of him. At least it was still well before dawn. They could cover a lot of miles today, which they needed to do now that he had decided where to deposit Miss Lively. Well after she dozed off, Sam had lain awake, considering his options. One thing he definitely didn't have time for was keeping a girl with dancing dark eyes and enticing lips with him. He'd spent too much time already remembering how slender her waist was, how delicate she felt on his lap. How pretty she was...

And what a rich, powerful daddy she had. An angry daddy, too, once he discovered what had happened to his little princess.

Finally, he'd concluded that the best place for Millie would be with one of his father's old friends, Gus Beaver. Gus and his wife, Louise, lived on a remote farm and would make certain Miss Lively stayed put, with her mouth shut, until Sam was able to free Jesse. Going to Gus's wouldn't take him too much out of his way, but he had no time to waste.

Sam stood up, dusted himself off and prepared to untie Millie, who hadn't stopped glaring at him.

"I'm not budging an inch until I've had a bath," she said to him before he could take so much as a step forward.

"A bath!" Sam exclaimed. "That's impossible."

"Why? There's a stream not far from here, you said yesterday. You can't possibly expect me to ride around the country dirty and smelling bad, can you?"

"Welcome to the unwashed masses, Miss Lively."

Her chin jutted out defiantly, in a manner he was beginning to know and dread. "I am *not* the masses. Every day since I can remember, my maid, Alberta, has drawn me a warm bath. It's not as if I'm asking for the moon. Just to wade in a cold stream. I wouldn't think that too much to ask."

"Well, it is," he retorted.

"Hmm." She tossed her mussed head of black hair behind her to indicate her utter disdain. "My daddy always says cleanliness is next to godliness. I suppose that just shows what class of person you are!"

"Sorry, Princess, I don't have time to be godly right at this moment."

"Then you might as well shoot me now," she argued petulantly, kicking off the striped wool saddle blanket. "I'd rather be dead than so dirty I'm attracting bugs!"

Sam could deal with bugs. An uppity rich girl with a powerful daddy bothered him a whole lot more. Yesterday he'd never have dreamed that taking the woman would make him feel as if he were traveling across Texas with a lit stick of dynamite, but that's how it seemed now.

Why hadn't he seen the signs? Her soft tan boots that looked like they'd barely ever touched dirt, her prissy side-saddle, the fine yellow dress that even in its simplicity was better than any of the dresses the womenfolk of his acquaintance had ever worn—those things all shouted mockingly at him now. Even in the darkness he could make out that damn yellow dress.

So, probably, could any person who saw them, even from a half mile away. Damn!

Sam bit back a ragged sigh. No use worrying about things he couldn't do anything about. Unless...

An idea occurred to him. A wicked idea, tailor-made to give the haughty little princess a cold douse of reality. Maybe next time she would think twice before she started making demands.

"All right," he said, with a reluctance he now didn't feel, "I suppose we could stop long enough for you to take a quick dip." He leaned down and untied her bonds, then reached quickly for his rifle, in case she had any sneaky ideas.

Apparently she didn't. Her smile of satisfaction showed through the darkness as she stood up and dusted herself off. "Now that's more like it!" she said, her voice a pleased chirp. "I won't be but a minute."

"I'll see to that. I'm not letting you out of my sight."

Her eyes became round and alert. "What? Surely you don't think..."

"Surely you don't think I'm going to let you swim away from me," he told her. "You just start walking to the creek."

She took one look at the barrel of his gun, turned, and began marching stiffly ahead of him. Funny, now that she knew she was going to have a witness to her morning bath—someone besides her maid Alberta—the woman seemed in less of a hurry to spiff herself up.

As the soft bubbling of the creek came into earshot, Millie's steps slowed to a crawl. Finally she stopped, and turned, a genial smile on her face. "Sam..." Her voice was far too pleasant to be trustworthy, and her manner was all flounce and flutter, now that she knew he had her over a barrel. "That's such a nice name."

"Thanks."

She nodded obligingly. "Sam, now that I've had time to give the matter further thought, I do believe I could wait another day, or perhaps even a week or so, before I take a bath."

He smiled back. "I've given it some thought, too," he told her. "And I've decided I wouldn't want to be responsible for depriving you of your daily dose of godliness."

"Oh, but I don't mind, honestly."

He shot his eyebrows upward, feigning shock. "What would your daddy say if he found out?"

Her black eyes grew fiery as all pretense of friendliness was dropped. "He'd rather that than that I stripped down in front of a criminal!"

"Don't worry," he said, smiling broadly. "I won't look."

She clucked skeptically. "As if I would trust your word—the word of a murderer!"

The tag stung. Would he ever be able to prove to the world that he and his brother weren't criminals? Obviously not, if Miss Millicent Lively had her way. "Just remember, Princess. This murderer will be nearby in case you decide to swim away. Now walk."

She tossed him a glare and marched forward again until they reached the edge of a stream. It wasn't very wide, but there was a spot where it formed a very small pond—big enough for Millie to splash around in. Sam nudged her toward it, then nodded.

"Take off your dress and hop in," he instructed.

After sending him an annoyed glance, she squinted down at the water at her feet. "This water is brown," she declared distastefully. "And there are probably snakes in there!"

"Just jump in. Most likely, you'll scare them all away," Sam said, growing impatient. "Now take off that dress and get in."

Knowing she had no choice—not with a gun pointed at her—she untied and slipped off her pinafore, then began to hurriedly undo the multitude of tiny pearl buttons down her front. There were enough of those to make Sam worry that Ed and Toby would catch up with them before they could all be unbuttoned. Finally, however, Millie was able to step out of the yellow frock, and Sam prepared to turn away.

Only, to his surprise, he discovered there was no need. Stripped down to her underwear, Millie had on more clothes than most women wore to church.

Her face flushed under his prolonged stare. "You said you wouldn't look!"

Sam was still in shock. "You put on all that gear just to pick a few pears?"

Her jaw dropped in astonishment. "Of course!" She looked down her front. Over a corset she wore a thin short-sleeved cotton camisole that gathered at her narrow waist, and under the corset there appeared to be a sleeveless shift. And that wasn't even counting the petticoats, which had to number three, at least.

Sam's expectations had by necessity been drawn from the women he'd seen undress in the past—but those women had been from a different class altogether from Millie Lively. He'd forgotten that the richer you were, the more uncomfortable you had a right to be.

"You'd better set aside one of those petticoats to dry yourself off with."

She complied, grumbling all the while. "All right. But I'm not going to so much as wade in that filthy muck. You can't make me."

"I don't care if you only wet your toes. *You* were the one who was all fired up to get clean."

He wasn't surprised to see that shedding a petticoat barely made a dent in her layers of skirts. He picked up her yellow dress and watched as she untied and stepped out of her boots, then reached out with one small, pale foot to test the water. It was still too dark for her to trust that there wasn't a snake nearby, so she took a tentative step forward—and, with a loud splash, was suddenly swallowed up by the pond.

"Millie!" Sam hollered, running to the edge of the bank. With all those clothes on, the poor girl was apt to sink like a stone! He looked anxiously at the wildly rippling surface, preparing to strip down to his long underwear and rescue her.

But before he could so much as tug at a shirttail, Millie surfaced again, coughing and sputtering.

"Are you all right?" he asked, still ready to dive in and save her. "Can you swim?"

Her shoulders poked above the water, and through the darkness she sent him a withering look as she coughed up the last of the water she'd swallowed. "I don't have to swim," she said. "I can stand."

"Thank heavens," Sam said, relieved. Remembering the dress, and the work he had to do, he turned away.

"I'm so touched that you care," Millie's voice said bitingly. "And it's such a relief that you didn't have to go to the trouble of getting wet just to fish me out."

"Yes, isn't it?" Sam agreed, smiling as he heard more splashing and sputtering behind him. He spread the yellow dress out across the bank and began to walk across it in a shambling shuffle.

The girl released a strangled cry. "What are you doing!"

"Mussing your dress. It's too clean."

"Too clean?" she exclaimed. "It's never been so filthy!" He bent down and flipped the dress onto its other side, and Millie groaned in dismay as he repeated the process. "Until now…"

"This way we'll be a better match," Sam told her.

"Just what I've always dreamed of," she said scathingly, "to look like I belong to the criminal class."

Sam finished with a little jig before stepping off the dress. "There," he said with satisfaction as he inspected the now dingier garment. "You won't attract as much attention now. It's hard to tell whether this is yellow or beige, I'll wager."

When his commentary was met with silence, Sam turned quickly. But Millie hadn't disappeared—she was standing very still in the water, her expression pained. And angry. Very, very angry.

"What's the matter?" he asked.

Her mouth clamped shut. Then she mumbled, "Nothing."

"You can come out now," he told her, holding out a hand. "Here, I'll help you."

"Don't you dare touch me!" she cried ferociously. "You, you—dress-musser!"

Sam smiled. "You wound me." Kneeling at the very edge of the bank, he grabbed her by the arms and lifted her bodily out of the water and onto dry land. Millie managed to get him at least half as wet as she was in the process.

He handed her the dress, which did nothing to soothe her. She looked at the garment in seething silence. "I loved this dress," she said at last.

Sam shrugged. "It's just clothing."

"That's all you know!" she retorted, her eyes flashing. "That dress was my very favorite. I sewed it myself—it took me months!"

Months? Sam wasn't sure about these things, but he doubted it took most women months to finish a dress. Especially women like Millie Lively, who had all the leisure the world had to offer.

But maybe he just didn't know what he was talking about. Needle and thread were tedious tools he'd always tried his damnedest to avoid using. "I suppose being called a dress-musser is better than being called a murderer."

"You *are* a murderer," she said, scrambling away from him up the bank as fast as she could. "Don't think I've forgotten those two deputies!" She began drying herself with the petticoat she'd put aside. "I'll bet hundreds of people are going to be combing the area for you today."

"We'll be ahead of them."

"Not for long. Word of my disappearance will get out, and then you'll be in big trouble."

Sam found it difficult to concentrate on the prospect of being hunted at the moment. Instead, his eyes kept glancing in amazement at Millie, whose shape was silhouetted against the lightening sky. The girl might appear to be mere skin and bone while buried under her mounds of clothes, but when those same clothes were wet and clingy, the womanly curves they revealed were definitely . . . eye-catching.

He remembered, back at the pear tree, thinking the legs poking out from it were mighty appealing. But that had been before he was faced with the spoiled princess that went with them. Most of the time she seemed more girl than woman. It would be hard to think of her that way now. . . .

He looked away, feeling his face redden. His throat was suddenly dry, and he cleared it uncomfortably.

"What's the matter?" Millie asked. "Are you sick?"

Ironically, anger over her dress seemed to have knocked the bashfulness clear out of her head, so that she stomped around, heedless of his gaping, as she whacked her dress against the trunk of a tree, hoping to flog some of the dirt off. Sam wished she'd go ahead and put the damn thing back on, already.

"No, I'm not sick," he answered, getting to his feet. "We just need to push on."

"*You're* the one who's wasted our time this morning," Millie lectured him primly as her fists rested on her curvaceous hips. "You can't blame me."

No, he couldn't. This was all his fault. If he hadn't gotten that fool notion about Millie's dress into his head, he could have gone on thinking about her as a . . . well, a troublesome hostage. A burden to be shed. But now he was going to be hard-pressed to look at her again without thinking of her as she appeared now, that camisole sticking to her collarbone and cleavage, her petticoats outlining her tiny waist, her hips and her shapely legs.

Damn. He trained his eyes away, on the spot where they'd left the horses. "All right. It's my fault. Now hurry up and get your clothes on."

She shot him an exasperated look. "First you want them off, now you want them on! And all the while you keep pointing that gun at me— How do you expect me to act efficiently under these circumstances?"

Patience, Sam told himself, turning away as he listened to her fuss over the scads of little buttons she had to contend with. The rippling pond mocked him now. If only there were time, he could use a therapeutic dunk in that cold water himself.

Tom McMillan, Chariton's sheriff for going on twenty years, was well-known for being a man of few words, so when the few he chose to tell his hastily gathered but handpicked posse were *shoot to kill,* Horace Lively was sure the sheriff meant them.

Poor Millicent, his little princess, all alone with that brutal outlaw. And her so unused to the rough conditions she was probably being exposed to! How would she survive?

He swallowed, fighting back a sick feeling in the pit of his stomach that had been there ever since the sheriff had come around with Millie's bonnet, asking a lot of questions. But, of course, he'd begun to anticipate the worst when Millie wasn't home for dinner that afternoon. Oh, he never should have quarreled with her! If only he could be sure she had survived thus far. He was an old man, had been through four years of battle during the War between the States, but he'd never faced anything so frightening as the prospect of losing his dear daughter.

He just had to stay calm, keep himself together, as he had been doing. Now if only he could convince Lloyd Boyd to comport himself in the same dignified way. Millie's fiancé had completely fallen apart when he discovered she was missing. Even now he was fondling the little redbird on Millie's bonnet, which he held in a white-knuckled grip.

"Shoot to kill?" Lloyd wailed, jumping up from where he was sitting on the wooden sidewalk in front of the sheriff's office. He looked beseechingly from Horace to the sheriff and then back again. "With Millicent nearby?"

"The sheriff knows what he's doing, son," Horace tried to explain. If only he could be certain of his own words.

Sheriff Tom continued instructing his men. "Now you all heard Ed and Toby's story. Sam Winter is a shifty, brutal character, just like that brother of his, and apparently he's a lot stronger than he looks. Any man who could overtake two lawmen on horseback while his hands are cuffed would have to be." He eyed his red-faced deputies sternly.

The sheriff thought the incident of the escaped convict made a laughingstock of him and his deputies in the eyes of the community. There *was* talk of incompetence going around, though not about Tom. That man had a will of iron, everyone knew, and tended to be overzealous in pursuit of justice. Especially when it involved somebody he didn't particularly like. And he very clearly disliked Sam Winter and his brother.

"Tom," Horace said, stepping forward, "don't forget Millicent is riding with the man. I don't want Millicent hurt."

"Oh, right," Tom drawled for the benefit of the others. "Try not to hit the girl. Now we're going to branch out in two groups...."

The perfunctory words failed to comfort Horace. As did the directions that followed. The trigger-happy sheriff was going to head the posse himself, and leave Ed and Toby in charge of Jesse Winter at the jail. Oh, Horace was glad that so many had turned out to join the search party, and he would be following the sheriff so that he could hear about events as they developed. Still, all the men in front of him seemed more interested in the prospect of catching the escaped criminal than ensuring the safety of his daughter.

All except Lloyd Boyd. And precious little good the hysterical young bank clerk was going to be in the search.

"Poor, poor Millie!" Lloyd wailed, combing his hands through his pale hair in a gesture of anguish. "Will we ever see her again, see her lovely face, hear her bright, tripping laughter?"

How a man could think so flowery in the midst of a crisis was beyond Horace's understanding. "We'll find her, Lloyd. Pull yourself together."

"I know. I must be strong. For Millicent," Lloyd said in an earnest attempt to tamp down his emotions. "But if there were only something more I could do!"

Lloyd's hysteria, signaling as it did a genuine concern for Millie, touched Horace's heart. He had been right to tell Millie that the young man would make a good match for her. Millie got engaged and disengaged with dizzying regularity—and Lloyd was an upstanding, sober young man. Or had been. Now he seemed to crumble before Horace's eyes.

"You're doing all you can by riding with McMillan's posse, son," Horace assured him. Then, looking at the young man's red, anxious face, he added, "Just remember to stay out of the way."

Unoffended, Lloyd nodded. "I'll stay right with you, sir."

Horace took a deep breath. Though it grated on his nerves, the boy's hysteria was easier to stomach than the bloodthirstiness of the other men gathered.

More than his own deputies' embarrassing loss of their prisoner, Sheriff Tom had used Millicent's apparent kidnapping as a call to arms. But now that they were all assembled, no one seemed especially concerned about whether she was dead or alive. Except Lloyd.

And one other man. But Horace didn't notice him, and neither had anyone else. He had disguised himself so that he could blend into the crowd as just another citizen, and was hanging back—but not too far back—listening and watching, examining the gray-haired, droopy-eyed colonel's wary reaction to the sheriff's directives.

Horace P. Lively was worried sick about his daughter. Anybody could see that—even a man who could barely see at all. The old gentleman was as despairing in his silence as the younger man next to him was in all his breast-beating grief. Lively didn't think the sheriff was going to find his daughter.

Maybe he would, maybe he wouldn't, the man thought. But the old codger was right about one thing. The sheriff didn't give a flip about Millicent Lively. Just about Sam Winter.

The stranger saw things differently. Whether Sam Winter lived or died was of no importance to him. But Millicent Lively—now *she* was another matter entirely. . . .

"I'm certain I'll catch cold now after being wet the entire day," Millie said crossly. She knew she was whining, but she couldn't help it. She was bound to a tree trunk, and uncomfortable, and hungry again.

Wasn't Sam Winter human? Didn't he get hungry, or tired, or cold?

How would she know? she wondered in frustration. They had been riding side by side for two days now, and she knew as little about him tonight as when they'd left Chariton. His continued silence alarmed her. It wasn't just that she couldn't understand a person who didn't talk—although that *was* puzzling—but, even stranger, that he seemed genuinely to want to say things to her. Otherwise, why would she have caught him watching her in that odd, almost pained way so often today?

Unless she looked funny. That was always a possibility, given that she'd dressed this morning so hurriedly, without a mirror, in a mud-caked frock. Even her normally perky, fashionably curled bangs drooped down to her eyebrows. But whose fault was that?

"Sam..."

He was leaned up against another tree, his long, lanky legs stretched out in front of him. "What?" he said, his voice annoyed and completely devoid of curiosity.

"Well, if you're going to be that way about it, never mind," she answered peevishly.

She heard a long sigh, then noticed that he sat up straighter. "What is it?" he asked, his tone only slightly more patient.

She sniffed proudly. "I only wanted to ask you if you thought I looked all right, but you don't have to tell me."

"Why? Are you sick?"

"No, I was just concerned with my appearance." When he failed to say anything, she added, "You know...my physical appearance."

"You look fine."

"How would you know? You didn't even glance at me!"

Reluctantly, he turned his head. She could see his gray eyes watching her across the darkness, with that same strange look in them that she had noticed so many times that day as they rode.

He really wasn't unattractive, even though he was badly in need of a shave and generally scruffier than when she'd first seen him. His face was almost handsome, in a common sort of way. It had taken her a while to get used to his rough, sun-darkened skin. He was almost bronze, which provided a stark contrast to his other features, gray eyes and light brown hair.

The odd look in his eye she chalked up to the same discomfort she felt. "You know what your problem is?" she asked.

The question brought a sharp laugh. "I know what several of them are, Princess. There's the fact that the law is after me, that my brother might hang. Oh, and there's you to deal with—"

It annoyed her when he called her "Princess" now, especially when he said the word with such a sneer of derision. "You're hungry," she said, interrupting him. "What you need is some real food."

"Too bad. We don't have any, and we don't have time to forage, either."

"You'll never make it far on an empty stomach," Millie told him. "We need to stop in a town."

"No," he said flatly.

As far as Millie could tell, getting Sam to take her into a town was her only chance of escape. "Why not? I wouldn't do anything stupid," she promised, lying baldly. She'd pictured it so many times during their long ride—getting away from him, running like a crazed woman down a sparsely populated, dusty street of a strange town, flapping her arms and yelling about the madman who had abducted her. Her daydream always ended with Sam being caught by a mob of angry townspeople, which made her feel a little sad, but relieved. Sam *had* kidnapped her, after all.

Daddy was probably worried out of his mind. It nearly made her cry to think about it. Yet she couldn't help wondering what was going on in Chariton—Sam's escape must have created quite a stir. Just her luck. Something exciting finally happens in that dull little town, and she gets abducted!

Oh, well. She was sure her father was doing something on her behalf, which did make her the center of attention, even if she wasn't there to enjoy it. Her best friend, Sally Hall, was probably going crazy with wanting to know what had happened to her. Alberta would be fretting, too. Oh, and Lloyd Boyd. Her situation would suit the misfit bank clerk's love of drama.

And with good reason! She had never been so dramatically worn out and hungry. She'd spent many leisurely days riding her gray mare, but never on punishing rides like these. Poor Mrs. Darwimple! Millie felt almost as sorry for her horse as she did for herself. She simply had to convince Sam to head back to civilization.

"It would be stupid trying to get away from me," Sam told her. "And don't tell me that's not what you're planning, because I can see it in your sneaky eyes."

The accusation fascinated her. "You think my eyes are sneaky?" No one had ever called her that before. Imagine, being branded sneaky by a desperado! "You know, I do believe that's the first thing you've noticed about me."

"Hardly." He laughed bitterly. "Besides, I didn't mean it as a compliment."

"Oh, that's all right. A girl does like to be noticed, though."

He tossed his hands in the air. "You are the most confounded woman I've ever run into. Don't you know you're in danger? You should be angry!"

"I was."

"Then you should have stayed that way."

She made a tsking noise. Stay angry for two whole days? "*That* wouldn't be very pleasant for either of us." She had never had any call to endure that much emotional turmoil. Until now, of course. "Though I am mad about your decision not to go into town. I wouldn't do anything to get away, Sam. On my honor."

"I know, I know," he muttered. "You're renowned for your trustworthiness."

"That's right."

"And your riding expertise."

"Well, of course, I don't like to brag—"

"Forget it."

She couldn't let him see her frustration—which was escalating rapidly. She'd never yet met a man she couldn't wheedle into doing what she wanted. Sam might prove the first. Usually all it took was a little pleading, but he wasn't softening a bit. Perhaps it was time to take more dire measures—like showing him exactly what kind of woman she was.

"Sam..."

After rolling his eyes, he looked over at her in irritation—until he saw that with what little mobility she had she was lifting her skirt up past her knee. Irritation turned to slack-jawed curiosity.

"I bet I can change your mind about going into town," she said sweetly, flexing her small foot enticingly. "I have something for you...."

His eyes bugged at the glimpse of leg, but he shook his head vehemently. "S-see here now," he stuttered in dismay. "Put your skirt back down!"

"It's just my legs," Millie said. "Same ones I had this morning. You didn't seem to mind them then."

His mouth clamped shut. "Never mind. Cover up."

"But I wanted to show you something," she argued, untying the small satchel at the waistband of her petticoats. She removed it, straightened her skirts and held out her offering primly.

"Oh..." he said, looking sheepishly at the velvet bag.

"It's money. Count it," she told him, "and you'll see that you can trust me."

Tentatively he reached out and took the bag from her, weighing it for a moment in his hand before loosening the drawstring. He upended the little purse and listened appreciatively as the heavy coins fell into his large hand.

"There's twelve dollars here," he said.

Millie smiled. "There! You see? I've shown you how much money I have. You can borrow however much you want. And the next time we see a town, we can just detour a little and buy ourselves some supplies. Maybe even stop over at a hotel..."

But even as she spoke, she got the oddest feeling that Sam really wasn't giving much credence to her words. He calmly put the coins back in her purse, folded it over and placed it in the pocket of the deputy's saddlebags he kept by his side.

"Aren't you going to give me my money back?" she asked.

He looked at her as if she'd just sprouted two heads. "Hell, no!"

"But that's stealing!"

Sam laughed at her. "Millie, didn't that daddy you're always going on about teach you to have a lick of sense? For two days you've been calling me a murderer, a criminal, a desperado. What did you think was going to happen to your money when you handed it over?"

"I showed you that money as an act of faith," she argued. "So that you could trust me if we passed a town. I only wanted something decent to eat."

He shook his head. "Good Lord, listening to you, a person would think you'd never been hungry before."

For a moment, Millie racked her brains. "I haven't," she told him, a little surprised by the discovery herself. But why would a store owner's daughter have to go without? "Until yesterday. And I must admit, I was rather excitable then— a little nervous about being kidnapped, naturally—so I didn't notice so much. But today is entirely different."

"Are you saying you're not nervous anymore?"

"Well . . . maybe a little. But I'm just so hungry I don't care," she added with a moan. "And sore, and tired."

"Then go to sleep."

"I will when I've gotten my money back," she insisted.

The petulant refusal brought her captor to his feet. He stomped over, fists balled at his sides, and towered over her. "Let's get this straight. You're not going to see that money again, unless I do think it's safe to go into a town. But that's for me to decide, you understand?"

His harsh tone irritated her—and scared her a little, frankly. She'd never seen such a hard look in his eye, or noticed him so on edge. She had half a mind to answer that *she* was a little on edge herself, thanks to him, but that *she* had the good manners to mask her foul humor. At the same time, something told her he wouldn't appreciate a lecture on his bad breeding at this precise moment.

She tilted her chin up and contented herself with a curt "fine." What more could she do? She was tied to a tree.

But, apparently, he wasn't through with her. "You seem to forget sometimes who I am, and what you're doing here."

"As if I could!"

He paced restlessly in front of her. "Don't you understand? You should hate me. You should be trying to escape, not giving me money."

"I didn't mean to *give* you the money," she said.

"You shouldn't have shown it to me, then," he said sternly. "I'm a criminal, remember? A *murderer.*"

"You say the word as if you really weren't one," she said.

"What would you think if that was the truth, Millie? What would you say if I told you both my brother and I were innocent, and that I was on my way to bring a real murderer back to Chariton?"

"I'd say that was a likely story!"

"I didn't kill those deputies," he told her.

She scoffed. "Next you'll be asking me to believe that I came along by my own free will."

"No, I'm afraid that was entirely my fault," he said. "But just consider this. Why do you think I brought you along, instead of doing to you what I did to the deputies?"

"Obviously," she said, "because I'm such a valuable hostage."

"So we're back to that again." He emitted a ragged sigh, then returned to his spot on the ground across from her. She could see him shaking his head as he lay back down. "Go to sleep, Miss Lively."

He had dismissed her rationale as if it were absurd—as if she weren't valuable to him at all. Despite the night chill, her cheeks grew warm at his lack of appreciation. It was almost as if he wished she didn't have a wealthy father—a man most kidnappers would be proud to have their hostage related to! Instead, he was treating her as though she were a millstone around his neck. What an odd criminal.

What an odd man. She couldn't forget the look on his face as she'd pulled up her skirt—as if looking at her leg were somehow painful to him. In a fit of self-doubt, Millie glanced over to Sam to make sure he wasn't looking, then lifted her skirt again to check her legs for herself. They appeared fine to her. Better than fine. Irving Draper, her intended two fiancés back, had even had the audacity to remark on her shapely legs once, moments before she slapped him silly. It amazed her to think that a boring, conventional sap like Irving could appreciate her, while virile, dangerous Sam looked at her as if he wished she would cover herself with a potato sack. She could only guess that she didn't compare well to other women of his acquaintance, who, given his character, probably consisted of floozies in fleshpots.

Now if that wasn't insulting, what was?

A long, slim leg, pale and shapely in the moonlight. Sam didn't think he'd forget that sight as long as he lived. Sweat popped out across his brow just from thinking about it. Millie was completely oblivious, of course. How could a woman be so prim, so haughty, and yet at times so completely heedless of propriety?

Because she was a pampered rich girl, he told himself. A young lady who considered herself so far above him that she didn't find anything at all wrong about prancing around in wet, clingy clothes, or hiking her skirt up to her thigh. He was so far out of her circle of consideration that he might as well have been another species entirely, as far as she was concerned. Frogs and toads didn't mix; escaped convicts didn't mix with rich men's daughters.

He would do well to put stock in that way of thinking himself. He had problems aplenty aside from Miss Lively. He had a murderer to catch.

He reached down and felt the small lump in his pocket and was reassured that the ring was still there. His evidence. In his mind's eye, he could see the inscription on the inside. T to D, it read in bold script. He had a good idea that *D* stood for Jesse's old partner, Darnell Weems. But he couldn't be certain. And who was T?

Finding Darnell Weems was only half the battle—assuming he could even make it out to Little Bend, Darnell's home, without being caught by the law. Most likely, Darnell wasn't going to confess to killing his friend's wife. Why should he, when Jesse was about to hang for the crime?

Jesse hadn't been able to understand why his friend would have traveled halfway across a state to murder a woman he'd never met. He and Salina had married after he and Darnell parted ways. Yet he swore he'd seen Darnell riding away from the house while he was out hunting the night of the murder. Then, when he returned home, he'd found Salina, and the nightmare had begun. The law had arrived, and when it became clear that the sheriff meant to have his revenge on Jesse by painting him as a wife killer, Jesse, still half out of his mind with grief, had run. The ring had been discovered later by a kind old neighbor lady who was by Jesse's to clean up the place. She'd promptly brought the engraved band to the jail, but the mysterious clue had interested Sam more than it had Jesse, who by the time it was found was beyond caring about his own life.

Jesse always wanted to think the best of people. But Sam had no illusions. After their parents died, Sam had tried to bring his little brother up to be practical. Jesse had the dreamer in him, though, and had gone his own way. He'd met up with Darnell in Colorado, and for two years the two of them had tried several schemes together—from cattle driving to gold mining. Finally they'd won two plots of land in a poker game. To decide who got which, they had flipped for them. That was the last they'd seen of each other, except for Jesse's last brief glimpse of Darnell in the night. Maybe Darnell harbored some resentment for getting the lesser plot of land out west.

Even so, Jesse didn't want to think the worst of his old friend. All along, he'd sworn that Darnell wasn't a bad character. But Sam didn't believe it for a moment.

He was going to find Darnell Weems and, come hell or high water, he would squeeze a confession out of him. There had to be a reason behind Salina's murder. And whether Jesse liked it or not, Sam intended to prove it was his friend's doing. Or else die trying.

Chapter Three

Thou shalt not covet thy neighbor's wife. Bob Jitter remembered those words from when he was a kid. Back then he hadn't known what coveting was all about, but he did now. Yes, sir, he sure did.

Jitter hung back in the cabin's small kitchen and watched the newlyweds fight. Watching and coveting was about all there was to do around the place these days. Darnell's cattle had up and died, the little garden they'd cultivated in the spring had dried up by July. If it weren't for Darnell's wife, Tess, Jitter was sure he would have left. Though he considered Darnell a friend, as well as his employer, that didn't change the fact that there was little around the place for him to do. But ever since Darnell had brought his bride home at the beginning of summer, Jitter had found himself stuck on the old place as surely as if he were knee-deep in mud.

"C'mon, Jitter, back me up here," Darnell said, turning away from his wife to plead with his friend in the corner.

"I ain't sayin' nothin'," Jitter replied. A person would have to be a fool to go up against Tess. Maybe an even bigger fool to marry her. But she had the looks and a figure men were apt to make fools of themselves over—himself included, he feared.

Many was the night he lay dreaming about her, dreaming about what if she weren't another man's wife. Probably she wouldn't spare him a second glance. But at least then he'd have a right to his dreams, to conjuring up the image of himself winding that long, silky blond hair through his fingers, and staring into those icy blue eyes. She was only a few inches shorter than his own six feet, and every inch of her soft, womanly curves. He doubted he had ever come so close to a woman so beautiful, yet she was completely out of his reach.

Once, she *had* been in his reach. Jitter and Tess had checked into a Buffalo Gap hotel together as man and wife, "Mr. and Mrs. Darnell Weems," while Darnell went to take care of his old partner. Of course, his being in the hotel with Tess had been pretense, an alibi, but as he sat up all night in a chair, watching Tess as she lay across the big double bed, her blond hair flowing on the pillow, the temptation had been achingly real.

"What kind of man are you?" Tess shouted across the room at her husband, startling Jitter out of his guilty thoughts. Her blue eyes flashed with contempt at the slightly hunch-shouldered man standing across from her.

"I done what you wanted, Tess," Darnell argued.

"Don't try clearing your conscience by heaping your sins on my head, Darnell Weems."

"But you was the one who said that if we'd have got Jesse's land in Chariton instead of this patch of dust in Little Bend, we'd be a lot better off."

"I'm sure you would have figured that out sooner or later," Tess replied snidely.

But Jitter wasn't so sure. It was Tess who, as a disgruntled new bride, had made the discovery that the deed to their land was actually in both Darnell's and Jesse Winter's names. At first she had only wanted to ensure that Jesse didn't come snatch the land out from under her in the event of Darnell's untimely demise. But after hearing the story of how Darnell and Jesse had won two parcels of land on either side of the state from a man who signed over the deeds in their names, and then flipped a coin to see who would get which, Tess had hatched an even better plan. Because if the deed to Jesse Winter's land still bore two names, then Darnell—and she, too—would have a legitimate claim to it in the event of Jesse Winter's untimely demise. Which she had soon convinced Darnell to arrange.

"You said you would be happy if'n I did what you wanted," Darnell said, hurt. "But you ain't happy. I'm beginning to think you ain't never been happy."

"Not since I laid eyes on you, I haven't!" she replied in a fury. "You bungle everything you put your hand to. You couldn't even kill the right person."

Darnell's shoulders tensed. "But I told you, I just saw a body in bed and assumed..." His voice trailed off helplessly as something inside him seemed to deflate. "And then... then it was too late."

"You should have waited until Jesse got back."

"But I couldn't. I'd just done murder, Tess. You know what that means?"

She crossed her arms and sent him a withering stare. "In for a penny, in for a pound, I always say."

"But she was just laying there, bleeding. His wife. I just sat there thinkin', what if it had been different. What if that had been you, hon?"

"Then I hope whoever had gone to the trouble of snuffing me out would have the sense to wait around for the right victim to come along."

Darnell, his rusty-haired good looks marred by his hangdog expression, ceded the point. "Well, I didn't."

"And now you won't even listen to reason. We can go get that land, Darnell. Good land. You said yourself he ain't got no relatives, 'cept his brother, who's going to jail, too. You're his partner, and you won that land together. You got as much right to the place as anybody. More. Your name's on the deed. Just because you flipped some fool coin, that doesn't mean anything."

"But I murdered his wife, Tess."

"Stop saying that!" Tess paced back and forth, her long legs crossing the room with few steps, and looked back up at her husband periodically in annoyance. "Worrying about that is making you sick, weak. Jitter and I spent the night in that hotel, so there couldn't be any problems. Buck up!"

"It ain't so easy," he snapped back.

She stopped her pacing and turned on him, her fists planted firmly on her hips. "Well, it ain't so easy for me, either, sitting here and watching a golden opportunity pass us by. I didn't marry you so's I could be poorer than I ever was, you know. I thought you were somebody that was going places."

"It's just been a bad year, that's all," he said, his tone full of resentment.

"Well, it's not gonna get any better with you sittin' around on your duff all day, too afraid to go and get what should have been yours in the first place."

"You can't expect me to just waltz into Chariton to see my old friend hang, Tess."

"You were happy enough to waltz in when you were aimin' on murdering him." The truth finally shut Darnell up, and Tess took advantage of the moment to ram her argument home. She walked over to him, sidling up real close, and meekly took his hands. "Oh, Darnell," she said, her voice pleasingly appeasing, "I just want what's best for both of us. You know how I want a family."

Darnell scuffed one foot against Tess's immaculate kitchen floor. "Aw, I know."

"But I can't see us having a family out here," she said, staring at him with those blue eyes of hers. She could make them go all gooey when she wanted to.

Times like these, Jitter could understand clearly how Darnell could have been hoodwinked into marrying a woman who had nothing but contempt for him. He had to give Tess credit for being the slyest thing he'd come across this side of a sidewinder. And she was a hell of a lot prettier.

"If we wait to make our claim, the land will be sold," she insisted gently.

"There's other land."

"Not land that should have been yours to begin with."

"It's a bad idea, goin' back there."

The two of them stood toe-to-toe, almost nose-to-nose. Darnell had the advantage in height. But when Tess's eyes started misting up, that slight edge was overshadowed.

She took a step back and wiped a tear from the corner of her eye. "I guess you just don't want me to be happy," she said in a wounded tone.

Darnell released a raw sigh. "Aw, hon. Of course I do. Didn't I marry you? Didn't I add on this nice kitchen for you? Nothin's more important in the world to me than you."

"That was months ago," she said, squeezing another teardrop out. This one she allowed to fall dramatically down her pale cheek. Jitter could almost feel its warm progress down her soft skin. "You sure don't act like you love me anymore, Darnell."

That little tear was Darnell's undoing. He stepped forward and gathered his wife into his arms and kissed the blond hair at the crown of her head. As the two embraced, Jitter felt his breath hitch in his throat, and his gut wrenched so uncomfortably that he had to look away. But not for long.

"I do, you know I do," Darnell said soothingly. "I just don't want to risk too much at once."

She sniffed, all the while running a long-nailed hand up and down Darnell's back. Jitter shivered.

"But we gotta take risks sometime," she said, "if we're gonna get ahead. Don't you think so, Darnell?"

He hesitated—or maybe he was just a little bit distracted by that hand skimming his spine. Finally, he caved in. "I guess you're right."

She hugged him more tightly. "Oh, I'm not even sure I want to go, anyway," she said. "I don't have a nice thing to wear—we'll never fit into polite society with me lookin' like an old shoe."

Now that Darnell was licked, he was all smiles. "Sweetheart, I'm gonna sell everything left here that could raise money, and before we go back east, we'll stop in Little Bend and buy you the nicest dress there."

She beamed up at him. "Oh, Darnell, you're so good to me!"

Darnell bent down and kissed her on the lips, long and hard. The two remained in an embrace until Tess pulled back, flashing her husband a delectable smile.

Finally, Darnell glanced around, remembering that someone else was in the room. "You okay, Jitter? You look all pale and clammy."

Jitter shook his head. He didn't care how mean she was. He would have done anything to trade places with Darnell at that moment. Good thing he could still call to mind scraps of his Bible learning. *Thou shalt not . . . shalt not . . .*

From the top of a long grassy hill, Sam looked down at a rough log building. A sign out front, above the door, announced it to be a store—but it couldn't be much of one, given its size and its location. Yet the place was bound to have something that would make the next few days a little more bearable. He was beginning to feel as worn out and empty as his hostage looked. And with any luck, he could be in and out before the proprietor even took notice of him.

With any luck... That was a good one! When was the last time he'd felt lucky? Moments before making the acquaintance of Millicent Lively, that was when.

He sneaked a glance at her now, trying to detect whether her expression was at all smug. She was getting what she wanted, after all. But no, her face was perfectly serene, devoid of any outward show of triumph. She stood, her thin shoulders straight, her head erect, looking directly down at the little building. Her yellow dress was dust-covered and raggedy, yet he hadn't been completely successful in disguising it; bright patches still showed through.

"I guess I'll tie you up back here," he said.

She turned on him, her eyes round. "Tie me up? Why?"

"So you won't gallop away when I'm gone."

"But I want to go with you!"

He rolled his eyes. He should have expected her to be difficult on this point. "You know I can't let you do that."

"Why not?"

"Look—it's just a little trading post. You won't be missing out on much." He shot her a keen glance. "Unless you were planning on trying to escape."

"I told you I wouldn't!" she cried. "I gave you my word. You can't just leave me out here, tied up to some tree."

Sam leaned forward on his saddle. "Why not?"

"Well . . . I'd scream."

"Not if I muffled you."

"You *would* do that!" she said in disgust. "But just the same, it's a bad idea. What if someone saw me out here? There's no place around where you could hide me and Mrs. Darwimple."

She had a point there. And she knew it.

"If someone should happen upon me, once I was free you'd be caught for sure," she continued. A second later, she added smartly, "And then you would have lost your very valuable hostage."

Millie apparently wasn't going to let go of that pet theory, no matter how many problems she caused him.

"If you go down there with me, I'll be watching you every minute."

"I know."

"Don't think you can escape."

"I don't," she answered, tossing her head testily. "I'm no fool. Besides, didn't I tell you that you could trust me? I have a repu—"

"I know, I know," Sam interrupted. "You're as honest as a looking glass."

She shrugged immodestly. "I'm only repeating what people tell me."

He smirked. "Guess what? I'm honest, too."

Millie's eyebrows raised dubiously. "I didn't say I was gullible!"

"You see, Millicent, I have a theory that most people are honest...until chance forces them to be otherwise. Good people lie when they're in trouble and can't see any other way out. Some people, the lucky ones who never have to face serious troubles, never are really tried."

As he spoke, Millie's jaw went slack. "Are you insinuating that *I* have never had real troubles?" she asked in astonishment. The very thought made her laugh incredulously. "Believe me, Mr. Winter, if anyone's life was ever a strain, it's mine! You had no way of knowing this, of course, but my mother died right after I was born, and since I was a little girl, I've borne the responsibility of running my father's household, and being his hostess."

Sam waited for further tales of woe, but apparently planning her father's dinner parties was the extent of the strain in Millicent Lively's sheltered life. "That's it?" he asked.

"No..." She sighed. "This might come as a shock to you, but my life is hardly as exciting as it might seem to an outsider."

"You're telling me that on top of having responsibilities, you're bored," he guessed.

"Boredom is a strain!" she said.

"Listen, Princess," Sam replied, anxious to get moving. "There are a lot of people in the world who would pay to have your troubles."

"Well, of course! I know that. That's the whole point of being rich. But you can't say my life is carefree."

"Maybe not now, at any rate," Sam allowed, swinging down from the black. He took Millie's arm. "Get down."

"Why?" Her face showed alarm. "I thought you were going to take me."

"I am. But you'll have to go bareback. That saddle sticks out too much."

She let herself down and watched as he ungirthed the saddle and slid it off the gray's back. "I've never ridden Mrs. Darwimple without a saddle," she said.

Somehow, it didn't surprise him. Millicent Lively probably had a groom to saddle and unsaddle her horse at her every whim. "Chalk this up as part of that troubled life you were whining about."

Millie crossed her arms petulantly. "Just because you've gotten yourself into a mess, that's no reason to be sarcastic."

Without a word, he turned and walked toward her, his arms outstretched.

"What are you doing?" she asked, stepping backward as if she suddenly expected to be mauled out here in an open field.

"I'm going to put you on top of that horse," he said, hoisting her light frame onto his shoulders and heaving her onto the dappled mare. "We don't have time for you to try to fuss about how you're going to get up there on your own."

She pounded a fist against his back until, with a final shove, she found herself seated on the horse. Sideways.

"You could have given me some warning before you started throwing me around like a sack of flour!" she protested, her face flaming as she awkwardly straddled the horse. Her skirts hiked up her legs, and she struggled to cover herself.

Sam looked away. Not that it did any good. He wouldn't forget what those legs looked like anytime soon. "Just remember," he said, nudging the black into a walk. He held up Toby's derringer for her benefit. "Once we get near the store, my finger won't be far from the trigger, so stay close and keep your mouth shut."

She shot him a wry glance. "Since you put it so sweetly, how could I do otherwise?"

"Murderers aren't supposed to be sweet," he reminded her, hiding his amusement as he urged their horses into a trot and watched Millie bounce and slip all over Mrs. Darwimple's back.

Millie fumed all the way down the hill. Not just because Sam refused to slow to a pace that would allow her to keep her seat without having to hug Mrs. Darwimple's neck for dear life, either. Worse. She couldn't shake the feeling that Sam had been trying to insinuate that she was spoiled.

Her!

Millie had known coddled people before, and she definitely wasn't one of them. Her aunt Clara in New Orleans had never even brushed her own hair. How was that for spoiled? Or what about Sally Hall? Now *there* was a pampered girl. When Sally was upset over her broken engagement to Warner Simms, her parents had sent her to Europe for an entire year! Millie had tried that trick on her father, but after eleven broken engagements she hadn't been sent anywhere besides her room. And now he actually wanted her to get married!

Besides, if the hallmark of a spoiled person was that she didn't do work, then she just didn't fit the bill. Far from it. Why, the very moment Sam found her, she had been picking pears that, once she'd run away long enough to bring her father to heel, she'd intended for a dessert for the family dinner. If that wasn't work, she didn't know what was—and look what a dangerous task it had turned out to be! She would have to remind Sam of that.

Of course, if she did tell him she would probably be forced to explain that she wasn't actually going to do anything with those pears except hand them over to their family cook, Sonya. She herself didn't know one end of the kitchen from the other. How could she? She'd been a motherless child, and after Sonya had caught her burning a batch of muffins all those years ago...

Well, anyway, lots of women couldn't cook.

Not that she actually cared what Sam thought, anyway. Why should she? It wasn't as if being a criminal were a noble way to spend one's time. It was far better to be a lady of enviable leisure than to run around killing people!

The thought made her feel much better about herself, and she glanced over at him with a renewed sense of self-satisfaction. Or as much as she could muster, looped as she was in such an undignified position around her poor horse. Sam rode straight and tall atop his black horse, his eyes scanning the horizon for signs of other riders approaching the small building.

Watching him, it was hard to believe he was the ruthless outlaw she'd seen murder two deputies with her very own eyes. Yet so much was deceiving about Sam Winter. He spoke like a man of some education, and his manners weren't unrefined. Not completely, at any rate. Of course, traveling out in the wild didn't bring out the best in anyone, least of all herself. She was certain her daddy would have some choice words to say to her if he could have seen her traipsing around in her underclothes yesterday morning.

That was another strange thing about Sam's behavior. In most of the books she'd read, criminals didn't treat women so...gingerly. Sam had barely even spoken to her unless circumstances forced him, and he certainly hadn't made any advances on her person. Thank goodness! She didn't know what she would have done if she'd been kidnapped by someone more unmannerly.

In fact, if Sam weren't her captor, she would have been tempted to say that his rough edges were rather endearing. True, he was overly gruff toward her at times, and perhaps a little too unconcerned about her comfort, but she couldn't deny that she found his wry humor charming, in its own peculiar way. And his dismissive way of treating her was a bit refreshing, frankly. Most men she knew made perfect fools of themselves trying to be nice to her and treat her as though she were a delicate flower. Not Sam. The moment he tied her to a tree and threw a horse blanket over her, she'd known he was different from all the others.

Millie sighed. Just as she had expected, it would be a little sad to part company with this strange man. And she would be terribly sorry to see him follow his brother to the gallows, as he no doubt would. Perhaps he might even beat Jesse there. Killing two sworn officers of the law topped wife-murdering any day, in her book. Even so, she couldn't deny having fallen under Sam Winter's spell, just a tiny bit.

What woman wouldn't? He was handsome in a rugged way that she just didn't run across among the men she knew. And his voice was deep, melodious. And his gray eyes practically lit up when he teased her. And when he touched her, as he had when he lifted her onto Mrs. Darwimple...

Oh, it was hopeless. What was the use of dwelling on details? They might serve her well when she was relating the events of her exciting abduction to Sally, but in the meantime, she was better off not romanticizing the man too much. After all, he'd be as good as dead once she was through with him.

Right now she had to concentrate on the task ahead of her. She couldn't forget Sam's threat; alerting the proprietor of the store that she had been kidnapped was going to be no easy task, with a gun trained on her the entire time. She only hoped that the person who owned the store was big and strong—or at least bigger and stronger than Sam.

As they slowed to a walk in front of the low building, she got a better look at the sign. *Ned Sparks' General Store.* She felt as if her whole future were in Ned Sparks's hands.

Sam eyed her cautiously. "You remember what I said?"

She straightened. "Of course."

"Good. Get down—and don't make any fast moves. And don't talk unless whoever's inside talks to you first. Understand?"

She gritted her teeth and nodded. Then she slipped off her horse. There was no other way to describe it. She put one leg back and lost her grip on the animal's slippery hide and shot to the ground with a thud. As she landed, she half expected to hear gunfire, although that particular fast move hadn't been intended. But instead, Sam appeared beside her and kindly yanked her back up to her feet.

"Sorry," he said as she dusted her backside off heatedly. "I forgot that your excellent horsemanship might not extend to the fine art of dismounting bareback."

"Never mind," she muttered. She wasn't going to argue with the man now. She needed him to think she was going to do exactly as he wanted. "Let's just get this over with."

"You first," he said, gesturing for her to walk ahead.

With some trepidation, she pushed open the door of the little store. Once she got a look at the dark, dusty place, she was doubly certain that she needed to be rescued soon. She couldn't imagine them buying anything there that she would actually want to eat.

"Well, hello there!" a voice cried out.

Millie looked around, but could see nothing—nothing besides old warped shelves stacked with dusty cans and jars, barrels full of who knew what, and bolts of mildewy cloth propped up against the walls. Finally, a head peeked over the long counter to her right—an old, wrinkled, bald head.

"You're Ned Sparks?" Millie couldn't keep the disappointment out of her voice. *This* was the man who was supposed to overcome her kidnapper and rescue her? Not likely! The man was seventy if he was a day—not to mention the fact that he was at least two inches shorter than she was.

Sam's hand clamped firmly around her arm, a reminder of his don't-speak-unless-spoken-to rule.

"Sure, I'm Ned," the man replied genially, plainly not realizing his reply sank Millie's hopes completely. "How do?"

"Just fine," Sam said, his manner equally friendly. "We just stopped for a few provisions."

"Are you the only person here?" Millie asked boldly, ready for gunfire. At this point, she hardly cared. She couldn't believe her bad luck.

"Sure am, little lady. Would ya'll be headed east or west?" Ned asked curiously.

"West," Sam replied.

"Well...I just come from the east myself!" The man beamed a partially toothed smile at them. "Fort Worth. You folks are lucky you found the store open. Just got back this morning."

"You don't say?"

"Yessir. Got me a ride on a fast wagon yesterday. Drove all night."

Sam nodded. Millie could feel the tension in his hand on her arm, the fear that this brush with the store proprietor was costing him. Was he worried that the man had heard about the kidnapping, Millie wondered, or was he concerned that she might blurt something out to the old man? If it was the latter, she would be perfectly willing to put Sam's mind at ease. She didn't see much point in trying to enlist the old fellow's aid.

When Sam failed to respond further, Ned continued, "I was off visiting my married sister. Lives in Fort Worth. How 'bout you? Where out west are you headed, exactly?"

Sam hesitated, his mouth slightly opened, then blurted out, "We're eloping."

Millie shot him a shocked glance, her mouth agape. Not only had he not answered the man's question, he'd come out with something totally unexpected. Yet she soon saw the wisdom in Sam's improvisation. If he'd intended to get the proprietor's mind off precise destinations, he couldn't have said anything better. When she looked back at Ned, he was all smiles.

"How 'bout that!" he cried. He let out a little whoop, then winked at Millie and leaned forward to whisper confidentially, "I was wonderin' why he was holdin' on to you so tight, but now I know. He's scared a handsome fellow like me's gonna steal his little bride away!"

He chortled merrily and winked again as Millie laughed limply along with him. Even Sam managed to force out a chuckle or two.

"Well, well," Ned went on. "What can I get for ya?"

Sam smiled, relaxing a little at Millie's continued silence. "Well, Ned," he said, shooting her a satisfied smile, "we just stopped by to get the wife a little grub."

"Don't want to take time off from the honeymoonin' to go huntin', is that it?"

"How did you guess?" Sam replied, squeezing Millie around the waist.

Millie felt her face flame at the implication—as if she would honeymoon with a desperado! Yet at the same time, she kept her tongue. This poor old man didn't know about her predicament, and couldn't do anything about it even if he did. The best she could hope for at this point was some good food.

She scanned the dusty shelves, full of jars with questionable contents, hoping to see something that caught her eye. Instead, her gaze alit on something far more interesting.

"A newspaper!" she exclaimed.

Ned turned to it with interest. "Just brought it back from Fort Worth."

"Would you mind if I read it some while my husband does the shopping?" she asked, squarely returning Sam's unamused stare. "I'd like to see if anything was written about our *elopement*."

Sam's eyes sparked in warning, but Ned remained oblivious as he handed over his precious paper. "Go right ahead," he urged. "Me and your husband will round you up some real nice vittles."

Millie's heart raced excitedly as they moved away, leaving her to leaf through the pages in private. There was sure to be news of her kidnapping from Fort Worth. If she could just figure out a way to scrawl a message across the newspaper, maybe the old man could help after all....

She didn't have far to look. *Prisoner Escapes in Chariton,* the story beneath the fold on the first page began. The next line in bold read, *Young Lady Abducted, Two Deputies Escape Attack Unharmed.* Millie quickly scanned the story, looking for her name, which wasn't mentioned. Just that she was a daughter of Old Lightfooted Lively. Now wasn't that silly? How was anyone expected to find her if the paper didn't print her name?

Her eyes were moving quickly across the page when suddenly she stopped, then looked back up, certain she had misread. *Two Deputies... Unharmed.*

Unharmed. But how could that be?

She had seen the "attack" with her very own eyes—had seen Sam brutally fell the two men, beating them repeatedly. They hadn't moved a muscle after that. Not when he'd dragged them over to that tree and—

The blood drained out of her face so quickly that she thought for a moment that she might faint. She refolded the paper, then leaned back against the counter, attempting to gather her racing thoughts.

First he'd beaten the deputies. Then he'd dragged them to a tree and tied them up. *Tied them up!* Why would he have bothered to tie up two dead men? Or shoo away their horses?

The answer was so simple. They had never been dead at all. Sam hadn't murdered anyone.

Oh, how could she have been so silly? How could she have made such a terrible misjudgment?

Across the small room, Sam and Ned conferred over various jars and kegs. At one point, Sam sent her a worried glance, as if he could tell that all was not right with her. But then he was forced to haggle with Ned over some sad-looking dried meat that made Millie's stomach lurch once again.

This new development threw everything into confusion. Sam was innocent of what she'd accused him of. She had proof of that now. Was his story about his brother being innocent also true?

She looked again at Sam. His proud, straight back. His head of dusty hair, his sun-darkened skin, his intelligent gray eyes. Was he an honest man, as he had claimed? Could she have misjudged him so completely?

It appeared she had.

She blushed to think about the hateful things she had said to him, the names she had called him. So many times he had told her the truth and she had turned a deaf ear, unswerving in her certainty about what she had witnessed. Only what she had seen had been entirely wrong.

His gray eyes were watching her again, and his forehead was creased with worry. He was worried about her? Something in her breast fluttered, and she looked away, stunned by the suddenness of it all.

Sam was innocent. That didn't change the fact that she was his hostage, of course, although it seemed to change practically everything else. How strange to think that she really had nothing to fear from Sam Winter after all. How strange . . . and how wonderful!

Chapter Four

"Isn't this just the loveliest day you've ever seen?"

Sam sent his charge a doubtful glance. Up till now, Millie had said not a word after they left Ned's little shack—just hummed and smiled—and though he appreciated the novelty of her silence, he knew the gears of deception must be grinding away in that twisted feminine mind of hers. The perky tone she chose when she finally spoke confirmed it. Something was up.

"I don't know when I've seen such a lovely day," she went on enthusiastically, sending him yet another of her beatific smiles.

That was another thing. Why was she looking at him in that simpering, cockeyed way? "You were cranky enough this morning."

Frankly, he was surprised that she hadn't attempted some sort of escape back at the store. She'd had ample opportunity to try to get Ned Sparks to hear her story, or to leave him some furtive message. Not that the old fellow could have been much of a help to her.

He frowned as they neared the place where he'd deposited her saddle. After knowing Millie only two full days, the idea of her not having an ulterior motive behind all this sudden complicity struck him as unlikely. These rich girls learned to use all sorts of roundabout tactics to get what they wanted from men.

Unfortunately, forewarned wasn't always forearmed. He found himself increasingly vulnerable to those thick-lashed dark eyes of hers. While he rode, he often thought about them—and how they would look just before he kissed her. Which wasn't going to happen, although his rambling thoughts did explain why he'd told that old man back there they were newlyweds. And probably why the old man could believe it, too. When Sam put his arm around Millie, there'd been nothing fake about the fierce stab of desire he felt for her.

Poor kid. She'd probably go screaming into the horizon if she knew what a case he had for her. He glanced warily at her.

Millie beamed. Her dark brown eyes seemed almost to sparkle at him with something that he would have sworn resembled admiration...if he hadn't known better. That was why it was so important to get his mind off her lips and focus on what was going on inside that brain of hers.

At the top of the hill, Sam reined in his horse. Millie stopped right next to him, and slipped off without his even having to ask her. Carefully he dismounted himself, certain now that she must have some trick up her sleeve.

He walked over to the saddle and lugged it back over to Millie's horse.

"Here, let me help you with that, Mr. Winter," she said, coming forward with outstretched hands.

This was too much. "Don't let's stand on formality, Millie," he answered politely. "You can just call me Mr. Murderer."

She blushed and cast her eyes modestly toward the dirt at his feet. "Oh, no," she said earnestly, "I would never call you that."

He let out a sharp laugh as he hefted the silly saddle onto Mrs. Darwimple's back. "Changed your mind about me, have you?"

She batted her thick black eyelashes twice before looking back at him. "Yes, I have."

What kind of game was this? "If you think a lie like that is going to make me let my guard down, think again."

That pointy chin lifted a little higher. "It's not a lie. I know with perfect certainty that you didn't kill those two deputies."

"Did a little bird tell you?"

"No, the newspaper did."

He looked at her in alarm.

"There was a whole long article on the front page about us—only I guess they didn't mention my name because that would have been detrimental to my reputation." She planted her hands on her hips in irritation. "Now I ask you, does that make sense? How else do they expect me to be found?"

Sam's brows knit together worriedly. Being front-page news didn't flatter him half as much as it did Millie. "Did the paper have a description of us?"

She sent him a look that let him know precisely how absurd his question was. "Most people in the area know what I look like."

"Sure, but we're not in the area. Ned Sparks didn't suspect us—but maybe he hadn't read the article yet."

"That old man? He probably couldn't see us well enough to identify us, anyway. Besides, he thinks we're newly married." She laughed. "And didn't I play my part well? I thought you would have mentioned that."

"You were fine," Sam said, distracted. "You should have snatched that paper, though. That old guy might be better at putting two and two together than we give him credit for." Sam took to his task more hurriedly. "We've got to put some distance between ourselves and this place."

"Good," Millie said cheerfully, "I'm anxious to get home."

Sam stopped in the middle of tugging on the girth. At first, he wasn't sure he'd heard her right. But the breezy way she stood nearby, inspecting her fingernails, convinced him that he had. "What the hell are you talking about?"

"Aren't we going back to Chariton?" Her wide, dark eyes were unfazed by his gruff words. "Surely you see this changes everything. I believe you, Sam."

"That's wonderful," he said. "What do you want, a medal?"

"No, I merely want to go home, and now there's absolutely no reason for us not to. Why should we be gallivanting across the countryside, now that you have a witness who can vouch for what happened? This has all just been a big mistake, and I'm perfectly willing to tell everybody so."

At first he was dumbfounded. Just a big mistake? Finally, after staring in shock for a few minutes at her standing in front of him, her face the picture of complacency, he bit out a bitter laugh. "Oh, now that's a relief."

Her thin shoulders squared proudly. "I should think it would be. I'm willing to explain to my daddy, the sheriff and even a judge if need be that there's been a terrible miscarriage of justice. I'm sure they'll understand."

Sam couldn't think of what to say. She really seemed to believe that all they had to do was go back and all would be forgiven. "Don't you realize that your father has probably organized a posse to hunt me down?"

"Oh, yes!" Millie nodded. "The story mentioned that. Twenty men, it said."

"Twenty men, all with orders to shoot to kill."

"To *kill?*" The idea seemed to startle her. "But you're innocent! I can tell them that."

"Princess, you don't understand. They're going to shoot first and ask questions later. If we go within two counties of Chariton, you'll be explaining my innocence over my carcass. It won't be a pretty sight."

Millie frowned distastefully. "My daddy is a reasonable man. Maybe if you sent me first—"

"Oh, no," Sam said. "Knowing you, you'll start talking, and soon as you know it you'll be leading that posse straight to me."

She rolled her eyes in exasperation. "But if you don't go back, or at least send me, we'll just have to keep running."

"That's right," he said. "But it's not going to be *we*, Princess. It'll just be me."

She crossed her arms over her chest. "And where will I be?"

"With friends," Sam told her.

"Oh, thank heavens!" she said, obviously relieved. "I'll go directly to Sally Hall. She's a notorious gossip, but if I twist her arm and tell her how absolutely imperative—"

Sam shook his head in disbelief. "Are you completely addlebrained? I'm not sending you to *your* friends," he informed her.

Millie blinked. "Oh."

"Actually, Gus Beaver was a friend of my father's, but I count him as one of my own, too."

Her expression, so recently smug and self-assured, now flushed with confusion and just a touch of panic. "Where does this Gus Beaver live, if I might ask?"

"About a day's ride from here."

"In a town?" she asked, her voice growing shrill with concern.

"Nope. He's about as isolated as can be. That's why I'm taking you there—so you'll stay put."

"Well, I won't go!" she said, coming forward, some of the old anger flashing in her dark eyes. "This is the most ridiculous plan I've ever heard of. Here I am offering—no, practically begging!—to tell the world that you've been wrongly treated, and your only reaction is to abandon me alone out in the middle of nowhere with some old man you barely know!"

"I trust Gus. And you won't be alone—he's married."

"Why can't I at least go with you? That way, if you're caught, I could—"

"Because without you along I stand a better chance of *not* getting caught. You stick out, Millie. Somebody's bound to notice you sooner or later. I'll move faster on my own."

"But as I was trying to explain, if you were apprehended, I could vouch for your character."

Sam was anxious to get going again. "We don't have time to stand here all day arguing, so listen tight. It's not only my own hide I'm concerned about. I have a brother in jail, and he's going to be swinging from a noose in eleven days if I don't manage to bring in the man who really killed his wife. That's going to be a hard feat in itself, but saddled with you, Princess, it becomes nigh on impossible. Do you want to be responsible for a man's death?"

She drew back, stung by his blunt words. "I only wanted to help."

He handed Mrs. Darwimple's reins to her. "Fine. Just keep doing what I tell you to do."

"You don't have to treat me like a hostage anymore," she assured him, grudgingly accepting the reins. "I'm on your side."

Somehow, her words failed to give Sam the solace he suspected was intended. Having Millie Lively on his side was about as comforting as having an ant in his boot. And, to his way of thinking, about as helpful.

Millie wrinkled her nose and, with her fingertips, held her once pristine white ruffled pinafore away from her person. The garment was letting off a dreadful odor that she felt sure not all of the scrubbing in the world could get rid of.

She couldn't really complain. It had been her idea that Sam teach her how to clean the fish he had caught that evening in a stream they had stopped near. She'd been so excited at the process of a square meal—not to mention a chance to prove how helpful she could be to Sam—that she had eagerly volunteered for the task. But that was before she'd known what a smelly, disgusting experience it would be. Sam could have at least warned her! Her poor pinafore, a mess from all the fish guts and the wounds Sam's knife had inflicted on her own poor hands, had been rendered unwearable, not to mention unattractive to anything but a swarm of flies.

No doubt Sam would tell her to wash it a couple of times. But with what? The man had thought to pick up things like fishhooks and a knife and ammunition for his stolen arsenal at Ned Sparks's store, but had he thought of soap? Millie had no intention of lugging a stinky, sticky pinafore around until she got to the Weavers' or the Beavers' or whatever their name was. She didn't care if Sam did think only a spoiled rich girl would be so shameful and wasteful. It was her pinafore, and she was leaving it here.

She just wouldn't let him know about it.

She scoped out the ground around her. Everywhere the earth was dry and hard, or covered with thick yellow grass she would never be able to claw through to bury the pinafore. The only thing left to do was stash the thing away under a bush and hope Sam didn't see it. It was nearly dark, anyway, and they would leave well before sunrise. Chances of him spotting it and forcing her to bring it along were slim.

She wasn't certain why Sam's opinion suddenly mattered so much. Maybe it had something to do with the quavery feeling she got every time she looked into those hard gray eyes of his—like her knees were about to collapse underneath her. No man she'd known had been capable of making her feel so fluttery inside.

After hastily pushing the pinafore beneath some leafy branches of a low bush and covering it with loose dirt and dried leaves, she hurried back to their makeshift camp.

Sam barely glanced at her as she returned. He was hunched over the smallest campfire she'd ever seen, fanning what little smoke the burning embers of mesquite wood gave off by waving a leafy branch over the fish, which, after she had scraped and mutilated the poor thing, now seemed pathetically small. Hardly worth the effort, really.

"You were gone long enough," he said.

Sam obviously didn't want to admit it, but Millie was certain he was glad she believed his story. In fact, she had a vague hope that she was winning the man over. Didn't that comment about her being gone a long time indicate he had been restless for her return?

The thought gave her a little lift. "A woman likes to have some time to herself, you know," Millie said, plopping onto the ground nearby and arranging her filthy dress neatly around her.

"Woman?" he muttered, poking at their dinner. "You're still a kid."

"I am not. I'll be twenty in December."

Now that got his attention. "You?" he asked, his voice drawling with an amazement Millie wasn't certain reflected well on his estimation of her maturity.

She nodded. "How old did you think I was?"

He shrugged. "Frankly, I haven't given it much thought."

That wasn't very flattering, either. "I've thought plenty about how old you are," she informed him.

A grin touched his lips, and he lifted a rusty brown eyebrow. "And what did you come up with?"

"I've decided you're probably younger than you act," she said generously. "I bet you're no more than twenty-eight."

"I'm thirty," he told her flatly. The grin was gone.

"Oh." But "Oh, dear!" was what she might have said, if she hadn't managed to stop herself. *Thirty!*

That made quite a bit of difference. Back when she thought he was twenty-eight at the most, her kidnapper had had a certain dashing romantic appeal. But thirty... Why, the oldest boy she'd ever been sweet on was Josiah Armstrong, and he'd only been twenty-three. Thirty was so old! After all, she could remember when her *father* was thirty. Couldn't she? No, maybe he'd been older—forty perhaps. But thirty was nearly forty. Both were old. Very, very old.

"Would you stop looking at me like that?" Sam shouted.

Millie was startled. "What's the matter?"

"Those eyes of yours were about to bug out of your head," he bit out. "I didn't say I was ninety."

"I know, but…" Well. She didn't want to make him feel any worse than he probably already did.

"I don't see why it matters, anyway," he grumbled, swatting the air above the fish again.

"It doesn't. Of course it doesn't," she agreed quickly. Seeking a safer topic, she said, "You haven't asked me how my hands are."

He looked up, squinting at the little nicks at the edge of her palms. "How are they?"

"Painful!" she cried with a groan. "I've never gone through so much fuss and bother for one measly meal in my entire life. All I've been through for that fish has completely robbed me of my appetite. Though I might like one of those apples from the store."

He reached into the saddlebag at his side and tossed a piece of fruit over to her. It was bruised and pulpy from its bumpy ride on Sam's saddle, but she bit into it happily, savoring the sweet, juicy flavor. "Sam, can I ask you something?"

Instead of answering, he half smiled, breathed deeply and shot her a patient stare.

She took that as a yes. "You said this afternoon you had to find the man who really killed your brother's wife. What makes you think you know who did it?"

He let out a ragged sigh, then dug deep into his pants pocket with his free hand. "Because of this."

He held something out to her—a ring. She took it from him and inspected the plain gold band, as much as she could in the dying light.

"It was found by the bed in my brother's house—after Salina was murdered."

"It's not your brother's?" she asked.

He shook his head. "Inside there's an engraving. 'T to D,' it says."

Millie squinted to read the lettering. "And you think the murderer is 'D,' and he accidentally left it at your brother's house on the night of the murder?'' She sat up at attention. Now *this* was interesting!

"My brother had a partner once," Sam explained. "His name was Darnell Weems. And on the night of the murder, as he was riding back up to the house, Jesse said, he saw someone who looked like Darnell riding away."

Millie clutched the ring in her small fist and held it up in triumph. "Then here's your proof!" she said excitedly, jumping up. "Now I *know* we have to go back to Chariton! Once Sheriff McMillan finds out about this, he'll have to let your brother go! And you, too—they can't imprison you for harboring a fugitive who shouldn't have been a fugitive in the first place."

Even in the face of her enthusiasm, Sam shook his head. "Before you bust a gut, you might be interested to hear that Sheriff McMillan knows all about the ring."

Millie blinked at him in confusion. "He saw it?"

"Sure, I showed it to him. He said it didn't prove a thing."

"But he's wrong!" Millie cried.

"Lucky thing I kept it hidden and didn't hand it over to him. I have a feeling the good sheriff might have conveniently lost it."

She sucked in a shocked breath. "Sheriff Tom wouldn't do that!"

Sam snorted in derision.

"He wouldn't," she insisted hotly. "I know him. He's been over to supper several times."

"Maybe he's different across the dinner table than through iron bars, Princess. Believe me—if I'd had twenty rings with the name Darnell Weems, Murderer engraved on them, your good sheriff wouldn't have been swayed one little bit."

"It can't be true," Millie insisted.

"Oh, no?" he asked. "Then I suppose you weren't at my brother's 'trial.' When Jesse testified that he'd seen Darnell riding away that night, the sheriff said my brother was just trying to pin the blame on some phantom rider nobody else had seen. And when I tried to show the judge the ring, they claimed I could have had it engraved myself.''

''That's outrageous!'' Millie said in disbelief. ''Why would Sheriff Tom turn a blind eye like that?''

''Because two years ago, in another murder case, my brother testified against Sheriff Tom's son. Of course, young Raif McMillan got off scot-free for gunning down a man in a barroom in broad daylight, but don't think your sheriff didn't remember the incident when my brother was brought in.''

Millie remembered when Raif McMillan had gotten off. She'd been glad—Raif wasn't bad, really. And nobody she knew was acquainted with the man who had been killed. But now the incident took on a more sinister cast; she wasn't sure what to believe.

One thing she did know, Sam wasn't lying to her about his brother's innocence. She might not have conclusive proof, but she was done doubting him. Instinct told her he was telling her the truth. Instinct, and a ring, and a prickly feeling inside that indicated she hadn't ever really taken an unfiltered view of the men who ran her boring little town. Sam's revelation about Sheriff Tom was a rude awakening.

Slowly, she handed the ring back to him.

''I've been carrying it with me, hidden, for weeks, just waiting for my chance to escape. Thank God it came while there's still time.''

''Eleven days isn't much,'' Millie said. Now she knew why he was always so cross when she was slow to move in the morning, or complained about being tired and wanting to rest. She never would again. ''How are you going to manage?''

His jaw sawed back and forth for a moment before he looked at her with his steely gray eyes and answered, ''After I dump you off with Gus, I'm going to ride like thunder to a town out west called Little Bend. That's where Jesse said Darnell owns some land. After that, I'm not sure. All

I know is that I'm bringing the man back with me if I have to tie him up and drag him."

His determination impressed her, even distracted as she was by his intention to "dump" her. She hopped up in dismay. "Oh, I wish I could go with you, Sam!"

He shook his head firmly. "Forget it."

"But I could be helpful, I know I could," she insisted. "You have to admit I'm a good rider. Now that we have a few provisions, I won't complain about the long days and lack of sleep, I promise."

"That's not what concerns me," Sam said.

"Then what? Surely you don't want to face this Weems man alone if you can help it. Wouldn't I be better than nothing?"

A smile touched his lips as he looked up at her.

"I would, and you know it!"

"Okay, maybe better than nothing," he grudgingly admitted. "But you can get the notion out of your head. I'm not going to mix you up in this."

"But I want to be mixed up!" she cried.

"You're a lady," he told her, "and the man I'm after is a murderer. If you get hurt, I'm responsible. Don't forget about that daddy of yours—I don't think he'd be as forgiving as you seem to think."

She kicked at the dirt peevishly. "I don't care what anybody thinks, Sam. This is important. A man's life is at stake."

"Yeah, a man you've probably passed on the street of that little town of yours a hundred times without noticing." In spite of his searing comment, his expression softened as he looked at her. "Give it up, Princess. This isn't your fight."

She folded her arms crossly. "What am I supposed to do after you stash me away—just wait for news that you've been killed?"

"You'd be better off forgetting I ever existed. Most likely I'll wind up in jail—or like you say, dead—but even if I don't, I doubt a girl like you would profit much from our association."

"Well, I think differently. In spite of what you may think, I know lots of people who aren't particularly rich or important."

"Oh, yes," Sam joked. "I heard you mention your maid Alberta several times."

She rounded on him, angered by his words, and by the tiny sting of truth in them. "Maybe you've been right to accuse me of being spoiled, and maybe a little snooty. My daddy's always tried to shelter me, I guess. But I'm not like that so much anymore."

Sam stood, laughing.

"I'm not!" she cried. "I'm a different girl entirely than the one you pulled out of the tree three days ago, Sam. I see things differently now. I *am* different."

"You really think so?"

"I know it," she declared.

"And what's caused this miraculous change?" he asked, coming closer.

It surprised her that he would even ask. "You did."

"You can't mean that." He shook his head again—it was a habit she was growing thoroughly tired of.

"It's true," she said. "You're the only person I've ever known who's treated me the way you do, like I'm no one special. Sure it makes me angry, but in some ways, it has its advantages. Like tonight, for instance. When you were telling me about your brother, you didn't mince words, or try to shelter me from the facts. You'll even insult me if you think it's necessary. That must mean you respect me on some level."

He tossed up his hands. "Princess, I think that's the screwiest thing I've ever heard you say!"

"There, you see?" she pointed out. "No one but you would ever say something like that to me. You treat me like an equal."

He let out a howl. "I'm only telling it to you straight, so you'll appreciate the danger you're asking me to put you in."

Oh, now he was back on that again. "But I wouldn't care about danger as long as I could be with you," she said in a rush, taking his arm.

At the contact, he looked down at her hand in surprise. They both froze for a moment, their barrage of words broken by the way she'd reached out to him—or was it the plain-spoken confession she'd just made? Millie wasn't quite sure which had caused the distinct shift in air around them, but she suddenly felt a tension snapping between them that hadn't existed before.

Slowly, his gaze lifted to her eyes. "You're playing with fire, Princess."

"I am?"

Her mouth was dry, and as she felt the intensity of his steely eyes, and the strength of the corded muscle beneath her hand, she attempted to swallow. The result was an ineffectual gulp of smoky air. Feeling less sure of herself, she took a step backward...but he followed stealthily after her, like a bobcat preparing to pounce on its prey.

"You can't go prancing around in your wet underclothes in front of a strange man—" he gritted the words out "—or hiking up your skirts, or telling him that you want to travel across the state in his company."

Millie swallowed. "I can't?"

Her heart tripped unsteadily, and for a moment, she considered trying to flee. Especially when she recognized that gleam in his eye. She'd seen it before, with modifications. Every boy who ever kissed her had shown a hint of that gleam—except they had never looked quite so predatory as Sam.

"If you chase a wolf, Millie, sooner or later he's going to turn on you."

Her heart drilled against her ribs. Sam *was* going to kiss her—she was certain of it now. Only he was taking his time about it! "Wh-what happens then?" she asked, her voice coming out a little more unsteadily than she'd expected.

"This," he said, grabbing her by the waist and pulling her roughly against him.

Millie didn't even have time to catch her breath. Sam's mouth descended on hers with a fierceness she hadn't expected; even if she had gotten a gulp of air, he probably would have sucked it right out of her. For a moment, all she could do was grab on to his arms and take in all the new sensations—his firm lips against hers, his breath, the sting of his whiskers against her soft skin, the solid hardness of his chest pressing into her bosom. The effect made her dizzy, as though her whole being had suddenly melted to a hot liquid that was pooling and swirling inside her. Never in her life had she felt so *engulfed* by another person before. She wasn't sure how much more she could take.

And then something extraordinary happened. His mouth pressed against her taut lips, opening them, inviting a sort of commingling of tongues such as she had never in her life imagined. She gasped in shock. How frighteningly intimate, how...

How wonderful! With a growing fierceness, Sam teased and tasted and clasped her to him in a way that made her feel as if they were one person. Her hands moved up his arms, and her body answered his embrace by pressing forward to become yet closer to him.

One callused hand reached up to cup her face as he pulled away from her. "Don't you see what I'm trying to tell you, Millie?" he asked, his voice raspy and hard.

Her mind was in a sensual frenzy. And his lips were still only inches away. "Oh, yes!" she cried excitedly.

This time, she launched herself at him, skipping the part where they were supposed to clasp lips the old boring way and going straight to the heavenly method Sam had just taught her. Her hands twined together at the nape of his neck and she was so eager to get nearer that she was practically standing tippytoe on his feet. She kissed him long and hard, reveling in the boneless, feverish way he made her feel.

A long, rasping groan broke through the night. It was Sam. To her utter dismay, he locked his hands on her shoulders and pried her firmly away from him.

Her knees shaky, Millie tripped backward, breathing heavily. Without thinking, she reached a hand to her mouth and brushed her moist lips with her fingertips, then felt her warm cheeks against her knuckles. A broad smile broke across her lips.

Sam's eyes rounded in alarm as he waved his hands and took a hopping step away from her. "Millie..." he growled warningly.

Giddy laughter erupted from her lips, and she lifted her limp shoulders helplessly. "Oh, Sam, I never knew!" she cried. "How magnificent!"

He shook his head in confusion. "No, look, you're not taking this the right way."

She came toward him. "Then show me the right way."

He sidestepped her advance. "You crazy girl!" he said in terse exasperation. "Don't you know how a girl like you is supposed to react when a man makes a pass at her?"

Millie nodded eagerly. "Now I do!"

He rolled his eyes toward the moon. "You're supposed to be outraged," he lectured. "Don't you see? I was taking advantage of you. Using you. You should have slapped me."

She sucked in a breath. As his words finally sank in, she remembered his warnings about playing with fire and was sick with disappointment. The most earth-shattering event of her whole entire life, and he'd only been trying to teach her a lesson. What a miserable failure of a pupil she'd turned out to be! "Slap you?" she muttered. "I guess I didn't think of that."

"Good grief," he said. "You're even more innocent than you seem. That's why you can't go gallivanting around the country with a wanted man, Millie."

"Are you saying I shouldn't trust you?"

He ran a hand raggedly through his hair. "Of course not. I just—" His words broke off, and he grumbled a few curses beneath his breath before looking back at her. "Oh, forget it. We might as well call it a night."

In a swift motion, he turned and kicked dirt on the fire, smothering both the flames and the charred little fish. "Probably would have tasted like a hunk of burned wood anyway," he muttered. Then he took her arm.

"What are you doing?" she asked as he dragged her away from the campfire.

"Tucking you in."

At the trunk of a mesquite tree, he pushed her down and began the usual ritual of battening her down for the evening. She blew out a weary huff. "I told you that you didn't have to treat me like a hostage anymore," she said. "I want to help you."

The dubious look he sent her spoke volumes, but still he answered, "That's what worries me. At least when you thought I was a low-down murdering varmint I could predict what you would do."

Her lips twisted in a frown as he finished tying her off, then stepped back to admire his handiwork.

"That should hold you," he said. When she didn't answer, he returned to the fire and brought back one of the blankets, covering her legs. She tried not to look at him, but the nearness of arms that had so recently held her tightly had a residual effect that she fought bitterly against.

"Well, good night," he said before returning to his place.

She wouldn't stoop to answering him. He might kiss well, but her initial estimate of him had been correct, she saw now. Sam Winter was an odious man.

And yet, everything she'd told him was true. So much had changed since she'd known him. She felt different now— more mature. Now she understood that matters didn't always fall into simple categories of right and wrong. Sometimes sheriffs could turn a blind eye to justice. Appearances could deceive. A fugitive could turn out to be the good guy.

Sam had shown her all that. How could she simply allow herself to be shoved aside, hidden away at some old man's house, while Sam risked his life? She wasn't the same old Millie Lively anymore. She couldn't blithely go on as if she'd never met Sam, never let him kiss her the way he had.

That kiss! She would never be able to get it out of her mind. The sweet pecks she'd received from all her prior sweethearts seemed laughingly innocent and uneventful to her now. Maybe having the maturity of thirty years wasn't such a drawback after all. Anyway, she wasn't exactly a babe in the woods herself. A girl who had been engaged as often as she had was pretty experienced, by Chariton standards. Sally Hall, who at last count had been kissed by only four boys, had once even called her loose.

Her lips stretched into a wicked grin. What would Sally say about her now?

She stretched and sighed. Somehow, even the idea of getting back to Chariton so that she could relate her adventures to Sally didn't sound as appealing as it had once.

Sam *had* to care for her, at least a little. She knew he did—that kiss couldn't have been entirely to teach her a lesson. And if it had, didn't that show he was concerned for her well-being? After all, by telling her that she couldn't trust him, he was admitting, albeit indirectly, that he probably wouldn't be able to control his animal passions around her.

Which meant that he was more attracted to her than he was willing to admit.

Now *that* thought gave her hope.

She tapped her foot anxiously. Looking at the situation in this new light, it seemed that his stowing her away at his friend's would be as tough on him as it would be for her. He was actually making a sacrifice for her sake—making certain she was safe so that he could go out and face his demons alone.

He was willing to give her up for her own sake. She would have to be equally brave. Sam wasn't willing to see reason, to accept all the good her position and status as a Lively could do for him. Probably he was wary because he had had a bad experience with Tom McMillan. But all men weren't crooked like that, especially not her father. And once she told her daddy about what had happened to Sam and his brother, she had no doubt that the venerable old gentleman would move heaven and earth to see that justice was finally served.

It nearly made her cry to think about what she could do for Sam, if only she had the chance.

Stubborn, infuriating Sam, she thought with a wistful sigh. He'd warned her that if she stayed with him, the days ahead would be dangerous. But he was wrong. The real danger, she feared, was that she was losing her heart to a desperado who was intent on fighting her every step of the way.

"Sam?" she asked lightly, curious to know whether he was having the same difficulty dropping off to sleep that she was.

His reply came promptly out of the darkness. "What?"

"Next time, I'll slap you."

A pause ensued. "There won't be a next time," he said.

Millie smiled. They would just see about that!

Chapter Five

"I bet we've been riding for five hours!"

Millie's shoulders drooped, and she looked as if she could scarcely keep her eyes open, which to Sam indicated that she probably hadn't slept any better than he had. He nodded curtly, but didn't answer. They couldn't stop. Five hours or not, Millie seemed to be keeping pace somehow. And if his own pace wasn't quite as steady as it usually was, she herself was partly to blame for that.

All night long, he'd lain restless against the hard ground, his thoughts uncontrollable. One minute they would all be focused on Jesse, and the forlorn way his brother had looked stuck in that jail as Sam was escorted away by Toby and Ed. Then, the next thing he knew, Millie would pop into his head, her sweet cupid lips and dancing dark eyes a vision he just couldn't shake. He'd start remembering how soft and inviting she'd felt in his arms, and worse, how she had responded to his kiss—like a woman who had just found an irresistible new way to pass the time.

He had been shocked out of his boots when she threw herself at him that way. Shocked, but not displeased. Hell, he couldn't deny it. He'd *wanted* to kiss her. Had thought of little else for days. And just for a tiny second, he'd considered not stopping that kiss and seeing where they would end up.

But he knew the answer to that—both of them sprawled half-dressed on a blanket, on the hard earth. And afterward he would have been filled with regrets instead of restlessness. Of the two, the latter was far preferable. Bedding Millie would have brought so many problems crashing down on him that he would have cursed himself for being all kinds of a fool for the rest of his life...which, once her legendary daddy got hold of him, couldn't be expected to last long. Especially if his daughter was returned to him in any way defiled.

No, he was better off not sleeping for a few years than acting on the notions that kept popping into his head when he looked at Millie Lively. Or even when he didn't.

Maybe it was time to get married. Jesse always told him he should—and now Sam knew why. If a man waited too long, his perspective would become all skewed and he'd start taking a yen to the first female who crossed his path, no matter how ridiculously unfit for him she was.

On his farm, he didn't avoid women, but he didn't exactly seek them out, either. His place was a little isolated, nestled at the edge of the hill country, sixteen miles from the nearest town. And he liked living the life of a bachelor. He had his own spread, a nice house, and nobody to tell him what to do. When he finished a hard day's work, he wasn't forced to be nice and pleasant to anybody. Of course, there was nobody waiting around to be nice and pleasant to him, either—except Burt, the man who cooked for Sam and whatever hands were hanging around the place. But Burt Lewis hadn't been pleasant to anybody since he'd had his last tooth pulled twelve years ago.

Occasionally Sam would go into town to drink and socialize and occasionally scratch an itch that could be taken care of on the second floor of a saloon. He wasn't one of those poor fellows who were forever attending church socials in hopes of finding a lifelong helpmeet. Too often he'd seen men like that finally get hitched, thinking they were getting a warm companion for cold winter nights, only to find out a year later that they'd saddled themselves to a permanent yearlong nag.

Maybe Sam just hadn't spent long enough stretches around women to see how irreplaceable they were. His own mother had died when he was three, leaving his father to care for Sam and the newborn baby Jesse. And when their father died, Sam, at seventeen, had finished the rearing duties, until the day the restless Jesse saddled up and rode off to make his own way in the world.

Should he have tried to keep Jesse at home? The question plagued him now. Maybe if Jesse hadn't ever met up with Darnell Weems... But such speculation was pointless. Nobody could live another man's life for him. Sam had a hard enough time living his own.

And that life would be even more difficult if he saddled himself with a woman like Millie. The notion itself made him want to hoot. Millie Lively was a proper young lady, despite all her exuberance at being kissed for what, by her earthy reaction, he could only suppose was the first time. She'd grown up with maids, men who complimented her every little move, and a daddy who called her "Princess" and meant it. She was not the type of girl a man like Sam could take to heart—much less take back to a farm that offered none of the niceties Millie had grown up with.

So why was his mind so stuck on her? Why, in unguarded moments, did he discover that he'd been imagining how it would be to turn over in his comfortable bed back on the farm and see her thick black hair spilling across his pillow, her red lips turning up in a satisfied little smile? In fact, the entire morning he'd been imagining the two of them in carnal embraces all over his rambling house, on every stick of the old familiar furniture, in every room, including the kitchen.

That just wouldn't do!

With all the mental fortitude he could muster, he forced his thoughts in a different direction. His imagination strained to picture Millie Lively at more useful tasks than satisfying his misplaced lust. It wasn't easy. Millie just didn't look right with a hoe in her hands, or wiping her brow as she removed a loaf of bread from a hot oven. Whenever he tried to picture her by the fire, mending clothes or perhaps just sitting quietly, he almost shrieked with laughter. Millie as a dutiful farm wife was something to behold.

When Millie married, it would have to be to a rich man, a city man, not to mention a man with considerably more patience than Sam possessed. She required a man willing to lavish money and attention on her. And, most of all, Millie would want a husband she could gently manipulate, and Sam just wasn't willing to be the docile piece of string she could twist around her delicate yet deceptively strong little finger.

Besides, when he married—*if* he married—it would have to be to a solid, hardworking farm girl. Someone who knew the meaning of hard labor for little payoff other than the satisfaction of seeing something grow. Someone who was content keeping herself entertained, and didn't mind the long stretches of boredom interspersed with spurts of frenzied nonstop work that comprised farm life. A good solid female of modest character and sensible temperament...

Sam frowned. No wonder he'd reached the age of thirty without getting hitched. His ideal wife just wasn't very appealing.

Beside him, Millie sighed as Mrs. Darwimple jogged along. Sometimes Sam thought that little horse had more stamina than the rest of them put together.

"What's the matter now?" he asked, his voice coming out more sharply than he'd intended.

"Nothing," she responded, the single word clipped and proud, yet nevertheless reminding him that this was the longest conversation they'd had so far this morning.

He glanced over and took a long look at her. Something was different. Something... Suddenly, it struck him. "Where's your, uh..." He pointed to her chest. "Your apron thing."

"Oh, my pinafore?"

He nodded. Millie swallowed. "I, uh, lost it."

"Lost it? Where?"

She pointed at the landscape behind them. "Back there somewhere, I think."

Sam scowled. "I should have known you'd be leaving a trail."

Her head snapped around. "A what?"

"A trail. You know, so people would know which way we're headed."

Millie shook her head furiously. "Oh, no, Sam—I would never do that. Well, I mean . . . not now."

Good grief. "What else have you left behind?"

She bit her lip anxiously. "Well, that first day I did drop a bonnet near where you kidnapped me. But honestly, Sam, that was all. Absolutely all. I only left my pinafore because it stank so bad—"

Sam let out a biting laugh.

"It's the truth!" she pleaded. "We could go back—"

"All right, forget it," he said. This wasn't a joyride. Millie knew that. He had only ten days to prove Jesse's innocence, and every minute of every hour of every one of those days was crucial. He didn't have time to be backtracking for lost items of clothing.

He looked over at her, fully prepared to give her a lecture on the desperate time frame he was dealing with. But her weary shoulders and her normally pert lips fixed in a tired, frustrated frown choked him into silence.

Inside, he sort of felt the way she looked. But Millie wasn't going to admit she was tired. Not after last night. His gaze tarried on her pretty face. Her white skin had burnished a light pink on her nose and high cheekbones after days of exposure to unrelieved sunlight. Her hair still had a dull shine, but she wore it differently now, pulled back at her nape, but otherwise flowing free down her back.

His thoughts raced back to the night before, and his gut tightened uncomfortably. Millie might not be his ideal for a wife, but that wasn't tamping down his desire any.

Stop, he thought. *You're letting her get to you.*

But it wasn't Millie's fault he couldn't concentrate, a little voice told him. He had been the one foolish enough to instigate that crazy kiss, after all. She was just a kid—a beautiful spoiled girl. And here he was, treating her as though *she* had done something wrong, as if her prettiness and youth and enthusiasm—born out of her misguided belief that she could influence the authorities to set him and Jesse free—had somehow offended him.

Actually, just the opposite was true. Things were as dire as ever, but since Millie had left Ned Sparks's store, he'd felt one less pressure. Even if she did have a naive, hare-brained sense of good triumphing over bad every time, Millie meant well. And despite the fact that he had kidnapped her, she wanted to help him. Sam just doubted she could.

And how was he repaying her faith in him, her desire to help? By driving her ruthlessly, when he knew she was probably worn out, though it was still before noon. And by jumping down her throat for making a simple mistake about that pinafore. He felt like a heel.

"Whoa!" he cried, sawing on the black's reins.

He stopped so quickly that Mrs. Darwimple trotted right past him, then spun abruptly when the tether that connected the horses snapped taut. Millie was nearly thrown, but managed somehow to keep her seat.

She really was a good horsewoman, Sam thought admiringly.

In fact, she really wasn't the terrible burden he'd thought she'd be....

"Well?" Millie asked, her voice impatient.

Sam looked at her, surprised at the dangerous path his thoughts had been winding down. "I just thought you might like a short break."

"I don't need one," she said.

"Well, take one anyway," he retorted, displeased by her ornery reaction. "Your horse could probably use a rest, even if you don't want one."

Her eyes narrowed and her lips puckered unhappily. "I should have known you were only thinking of the horse."

Sam swung down and untied the tether. "Walk her down to the creek for water," he instructed.

He would take a more circuitous route to give Millie some privacy, not to mention to get away from her. Crazy girl! he thought in annoyance as he walked the black away. Millie's thoughts never seemed to progress in straight lines. Why couldn't she just thank him for stopping? Instead, her brain had to zigzag around everything he said, thinking he was somehow insulting her by offering her a rest.

Which was just another example of why he would be glad to be rid of her. His life was mixed up enough without her in it.

Suddenly—from out of nowhere, it seemed—he heard hoofbeats.

Sam's first instinct was to duck behind a tree, out of plain sight. He muffled the black, then tilted his head, listening. His heart slammed against his chest in panic. Where was Millie? Damnation! Why hadn't he been more careful, more alert?

The hoofbeats weren't getting closer. In fact, they were fading quickly. Taking in the growing silence around him, Sam clenched his teeth and bit out a curse.

Millie!

Fast as lightning, he mounted the black and kicked the tired horse into a gallop. He spotted her, skirts flying, headed back where they'd come from, following their old path but keeping closer to the creek. Sam didn't bother to question what was going on in that sneaky head of hers. All his concentration was bent on catching her.

She'd had a nice head start, thanks to his own cussed thickheadedness. Now she'd heard him giving chase and had spurred her little mare into a wild gallop. From his view, it seemed the horse's hooves never touched the ground.

But the black was bigger and, though tired, he still had a little drive left in him. Sam pushed him relentlessly, bemoaning every yard of earth they were backtracking in Millie's crazy attempt to flee. Didn't she know every minute, every second, was dear to him?

Of course, he thought grimly as he came ever so closer. But ever since yesterday he had been working on the assumption that Millie was on his side, as she'd claimed over and over. How gullible could he be!

Millie tossed a glance over her shoulder, her eyes rounding in surprise as she saw how close he was. Then she turned and pressed on, her head low against the mare's neck.

Sam had raced horses before—for fun—and he had occasionally been called upon to chase a stray animal back to the herd. But chasing a woman was a lot tougher than chasing a heifer. The closer he got, the blurrier she became. And she seemed to know precisely when to veer away from him, to throw him off. Her little mount could leap obstacles in its way that Sam and the black, directly behind, were forced to sidestep.

Finally the black's muzzle was even with the little mare's flank. Now what? Millie was small enough to grab, if he could get that close, but it would be like her to resist and end up getting herself trampled. He could try getting hold of her dress, or the rope flying behind her that was still attached to the pommel of her saddle, but he feared that might end in disaster, too. Finally, he decided to make a jump for it.

As soon as he was dead even with her and pulling ahead, he said a quick prayer, swung his leg over and pushed off. Millie yelped in astonishment and shock when she saw what he was doing.

Which was probably a good thing. If she'd had the presence of mind to try it, a simple poke in the arm would have sent him flying. He wrapped one hand firmly at the pommel of her saddle and swung around behind her.

It was not a clean landing. Millie's saddle seated one, and he came down on the edge of it, then was bumped down onto Mrs. Darwimple's haunches. Suddenly, he felt Millie's elbows pull back sharply, jabbing him in the ribs as she sawed on the reins. The mare whinnied in protest, then stopped short, rearing slightly and nearly sending them both flying.

Once Mrs. Darwimple was finally stilled, Sam took a deep breath. Too soon. To his shock, Millie hopped off the saddle and commenced running.

He sighed furiously, tempted just to let her go. But the same instinct that had made him hop on the black and chase her to begin with urged him to slip off the mare's sleek back and hobble after Millie on foot. At least here he had an advantage. Though Millie was swift, she was hampered by too many clothes, years of gentle living, and legs a sight shorter than his own.

As she heard his footsteps behind her, she ducked into a grove of mesquite trees and scrubby bushes, using her smaller height to good advantage. But while Sam cursed and slowed down to duck beneath a branch, Millie was running too fast to see where she was going.

"Watch out!" Sam cried.

Too late. Slapped in the face by a still-leafy branch, Millie was blinded and therefore could not avoid running headlong into a hawthorn bush.

A howl issued out of those lips the likes of which Sam had never heard. The bush's spiny branches seemed to have caught Millie in a thousand places, and she stopped stockstill, trying to figure out what to do next.

"Here, let me help," Sam offered, stepping forward and grabbing hold of her skirt.

"Are you insane?" Millie asked, whipping around. She whacked him on the head for good measure. "You could have gotten us both killed!"

"*I* could have?" Sam asked, his voice arcing into an astonished bray.

"Who else?" she cried, throwing out her hands in exasperation—a gesture that inadvertently caused her to prick the back of her hand. She held it out, shaking it, and scolded, "Oh, if you had just let me go, I could have done some good! Now all you've done is waste time!"

"*I* did?" Sam was dumbstruck. "Princess, *you* were the one who ran away, not me!"

"I just wanted the opportunity to go back and find the posse so I could tell them they're chasing the wrong man."

Sam's lips scrunched into a disbelieving frown.

"It's the truth!" Millie cried. "You're so pigheaded, you'd never let me help you on your own. So I was taking matters into my own hands."

He didn't know whether to believe her dizzy explanation or not—but he was definitely leaning toward not. And it would do her good to know it. "You can bring down the curtain on your little act," he said.

Her eyes widened. "What act?"

"Your 'I believe you' act. I fell for it yesterday, but I'm wise now," he said. "I'm not swallowing any more stories about pinafores accidentally left behind, or—"

"I just made a mistake."

"From now until we get to Gus's, it's going to be just like it was before you had your revelation in Ned Sparks's store."

"But that's so foolish and shortsighted. If you'd just listen—"

"I *have* listened to your ideas, Millie," Sam snapped. "They're very reasonable. And if we were dealing with reasonable people, and if I trusted you, I'd say sure, go ahead. But reason isn't a posse's most notable trait. And you haven't exactly bowled me over with that honesty you used to brag about."

"But—"

"No buts," Sam said, cutting her off. He wasn't in a mood to listen to any more of her arguments about getting them into this mess. The clock in his head, the one that counted the hours and minutes that he had to get his brother out of that jail, was ticking away. "Once we get you unstuck, we've still got to find the horses."

She opened her mouth to protest, but her words were cut off as he attempted to free her arm from a bramble. "Ouch!" she cried. "Don't you have any mercy, Sam?"

He looked up at her, his eyes squinting against the leaf-dappled sunlight filtering through the trees overhead. Despite her hair being gnarled in a limb, she looked pretty. But dwelling on Millie's physical appearance and his unaccountable attraction to her was what had gotten them in this mess to begin with. From now on, he would train his mind on business. And Millie, if he thought about her at all, would be just what she'd been the minute he laid eyes on her—a burden.

"Not anymore, I don't," he said.

"We're almost there."

Millie scowled. Sam didn't care one whit about her, wasn't even the least bit grateful that she was trying to save him from his flee-or-fight impulses, which were absolutely wrong in his case. She was certain of it. But she might never make him understand that. He was as thickheaded as a mule.

And now he seemed to genuinely believe that she'd just been putting on a show, pretending to believe in his innocence. If that wasn't absurd, what was? Millie wasn't one to take up causes willy-nilly, unlike some people she could mention. Miranda Rogers, for instance. After Miranda got married to a rich rancher outside Chariton, all she did with her time was think up do-gooder schemes. Last year it was "Save the first house built in Chariton," which, in Millie's opinion, was nothing more than a miserable little sod hut.

No, no, no. Millie just didn't believe in do-gooder schemes. But Sam's case was different. The cause of getting him and his brother out of this terrible trouble stirred the fires of determination inside her. Somehow or another, she would help him, whether he wanted her to or not.

"If you think I'm going to stay at this place, you're wrong."

He shot her a withering stare. "I'll see to it that you stay."

"Ha!" Millie said triumphantly. "You can barely control me now, when I'm practically strapped onto your saddle. How can you be certain I'll do what you want when I'm out of your sight?"

"I'm going to give Gus instructions."

Gus. She wasn't sure she was going to like this man. Especially not if he was going to do every little thing Sam told him to. "Is Gus a handsome man?" she asked curiously.

A wicked grin spread across Sam's mouth. "Your princess act won't work on these people, Millie. You'll have to try something else."

"Don't think I won't," she shot back.

He chuckled—it was the first halfway-pleasant sound he'd made since her escape attempt. "Oh, I'm sure you will. But Gus'll make sure you're kept in line. He and his wife both."

She'd almost forgotten about the wife. Now the odds would be two against one. Life just wasn't fair. "I don't see why you're making it so hard for me to help you," she complained.

He turned, his gray eyes glittering harshly. "Once and for all, I don't *want* your kind of help. That's why I've gone out of my way to bring you somewhere secluded. If you really wanted to help, you'd shut up and stay put."

Well! Millie shot him a cold glare, chin up, and turned her head slowly away. She just wouldn't dignify that comment with an answer. Except maybe one. "I'll have you know that no man on the face of this earth has ever used the words *shut up* to me before," she said, squirming impatiently in her saddle.

"First time for everything," Sam muttered.

Her lips pursed. "But, of course," she continued coolly, as if she hadn't heard his little gibe, "if ever a man was going to, it doesn't surprise me at all that man would be you."

"What's that supposed to mean?"

She tossed her head, glad to have gotten a reaction out of him at last. "It means that, naturally, a man who would say such a thing would be rather . . . uncouth."

"Uncouth, am I? Listen, Princess, just because I happened to find you under trying circumstances doesn't mean I always live this way. I happen to be the owner of a fine farm with a large house with four bedrooms, a sitting room, a kitchen . . ."

"Go on," Millie prodded, finding herself highly interested in the architecture of his home.

"Never mind," he said. His mouth clamped firmly shut.

Somehow, in all these days, she had never asked Sam about where he lived, or what he did. He was right. All her focus was on what was happening between them, on the road. Now, as they neared Gus Beaver's, she realized she had wasted so much time. She knew so little about Sam!

"I don't see how you can just dump me off like this!" she moaned in dismay.

He didn't even look at her. "Oh, it won't be hard. In fact, I imagine once I get rid of you I'll feel better than I have for days."

Millie practically howled at that statement. "Don't think this has been any picnic for me, either!"

"I know it hasn't," Sam said. "I hope you'll remember that while you're at Gus's. You'll be a lot more comfortable if you just stay there."

Her eyes barely registered the column of smoke she saw rising from somewhere over the hill they were climbing, yet she knew this was Gus Beaver's place they were coming upon, by the heavy feeling she had in the pit of her stomach.

Left behind. Abandoned. *Dumped.* That dreadful word kept repeating itself in her brain. Oh, this was horrible! And yet, after his mean words, she knew she didn't want to stay with Sam.

Or maybe she did. That was her problem. Nothing Sam did or said could make her completely angry. He only annoyed her in little bursts. Then, minutes later, she would seem to forget his every offense. It was so irritating.

She had the sinking feeling that this was what it was like when a woman started caring for a man. Really caring. Not just the feeling a girl had before she got engaged. This was something deeper, like what her daddy always said he felt for her mother—a kind of fellow feeling that defied even death.

Would her feeling for Sam defy being dumped?

She was torn. On the one hand, it would serve him right if she forgot all about him the minute he rode away. That was what she was determined to try to do. And yet, there was something irresistible about being swept up in a grand cause like his, about being part of an adventure. And when Millie was faced with the irresistible, her usual course was not to resist.

They crested the hill. Millie wasn't certain what she had expected the house of a man named Gus Beaver to look like...but never in her wildest dreams had she thought of *this*. This house—and that was putting it in wildly flattering terms—resembled nothing in her experience so much as that sod hut back in Chariton that crazy Miranda Rogers was always trying to save. Sam wanted her to stay *here*?

Her head swung around. She didn't even try to mask her horror and dread.

Sam, wicked man that he was, smiled at her open-mouthed gape. "Looks mighty inviting, doesn't it?" he asked. His row of even white teeth showed in a devilish grin. Then, before he kicked his horse into a trot to finish the journey down the hill, he added with mean glee, "Or is it too uncouth for you, Princess?"

Chapter Six

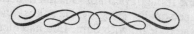

Hard as it was to believe, the inside of the shack was even more wretched than the outside. After the complete one-glance tour necessary to view the interior, Millie decided that *hovel* might be the most accurate description. The one room was crammed with a bed—one small bed—a stove, a table and chairs, two chests, and some shelves that were packed from one end to the other with everything from clothes to the family Bible to tableware.

Millie's nose wrinkled unhappily. The house smelled ripe and salty, like old pork. She looked toward the pot sitting on the stove and saw some unrecognizable type of stew brewing there, giving off a pungent odor. Finally, she glanced up. There, hanging from one of two rafter beams, alongside pans, an old shotgun and assorted dead animal skins, was a hunk of something of a brownish-pink hue. Millie looked away quickly. Between the scary stewpot and the hanging hunk, her stomach was beginning to grow queasy.

She was *not* going to cry. At least, not until Sam left. There was no way she would let him see her horror at being abandoned in such primitive accommodations. And that was just what she thought of the house. Its occupants were another matter still.

Gus and his wife, Louise—or Lou, as Gus and Sam called her—certainly looked like they belonged to their hovel. And if Sam hadn't told her differently, she would have sworn that the pair were brother and sister, rather than husband and wife. Their old faces looked like they could have been carved out of the same granite boulder; there was nothing soft about either of them. Both shared the same dark skin, tanned and wrinkled like worn leather from years of outdoor labor. Their mouths were set in the same grim line— although Millie thought perhaps Gus might actually be the winner in the personality category. He at least had said hello to her when she rode up with Sam. Lou had merely looked Millie over with her dark, beady eyes and pronounced her "skinny and useless."

The pair begged Sam to stay for some dinner, but Sam wouldn't. "I've got to push on, Gus," he said, having already divulged the whole mess his life had turned into.

To Millie's mind, Gus and Lou seemed to swallow the unbelievable, outrageous tale of murder, wrongful conviction and escape with striking placidity. Listening to him, they had shaken their heads and sucked on their pipes in perfect unison.

"That's what happens," Gus had said sorrowfully. Lou kept shaking her head and made no comment.

The thought of being left with these two rural stoics was throwing Millie into a panic. How could Sam do this to her? Surely, she thought, it was some kind of joke. He was just *saying* he was going to leave her to get back at her for all the times she'd annoyed him.

This had to be just another one of his lessons. Yes, that was it—repayment for her remark about his being uncouth. Or for her attempt to escape. Sam was probably getting a wonderful laugh out of seeing her gaping in disbelief at dead meat and raccoon skins....

But there he was, talking about "pushing on," not even sparing her a glance. In fact, it seemed that he was making a point of not looking at her, which was even worse. He was depriving her of the opportunity to use her best resources on him—the brown eyes that she could widen into such a look of helpless distress that no man could refuse her anything. At least, no man up until this point. Until Sam.

The three of them began shuffling out of the cabin again, toward the horses, and Millie began to panic for real. Especially when the subject of herself came up.

"Guard her with your life, Gus," Sam instructed the old geezer. "If she gets out, it could mean my doom."

Doom? A lot *he* knew about that word! *She* was the one who was going to die if he left her here.

Able to stand it no more, she catapulted herself from the solid doorframe of the cabin, past Gus and Lou, and attacked Sam, wrapping herself around his back.

"What the—?" Sam cried, attempting to twist around.

Millie attached herself to him with the rapacity of a sticker burr. "Don't leave me, Sam. Oh, please, please, please!" When she was certain she was worked up enough, she allowed Sam to turn and push her away slightly, looking into her face, into her eyes, which in turn looked pleadingly into his with what she was sure was genuine pathos.

Not that you could tell it by his reaction. The little muscle in Sam's jaw twitched, and he slowly began to wrench her away—no easy task. Her shock at his icy response to her pleas caused her to freeze, her fingers digging into his arms with fierce strength.

Finally, she felt a strong hand clamp down on her shoulder and pull her, with one mighty tug, backward. Surprised, Millie glanced up and saw Lou looking down at her with an even more than usually disdainful frown. "Useless," the old woman repeated.

"The minute she gets away, she'll go running for that posse," Sam told them. "She tried to just this morning."

"I did not!" Millie yelled. "I was trying to get away so I could tell my daddy—"

"Her daddy's real important," Sam told them. "One of the powers that be. The sheriff is always invited to their dinner parties."

At the words *dinner parties,* Lou's grip on her tightened.

"Not always," Millie said resentfully.

"We won't let her out of our sight, Sam," Gus assured him.

"Out of our gunsights, neither," Lou assured him as he mounted his horse.

Millie sucked in a shocked breath. "You can't mean—"

"Whatever it takes," Sam agreed, cutting her off. He didn't look at her when he said it, either.

He wouldn't dare, Millie fumed. After all she wanted to do for him, too! She could have been his salvation.

"Good luck, son," Gus said, patting the black's neck. "We'll take care of the girl until we hear from you."

For the first time since they'd arrived at Gus's farm, Sam's mouth twisted in one of his old familiar wry smiles. "Well, I'd give it a few months. If you haven't heard from me by Christmas, you can assume I'm dead and that it's safe to let her go."

Dead? How terrible!

Christmas? How even more terrible! But she had no intention of spending three days here, much less three months. She didn't care if they had cannons trained on her instead of shotguns.

Sam took up the reins of the black, wheeled around and, without another word, trotted away. Just when he was halfway back up the hill, his arm shot out to one side in a curt wave. But Millie didn't kid herself that it was meant for her. Sam didn't care about her at all. She knew that now....

She crossed her arms over her chest and lifted her chin. Fine. If he could just ride away without giving her a second thought, then she could certainly go about the business of forgetting him.

"Humph."

In her grief at watching Sam ride away, Millie had nearly forgotten about Gus and Lou. As if that were possible! Her jailers exchanged silent glances.

"Humph," Gus replied to his wife's prior grunt. "Well, he's gone."

"That he is."

If this was what passed for conversation around this place, Millie was sure she would go out of her mind. Perhaps they were just uncomfortable speaking around her. If that was the case, it was up to her to break the ice. She steeled her spine and forced a chipper smile. "It's right nice of you-all to put me up on such short notice."

Lou eyed her distrustfully. "Humph."

Millie swallowed and soldiered on. "What Sam was saying before—about my being his doom?" She sent them another of her most fetching smiles and waved a hand dismissively. "That was just Sam talking! You might not have been able to tell it, but Sam likes me. He really does. So I'm sure there's no need to—"

"Gus, bring me my daddy's shotgun."

Millie's eyes widened. "I thought that was just a little joke!" she lied. She'd *hoped* it was just a little joke.

Lou shook her head. "I reckon if Sam said to watch you, we'd better do just that."

"Well, *watch* me, certainly, but..." Her words petered out as Gus returned with the old rifle she'd seen hanging with the skins and cooking utensils. Heart sinking, she watched him hand the weapon over to Lou, who immediately raised it, training the barrel at Millie's chest. For a brief moment, Millie envisioned herself hanging by her toes from one of those rafters, somewhere between the rabbit skins and frying pan.

She swallowed, trying to push the unpleasant thought away. As low as her opinion of Sam was at the moment, he wouldn't have left her with people who would do her any real harm.

Would he?

"Well!" Millie said, trying to sound a cheerful note. "What are we going to do with ourselves this evening?"

Her bubbliness didn't even bring a smile. "Turn around and I'll show you," Lou said, butting Millie's arm with the end of the rifle.

Not having a whole lot of choice in the matter, Millie turned and marched as directed to the back of the house. Lou stopped by a stump that had a long-handled hatchet embedded in it.

"Oh, is Gus cutting wood?" Millie asked when Lou failed to explain why they had stopped at this particular point.

"Nope, you are."

At first, Millie simply stared at the woman, whose leathery old face was particularly hard to read. Then, suddenly, she laughed, understanding the ridiculousness of the situation. Lou was making fun of her! It gave her hope to think that the woman had a sense of humor after all, even if this particular joke was at her own expense.

But as her laughter lengthened and thinned and finally trailed into an uncomfortable silence, Millie looked again at the ax, then at Lou, and cold understanding began to dawn. This was no joke. Gus hadn't followed them around the back of the house. Lou truly intended Millie to *work*.

Well. A terrible misperception had apparently occurred. "I've never done this," Millie explained.

"It's not hard," Lou said, wrinkling her nose and sniffing loudly as she shifted her feet and her stance settled firmly into her hips.

Millie gaped at her. Of course, she had heard of women doing this kind of work. No one she knew, naturally.

"Go ahead," Lou said, goading her.

"Don't you think we ought to switch places so you can show me how first?"

Lou was not to be fooled. "I ain't lettin' you hold a gun on me, sweet thing. Just pick up the ax and commence to choppin'."

Sighing as audibly as humanly possible, Millie turned and put her small hand around the handle of the ax. Perhaps this wasn't as hard as it looked. It couldn't be any more unpleasant than cleaning that stinky fish had been. She grabbed the hatchet and tugged, to no result. The instrument was firmly imbedded in the stump.

"Put some muscle into it," Lou told her.

Gritting her teeth and bracing her legs against the base of the stump, Millie gave the ax another try. And another. A bead of sweat popped off her brow and hit her damp, already chafed hands.

Finally, Lou's big paw closed over hers and exerted a little pressure. Like Excalibur in King Arthur's anointed hands, the hatchet released magically from the stump, nearly sending Millie reeling. She looked at Lou's corded forearms and gasped with awe.

"You're like a mule!" Millie exclaimed before she could think better of it. Hearing the insulting words hanging in the air, staring into Lou's dark eyes, Millie shrank back in horror, mentally prepared for buckshot to explode from the barrel of that gun.

Instead, Lou merely nodded toward a log on the ground. "Don't think flattery will get you anywheres with me, missy," she said. Then she spat—something Millie had never seen a female do before. "Now get to work."

And, not seeing any earthly alternative to this ultimatum, work Millie did. She chopped and chopped and chopped, until her whole body felt weak and woozy. "Lord, this is hard!" she cried, hanging over the stump to rest her arms.

"My daddy always told me I was the best woodchopper in Texas," Lou bragged.

Millie bit her lip, thinking. This was the second time Lou had mentioned that father of hers. "Is your daddy still alive?"

Lou laughed. "Lord, no! He's been gone since the battle at Vicksburg. All I got left of him is this here gun."

Millie tried to look admiringly at the cold metal aimed at her chest. "My, my. That's a very nice memento."

For a moment the woman stared at her uncomprehendingly. "This ain't no memento. This happens to be one of the finest carbine rifles in the county." The woman visually caressed the steel of her weapon, as if in fond memory.

Millie smiled. "I'll bet!" She still had hope that she could win Lou over somehow—and maybe their warrior daddies was just the connection she was looking for. "You know, my daddy was in the war, too."

Lou spat again and lifted the barrel a notch. "So was everybody's, missy. Now get back to work. This ain't a holiday." The fleeting gentleness was gone from the woman's face, replaced by the same hard lines as before.

Millie sighed and straightened—though after a day of swinging and chopping, she feared she would never be truly upright again.

How could Sam have done this to her?

Millie silently moaned the anguished question for what had to be the three-millionth time that evening. Every muscle in her body spasmed, causing shooting pains that not even the slug she'd taken from Gus's whiskey bottle could calm. Her head throbbed. And, to top it all off, she was hungry. Hungrier than she'd ever been in her life. But she wasn't about to eat that coon stew, or whatever it was that had been cooking on top of that stove all day long. Although—and Millie took this as a certain indication of how desperately hungry she was—she'd actually considered it.

Lord knew Gus and Lou had slurped the stuff down by the bowlful, oblivious of her silent agony. Millie doubted three words had passed the couple's lips the entire time they were chowing down. And afterward, Lou had gone back to work and Gus had disappeared again. Lou said Gus spent the day checking traps. Could he do that at night, too? In the back of her mind Millie suspected he just wanted to get away from his wife.

Lou was unrelentingly grim. And work-minded! Millie had never worked so hard in her life! Alberta would never believe it, not in a million years. And Sam...well, his name was mud anyway. She hoped she never saw the man again. And he could count himself lucky if he never ran into her, because the moment she ever laid eyes on him...

Tears sprang to her eyes, and she rolled over on the hard dirt floor and sighed. Oh, what was the use? She'd do anything to see him again. She had tried to be angry—had worked herself up into a good lather there for a while, sometime after the thirtieth log—but, truly, she was worried sick.

She kept thinking about what Sam had said the posse would do if they ever ran into him. "Shoot to kill," he'd said. But they couldn't kill Sam. And they wouldn't, if only she could reach her father. Or, better still, if she was with Sam. Her daddy would never allow Sheriff Tom to use deadly force if there was a chance she might be hurt.

At least she hoped not. She remembered Sam's warnings about the kind of man the sheriff really was. It seemed so unbelievable, but then, Millie's whole world seemed to have been turned topsy-turvy.

Gus returned. Millie heard the tread of his heavy boots and smelled his pipe tobacco. Then Lou spoke to him.

"You watch the girl, Gus. I'm all worn out."

No answer. But the footsteps retreated away from the bed, nearer to Millie. She felt a slight vibration beneath her as Gus joined her on the floor. She lay in silence for several minutes, until the quiet stillness around them was broken by a loud, startling honking noise. Lou, Millie discovered, snored.

After a few repetitions of the boisterous sound of Lou's somnolent breathing, Millie flopped over again. Her stomach growled.

"Don't let it bother you none," Gus whispered. "Once you do, it's all over."

Her eyes popped open. Gus, sitting up with his back against the wall three feet away, was looking off into some other corner of the room. The shotgun was propped against his outstretched legs. How had he known she was awake?

"I let it get to me one night, and now I haven't slept a wink going on thirty years."

"Thirty years!" Millie squeaked, attempting to keep her voice low.

"Yup. That's the joy of workin' out in the woods. I can catch a nap while I'm waiting for those bunnies to step into a snag."

Millie smiled. This was a man after her own heart. Suddenly, she found everything about Gus completely pleasant, from the peculiarly strong smell of his pipe tobacco to the three-day whisker growth that reminded her of Sam.

The thought of Sam caused her brow to wrinkle. "I'm worried about Sam, Gus. Do you think he can make it to that town?"

"Little Bend?" Gus shrugged. "Ain't far. He might."

The words didn't inspire optimism. "I hope he knows what he's doing," Millie said.

"Sam is one man who knows his way about," Gus told her. "He's been on his own for a long time now."

Millie blinked. Just today she had been kicking herself for finding out so little about Sam. Now here she was, sitting with someone who knew him well. "You mean his parents died?"

"Mom died when Jesse was born, and father died when Sam was seventeen. The boy took over a farm and raisin' his young brother."

Seventeen. The thought gave Millie pause. That was two years younger than she was now. When she was seventeen . . . well, she'd hardly been a thinking person, now that she remembered it. She had only been engaged once then, to Wilbur Tooey—evidence in itself that her head wasn't on straight yet. And seventeen was the year she and Sally Hall had decided to run away to San Antonio to join a convent; but they had returned home after an hour and a half, when Sally, who had always been on the plump side, realized she would have to give up sweet foods. When she was seventeen she'd been just a girl, and Sam had probably only been a boy . . . until responsibility was heaped on his shoulders.

No wonder he thought she was spoiled. And young.

Of course, things were a little different now. After the work she'd put in today, Millie practically felt like an old woman.

"Do you know Jesse?" she asked Gus. "Do you think he's innocent?"

Gus swerved his gaze toward her. He even had dark eyes like his wife's—only there was a trace of warmth in them. And pity. "I don't know the boy too well," Gus admitted. "But I know Sam, and if Sam says Jesse didn't kill his wife, then he didn't."

Millie nodded. "That's what I think."

"Then why are you trying to get Sam caught?"

"I'm not," she explained. "Just the opposite! I just want to use my influence to help him. My father is Horace Lively."

His eyes rounded in recognition. "Old Lightfooted Lively?"

Millie nodded. "And if I could tell him that Sam was innocent, he wouldn't let them hurt Sam. That's what I was trying to do today, get to Daddy."

"There's no tellin' where that posse is now. Maybe they've even given up."

That would be too good to be true. Millie wanted to believe it, though. Because if there was no posse, Sam would be safe until he reached Little Bend and found that Weems man he was looking for. After that, she had no idea what would happen.

"Sam loves his brother more than anything, doesn't he?" she asked.

"Sure. Jesse even left him for a while, wanting to set out on his own like young men will do. It nearly broke Sam's heart to see him go. Like losing a brother, a best friend and a son, too, I guess. But he took it on the chin, because he knew it was just one of those things a young man had to do."

"Sam never left home, though."

"No, but Sam's different. He knew his place early. There's nothing flighty about him. Never was."

That was the truth! And now, after working hard for a whole day herself, she could see why, after a lifetime of work and responsibility, Sam was cranky so often.

"You seem awfully concerned about the man, considerin' you're his hostage."

"I believe in Sam," she said, knowing she meant it with all her heart. She had thought—no, hoped—that she might be able to forget him once he had left her. But how could she? He was unlike any man she had ever known.

Her thoughts raced back to the night before, when he'd pulled her into his arms and kissed her like she'd never been aware a person could be kissed. Her whole body went gushy and feverish just from thinking about it.

"I believe in him even more now that I've heard about how he raised Jesse. It's no wonder he's so frantic to get him freed."

"There's never been bad blood between them," Gus agreed.

Poor Sam. He was so alone. "I hate to think of him out there riding by himself."

To her shock, Gus said, "Me, too."

"If I could only join him!" she said. "He thinks I'm a nuisance, but I'm not. And if I were with him should the posse ever catch up with him—"

From the bed, Lou emitted a loud, sputtering honk. Millie realized that her voice had been rising in pitch until she was nearly shouting.

"Best not think about it," Gus said, cutting her off. "The only thing to do now is just to roll over and get the best night's sleep you can." He darted a glance at the bed. "*If* you can."

Millie frowned and flopped back over, pulling her thin covering up over her shoulders. It wasn't snoring that would keep her awake this night. Nor was it her hunger, or her aching bones, or even the hard floor beneath her. Anything was an improvement after being roped to a tree.

No, the very thing that kept her wakeful was the memory that just wouldn't leave her—that of two steely gray eyes glistening at her as she was enveloped in a devastating kiss.

After days of fruitless searching, Millie's pinafore was found beneath a bush, not far from the remains of a small fire, and the garment was spattered with stains that looked like dried blood.

"Oh, my poor, poor Millicent!" Lloyd cried.

Horace's own heart cried out something similar, especially when Sheriff Tom strolled over.

"It looks bad, Colonel," the sheriff said.

Obviously, Ned Sparks, the storekeeper, had been wrong about that runaway couple, who he had sworn appeared too much in love to be a fugitive and his hostage. Now the grim faces of the posse milling around him indicated to Horace that Ned Sparks might have been the last person to see Millie alive.

Why? Why would Sam Winter have killed her? And why would Millie have cooperated with him in front of Sparks?

"I don't want to give up too soon," he told Tom.

The sheriff looked at him with a gaze hard with pity. "I'll tell my men we'll keep looking for both Winter and the girl."

Horace twisted the once white pinafore in his hands, hating the sight of it, not to mention the sickening smell. He couldn't bear the looks of the rest of the posse, either, as they glanced anxiously at him periodically while Sheriff Tom was addressing them privately. One man seemed to be watching him especially close, peering at him through a pair of the thickest spectacles Horace had ever seen. Vaguely he remembered spotting the man in town when the posse was gathered. That he didn't know the man didn't surprise Horace. Several men from surrounding towns had joined the hunt for the escaped felon. It was a matter of collective security in the area.

"If only there were something more I could do!" Lloyd moaned. "Poor Millie, my childhood friend, my sweetheart. If only—"

If only he'd shut up, Horace thought with annoyance.

Thunderous hoofbeats sounded over a hill, followed by shouts. "Sheriff! Sheriff!"

Horace felt his heart lift in his chest. Was this news of Millie? Had they found her?

All the men surged forward. Two riders—two of the men who had been sent out on a wider search of the area—appeared, galloping toward them so fast that they nearly toppled over their mounts' necks when they stopped short beside the group on foot.

"Did you find her?" Lloyd said, running forward.

The two riders, seeing the swarm of anxious faces around them, and the obvious air of expectation, colored slightly. The one who had been doing the shouting suddenly closed his mouth and looked down at the ground.

"Well, what is it?" Tom asked impatiently.

The other one, avoiding Horace's gaze, looked straight at his boss. "We found this, sir." He held out a long, faded blue hair ribbon. Where it was tied in a knot, a hunk of long brown hair was attached. "It was stuck on a hawthorn bush."

For some reason, the hank of hair looked especially sinister to Horace. It didn't help matters, either, when poor Lloyd gasped and cried, "He practically scalped her!"

At the stricken looks all the rest of the men sent Horace, he knew they agreed. Most, probably, had known they would find gruesome artifacts like this along the way.

Sheriff Tom pulled Horace aside, but Lloyd was not going to be shaken off. "You're giving up, aren't you?" he wailed.

"Now, son, maybe not," the sheriff assured him.

But Tom's *maybe* spoke volumes. A safe distance away, Horace could see the heads slowly shaking. Everyone had given up on Millie.

"We won't stop looking until either the girl or Winter is found, Colonel, you know that," Tom said. "But we've got to be practical. From now on, we've got to be sure we don't undermine the search by asking folks if they've seen a couple when we might ought to just be looking for one man."

He squeezed Horace's arm, patted Lloyd on the shoulder and moved back to his men. After a few brief words, everyone spread out to prepare to ride again. All except one, the man with the glasses. He approached Horace alone.

"Colonel Lively?"

Horace looked up. Strange little man. He hoped he wasn't here to give condolences. No matter what Tom thought, Horace hadn't given up completely.

"Colonel Lively," the man continued, "my name is Barney Tibbetts. I was wondering whether I might have the opportunity to examine Miss Lively's pinafore."

Horace liked the way he said "Miss Lively." Tom had been referring to her as "the girl" for days now. He wasn't quite sure what the little man was up to, but he handed over the garment.

Efficiently Tibbetts held the pinafore inches from his spectacles and peered at it, especially the stains. Then he held it even closer and sniffed. "Just as I thought," he said matter-of-factly.

"Colonel, are you coming?" Sheriff Tom shouted.

Horace looked from the sheriff to the little man, then back again. "We'll be right along. No need to wait."

The riders moved away, but Horace knew he wouldn't lose the search party. It was still early, and Tom, though a dogged, patient searcher, didn't like to push his men too fast.

"What did you mean by that statement, Tibbetts?" he asked, turning his attention back to the spectacled man.

"If I'm not mistaken, this pinafore smells of fish. I believe the stains were the result of your daughter preparing dinner, not her murder. Furthermore, the discovery of one of Miss Lively's hair ribbons a few miles from here is a rather hopeful sign, in my opinion."

"How so?"

Tibbetts cleared his throat and pointed. "Winter seems to be heading west. The ribbon was found northwest of this spot, where they presumably would have arrived at least thirty minutes after they left here. Therefore, if she was murdered here, why would she have lost her hair ribbon later?"

Horace tried not to get his hopes up just because Tibbetts was saying precisely what he wanted to hear. But the man made sense. Even Lloyd thought so—he could see it in the boy's eyes.

"Maybe Millie's been leaving us a trail. Colonel, do you think it could be true?" Lloyd asked, as if his own opinion weren't to be trusted in any case.

Instead of answering, Horace turned to Tibbetts and asked, "Who are you?"

"Barney Tibbetts. I used to work for Pinkerton."

"Ahh," Horace said. A detective! For the first time in days, he began to experience real hope.

Lloyd asked eagerly, "Could you find Millicent for us— I mean, if the colonel were to pay you?"

Tibbetts hesitated. "It's not just money I'm seeking."

Horace's gaze narrowed. "What else?" He hope he hadn't been rooked into some kind of blackmailing scheme.

"A letter of recommendation if I succeed." Frowning, he explained, "You see, a few years back, my sight began to deteriorate. After I failed to find a runaway wife for a very wealthy client—for reasons completely beyond my control, I assure you—Mr. Pinkerton decided, erroneously, that my weak eyes were a hindrance to my performance on the job. But, as I hope I just demonstrated, a good detective works with more than mere eyesight."

"Of course!" Lloyd asked. He was as excited as a puppy with a fresh bone.

Horace was a little more skeptical. But what the man said *seemed* reasonable. And what other choice did he have? He could hire another detective—one with all his senses in tip-top shape—but that would take time. And he feared time was one thing he didn't have. But he did have money, and as for the letter... "If you find my daughter, sir, I will write you a thousand letters!"

Tibbetts looked at the hand that had been extended for him to shake on the deal. He cleared his throat. "One should suffice. As well as four hundred dollars."

Horace sputtered in surprise. "Four hundred dollars!"

"To find Millicent?" Lloyd asked, his mouth agape. "That's a pittance, Colonel!"

A pittance for whom? Horace thought. It seemed his future son-in-law was quite comfortable throwing his money around.

"And just think," Lloyd continued. "*I* could go along with him and help in his detecting."

Horace nearly choked. "No, no!" he cried. "You'll stay here, Lloyd, with me." The last thing he needed was to hire a detective and then have Lloyd Boyd botch the job. All thought of haggling over the price of finding Millie disappeared. "Bring back my daughter and you'll have your four hundred dollars."

But as he finally shook the detective's hand, sealing the bargain, it occurred to Horace that for four hundred dollars he could probably pay ransom for a true-blue princess.

Chapter Seven

Sam awoke and stretched, a lazy smile working across his lips. He never had been one for dreaming, or thinking about dreaming, but this particular dream he'd just had was awfully nice. In it, Millie had been like she was that first morning, by the water, half dressed and with her clothes clinging lovingly to every curve of her body. He'd gone up to her and pulled her into his arms and—

Suddenly, Sam sat bolt upright. "Millie?" he said aloud, but immediately he knew he was completely disoriented. The princess was with Gus. He was on his own now...and some job he was making of it!

The sun had already risen. He hadn't slept this late since he'd made his escape. Of course, he didn't have Millie fidgeting on the ground nearby this morning, either.

He jumped up. Yesterday evening he'd covered a lot of territory, although not as much as he'd hoped. Maybe he'd expected too much from getting rid of Millie. Maybe he had thought that once he was unencumbered he would sprout wings and fly to Little Bend. Obviously, that wasn't going to happen. Instead, he was moving about the same speed— Millie really hadn't slowed him down that much at all, like she'd said. Except that he'd gone out of his way by half a day so that he could leave her with Gus.

The odd thing was, he felt more jumpy now. Having Millie's company—exasperating as it was—had buffered his fretfulness. He might be less noticeable riding solo, but his nerves weren't registering that fact. Now he jumped at every jackrabbit that crossed his path. His heartbeat raced each time he heard a noise. Instead of braving open land, he moved in fits and starts, sprinting from one tree to the next, like a thief in the night.

Of course, to the people who were after him, he was worse than a thief. The course his life had taken shocked the hell out of him. How had he gotten himself in this predicament? One day he'd been a law-abiding citizen; the next, he was clunking lawmen over the head and stealing off with young ladies as if he'd been born to the criminal life.

He wished he could have explained more about himself to Millie, so that she would truly understand that he wasn't like the crude barbarian she'd once accused him of being. That he wasn't used to sleeping on the dirt any more than she was. Or that he liked to laze about late in bed on a Sunday morning just as much as the next man. Or that he usually ate like a horse, big meals shared with the few other workers who happened to be at the farm.

Of course, it didn't really matter to him *what* she thought. Not really. But a man—even a man most people thought was a criminal—had some pride, after all.

He shook his head. It was useless thinking about her. He would never see Millie again—except if she showed up for his hanging someday.

He tightened the saddle on the black, trying to concentrate on the task in front of him and not let his thoughts drift. When they did, they always returned to the bleak idea of his brother in jail, or, more frequently, to Millie. Lord, he'd spent more time thinking of Millie since he'd left her than when he was with her twenty-four hours a day. Several times he'd wondered why he'd gone to so much trouble to get rid of her after all.

But, of course, he knew the answer to that. Millie was safer with Gus and Lou than she was with him.

She was also twice as miserable. She probably hated him for leaving her there—Gus's place wasn't much, he'd remembered once he got there. And Lou wasn't the friendliest woman in the world, either. But God bless her. Sam had been torn near in two when Millie pleaded with him to take her along. A few seconds more and he would have relented. But he'd been saved from that mistake by Lou's firm hand pulling her back from him.

If she hadn't, no telling what would have happened. He couldn't stop thinking about that kiss, and fearing it would happen again. Thinking about Millie that way was dangerous. And not just because her daddy wanted him dead. He and Millie just weren't suited, and there was no reason for him to start fancying that they were, just because they'd been stuck in each other's company for a long spell.

No, they were both better off this way. He would just have to keep reminding himself of that fact.

"It's shameful, that's what it is!"

For a blissful moment, Millie couldn't remember where she was. Instead, she was floating on the most heavenly little cloud, eating something light and sweet and decadent. On the next cloud, attached by a length of rope, floated Sam, who was looking at her and smiling from ear to ear.

Then, as piercingly as Lou's voice cutting through the peaceful morning air, memory assailed her. She was at Gus's.

"A girl oughtn't to sleep the whole day away!"

When Millie looked up, carefully avoiding Lou's gaze, she noticed Gus putting on his wide-brimmed hat and readying himself to go out for the day. To sleep, Millie knew now.

"It's about time you got your bones up off the floor!" Lou told Millie. "You better hurry, or Gus'll leave without you."

Even though she feared she'd never felt so stiff and dirty and hungry—at least not since yesterday—happiness surged in Millie's heart. "You mean I get to go with you?" she asked Gus.

"Do you think I want you with me another day?" Lou asked testily. "I need to get *some* work done around here."

Millie bounded off the floor in nothing flat, not even bothering to point out that she had done quite a bit of the woman's work for her yesterday. She folded her blanket, combed a hand through her hopelessly tangled hair and trotted off after Gus.

"And don't forget what Sam told us!" Lou yelled after him. "You keep a close watch on that girl."

"I will," Gus said, striding away with the shotgun at his side. Yet, instead of Gus keeping an eye on his captive, his captive was chasing to catch up to him.

This was just too good to be true! Finally, she was away from Lou's tyrannical oversight. Not only would she not have to worry about being worked to a nubbin, she could even contemplate escape again. All she had to do was wait for Gus to fall asleep—then she would be able to make a run for it. Of course, she wouldn't have Mrs. Darwimple....

"You'd better bring that little mare of yours along today," Gus called over his shoulder just then, causing Millie to stop in her tracks, her mouth agape. "Give her some exercise."

"Good idea!" Millie agreed enthusiastically. This was going to be even easier than she'd thought!

She greeted Mrs. Darwimple, wishing she had something to offer the dear animal. Of course, Mrs. Darwimple, who even at that moment was nibbling on the sweet yellow grass beneath her, was probably better nourished than Millie. And, after a day of relaxation that Millie hadn't herself enjoyed, the mare was also the better rested, and showed it by prancing gamely after Millie mounted her.

"Better conserve your energy," Millie instructed the dappled mare. "You're going to need it this afternoon." If all went as she wanted it to.

She trotted up alongside Gus. From his pocket, he produced a bright orange carrot. "You can half it with your friend there," he told her with a wink.

This was almost uncanny. She'd just been wishing for a treat for Mrs. Darwimple, and here he was, offering her one! Could he read her mind? Of course, if he could, he would probably also know that a carrot wouldn't begin to soothe her grumbly stomach.

"Snuck you out some corn bread, too," he told her, nearly causing her to weep with gratefulness. "I noticed you didn't take to Lou's stew last night."

Once she'd finished chewing a mouthful of corn bread, the whole piece of which she had stuffed past her lips as soon as possible, she swallowed and shook her head, not wanting to be a bad houseguest. "Oh, no—I'm sure it was quite good."

He let out a bark of a laugh that caused Mrs. Darwimple not a little alarm. Millie, too. "Awful stuff. You were right not to try it. A thing like you probably isn't used to vittles like that."

Millie pursed her lips. Kind as Gus was attempting to be, she did have to take exception to his language when referring to her, which was very reminiscent of Sam's. "What do you mean, Gus? What kind of person do you think I am, exactly?"

He shrugged. "Dunno. Guess you're kind of...soft. Feminine, like."

As if she could help that! Millie thought with exasperation. But on second thought, she realized he only meant that she wasn't a tough old bird like Lou. And thank heavens for it! "But I'm not as weak as you and Sam seem to think."

Gus's grizzled old face cracked in a grin. "Oh, you're not?"

"No," Millie said emphatically. "Just look at what I did yesterday. Lou would never admit it, but I chopped every bit as much as she would have herself, and probably wasn't that much slower at it. And I had a gun pointed at me!"

Gus chuckled. "So Sam thinks you're nothing but a weak female, does he?"

"It's very annoying!" Millie cried. "He's so critical of me, just because my daddy has money and a nice house and I was raised . . . well, not to worry about things."

"I know Sam," Gus told her. "Know him better than you do, obviously. You've got him all wrong."

Millie shook her head. On this point, she was absolutely certain. "Oh, no. He thinks I'm useless, just like Lou does. He wishes he'd never met up with me."

"But you're determined to prove that he'll be glad to see you yet, is that it?"

"Yes!" Too late, Millie realized the trap she had just so eagerly leapt into. "I mean, no. Of course not. I have no intention—"

Gus shook his head. "He might be glad to see you, but he won't admit it. Same as he wouldn't turn around and look you in the eye yesterday when he rode off."

Millie's eyes widened in surprise at this observation. Yesterday she'd noticed that he didn't look back at her, but she'd given his inattentiveness an entirely different—not to mention more depressing—interpretation. Now she was beginning to see another possibility. . .

But it just seemed too good to be true. "Do you really think he was sorry to leave me?"

"Sure," Gus said. "See, I was in the war, same as your pa. And if there was one thing I learned then, it was that there were two types of people in times of trouble. Them that wanted always to be with everybody else, to have companionship and take their mind off their worries, and them that kept to themselves, to avoid gettin' too close to anybody."

"You mean because they're scared?"

He nodded. "Guess which one our boy is."

She wasn't quite sure it was that simple. "I think maybe he just doesn't like me."

"Man's got eyes, hasn't he? You can't tell me he hasn't tried to kiss you."

Millie blushed. "Oh . . . but that was just . . . to teach me a lesson. He thinks I'm spoiled."

This time Gus's cackle echoed through the spindly grouping of mesquite trees around them. He stopped in the center of the wooded area. "Got one," he said, bending down and producing a rabbit.

Millie frowned at the sad sight of its stiff, furry body, which Gus was inspecting as if it were worth its weight in gold. She shuddered. "Why did you laugh just then?" she asked, trying to get her mind off the unfortunate creature and back to her own more fascinating misfortunes.

"Huh?" Gus looked at her briefly, squinting through the dappled sunlight that filtered through the tree leaves and struck his eyes. He smiled and shook his head. "What you said about Sam teachin' you a lesson. I don't think I've ever heard of a man kissin' a woman to improve her education."

"That's what he told me," Millie said.

"That's more of that pride of his. Didn't want to admit he couldn't help himself."

Wouldn't it be wonderful if that were true! But Millie was still skeptical. "I wonder where he is," she said, scanning the horizon. If she did manage to escape Gus, how would she ever find him?

Gus told her. "If he's going toward Little Bend, he'll be heading due west now." To Millie's utter amazement, as they walked, Gus described the landmarks Sam would be passing at length, down to the knotholes in particularly noticeable trees, old dry wells that had stood unused since the last drought, and several abandoned buildings.

"He'll try to skirt those, of course," Gus informed her, "because they create perfect cover for somebody trying to ambush him. But he'd note them, and steer around them. Also, you got to take into consideration that he's a man traveling alone."

"What does that mean?" Millie asked, growing bolder.

"He'll be fretful-like. Won't want to be seen in the open at all. He'll be like a little rodent, flitting from one place to the next to hide, never letting his guard down."

It didn't sound too different from the way they'd been traveling all along, but she would remember to look for him to be extra careful to camouflage himself. Suddenly, she became anxious for Gus to tire out on her. Wasn't it time already for one of his naps?

But no, they walked on and on, Gus rambling the whole time about the hazards of riding alone out west. Millie couldn't believe he actually thought Sam would have any trouble, but she soaked up the information nevertheless, for her own benefit. When would she be able to make a run for it? Sam had such a lead on her, she worried she might never catch up now.

Gus found a second rabbit and, to her utter disgust, tied both dead creatures onto the back of her saddle. "Those'll make good eatin' for several days. You tell Sam to enjoy 'em."

Millie nearly replied tartly that Sam was welcome to every bit of those sad little carcasses. Then she drew a sharp, shocked breath. "Do you mean—?"

"You take this shotgun, too," he continued, handing her the heavy, antiquated weapon.

"Oh, Gus!" Millie said, feeling the heavy weight of the warm metal in her hands. Then her conscience began weighing on her, too. "Oh, but, Gus—this carbine rifle belonged to Lou's daddy. I couldn't take it."

"Don't you know how to use it?"

"Yes, of course," she said.

"Well, then," Gus said, stepping back and holding his hands up helplessly, "you got me. If you want to kick that horse into a gallop and ride off after Sam, there ain't a dad-blasted thing I can do about that." He shook his head and winked. "Serves me right for talkin' a blue streak instead of payin' attention to where the gun was. Lou'll fuss, but she'll get over it. Eventually.''

"Oh, how can I thank you?" Millie cried.

"Don't thank me," Gus said. "Just do a good job of escapin'. I don't like to think of Sam out there alone."

"I won't thank you, then," she agreed. "Not because you don't want me to, but because there's nothing I could say that would possibly match how I feel."

He sent her what she now knew passed for a whole-hearted smile. "That's about the purtiest thank-you I ever got, anyways." Then he raised his hand and waved her off. "Good luck."

In too big a hurry now to stay and argue over whether he should accept thanks for that sentiment, she turned in her saddle instead and told him, "I'll need every scrap of *that* I can get my hands on!"

But maybe she would need a little less luck—and more common sense—now that Gus had told her exactly which way to go.

Doing no damage to her modesty, Millie had always considered herself one of the bravest women of her own acquaintance. She knew plenty of women who shrieked every time something unexpected crossed their paths. Take Sally Hall. Now there was a nervous Nellie! Sally was startled by every little thing, including but not limited to spiders and almost any variety of bug, small furry animals, dark enclosed spaces, heights, and bald-headed men.

Millie had even run across some men who fell somewhat shy of fearless. Lloyd Boyd was a perfect example. One night he had been walking her home from a picnic when his hat was brushed off his head by a low, leafy branch. Lloyd had immediately jumped to the conclusion that they were being attacked by bandits—and had nearly jerked Millie's arm out of its socket trying to pull her a safe distance away from the marauding tree. Naturally, Millie hadn't mentioned that incident to anyone, considering that Lloyd was her fiancé. A girl had some pride.

But now, as she passed sinister silhouettes of trees on the dark horizon, Millie found she was nearly as much of a fraidy-cat as Lloyd. Everything alarmed her—the sound of a twig snapping beneath Mrs. Darwimple's hoof, the phantom shadow of a bird flying above, the eerie call of a distant wolf. Sounds and noises she normally wouldn't even notice now struck her as unbearably frightful.

Well. Not unbearable, Millie thought, straightening her spine and relaxing the tense, shaky hold she had on the reins. She wasn't a complete ninny. She knew perfectly well that a wolf wasn't going to come eat her, or a bat swoop down on her, or a *bandido* jump out of a bush and seize her....

Yet she kept remembering what Gus had said about Sam probably hiding within concealing foliage, which made her wonder. After all, what was the possibility that Sam was the only desperado out this way, heading into the sparsely settled West? Sam was only going there to find a man, but other, more unscrupulous men might be going there to hide out....

What of this Weems person himself? So far, she'd only considered the danger he posed Sam. What about the danger he posed her? He and Sam might have met up already. Was it possible that Weems might have heard of her, or be out looking for her?

Naturally, it would be difficult for anyone to recognize anyone else on this inky night. The swath of darkness that made her imagination conjure up such terrible possibilities also shielded her from the very things she was afraid of. No one could see her. She was perfectly safe. In fact, all her terrible thoughts probably sprung from the fact that she was overly tired. It had been a long day of hard riding, being constantly on the lookout for Sam, yet still careful to keep pushing forward, with one eye on the way Gus had mapped out for her.

Darkness made that more difficult, too. She kept doubling back, covering areas twice to make sure she hadn't overlooked Sam beneath some bush or behind a rock—anyplace that was big enough to shield a man had to be investigated. They were growing increasingly difficult to spot, and soon she would have to give up, claim one of those bushes for herself and call it a night.

Not that she would get much sleep. Between imagining night crawlies and fugitive abductors and worrying about—

Before she could finish her catalog of sleep inhibitors, something grabbed her arm and tugged her roughly—and this wasn't a tree branch! Millie found herself being pried off Mrs. Darwimple, though in defense she crooked her knee around the saddle so tightly she feared that it wouldn't come off even if she did. She lashed about, trying to make it as difficult as possible for the *bandido* to drag her off.

"Let me go, you filthy coward!" she cried.

"What the hell—?"

The man's familiar voice caused her to freeze, as did the poke of cold metal against her ribs. Millie, strung out like a hammock between the stranger's arms and Mrs. Darwimple, struggled to look up, to see into the face of the man who had her. It couldn't be! Yet her speeding heart and sudden relief told her it was.

Sam!

Through the darkness, she focused in on his eyes, so shadowed they appeared black, not gray. But it was him, all right. The hard set of his jaw, the breadth of his shoulders, the hank of hair that fell across his creased forehead as he looked down at her in shock—all were unmistakably Sam Winter. She could have whooped for joy. In fact, she did.

And for that brief moment when she let her knee relax and slid easily off Mrs. Darwimple and into Sam's arms, she could have sworn she detected a hint of happiness in Sam's eyes. Maybe Gus was right and he really was glad to see her.

The sparkle in Sam's eyes turned into that old suspicious glare as his hands moved over her arms and held her stiffly away from him.

"What the hell are you doing here?"

"I was looking for you."

He closed his eyes, took a breath as if to summon up patience, and then opened them again. "I realize that," he said. "How did you get away from Gus?"

She tossed her head with not a little pride. "How else?" she asked. "I charmed him."

Sam let out a clipped bark of disbelief.

Undaunted by his skepticism, she explained, "Just because you don't appreciate me, Sam Winter, that doesn't mean the rest of the world is blind. After a morning with me, Gus practically begged me to go after you."

"Now *that* I can believe," Sam quipped.

She huffed out a breath. "Because he could see how helpful I could be to you."

Sam shook his head. "And I thought Gus was on my side."

"He is!" she cried. "Haven't you been listening to a word I've said?"

Of course not. He wasn't even looking at her anymore. Instead, he was peering around them, in that ever-watchful way of his. She supposed the novelty of her arrival had already worn off.

"Follow me," he said, twitching his head toward a group of gnarled young live oaks. He took Mrs. Darwimple's reins and led the horse away.

Millie trotted silently after them. She was dismayed that she had failed to see Sam even when he was right on top of her. How had he done it? Of course, he'd had the advantage of hearing her coming and being able to lie in wait for her. But just who had he thought she was—and what had he intended to do with his captured rider?

"Sam?" she ventured to ask when they were in the little treed oasis he had picked for the night. "Who did you think I was?"

"I didn't know."

Growing bolder, she asked, "Did you think I was a member of Sheriff Tom's posse?"

"I didn't know," came his clipped reply.

"Then why did you grab me off my horse?"

There was a pause. "To find out, I guess."

She shook her head. Gus, though he might have overestimated how fond Sam was of Millie, had apparently been right about one thing. Alone, Sam had obviously been as jumpy as she was. "That was a mistake."

This time, the silence stretched longer. Much longer. Sam didn't take too well to her criticism of his judgment. "I guess I knew somehow it was you," he said slowly.

Millie laughed and dropped to the ground. Men! "No you didn't," she told him. "You were completely surprised to see me. You exclaimed, 'What the hell?' I remember it perfectly."

"Maybe I did," he admitted. "Just because I thought it might be you doesn't mean I couldn't have been surprised to find that it actually was you."

"*That* is a lame explanation, Sam," she said, feeling rather pleased with herself. Sam was just as jumpy as she had been. Probably almost as jumpy as Lloyd Boyd. And thinking of Sam on the same level as Lloyd suddenly made him seem more manageable, and her own position more secure. "Besides, I felt your gun in my back," she said saucily. "Was it the thought of me you almost shot, and not the actuality?"

"You're finally coming closer to the truth." His lips twisted into a mask of perturbation. "Does Gus hate me? I can't imagine what he was thinking sending you here!"

"He was thinking of what a help I could be to you. You haven't even looked at the rabbits I brought."

Sam swung his gaze back to Mrs. Darwimple's saddle. "You caught those?"

She smiled enigmatically. "I wasn't idle while I was at Gus and Lou's, you can count on that."

For once, he seemed impressed. But that apparently didn't change his feelings about her being there. "How in tarnation did you know where to look for me?" he asked, a little belligerently.

She harrumphed proudly. "I do have some sense of direction."

"Gus again," Sam grumbled, pacing in front of her. "I'll have to have a talk with that man."

"Aren't you glad at all to see me?"

He sent her a look of utter disbelief. "Glad!" he said, aghast. "Did you ever consider that I might have left you with Gus because I thought you'd be safer there?"

"Really?" she asked, a smile beaming across her face. This was the closest he'd ever come to showing any kind of regard for her at all, and she savored it greedily. "That's sweet! But I'd rather be here with you," she said, standing again.

"It's not just what you want that's at stake here, Millie. I'm trying to move fast...." He backed away from her as she came forward.

"Look," she said, "I caught up with you, and you even had a half day's lead!"

She had him stumped on that one. He stepped away and kept pacing furiously, yet silently, then finally shook his head and turned to her again. "All right. I'll admit you're fast, but I can't be worrying about you all the time."

"Then don't. I can take care of myself."

"Sure—just like you did when I pulled you off that horse of yours a while ago."

She crossed her arms and lifted her chin. "You did *not* pull me off," she pointed out. "I wasn't about to let go until I realized it was you."

He made a derisive clucking noise. "What am I supposed to do with you when I finally find Darnell Weems? I doubt you'll be much of a help then."

"You never know," she said evenly. He was just trying to rile her, she told herself. Like Gus said, Sam didn't want to admit that he was glad to see her. At least it made her feel better to think so. "I've surprised you before, you have to admit that."

"The only thing that surprises me is that you won't quit. It's like there's this little steam engine inside you that keeps you chugging along after me."

She smiled, not in the least displeased by his description. Her daddy often said that Millie's problem was that she didn't follow through with things. She'd start knitting something, only to find scraps of the project tucked away years later, unfinished. And cooking was beyond her. She never had the patience to remember what she'd put in the oven, or how long something had been boiling on the stove. Too tedious!

And, of course, there was the small matter of her eleven fiancés....

Which just served to show how much she really had changed. She was a completely new Millie Lively. Tenacious and purposeful. "Looks like you're stuck with me, Sam. But don't worry. It's like I told Gus. Someday, you'll be glad that you ran across me."

He looked at her with a disbelieving grimace. "What makes you think that?"

"Because if you ever get in a spot, I'll be there."

An eyebrow shot up. "And just what do you plan to do to get me out of this spot I'll be in?"

Her head lifted majestically. "You just leave that to me," she assured him. "Don't forget—I have influence!"

Chapter Eight

Sam awoke the next morning feeling as if someone had hit him on the head with an anvil. He attributed the terrible ache to Millie's surprise return.

He still couldn't believe she had found him. All night long he'd kept waking up and looking over at the long, thin lump a few feet away, trying to puzzle out the bewildering situation. His only answer to Millie's catching up to him was that Gus must have told her about some short cuts, which made sense. Gus knew this area much better than he did. But Gus apparently didn't know the effort it had taken Sam to leave Millie behind, or why else would he have let her get away?

When Sam opened his eyes, he still couldn't make out Millie, but not because of the darkness. Light was already brightening the eastern sky. Millie just plain wasn't there.

He sat up, alarmed, then took a deep breath—smoke and the aroma of cooking meat assailed his nostrils, reminding him of his hunger. Ever since leaving Millie off at Gus's, he hadn't eaten a full stomach's worth of food. He'd been too anxious to relax even that much. Frankly, without Millie there nagging at him, he'd practically forgotten about nourishment.

No wonder he'd been so slow, he admonished himself. He'd probably made himself weak as a kitten from hunger without even realizing it.

He looked over at Millie's silhouette as she leaned over a tiny fire. He could just make out the petite curves he'd been dreaming of for days now, could barely discern the dark hair spilling down her back that he'd thought so often of running his hands through. In a few minutes, he would be able to walk up to her and see her dark, shining eyes. He'd dreamed of those, too, ever since leaving her.

Last time they were alone in the dark together, he'd kissed her. He wanted to kiss her now, even though she did annoy him, and even though he was equally torn by the desire to eat that rabbit she was cooking, and even though his head was still pounding like thunder.

He eased slowly to his feet, trying not to jostle the pain that lay in wait for him every time he made an abrupt movement. There was no time for lollygagging and daydreaming this morning. Nor was there time to dwell on his own problems—and this weakness for Millie was definitely a problem—while his brother was still in jail. The hanging date loomed ever closer. Luckily, Little Bend loomed ever closer, too. The town probably wasn't more than a day away, if he made good time. He and Millie were not at leisure to socialize.

"Oh, you're up!" Millie chirped at him, squinting through the creeping dawn as he rose.

Her words met his ears as if someone were beating him over the head with a club. He grunted in response.

"I've got breakfast," she said, scurrying over and handing him a handkerchief with a bit of the rabbit he'd skinned last night on it. "Looks pretty good, too!" she bragged.

Sam looked at the charred piece of meat. Even from his short acquaintance with her, Sam had divined that Millie was not the most adept at the feminine arts—the practical ones, at least. While some women were forever fussing over a man, cleaning and cooking and trying to keep things orderly, Millie just fussed.

He took a bite of breakfast and felt a smile spread across his lips in spite of himself. Not bad! Of course, the rabbit was half burned, half raw, but beginners were likely to make mistakes.

"It's good, isn't it?" she asked, folding her arms in self-satisfaction.

Maybe his headache had been from hunger. He could have sworn the pain was lifting a little.

God, she was pretty. He had forgotten just how her head tilted to the side a little when she looked up at him, giving him a view of the graceful curve of her neck. He fairly itched to reach out and run his fingertips across that delicate jaw of hers that looked as if it had been molded out of something fine but tough, like ivory. And then his gaze alit on her red lips, sweet and inviting as she smiled up at him proudly. He had never felt so drawn to a woman before.

Which was precisely why he had tried to get rid of her to begin with! He had never met a female who so easily made him leave his common sense behind.

"It's fine," he answered, not about to let her see the effect she had on him. That dull throb started pitching camp in his head again. "But you shouldn't have made a fire."

"Why not? You did."

"That was days ago, and only because it was the one way I could think of to shut you up."

Her eyes rounded in offense as she watched his booted foot kick dust over the coals. "Well, I'm glad you appreciate my efforts!" she said in a huff. "I'd forgotten how cross you were in the mornings."

"Maybe if you'd remembered you would have stayed put," he grumbled, saddling up.

To his surprise, she fell in right beside him and started readying Mrs. Darwimple, without his having to press her. "No matter how much you gripe at me, you're nowhere near as grumpy as Lou."

The statement caused Sam to smile, and smiling caused him to wince. "She's a good hand at healing ailments, though."

He couldn't see her, but he could imagine Millie's lips pursing in displeasure. "What difference does that make? I'd rather be dead than have to put up with her for longer than a day."

"Men value useful women."

"Ha!" Millie cried. She might as well have smacked him on the skull with a rock. "Not in my experience. If men truly liked useful women, then the most sought-after woman in the world would be Alberta, my maid. She can do anything! But I haven't noticed men busting down the door trying to take her away from us. I even asked her about it once, and she said she'd only received two proposals her entire lifetime."

"That doesn't sound so bad to me."

Millie's mouth went slack in utter dismay. "Well, it should!"

"I've never received any," Sam said wryly.

"*That* doesn't surprise me in the least," she sassed back.

For a moment, Sam felt the sudden urge to forget his troubles and the miles they had to cover this day and pull Millie into his arms for a long, lingering kiss. His chest nearly hurt with the desire to fold her against him—and the activity might be just the thing to clear his head.

Then he heard Millie say, "As for myself, I would just die if I'd lived to be as old as Alberta and only received two measly little proposals."

"How old is Alberta?"

"Twenty-nine!"

Her tone let him know just how disgustingly old she thought that was. And her disdain for Alberta's scant romantic history made him wary. "How many proposals have you received?"

She let out a snort of derision. "More than that, I can assure you!"

No doubt, Sam thought. Rich town girls made sport out of breaking men's hearts. They knew just how to trap a man into believing she was exactly the woman for him, then kicking him in the teeth when he suggested as much. That was probably what Millie was doing now, with her rabbits and her helpfulness—tempting him. Stringing him along.

Well, he didn't have time for it.

"Aren't you going to ask the precise number?" she asked.

He gritted his teeth. "I am not."

She shook her head. "It would take me a while to remember them all, anyway."

He watched as she flitted about, picking up after herself, trying to erase the evidence of their presence there. And though she hummed a tuneless melody and appeared distracted—probably totting up her discarded beaux—she was doing a fairly competent job of covering their tracks.

Not that he was taken in, he reminded himself.

"Oh, Sam, look!" she said suddenly, pointing to the horizon to the east.

He glanced up and saw a heart-stopping display of deep gold and orange, casting the dark silhouettes of clouds in the foreground against the sky's brilliant tones. The sight was impressive, but Sam wasn't as much dazzled as he was disturbed. For the first time, he noticed that the air felt heavier, moist. He frowned.

"Don't you think it's spectacular?" Millie asked as she swung up on Mrs. Darwimple, her eyes never leaving the brilliant display.

"Oh, sure," Sam said, his unhappiness clear in his tone. "That pretty sky of yours also means we're in for some rain." His mood sank just a notch further. "A lot of it."

"Sam, are you sure you're feeling all right?"

Sam's head jerked up and, not too subtly, he straightened in his saddle. There was no disguising the fact that he appeared a little green around the gills, however, or that they weren't moving as fleetly as they had in days past. "'Course."

Millie glanced at him skeptically. And nervously. She'd never been good with sick people.

"What's the matter?" he grumbled, one of his eyebrows arching up in that way it sometimes did. It gave Millie a little hope. "Are you waiting for your chance to bolt again?"

She scoffed at the very idea. "Would I have chased after you all this way just to get away from you?"

"Hanged if I can figure out why you chased after me."

Men could be so dense! "You must know I'm not going to run, since you haven't seen fit to tie me down this time."

"Or maybe I'm just hoping you *will* run."

Her head whipped back around, and she caught him smiling teasingly. "It would serve you right if I did!" Millie said.

He winced at the shrill outrage in her tone. Poor man. He'd complained of a headache several times. She had no doubt that the weather must have something to do with his condition. All day long the dark clouds had loomed overhead, threatening to bust wide open, but rain never came. It was enough to make anyone tense.

Maybe she could help him by taking his mind off his pain. "You know what, Sam?" When he didn't answer, she looked over at him and saw him tilting in his saddle. "Sam!" she cried.

He shot upright.

"Oh, Sam, you look so bleary! Maybe we should find somewhere to stop."

He narrowed bloodshot eyes on her. "It's not even close to dark."

"But the clouds... If it rains and we get caught..."

He shook his head.

Stubborn. That was his problem. He was too proud to admit she was right. But what could she do? Even with him sick, she could hardly drag him off his horse and force him to stay put until he felt better. Yet she felt she herself might die if anything happened to him.

What was she going to do? Millie had seen a lot of tragedy in her life—although perhaps her daddy would call that being melodramatic—but she had never suffered the loss of someone she loved before.

The thought gave her pause.

It was the first time she had thought it so clearly. *I'm in love with Sam. I think.* Could it be possible?

She turned to take a good long look at the man who had stolen her heart. Then she gasped. Sam's head had sunk so far forward that he was practically hugging the black's neck, and he was listing dangerously to his left side.

"Sam!"

He didn't respond to her. He was going to fall off his horse!

Quickly, she headed Mrs. Darwimple over and grabbed the reins from Sam's hand, and then stopped and dismounted. Halting caused Sam to fall over even farther, and she had to wedge her shoulder underneath him to keep him from crashing to the ground with a thud.

She scanned the area around them, hoping for somewhere to take shelter. In the distance she could just make out a rise in the landscape. The dam of a pond, she wondered? If so, perhaps there would be some kind of vegetation on the other side, too. A tree or a bush—anything that could hide them even a little. As Sam said, it was still daylight, though you could hardly tell it for the dark clouds hanging overhead like a dreary shroud.

Trying to keep Sam steady, she moved slowly forward, and was pleased to feel a cool breeze whip past suddenly. It was hard work hauling a grown man this way.

Then she heard an ominous rumbling and frowned. Thunder. A streak of lightning struck on the horizon, followed by another clap. The cool breeze felt suddenly cold.

Then, at the worst possible time, the clouds finally released their dam of moisture. Rain poured down on them, cascading as if someone in the heavens were throwing buckets of water on their heads. In no time, Millie's dress was soaked through.

What were they going to do now?

It occurred to her, however, that "they" no longer existed. One of them was passed out cold. All the decisions were up to *her* now. And unfortunately, given the blue pallor of Sam's face, she feared the decisions she would be making would be matters of life and death.

Rain. Coming down in sheets. What were they going to do now?

Horace stood huddled in the doorway of the little home of the Beavers, two people he could only describe as irascible. They not only refused to talk to Sheriff Tom, they apparently hadn't spoken to each other in quite a while, either.

"Sheriff Tom says water is the tracker's worst enemy," Lloyd Boyd said mournfully. "We'll probably never find them now!"

Horace was tempted to tell Lloyd that "we" were about to be minus him, if he didn't get a grip on himself. "It will stop," he said, trying to exude confidence, as he once had done for his war-weary troops.

Unfortunately, Lloyd lacked a soldier's patience. No wonder he made such a terrible bank clerk, Horace thought. The man had a flair for fretful histrionics that just didn't suit standing behind a window all day. "The rain might stop," he wailed, "but who knows what toll it may already have taken? Millie could have caught pneumonia, or have been swept away in a river."

"We're nowhere near a river," Horace snapped.

"A creek, then."

Wonderful. All Lloyd could think about was Millie being swept away, while all the sheriff cared about was the possibility that Winter's tracks would be swept away. And where was Tibbetts, the detective? He seemed to have been swept away himself, considering how often he had checked back with Horace.

He bit back a sigh. Couldn't let them see the tension. It was up to him to keep hope alive.

The sheriff, shaking his head, came from the back of the room, where he had been attempting to question the Beavers. "All the woman will say is that she and that old coot she's married to aren't talking because he came back from hunting one day without her father's gun."

Lloyd gasped. "Do you think he shot Millie?"

"That old geezer?" The sheriff slammed his hat down on his head. "Now where in tarnation did you get that idea?"

"I don't know... The gun..." Lloyd's voice broke off.

"Stop being an alarmist, Lloyd," Horace said. "It does no good to panic."

But the very word seemed to set off just that in the poor youth's brain. "Oh, Colonel! I'm afraid our poor Millie is doomed, doomed! If only I could do something!"

"You can calm down," Horace said.

"But something important! I keep thinking of all the terrible things that could have happened to our poor Millie— what that horrible wretch may have done to her! And now this rain, this terrible, unending, ceaseless, miserable rain!"

"That rain'll wash those tracks away, sure enough," the sheriff repeated for about the hundredth time.

Suddenly, Horace could take no more. He reached out and clapped his hands on Lloyd's shoulders, shaking him sternly. "Lloyd, snap to! There *is* something more you can do."

Lloyd blinked, suddenly still. "A mission?" he asked. "Me?"

"Him?" the sheriff asked in disbelief.

"Yes," Horace said.

The young man nodded eagerly. "What is it? I'll do anything, I'll—"

"Go home," Horace commanded him.

He continued nodded. "And then?"

"Wait there."

Lloyd looked confused. "You want me to go home and wait? Back to Chariton?"

Horace felt a stab of regret—and more than a stab of relief.

"You're sending me home in disgrace!" Lloyd cried. "The humiliation of it all! The anguish! I don't know if I can bear it!"

"Now, now, son. It's just in case Millie makes her way back home. You'll be waiting for her."

Understanding dawned across Lloyd's earnest face. "Of course!"

"You can leave as soon as the rain lets up." Already Horace couldn't wait.

"If it ever does," the sheriff said.

Horace looked at the man, considering. Was there any possible way to get rid of him, too?

"If it doesn't," the sheriff continued gloomily, "I'm afraid Sam Winter just might be unstoppable."

Chapter Nine

"I've never been so cold and miserable in all my life."

Millie knew she'd said it before, but it bore repeating, even if nobody could hear her. And now she could add a new item to her list of woes—fear. She was terrified that something would happen to Sam. What would she do then? Where would she go, and how could she return to her old life?

Not for herself alone was she frightened, but also for Sam. So much rested on his shoulders. Her welfare, and his brother's, too. And justice. Sam said Jesse was so torn apart by grief he was beyond caring about his own life, or whether the true murderer came to justice. But Sam still cared, and some of the things he'd told her about what had happened in that courtroom in Chariton made Millie care, too. But she doubted she would be able to carry on Sam's crusade alone. More likely, if anything happened to Sam, she would be like Jesse. Torn apart by grief.

She would never have imagined feeling so much for a person, but the connection she felt with Sam was strong. Watching him in his fevered delirium was almost more than she could bear. His skin felt clammy, then hot, by turns, and what was worse, there was little she could do to bring him any relief. It was only by some miracle that she had managed to haul him to this little shelter, but the small hollow in the dam by the pond was barely sufficient to keep him out of the rain. She herself was mostly exposed to the elements, and was soaked through. Her petticoats, which had been the only dry thing around by the time she'd wedged Sam into the tiny space where he now fitfully rested, she had immediately taken off and used to cover him. But he couldn't be comfortable lying on the cold earth.

"Millie..."

At the sound of her mumbled name, Millie snapped to attention. Quickly, she pushed a wet, drippy hank of hair out of her eyes and leaned close to Sam's face. He looked terrible! His usually tanned skin was white as alabaster now, with only stains of color in his cheeks.

"I'm here, Sam," she said, trying to keep the hysteria she felt out of her tone. He needed to be reassured.

"Millie..."

The repetition made her heart flop with happiness. "Can you hear me, Sam?" she asked in a loud, firm voice.

He mumbled something that sounded like "dear." She smiled. "Oh, Sam—please talk to me."

"Dearly beloved, we are gathered..."

Her brow furrowed. "What?" He sounded as though he were reciting the wedding ceremony. "Sam, could you say that again?"

He seemed to sigh in frustration at her question, which would have been a good sign that he was returning to normal, except that his next words were "We the people...in order to build a more perfect union..." And then, after that petered out, he repeated her name again, and then Jesse's, following that with a recitation about planting corn that could only have come from *The Old Farmer's Almanac.*

Millie wiped his forehead, then sank back on her heels, trying not to let the disappointment get to her. He was just mumbling in his delirium. Her name meant no more to him than any of the other words that came spilling out of his mouth. Sam was out of his head with sickness.

And she was nearly going out of her mind trying to decide what more to do for him. As soon as the rain let up some more, she would build a fire, no matter how much of a risk they ran of being seen. At this point, she would have welcomed even Sheriff Tom coming along and finding them. She wondered whether she should have headed back to Lou, who Sam said was a good hand at healing people. But that was a whole day's ride, and would mean backtracking. She doubted Sam would appreciate waking up farther behind than he'd started out days before.

To give herself something to focus on besides her charge, she started to gather up sticks and twigs and even wet leaves. How she was ever going to be able to dry them out in order to light them was beyond her thinking at the moment. She could only pray that somewhere in all their stuff was a match. If there wasn't, she didn't know what she would do. This fire was her last hope.

In fact, Millie was willing to go further than that. The thought of lighting that fire was perhaps the only thing standing between herself and utter despair.

It was warm. Too warm. Beads of sweat popped off his brow, but he couldn't wipe them off. His hands were tied. Ahead of him was the gallows where he would meet his end, and all along the dusty streets of Chariton stood spectators, turned out in their best Sunday clothes for the hanging.

Or was it really a hanging?

Suddenly, the world went all fuzzy on him. When it came into focus again, he was still looking out on the well-dressed Chariton public, but his path had turned into an aisle, and he wasn't moving. As the people peered curiously at him, the figure directly ahead of him changed from a hangman's rig to, of all things, Millie—Millie in a white dress, clutching a big cascading bouquet, coming right at him with a demure smile on her lips as she moved in a slow hesitation step!

There was no doubt who he was supposed to be playing in this scenario, and he still felt as clammy and hot and sweaty as he had when he was marching to the gallows. Now not only his hands felt tied; his feet also seemed embedded in the ground, as if there were stakes in his heels.

His eyes popped open. Darkness. The air felt cool, but his body was surrounded by warmth. Not far away, the left-over embers of a small fire glowed through the dark, but providing more immediate warmth was Millie's body, her backside snuggled up against his chest and legs warmer than any blanket—and infinitely more arousing. Sam shifted uncomfortably, trying to ease the ache her nearness brought to him even in delirium.

What the heck had happened? The last thing he remembered was riding along like they had been for days. Sure, he'd had a little headache—but nothing that had made him suspect he'd pass out. How long had they been stalled here?

"Princess!" he barked.

Millie was up like a shot, propped up on her elbows and looking at him through eyes so round with surprise he could see the whites of them even through the darkness. "You're awake!"

He smiled, relief that the dream hadn't been real mixing with genuine gladness to see Millie's face, her cheek smudged with dirt. "Seem to be."

"Oh, thank goodness!" she cried. "I was so worried!"

He tried to sit up, too, but he still felt drained. And clammy from the sweats. "Did I have a fever?"

"Something fierce, Sam," she told him. "I wasn't sure how serious it was—"

"Got your hopes up?"

There was genuine concern in her tone as she admonished, "Don't joke about such things. I was nearly scared sick myself! I don't know what I would have done if anything had happened to you." She looked at him, and though it was dark, he would almost have sworn there were tears in her eyes. "I'm just so glad you're all right."

"How long have we been stopped here?" The question came out more clipped than he'd intended, breaking up the tender drama of his recovery for Millie.

Her lips twisted down. "Just tonight. It's been raining cats and dogs, Sam. I don't think the posse could have been following us through it."

He squinted, trying to scope out the world around him. One night? He felt as if he had slept as long as Rip van Winkle. But if what Millie said about the rain was true, then she was probably correct. It was hard to track anything in a downpour, and the night was dark as pitch. He could barely make out the horses in the distance, much less gauge how much rain had fallen. One thing he could see was that they had stopped near some sort of pond and were wedged beneath a slight overhang along its bank. "How did we get here?"

"I brought us."

He stared at her. "You?"

She straightened up. "Yes, and you can act surprised if you want to. It wasn't easy."

Sam was so impressed he was momentarily struck dumb. He couldn't imagine a slight thing like Millie hauling his dead weight around in the rain. How had she done it? And how had she found what had to be the one place for shelter in the entire area? Even so, the little overhang was only big enough for one, and she had made sure he was given the best spot. Not to mention somehow managing to light a fire—when, by her own admission, it had been pouring rain.

"How did you get those coals going?" he asked, nodding to indicate the warming embers.

She tilted her chin proudly. "Oh, that was the easy part! You had matches in your saddlebag."

"What about the wood? How did you find any dry enough to light?"

"I pulled some old branches out of here so I could have room to stuff you in," she told him matter-of-factly.

He tried to picture it, and smiled at the vision his mind conjured up. He'd heard that ants could carry objects ten times their size, and that's how he pictured Millie hauling him along, like a scrappy little ant in petticoats. Sensing something wrong with that thought, he looked down and immediately amended the image. Millie wasn't wearing the petticoats anymore—*he* was!

He scowled and began pulling them off himself, one by one.

She laughed at him. "I think they look quite becoming on you."

"You shouldn't have done that. How are you supposed to stay warm?"

"Don't worry about me. I did fine."

He couldn't believe that. The girl was accustomed to wearing more underwear than Queen Victoria probably did. "Put these back on," he told her. "There's no sense in your catching pneumonia just as I'm getting better."

"I've decided to do without them entirely. I like going about practically naked this way—it's so freeing!"

He didn't like the picture of Millie "freed" that leapt to his mind, and he fought against the uncomfortable feelings it stirred inside him. Apparently he was feeling *much* better. "Put 'em on," he insisted. "I won't be responsible for corrupting your sense of propriety."

"Oh, I don't care about that," she said. "Do you know what, Sam?"

"What?" He bit the one word out.

"I think I'm a changed person."

"That's what you said two days ago."

Her forehead wrinkled. "But this time I *really* think it's true. I believe I'm truly turning into a person who appreciates nature, and living for the moment. Can't you see the change?"

All he could see was her hair spilling down her back, the smudge on her face, the way her dress silhouetted her thin shoulders, bodice and hips like a glove. He swallowed past the lump in his throat.

"I'm beginning to think that you've got a touch of fever yourself—either that, or you're touched in the head!"

When he looked into her eyes, they glistened, all right, but with fervor, not fever. "Oh, no, I think I've finally come to my senses. All these years, I only looked at things the way my daddy and other people told me I should. But now I see that a lot of what they told me was pure nonsense."

"Like what?"

"Well . . . for instance, my daddy always told me that I should never spend too much time alone with a man. But tonight I slept right up next to you for hours, and nothing terrible happened. Daddy's just an alarmist."

"Millie . . ."

"And what if I don't wear a million layers of clothes?" Millie went on, heedless of his negative reaction. She jumped to her feet and pirouetted for him, her rain-stiffened skirt clinging to her like a second skin. "I like being able to move around unencumbered. And I think all those clothes disguise a woman's figure, don't you?"

"Millie . . ."

To his dismay, she lifted her skirts clear up to her knees, revealing the outline of those shapely legs that never failed to have an effect on him. He was feeling dizzy again, but how could he tell her to stop without admitting that he wanted nothing more than to pull her into his arms and ravish her?

"I think I'd like to wear breeches," she said, shaking out one foot and then another in a sassy little dance. "That way I would be able to move around better. Especially while we're out in the wilds. How would you like that?"

"I wouldn't," Sam said.

She glanced at him, as if amazed by his adamant tone. "Don't you think it would be better to have me unencumbered?"

What a question! One by one he tossed her the petticoats, then answered, "No, I don't. And don't ask me why."

She held the garments in fists by her sides. "You don't believe that I've matured at all."

"Matured!" He practically spat the word. "It sounds more to me like you've become one of those damn suffragists!"

"Maybe I have." Millie planted her hands on her hips. "At any rate, I know I'm not going to be closed-minded ever again, not even toward those horrible manly women."

Sam laughed. He hated to admit it, but maybe these past few days had been good for Millie. Hadn't she handled the crisis today as well as he would have, had their roles been reversed? And she wasn't asking for thanks, or whining about the hardships she'd been put through. In fact, she seemed to relish them. She even looked different; she appeared weathered now, not so much like a sheltered flower. The pouty princess had turned into an exuberant woman....

Which, from his point of view, wasn't an entirely good thing.

"Well, I guess I shouldn't expect *you* to understand," Millie said, flopping back down to the ground next to him. In response, he found himself inching away from her, from her nearness. "After all, you were just on the brink of death. I suppose I should be glad you're not talking your head off anymore."

Sam froze. "What?"

"You were saying all sorts of crazy things, Sam, like the Declaration of Independence."

His dream came back to him, the one in which he was getting married to Millie and felt so clammy and nervous. He felt clammy now, just thinking about it—or about what Millie might think if she knew. "I, uh, didn't say anything about a wedding, did I?"

Her brow wrinkled. "Come to think of it, yes, you did."

It wasn't often that Sam felt embarrassed, but he was sure his face must have turned crimson. Thank God it was still dark! He swallowed. "What exactly did I say?"

"Well . . . you started reciting the wedding service."

"And?"

She stared at him long and hard, as if trying to gauge why he was asking. "And then you supplied some information about the best time for putting in corn. Sam, are you *sure* you're all right?"

He took a deep breath and sighed. "No, I'm fine."

"You certainly did have a curious mix of things going on in your head," Millie continued, "but I just supposed you were remembering your brother's wedding or something. Isn't that right?"

He couldn't get the picture out of his mind. Millie, in her white wedding dress, walking toward him, that enigmatic, knowing smile on her face. Why had she been looking at him that way? What did it mean? And why had he felt so trapped? He couldn't help thinking it was some sort of premonition. But that was crazy! The chances of him and Millie getting married—especially against his will—were absolutely nil.

"Sam?"

He shook his head, clearing it. "That's right," he lied, "I was probably just dreaming about my brother."

"Oh." She sank back against the walls of the insufficient little cave and let out a sigh. He couldn't believe she, of all people, would let the matter drop—a dream wedding seemed just the type of thing Millie would latch on to. But instead, she seemed almost . . . disappointed.

Sam sucked in a breath, surprised by the idea that came to him. He'd guessed that maybe Millie had a little schoolgirl crush on him, but never had he imagined that she might be entertaining visions of wedding bells and white dresses. That was just too preposterous! Of course, that *he* had been doing exactly that in his dreams was an entirely different matter.

He'd just been out of his head.

"Say," he warned her, "I hope you aren't getting notions."

An imperious dark eyebrow arched upward against her pale, moon-shadowed skin. "Notions? What kind?"

"You know..." he said, not wanting to say it outright. "About you and me."

Her mouth clamped shut for a moment, and then she tossed her head saucily. "What ideas you have, Sam!" she admonished. "Did you actually think that because I heard you reciting a few words I imagined you whisking me away to a church?"

It did sound pretty dumb, now that he thought about it. He should have kept his mouth shut.

"Men are so conceited!" Millie cried in offense before he could even get two words in. "You and me? Why, I can't imagine how you came up with such wild thoughts!"

Sam shrugged resentfully. "It isn't that wild."

"But you know it is!" she scolded. "You've said so yourself."

"Since when have you ever paid any attention to what I say?"

"Well," she admitted, "I might not *look* like I'm paying attention, but in this case, Sam, you have no worries. I'm not sitting on Mrs. Darwimple fantasizing about you carrying me off into the sunset." She snorted at the image, which ruffled Sam's pride. "Anyway," she finished with a haughty sniff, "I couldn't even if I wanted to."

"Why not?"

"Because I'm not free to. I have a fiancé."

"A *what?*"

"A fiancé. You know, a man to whom—"

"I know what it means," he snapped. For a moment, his heart seemed to stop beating. Then, smiling, he waved a hand derisively. "I'll just bet you do."

"I do!" she insisted.

"I don't believe it," Sam said. "You're engaged to be married, and in all the time we've spent together you've never mentioned this person?"

"The subject never came up," she replied defensively, looking slightly uncomfortable.

Could it really be true? "Then you should have brought it up," Sam said.

"Why?"

He was beginning to suspect she actually *did* have a fiancé. And for some reason, the idea of some man—some town dandy, no doubt—laying claim to Millie rubbed his fur the wrong way. "Because he's your fiancé!" he cried. "Land's sake, Millie, seems you've told me about every other person in that sad little town. I practically know your maid's life story. I'd think somewhere in all that chatter you might have slipped your fiancé's name in."

"It's Lloyd Boyd," she said.

Hearing it didn't make him simmer down any. If anything, he felt such a sharp stab of jealousy that he began to boil all over again. "Lloyd Boyd?" he asked in disbelief. "That's his name?"

"I said it was, didn't I?" she returned, folding her arms over her chest crossly.

There was no way that she could have mentioned that name before and he would have missed it. Lloyd Boyd. It wasn't a name a person could forget. He probably wouldn't forget it for years to come. Although Millie seemed to forget about the man easily enough . . .

Maybe she'd only forgotten to mention him because she hadn't been engaged to this Lloyd person for very long. That had to be it! After all, he thought, feeling a little reassured, when he first met up with Millie, she had been on the flighty side. Chances were she and this Lloyd Boyd had become impetuously engaged right before she was kidnapped.

"I suppose you only met this man recently," he supplied, hoping she would confirm the statement.

"Oh, no! Lloyd's worked in my father's bank for years!" Suddenly, he could make out her white teeth in the darkness as she flashed him a smile. "Sam, are you jealous?"

"Hell, no!" He scowled fiercely at the very idea, and yet he couldn't help asking, "How long have you been engaged to him?"

"Three months."

His headache started up all over again. "Three months!"

"I don't see any reason why you should be so upset, if you don't give a flip about who I'm engaged to."

"Neither do you, apparently," Sam observed. "Did it ever occur to you that Mr. Boyd might be worried sick about you?"

"Of course. Lloyd is very emotional. Too emotional for a bank clerk, I've always told him."

"How much could you care for the man, if you haven't even thought about him—haven't even mentioned his name?"

"I care very much about Lloyd," Millie insisted with a smile.

"You evidently didn't care about him too much when you were kissing me," Sam blurted out.

Millie's mouth dropped open in shock. "Pardon, but I believe it was *you* who kissed *me*."

"Well, you sure didn't fight it any," Sam observed hotly. "Or maybe kisses just don't mean much to you. Maybe you just kiss all men you come across that way."

She looked so stricken that he immediately wished he could take back his words, especially when he remembered how she had actually reacted—like a person who had never been kissed at all.

"If you're trying to insinuate that I'm loose, you can just think again," she argued, her hands on her hips. "And I'm not a heartless fiancée, either. It just so happens that I know Lloyd and I will never get married."

"How's that?"

"Don't get me wrong. He's the nicest boy in all the world, and I'd trust him with my very life…but in the whole three months we've been engaged, he's only tried to kiss me once. And that was just a peck on the cheek!"

Now it was Sam's turn to stare at her in slack-jawed amazement. One puny kiss in three months? Why, he'd kissed her once in three days, and he'd been having a hard time keeping his hands off her since. He couldn't imagine being engaged to a woman as beautiful and flirtatious as Millie and not trying to snatch a taste of the pleasures to come. Hell, he'd been wanting to snatch them, and he didn't even have a right to!

No, he thought sourly, Lloyd Boyd was the only one with that right.

"If we're going to discuss a person to whom kisses mean nothing," Millie went on, "then I believe the subject at hand would be you, Sam Winter."

"Me?"

"It's been three days since you kissed me, and you haven't ever mentioned a thing about it!"

"It's not something you talk openly about, Millie," he lectured. "Especially to a woman who's engaged to someone else."

"You didn't mind kissing an engaged woman."

He rolled his eyes. "Because I didn't know you were."

"Would it have made a difference?"

Sam had a code about such things. He'd never stolen another man's woman, never even been tempted to. It seemed a low thing to do, besides which, he'd never met a woman he thought it would be worth the trouble to steal. Now he looked at Millie and wondered. Not knowing Lloyd Boyd, he couldn't say what kind of a fight the man would put up, but it would have to be a pretty fierce one to keep him away from Millie.

Millie took his silence as a negative response. She sank down against the shelter's clay wall and pulled the petticoats up to her shoulders like a blanket. "Never mind," she said. "You don't have to worry about embarrassing me by answering. I can see now that you really were just trying to teach me a lesson, like you said."

Sam remained silent. The truth was, he didn't want to embarrass himself by admitting that he probably would have kissed her, engaged woman or not, simply because he wouldn't have been able to help himself. Just as he hadn't been able to help himself wondering what it would be like to have her in his bed, or to make love to her all over his house.

Three months *was* a terribly long time for only one kiss, he thought, sinking back down to the earth himself. There were still a few good hours of dark left in which to rest. He closed his eyes and pictured Lloyd Boyd—a scrawny youth, pasty and pale and hunchbacked from counting money over a desk. A rival's dream.

Not that they actually were rivals. Not in any realistic sense. He knew he didn't have any chance with Millie—but trying to picture Millie as someone else's wife was not pleasant.

Did she really mean it when she said she would never marry Lloyd?

You have no right to her....

He had kidnapped her, for heaven's sake, taken her by force away from her father and a fiancé. What kind of man was he that he could now be dreaming of having her for his wife, this pampered girl he'd dragged away from the only life she'd ever known? Maybe he truly wasn't far from the barbarian she'd accused him of being from the first.

Or maybe, for the first time, he was seeing that Millie might not be so far out of his grasp. After all, if she was as stingy with her kisses as she claimed, one kiss in one week was a far better record of persuasion than one kiss in three months.

Far better.

Chapter Ten

Millie awoke feeling as if she'd been dipped in mud and hung out to dry. A clump of dirt from above must have fallen on her shoulder during the night, because she felt an odd weight there. She opened her eyes to see the sun sneaking up on the horizon, then, remembering, darted a glance over at Sam. He was lying on his side, still fast asleep. His skin once more had its usual tan appearance, though Millie noted that his expression in slumber made him appear almost boyish. More interesting still was the source of the weight she'd felt on her shoulder—Sam's hand, which was outstretched and lying protectively along the curve of her neck.

Something inside her ached at being able to watch him so unguarded, and she smiled sleepily, wishing they had all morning to rest this way. Yet just looking at him and feeling his heat against her made her feel strange, restless. It also reminded her of Sam's testy reaction when he had discovered she had a fiancé.

Millie smiled. Jealous? Though it had been dark, she would have laid down money that the man was green with jealousy. She might have told him that she had every intention of breaking off the engagement—had even run away when her father crossed her on the subject—but what would have been the point? She'd rather enjoyed his dismayed reaction when he discovered she was spoken for. Which was confusing in itself, considering that Sam didn't seem to treat her in a very loverlike way... at least, not the way she was used to.

She sighed quietly. The whole world seemed to have been shaken up and turned on its head. Not that she minded. Her father, Lloyd, her future...all that seemed very distant. As long as she was with Sam, she was content. She would even have liked to nestle closer against him, but she was certain that would wake him. Sam needed his sleep. What he didn't need was to see her looking like a dog who'd been rolling in the mud.

With extreme care, she slowly turned and lifted the hand away from her shoulder, returning it to its owner's side. Then she got up and began to tiptoe down the bank to the pond, which had risen much closer to their bed in the course of the past twelve hours. Millie stripped to her undergarments, laying down her dress carefully so that it would not accumulate any more mud, and waded into the water.

It was numbingly cold at first, but as she silently flailed her arms beneath the surface of the clear pool, it began to feel more bearable. She took another step, then another, until she was fully submerged. When she resurfaced, going through the motions of washing her hair, even if she had no soap, she felt much better already, so much so that she dunked her head underneath the water and lifted her face so that it would be the first part of her to feel the refreshing morning air again. Never again would she take luxuries like baths for granted.

When her eyes focused again, she saw Sam on the bank, still lying on his side but propped up on one arm, staring at her. For a split second, their gazes met and held. The intensity in his gray eyes made her insides go as liquid as the water around her, and Millie found she couldn't move a muscle, even though a part of her yearned to cover her nearly bare shoulders beneath the pool.

Perhaps her paralysis simply stemmed from the fact that the other half—the wicked half, she was certain—wanted to rise out of the water, her wet clothes sticking to her like a second skin, and preen sensually before the man in front of her. The very idea should have made her die of shame, yet she couldn't deny it. Sam had lectured her twice on the impropriety of prancing around in front of him in her wet undergarments, which meant that doing so must have some effect on him. And, suddenly, she found herself wanting to affect him in any way possible. She wanted to play with fire.

Sam's face tensed, and he jerked his gaze away, almost as if to pretend that he hadn't seen her at all. He ducked out from under the overhang and stood abruptly. Millie felt her limbs relax in equal parts disappointment and relief.

When she finally worked up enough spit to talk, she voiced the first words that came to her. "Are you feeling better?"

Grumble, grumble was the only answer she could hear as he disappeared momentarily over the other side of their dam. Which meant that he must be feeling more like himself today.

But there was something different about him, too—something she'd caught in that look of his. It had lacked its usual wry disdain. Instead, she would have sworn she'd noticed something akin to fondness in those gray eyes. Could their discussion of her fiancé really have changed his attitude toward her, just a little?

Right. And if wishes were horses, beggars would ride. Millie slogged back to the bank of the pond and shook herself out, drying in the air as best she could. It was a glorious morning, all things considered. The rain had left the earth glistening, and the world was redolent with the smell of sweet wet grass. Birds chirped, a few bugs scratched out fidgety dawn noises, and the orange sun low in the sky promised to shine bright, making the temperature for their ride to Little Bend more pleasant than it had been the day before.

She shook out her dress, trying to bang the dirt out of it. The task was impossible. Her pretty yellow frock, once one of her best, was now permanently a sick ocher color, with stains enough to make it appear as if they had been dyed as a pattern into the fabric. Oh, it was a depressing sight. Millie, standing in her wet pantalets and camisole, dreaded putting it back on. She walked over and grabbed a petticoat and slipped it over her head. One was all she would wear. The others she rolled up and tied to her saddle.

Just as she was finally pulling on her dress, she heard Sam's footsteps.

"Oh, pardon me—"

She jerked the garment the rest of the way over her head and looked up at him. But he wasn't looking at her. Instead, he was staring in the opposite direction, a bright red splotch coloring his cheek. It appeared as if he were ready to bolt.

"Wait, Sam," she said.

He stopped, but didn't turn.

"What's the matter with you?" she asked. "You're acting so peculiarly."

"I, uh, just wanted to talk to you about something."

"Well?" she prompted, finishing doing up the last button.

Still he hesitated. "Are you decent?"

"Yes, I am," she answered, folding her arms across her chest. His sudden bashfulness was making *her* feel self-conscious.

He turned cautiously, as if he didn't believe her. Seeing her encased in her yellow dress seemed to relax him a bit. He wiped a hand through his hair as he stared at her. And stared at her. That gray gaze couldn't stop traveling up and down her frame, making Millie feel weak-kneed all over again. Though she couldn't imagine what Sam thought he was going to see. After five days, her dress was hardly big news.

"Sam?"

He jerked back to attention. "I was just going to say. . . I think we should stay newlyweds."

The odd statement caused an equally curious thumping to commence in Millie's chest. "What do you mean?" she asked, a little breathlessly.

"In Little Bend," he explained. "We need a cover, and I thought we could pretend to be newlyweds again."

Of course! Millie felt silly now for her heart-thumping reaction to such a practical plan. Yet it didn't escape her notice that he'd immediately suggested that they be a married couple. After their discussion of her engagement last night, she found this *very* interesting. She bit her lip in thought. "Why not be brother and sister?" she suggested.

He stared at her blankly, then blurted out, "We don't look a thing alike."

"Siblings don't necessarily look alike," she answered.

She expected him to cave in to her suggestion, but Sam wasn't backing down on this. "But people try to figure out if they do or not, and we don't want to draw attention to ourselves. So we'll be the Johnsons, newly married, from Dallas."

Millie felt her nose wrinkle. "The Johnsons?" she asked. "While we're pretending, can't we be the Vanderbilts?"

To her astonishment, a smile turned up the corners of his mouth. "The Johnsons," he insisted. "Married a month."

"Why a month?"

"People will leave us alone that way, and won't think twice if we keep to ourselves."

"Then why shouldn't **we** say we've only been married a few days?"

His smile broadened. "Because then they'd expect us never to leave our hotel room."

His words instantly brought to mind waking up with him this morning, guiltily enjoying the feeling of his hand on her shoulder. If they really were married, they would be entwined intimately like that every night. More intimately, even, if her and Sally Hall's guesses were correct.

Millie blushed a fiery red. "All right," she said. "But I still think Johnson is a boring name. What will my first name be?" she asked.

"I'll leave those to you," he promised, then added, "within reason."

"Of course!" she said, bridling slightly. "When am I not reasonable?"

Surprising her twice in the space of a few minutes, Sam threw his head back and laughed. Millie frowned, until she began to notice some things. Sam's teeth were straight and white, and they seemed to light up his whole face when he laughed like this. A deep crease—a dimple?—appeared in his left cheek, and his gray eyes fairly danced. As his glance swept over her again, Millie felt her frown disappear, and before she knew it, she was laughing, too. But not at her own expense.

She was suddenly giddy with joy. Because suddenly she realized that Sam hadn't laughed like this since she'd known him. And it also occurred to her that days before, if Sam had woken up and found her in a pond, he would have gruffly told her that she was a vain, foolish girl and should put on her clothes before she caught pneumonia. But this morning he hadn't scolded, and had actually seemed to appreciate looking at her fresh, clean appearance.

It was a long while before her smile went away that day. Because the whole time they rode, a single word repeated again and again in her mind, retrieving that original burst of giddiness. That word was *newlywed*.

Little Bend was not a disappointment to Millie. The town resembled a smaller, dustier, more rustic version of Chariton, but it was definitely civilization. Along the main street stood several establishments side by side—a bank, a store, a small restaurant. Disjointed from those but also bordering the street was a building holding a blacksmith and a hotel. The town had its church entrenched firmly on the opposite side of town from a rough-looking saloon. Houses, uniform in their simple design and lack of embellishment, dotted the environs of the little bustling center of commerce.

Millie was so glad to see the place that she could have cried for joy, were she not so nervous. Darnell Weems lived somewhere in the area, after all. She saw the killer's face on every man they passed, half expecting each one to pull out a revolver and gun them down.

"Stop looking so anxious," Sam said in a low voice.

She shot him a surprised glance. "I'm not anxious," she said, her cracking voice belying the statement.

"Don't forget, Weems doesn't know me."

"Or you him," she pointed out.

"But we've got the upper hand, because he won't be expecting us." Gray eyes focused on her with concern. "Now who are we?"

Without having to think about it, Millie answered, "Eugenia and Lowell Johnson, from Dallas."

"How long have we been married?"

"A month," Millie answered with assurance. Their subterfuge was a diversion she had relished all day. To kill time as they rode, she had woven an imaginary history of their courtship and marriage, and Sam had seemed to enjoy it. He had even agreed to the names Eugenia and Lowell after rejecting only three other combinations. And on one of those—Napoleon and Josephine Johnson—she'd only been kidding.

Sam stopped them in front of the hotel. "We might as well go ahead and get you a room here now."

At the word *you,* Millie's blood went cold. "Aren't you staying here, too?"

"I've got to find Darnell, Millie."

"So do I!"

He looked at her as if she had gone bug-crazy. "You'll remain here," he said. "I thought you knew that."

Her jaw was slack with shock. Why hadn't she expected this? Sam had said all along that Darnell lived outside Little Bend, but he'd never mentioned her going with him to find the Weems ranch. "But you can't leave me here, just when you need me most."

"*Need* you?" he asked, incredulous.

"Haven't you learned anything from dumping me off with Gus?" she asked. "What would have happened to you yesterday if you'd gotten caught in that storm by yourself?"

His jaw snapped shut, but he shook his head. "We're getting you a hotel room, and that's all there is to it. I'll meet you back here if I can."

That *if* spoke volumes. *If* he didn't get captured by a posse, or killed by Weems. Heaven only knew what all could happen once they were separated again! She wouldn't allow it to happen.

But she wouldn't let him know that just yet.

"I guess I see your point," she lied, trying to strike the correct note of resentfulness. "But there's no reason for you to waste time here. You go on about your business. I can register."

"I want my name registered, too," he said. "It'll look more normal than you being a lone woman."

"Of course I'll put your name down," she said, throwing him a flirtatious wink, "I'm your wife!"

He smiled back with mock patience. "All right then, sweetheart of mine," he said, taking the money, *her* money, from his saddlebag and handing her what was left—a little over seven dollars. "Here's the money for *our* hotel room. I'm going to see what I can find out about the Weems ranch."

She took the money and smiled. "I'll take care of everything, Lowell. You just leave it to me." Before he could move away from her, she hopped up on tiptoe and gave him a wifely buss on the cheek, then flitted away into the lobby of the hotel.

A look at the place was enough to confirm that she wouldn't be spending even one night there. The lobby—and that was putting it generously—was a barren, dusty room with what looked to be a bar table that served as a place to check in. No one was there, but why should there be? She wondered how many people could possibly pass through Little Bend and actually decide to stay. This place provided no incentive. The most inviting piece of furniture in evidence was a narrow wood bench against one wall that appeared to have about an inch of dust coating it.

Millie turned and looked out the window, staring at Sam's broad, straight back until it disappeared into the saloon. Naturally. That was where men always got their information.

She had no intention of following him there, which left her at loose ends. She felt the money in her hand and thought for a moment. Maybe she should go to the store and see what she could find there. They might have something that would make traveling a little easier. She knew she would appreciate some soap, and a blanket to sleep on, perhaps. As her feet instinctively seemed to direct themselves toward the store, she thought about something else she'd been thinking about getting. Breeches. Wouldn't Sam die if he came out of that saloon and saw her standing before him in a pair of pants!

She smiled smugly at the thought. Oh, she had changed, all right. Who would have thought she would ever turn out so practical? Not that she was going to become one of those eccentric women she'd heard about who dressed like men all the time. But could anyone fault her, after having been kidnapped and riding for five straight days, for wanting to wear something that allowed a little more movement?

She knew what Alberta would say—that she was "behaving scandalous." But Alberta would have had a fit over her wadding up all her petticoats but one and leaving them on her saddle. And she doubted Sally Hall would speak to her on the street if she came across Millie in a pair of pants. Her grin broadened, and she envisioned herself strolling down Chariton in her boots, breeches, and perhaps a jaunty hat to match. With a veil—that would add an air of mystery.

So lost in this revised vision of herself was she that she almost missed *it*. But, of course, the very second she passed the large glass window fronting the mercantile, her imagination slammed to an abrupt halt, and a covetous whine caught in her throat.

"Oh, how darling!" she cried, to no one in particular.

But *darling* was the only word for the dress hanging in the window, right next to a bridle, a butter churn and three plump sacks of seed. It was made of fine, smooth linen dyed a beautiful butter-yellow color—her favorite! The sleeves were fitted close, but the cuffs were trimmed in white lace and finished off with the same pearl buttons that ran down the dress's back. The front was high-cut, a style that suited Millie's long slender neck. The skirt was tight-fitting, just as the bodice was, but in the back, about halfway down, there was a pleat, lined with the same lace that adorned the sleeves.

For what must have been minutes, Millie stood mesmerized, oblivious of the comings and goings of the other people entering and leaving the store, her mind unable to focus on anything but the gorgeous creation in front of her. It seemed years, not just days, since she had seen so fine a dress, and for a moment she couldn't remember where that possibly could have been.

Then it came to her. Her cedar wardrobe at home. It was stuffed with dresses every bit as nice. She looked down at the dress she had on, which had once been as fine a creation as the frock in front of her. Though it was old, the color—the original, unmuddied color—suited her perfectly. She had always felt her most attractive in her yellow dress.

Sam had seen her in this dress—but had he really noticed her? Perhaps that was her problem. Everything had been so frenzied when they met, he hadn't had the leisure to truly appreciate her. So when he ruined her dress that first morning, he naturally hadn't understood the ruthlessness of his action. That was also why he had taken so long to fall for her charms, compared to other men. Although even now she wasn't sure of him. His being jealous of Lloyd Boyd didn't mean he loved her.

Suddenly her hand, which was gripping the money Sam had given her, felt very heavy. Gone was all intention of running after Sam in pants. The next time she saw Sam, she wanted to dazzle him in a decidedly feminine way.

With renewed, if altered, purpose, she strode into the little store. Inside, a pudgy, balding man was talking to a blond woman about twice his size. Millie swept past them and headed straight for the dress to get a better gander at it. If anything, she found the garment even more dazzling up close, without a glass window in front of it, and was just reaching out to feel the smooth linen beneath her fingertips when another hand reached for it, too.

Millie looked down at the large hand gripping the dress's sleeve, just above her own smaller one. Then her gaze trailed up the mystery hand's long arm, all the way to the broad shoulders and blond head that rested atop them. Searing blue eyes flashed at her with antagonism.

Oh, what a nuisance, Millie thought. This amazon apparently was interested in the dress, too. "I beg your pardon," Millie said, holding fast to the dress. She looked to the proprietor, who was standing behind the blue-eyed Brunhilde. In situations like this, it was always best to turn to a mediator. He would surely be able to show this country woman something more appropriate for her. Though the blonde was definitely attractive—in that earthy, strapping way some women had about them—this dress would be a disaster for her. That butter-cream yellow would make her look completely washed out.

"*I'm* looking at this dress," the woman announced, with an imperious twang.

Obviously, this poor woman didn't know who she was dealing with. Millie had wrestled purchases away from better women than this. In this case, she decided, the best tactic would be simply to ignore the intruder. "Would you mind taking this off the mannequin for me, sir?" she asked the shopkeeper.

He looked anxiously from one customer to another, though Millie was shocked to note that he seemed to be favoring the blonde. "I'm afraid this other lady was interested in the same dress," he explained.

Millie smiled patiently. "Of course," she said. "It's quite becoming. Or it *would* be, if one had the coloring for it." Yellow was so obviously *her* color.

The other woman stared down at her with pure icy hatred. "*I* would like to try it on, Mr. Sims, if that would be possible."

"Of course."

Of course?

Millie nearly fainted. Was he just going to let the other woman have it—just like that? How did the woman expect she was going to squeeze herself into such a darling little dress? It nearly broke Millie's heart to think of this corn-fed country bumpkin taking it away from her. "I was going to ask the same question, Mr. . . . Sims, is it?" Millie asked.

The man looked at Millie with something like disdain. Disdain! "I was helping this other lady. Perhaps if you could stand aside, ma'am."

Stand aside?

Millie was perplexed beyond words, until she suddenly looked down and remembered her own appearance. Her dress was beyond filthy, and since she had done away with half her undergarments, it hung on her frame like a withered old bean on the vine.

They were still staring at her, waiting for her to release the dress. Millie allowed a gay little laugh to bubble forth from her lips. "You see, I've been traveling. Now, if you'll just tell me where I could try—"

"I'm sorry, miss, but I do believe this lady had the prior claim."

Her mouth dropped open in astonishment. "Are you saying—?" She swallowed. "Do you mean—?"

"Do you mind?" the blonde asked, looking askance at Millie's hand, which was still clutching at the dress. Millie looked down at it herself and did note that her jaggedy, grimy fingernails had seen better days. And her pale skin was brown and dry—hardly the hallmark of a lady. Not that the amazon's were much better. Just better enough to convince the proprietor of this little penny-ante dry-goods place that she was the preferred customer of the two.

Millie, already bridling with indignation, nearly exploded when the woman looked down her nose and told her earnestly, "This is quite an expensive dress. Probably more than you could afford, anyway."

"Ha!" Millie cried in outrage. As if she couldn't have bought every dress in the place. "How much is it?" she asked Sims challengingly.

"Twelve dollars."

"Twelve dollars!" Millie said. "That's nothing for such a beautiful dress. Why, I'll—"

Her words were cut off abruptly. Twelve dollars might be a steal, but steal she would have to if she wanted that dress. She was five dollars short. She swallowed, relinquishing her grip on the linen—such pretty linen, she thought mournfully—her face red with humiliation.

"Well. Actually, I was looking for something more practical," she finished, trying to cover her monetary shortfall. The smug smirk on the other woman's mouth made it clear she wasn't buying the excuse, however. Millie added, "The linen on that dress is nice, but for twelve dollars I would certainly expect something cut more fashionably."

The woman raised her head proudly and turned to Sims. "Mr. Sims, this is as fine a dress as anything I ever saw in Fort Worth the time I was there."

"Then you must have been there a very long time ago," Millie said.

With that parting barb, she skulked away, examining the rest of the man's stock of ready-made clothing, which was sparse indeed. Certainly there was nothing there that she would have put on her back under normal circumstances. Mostly drab muslins in brown and black. A blue print that would have been fine for that blond woman, but whose busy pattern would have overwhelmed Millie. She frowned unhappily. The unkindest cut of all was that none of them was under seven dollars.

What a terrible thing it was to be poor! Even hideous country sacks were unattainable for her.

After installing the other customer in a back room to model the yellow dress, the proprietor came back to Millie. "Findin' anything?"

"Uh...no," Millie said, careful not to let the man see her wounded pride. She lifted her head. "All of these seem so... Well, I never cared for muslin. I'm actually used to much finer things."

The man sized her up from head to toe and nodded. "I got a calico dress 'bout your size for six dollars and eighty-five cents."

Millie's heart leapt. "Really?" she asked excitedly.

He went behind the counter and pulled it out. Although the little green-sprigged print wasn't too terrible, the dress was achingly plain in design. The type of thing her old granny used to don for church on Sunday—and about as up-to-date.

But what a bargain! Millie thrilled at the idea of actually wearing something clean for once. And anything was bound to look more attractive than what she had on.

"*That* is just adorable," Millie said, pretending an enthusiasm for the dress's design that she actually felt merely for its cleanliness. "I do believe that is just what I've been looking for."

"It is, huh?" the man asked skeptically. "I guess you'll be wanting to try it on."

"Oh, no," Millie said. "I'll take it." She held out her money, then thought of the hotel room she had never checked into. "Actually... I think I will try it on."

As she went toward the back, the other woman came out, resplendent in her yellow dress. There was no denying that the woman was dazzling, Millie decided now. Yet she also noted with a certain glee that the darts on the bodice were stretched to popping, and the hem came clear above her ankles. Well. If the woman wanted to pauper herself to look ridiculous, who was she to argue?

Millie sashayed back into the tiny closet the man had pointed her to and changed into the calico. Just as she had expected, the clean fabric against her skin felt glorious—even if it was green instead of butter-cream yellow. She came back out feeling like a new woman, flouncing in front of the full-length mirror on one side of the store. It was quite a shock to see herself in such a getup; she looked as if she should be leaning over a washtub, with several dirty babies pulling at her practical, ample skirt. Nevertheless, she was satisfied. She looked neat and clean—and green wasn't such a bad color on her, either.

And with twenty cents left over, she could finally afford some soap!

Sam almost didn't recognize her. He'd been standing outside the saloon, thinking over what he had just learned, when a rustle of green caught his eye. He glanced up and saw Millie coming at him in an outrageous new getup—or maybe it was only outrageous because she looked so out of place in it. Like a princess at a quilting bee.

Yet she managed to wear even this matronly outfit with a sassy jauntiness that livened up the dull bug-green color. Leastways, the fuller skirt and bodice of the dress emphasized her petite waist, which definitely made her appear vibrant and youthful and sweetly feminine.

As if he needed any reminder of that! All day long, memories of her rising out of the water that morning had played through his mind. He'd ached to jump right in with her, then carry her back to their makeshift bed and lick every drop of moisture off her. It had been all he could do to turn away.

"Hey there!" she called, smiling brightly as she came up to him. "Recognize your wife?"

Even though he had a feeling her new appearance indicated trouble, he couldn't help responding to her. She looked so much more lighthearted than he felt, just gazing at her raised his spirits. And as she came closer, he could see that she'd cleaned herself up. Her face and hands were scrubbed clean, her newly combed hair was damp around her hairline, and she smelled like roses.

Did the Little Bend Inn provide rose scented soap? He doubted it! His eyebrow shot up. "Where did you get the dress?"

"I went shopping," she said, tilting her chin defiantly.

"Shopping!" he repeated in disbelief. "Good Lord, Millie. I only gave you seven dollars."

"And I spent seven dollars," she told him.

"What about the hotel?"

"We don't need it. I'm coming with you."

He sighed. "Millie, I told you—"

"And I heard you," she said, interrupting him. Her fists were planted on her green-sprigged hips. "You're crazy if you think I'm going to let you ride off and face a killer alone."

"Shhh . . ." he hissed, gesturing for her to keep her voice down.

"I'm coming with you, and that's that. And if you don't let me, then I'll simply follow you, which would be even more dangerous. So I really don't believe you have a choice in the matter, *Lowell.*"

That was nothing new. Choice had been robbed of him the moment he found Millicent Lively in that damned pear tree. Ever since, his life had been a succession of *have-to*s; first he'd had to take her along; then he had to try to get rid of her; then, after she found him, he'd had no choice but to take her along again. And now it looked like she was in it for the rest of the way.

"Weems's ranch is miles out of town," he told her. "I intend to ride out close to it tonight, then confront him tomorrow morning."

"Good," Millie agreed.

"You just spent all our money," he said grudgingly. "I can't put you in a hotel anyway, so I guess you have to come along."

"Good!"

"No, not good. This is dangerous business."

"That's why you need me there," she assured him. "I'll be useful."

"Useful!" he exclaimed. "What do you intend to do?"

"Watch your back for you," she said without missing a beat.

Sam got a whiff of roses and swallowed. Much as he wanted to laugh at the idea of Millie looking after him, much as he wanted to tell her that a woman like her was no match for Weems, something inside him held him back. One more night. He didn't know what tomorrow would bring. He didn't hold any illusions that Darnell would be a docile hostage, or confess straight off to Salina's murder. He only knew that one more night with Millie was something he didn't want to pass up.

Still, he couldn't help joking, "A lot of good you'll be. Weems will be able to smell you coming!"

Naturally, she took his words as a compliment. "You noticed."

"How could I not?" he asked. "You're a walking hothouse."

White teeth gleamed behind her rosy lips. "When do we start?" she asked.

"Now, I guess. That'll give us more time to rest up." He offered her his arm, which she took. It felt natural to be holding her this way—like they actually were a married couple.

Ridiculous notion.

"Who told you about the Weems ranch?" Millie asked.

"Man in the bar. A dark, strange sort of fellow. At first I thought he was one of those mutes."

Millie's brow wrinkled. "I hope he steered you right."

"Why wouldn't he?"

After a moment's hesitation, she shrugged and smiled, squeezing his arm a little tighter. "You're right. I'm just being alarmist."

Sam felt uneasy. Maybe Millie was right, and he should be more wary of the information he'd gathered. But the loudest warning bells going off inside his head were the ones triggered by the tightening in his gut when Millie held his arm. Or the uneven rhythm of his heart when she smiled at him. Or the way the smell of roses fairly knocked him senseless every time he got a whiff of them, making him wish all sorts of nonsense. Mostly that he and the girl on his arm could really have been Lowell and Eugenia Johnson, newlyweds, just for one night.

Chapter Eleven

Bob Jitter took one look at Tess, sitting at the restaurant table with Darnell, and felt his mouth go bone-dry. The new yellow dress she had conned her husband into giving her the money to buy had proved worth every penny. That rich yellow fabric made her look good enough to eat; the rest of the world, even the white-walled, crisp white interior of Lonnette's Dinner Bell, the best and only restaurant in Little Bend, was a shabby thing by comparison.

Tess was all dolled up to conquer Chariton society. Everything that Darnell had thought of to sell around the old place, short of the house itself and its modest furnishings, had been hocked to finance their attempt to get Jesse Winter's land. Jitter hated to be the one to tell them there might be a change of plan.

Darnell spotted Jitter at the door and half stood, waving him over. Tess regally turned her head and sent him her even gaze. The familiar wave of repressed desire shuddered through his body as he tugged his hat off his head and came forward.

"Had any dinner?" Because Tess was in a good humor—she'd finally finagled him into doing what she wanted—Darnell acted as if he didn't have a care in the world.

"No thanks, I drank mine," Jitter replied, taking a seat. He tried to avoid Tess's face. Looking at her got his insides so balled up that he couldn't think straight. And he needed his wits about him now. They all did, he feared. "I learned some interesting things down at Hank's bar," he told Darnell.

Darnell didn't even glance up from his plate, which was heaped with mashed potatoes and steak. "Aw, those cowboys over there gossip like old hens."

"Wadn't a cowboy I was talkin' to," Jitter said, watching patiently as Darnell shoveled more food into his mouth. He waited for the man to swallow before he told him, "It was somebody lookin' for you."

Tess's fork fell to her plate, and Darnell looked as if that hunk of meat he's just swallowed had lodged in his throat. He reached for his glass and took a swallow of water. "Anybody you recognized?" he asked finally.

"Nope," Jitter said. "Man said he was from Dallas."

Darnell's face scrunched up in concentration for a moment. Sometimes Jitter couldn't understand how somebody so dense could have made it even this far in life. "I don't know anybody from there."

"I didn't think so," Jitter replied.

"You think he was lying?"

Tess tossed her napkin on the table and pushed back her chair. She was nervous as a cat. *She* was no fool. "Jitter knows something," she said in an impatient voice, not even bothering to look at her husband. "Spit it out, already," she demanded.

Jitter didn't particularly mind her tone. It normally wasn't pleasant to take orders from a woman—but Tess was no ordinary woman. Besides, her exasperation with her husband clearly showed that she thought Jitter was the sharper man. He turned away from Darnell and directed his information to her. "I think this man has something to do with that other business."

Every muscle in Darnell's face went slack. "You mean he's from Chariton?"

Even though they were the only patrons in the restaurant and there was little chance that Lonnette was eavesdropping on them from the kitchen, the gaze Tess aimed at her husband could have turned the sun to a yellow block of ice. Darnell shrugged sheepishly, but said no more.

"Sure do," Jitter said.

"How do you know?" Tess asked.

"He didn't seem to know Darnell at all—where he lived, what he looked like. He was askin' all sorts of questions like that."

"Why would he do that?" Darnell asked.

Tess frowned. "So he'd recognize you when and if he ran into you."

"That's it," Jitter said. "And then, after he left Hank's, I looked out the window and noticed he had a woman with him."

Tess's lips turned down. "A dark-haired girl, snooty-lookin'?"

Jitter wasn't sure about the snooty part. "She had dark hair and eyes," he affirmed. "A slip of a thing."

"The girl from the store!"

Jitter shrugged. He didn't know anything about that, but he figured it was probably the same woman. Strangers didn't arrive in this town every day.

Darnell appeared wound up enough to pop at any second. "What does a dark-haired girl have to do with anything? She and the man could be old friends of my parents." Though the temperature in the restaurant was comfortable, sweat beaded on his brow. "That's it? Didn't the man say what his name was?"

"Lowell Johnson."

"Johnson, Johnson," Darnell muttered feverishly. "That's ringing a bell...."

"Of course it is. Half the people in the world have that name!" Tess said.

"I have some other news," Jitter told them.

Poor Darnell looked as if he couldn't take much more. Tess sat next to him, her shoulders straight, her back erect; every fiber of her being seemed alert.

"Before that man named Johnson came in the saloon, there was talk of news from Chariton. Not about Jesse, but his brother."

Darnell's eyes were like round, frightened moons. "What?"

"Escaped."

Both of them sucked in breaths of shock. "That can't be."

"And what's more, word has it that he headed west. With a hostage. A young woman."

"That girl!" Tess guessed.

"W-wait," Darnell said, holding up a hand to stop any out-of-control speculation. "Maybe it's not him. A man named Johnson, traveling with a woman... is that so uncommon?"

"He asked for you by name," Tess said harshly. "And where your ranch was. His brother is about to hang, and he's figured it out. He's come to get you, Darnell."

Darnell looked from Tess to Jitter. "Do *you* think—?"

"'Fraid so," Jitter said. "Looked like the couple was headed out in the direction I told him your ranch was. Good thing you hadn't been in that saloon today, Darnell. Otherwise, somebody might've been able to tell him you were in town."

"That's right," Darnell said, hope dawning on him. "He's going to the ranch, but I'm here. We can just hole up in the hotel—they might never find us."

After a solid minute of staring at him in cold shock, Tess said, "You can't let those two get away, Darnell."

"Why? If they don't find me..."

"You killed his brother's wife, and now his brother is fixin' to swing," she said in a low, irritated voice. "I don't know what that little Miss Priss he's got with him has up her sleeve, but believe you me, that man isn't going to let you go.''

Jitter shook his head. "She's right, boss. Need to do something."

"B-but what if we go on to Chariton, as planned? After all, we were going to leave today. We'll probably be there before Winter figures out we're not at home."

"Yeah, and then he'll come after you, just when you're at the scene of the crime," Tess said coldly. "You have to get rid of him."

"You mean murder?" Darnell asked.

"I mean self-preservation," Tess she told him. "It's us or them."

"I know who I'm rootin' for," Jitter put in, sending Tess a wink to lighten up things a little. She looked like she was about ready to strangle that husband of hers, though he couldn't really say he blamed her at this point. Darnell had botched things up good from the beginning.

"I know," Darnell said. "Let's get the law on him."

"And be standing right there when he starts throwing accusations?" Tess asked.

Darnell's bloodshot eyes darted frantically from Tess to Jitter again. Jitter nodded, letting him know where he stood on the matter—right beside Tess. His boss ran a hand through his already tangled hair, then propped his elbows on the table and buried his face in his hands. "I can't!"

Tess's gaze had daggers in it. "Anyone would think you were afraid."

Darnell looked up and stared at her, bewildered. "I *am* afraid. Afraid of what's going to happen to me, to you. How can you respect me if I do this thing?"

"How can I if you don't?" she said coldly.

Shoulders hunched and face tense, he looked like a trapped, frightened animal. So much so that Jitter almost felt sorry for him, going against his conscience to please his wife. But what a wife.

Receiving such bleak stares from them both, Darnell finally straightened resolutely. Yet his next words surprised the hell out of Jitter. "I won't do it," Darnell insisted. "I ain't gonna make any snap decisions—not like last time."

He pushed his chair from the table and the rasping squeak of wood against wood echoed through the nearly empty dining room. Tess reached out a long-nailed hand and fastened her grip on Darnell's wrist. "Where are you going?"

"To the hotel. To drink."

He pulled his hand free and slunk toward the door. Tess, her cheeks flaming red, didn't watch him go. Instead, she turned her frosty blue gaze toward her plate, which was still heaped with untouched food. "I'll change his mind," she said aloud.

"Maybe I can help," Jitter suggested.

She turned her eyes toward him, considering his offer. Jitter felt his groin tighten uncomfortably. She was so beautiful it nearly made him sick. "I'd do anything for you," he said, his voice coming out as a shocking, gravelly sound. He swallowed, waiting for her reply.

Those blue eyes softened, just like he'd seen them do with Darnell, whenever she realized she might get what she wanted. But just then, he didn't care that she was thinking she could manipulate him. Fact was, he'd like to manipulate her into his bed.

To his shock and pleasure, she reached out her hand and covered his with it, ever so gently. A little smile tilted at her lips, making him go dizzy with wanting her. "I do appreciate your offer, Jitter," she said, "but I think I might be able to bring Darnell around. A woman has ways, you know."

Her hand squeezed his, and her thumb brushed in a lazy pattern against the inside of his palm. Jitter gritted his teeth. If this was just a hint of her "ways," that Darnell was one lucky son of a gun. Too lucky, if you asked him. Darnell didn't deserve Tess.

"Still," he said, taking a steadying breath. "If there's anything I can do for you, anything at all, you let me know."

One of her long-lashed eyes came down in an understanding, sexy wink. "Oh, I will, Mr. Jitter," she promised in a sweet, husky drawl.

Ever since they had come back from scoping out Darnell Weems's small homestead, Sam had been quiet. Too quiet. His distracted air made Millie nervous—and she was already jumpy enough about what might happen tomorrow. This wasn't how she'd envisioned the evening when they left town together that afternoon, with their saddlebags full and Sam looking like he appreciated her new dress.

Now she might as well have been wearing those trousers she'd thought about getting, for all he cared. He was doing his level best to gaze right past her, as though she weren't even there, and his inattention stirred a rising hysteria in her. Didn't he understand that this could be their last night together, that tomorrow he might—?

The thought of his riding out alone at daybreak to face Darnell Weems made her go stone-cold inside, but that was what he insisted he was going to do. She was glad at least that she hadn't stayed in Little Bend, so glad that he wasn't alone this night. Only... why wouldn't he speak to her?

"I'm nervous, Sam," she admitted.

Finally, his eyes cast her a quick glance. "Don't be."

"How can I not? You said yourself Weems is a murderer."

His lips twisted up in a wry imitation of a smile. "If he wasn't, I wouldn't be here."

She tossed her hands in frustration. "I know, but we have to be careful."

"Wrong," he said. "*I* have to be careful. Tomorrow I'm riding out to the house alone."

"But what would happen to me if something happened to you?"

His expression crinkled into a mask of worry. "Don't think that thought hasn't occurred to me."

Millie's mouth dropped as understanding struck her. "Is *that* why you've been so taciturn all night?" she cried, relieved to think that she had remained at the center of his thoughts, even if he'd refused to talk to her for hours on end.

"You shouldn't sound so happy about it."

She dropped down to the ground next to him. "But I am!"

He shook his head. "You're crazier than a jaybird, you know that?"

He sounded so like his old self again that she wanted to throw her arms around him joyfully. "I was afraid you were going to ignore me until daybreak."

Steely eyes glittered at her in the moonlight, sending a shiver coursing down her spine. "You're not easy to ignore, Princess."

Her whole body turned feverish as his gaze traveled slowly from the crown of her head to the tip of her now worn boots. There was something in that gaze of his tonight, some deep wanting in them that she felt answered a need deep in the core of her being. The sensation made her feel unbalanced and dizzy.

"Oh, I bet you could ignore me," she said, covering her nervousness with chatter. "In fact, you remind me somewhat of Leo Stubbs, and heaven knows, he was the world's champion at treating a person as though they didn't even exist."

Sam lips curled into an easy smile. "Who's Leo Stubbs?"

"He was my fiancé."

His smile froze. "I thought that fellow's name was Lloyd Boyd."

"Oh, no," she said, clearing up the matter, "Lloyd is my *present* fiancé. Leo was a year and a half ago. In fact, I think he was my..." She paused a moment to do some math. "My fifth, I think. Yes, that's right."

Sam blinked. "Your *fifth?* Fiancé?"

"That's right."

"So am I to take it that Lloyd is your sixth attempt at engagement?"

"Oh, heavens, no," Millie said. "Lloyd's my eleventh."

"Eleventh!" Sam cried. He recoiled from her as if she were some kind of venom-spitting toad.

She was beginning to feel a little self-conscious. She didn't want Sam to think she was so defective that none of the eleven would have married her. "I know it might sound like a lot, but..."

He didn't even let her finish. He shot to his feet and took her place on the little path she'd beaten out with pacing. "For a woman, I'd say it was about ten too many."

For a woman? "I didn't know there was a limit."

"Well, any decent, levelheaded female would realize that eleven was too many."

She sprang to her feet and, heedless of his superior height and bulk, marched right up to him, her hands planted on her hips. "How dare you insinuate that I'm indecent! It's not as if I ran off with these men, or behaved in any way improperly."

He smirked. "I get it. You might be fickle, but your reputation is otherwise unsmudged."

"The only smudges on it at this point are the ones *you* put there."

A thick brow shot up smartly. "How so?"

"You know..." Was he going to make her say it? "By kissing me."

He threw back his head and cackled. She watched in irritation as his handsome features—ones she had admired when he laughed earlier that day—beamed in obvious delight at her romantic shortcomings. "If a few little kisses are the only black marks on your slate, Millie, you can rest assured that your conscience should be as clear as a schoolgirl's."

A schoolgirl! Was that how he thought of her, after all they'd been through together? Oh, maybe it didn't seem like so much to him, but these past few days had been a revelation to her. Those "little" kisses they'd shared had stirred desires in her body that were far from innocent. She knew now what it was to want someone body and soul.

"I don't understand why you refuse to take me seriously, Sam."

He shook his head. "Maybe because you're the kind of girl who gets herself engaged eleven times."

"Stop calling me a girl," she said. "I'm not. I'm almost twenty. And anyway, I'm all through with engagements. I know now that I could never feel deeply for anyone but you, Sam."

Her words shocked him into silence. He stared at her, his expression anguished. "You don't know what you're saying," he said finally, quietly.

"But I do," she replied. "You're what I care about."

He shook his head disbelievingly. "Today, maybe, but next week you'll have forgotten. You'll be back to being your daddy's spoiled little princess."

"No, I won't." She stamped her foot in frustration, then felt foolish. Like the spoiled thing he accused her of being. "This isn't just about today, or what might happen tomorrow."

"Well, maybe it should be," he told her, his tone forcibly factual. "After tomorrow, I might not be around."

She rushed forward. "Don't say that!"

He stopped her with a hand on her shoulder and put his forefinger to her lips, silencing her. But the contact also sent a wave of desire crashing through her. "I'll have surprise on my side, sure, but the odds are still just fifty-fifty that I'll come out on top. But even if I do, what then?"

"I don't know what you mean."

"I mean, what happens in the unlikely case that everything turns out hunky-dory? Can you envision me calling on your father at that bank of his, asking permission to court you?''

''Why not?''

''After I kidnapped you?''

''He'll understand,'' she said, reaching her hands up to clutch his arms. She was terrified he was going to convince himself that they couldn't be together. ''Eventually. I'll make him.''

His gaze darted from her hands, clutching at his arms, to her lips, then back to her eyes. ''But what if you can't make him understand how the daughter he carefully raised to be a modest young lady has fallen for a fugitive? What happens then?''

She bit her lip. Why was he being so defeatist? ''Then I'll run away again.'' She leaned forward and nestled her head against his broad chest. ''I'll run away to you.''

She was amazed at how good it felt to be snuggled against his chest this way—more sensual, even, than waking up cradled in his arms had been. She shifted again, bringing herself closer, then felt a hand reach slowly, or perhaps reluctantly, down to her waist. His chest lifted and he let out a ragged sigh.

''It won't work, Millie.''

''What won't?''

She lifted her eyes to his. He was looking at her so peculiarly; his gaze was about ten times as intense as usual, and she blinked as she recognized finally what it was. Desire. That was the way he'd looked before he kissed her. Strangely, it was the exact mirror of how she felt inside, too—as if all her senses were amplified, heightened, inescapable. No one could have paid her money to step out of his arms at that moment, especially when his hand at her back pulled her closer. He seemed distracted, against his will, by her clean, soapy smell.

''Sam?'' she repeated when he didn't answer.

''Huh?''

''What won't work?''

He shook his head as if to clear it. "You and me. A girl like you—"

"Not a girl," she reminded him automatically, her voice strangely sleepy-sounding. With a pleasurable little smile, she moved her hands up and twined them around the back of his neck.

"Well..." He stiffened for a moment, especially when she began to massage the muscle at his back where his shoulder blades met. "You're... you're used to a different kind of life."

It amazed her. He was so much larger, stronger—the muscle beneath her fingertips was pure brawn. Yet as she manipulated it with her fingers, his head lolled beneath her touch, his hand tightened on her waist, bringing the result she wanted, bringing them closer. This was a kind of power she'd never tested before.

"But haven't I proven that I'm *veeery* adaptable?" she purred at him as she continued her ministrations.

"Mmm..." he agreed mindlessly, his neck swaying with the movement of her hands. Then he jolted back to attention. "No! Mostly you've complained every step of the way."

"I have not, and you know it. And I stuck with you," she said "You have to admit I did."

"But now..." His words were cut off as the forefinger of her right hand traced its way around his shirt collar, down to the front of his chest, where it looped itself around one of the buttons of his shirt. "Now things are different. Tomorrow..."

"I don't want to think about tomorrow," she begged. "Not now."

"*Especially* now," he said. "You're an innocent young lady. Now's not the time to get yourself tangled up with a desperado."

"You're only a desperado by mistake."

"That still doesn't mean it would be any less of a mistake for you to get tangled up with me."

Tangled up. The words tantalized her, suggesting in her mind bodies intertwined, a sensual snaggle of arms and legs. As close as she was standing to Sam, there must be a way to get even closer, to somehow ease the hot, liquid ache that was building inside her. Its insistence forced what remained of her modesty to shed away from her like an old, unusable skin. She rubbed up against him suggestively.

"Sam, don't you want me...that way?"

His eyes rounded in something between lasciviousness and dismay. "What way?"

"You know, like men want other women. Saloon women."

He groaned. "Millie!"

She smiled in what she hoped was a worldly way. "Don't sound shocked. I know all about these things."

"You do not," he admonished, cupping her chin in his hand. "Just kissing you, I could tell you were a virgin."

Her face flamed, both from embarrassment and a flush of desire caused by the feel of his rough fingertips against her face. "I said I knew about them, I didn't say I'd done them," she admitted.

"Damn it, Millie," he said, his voice raspy with exasperation, "can't you see I'm trying my level best to be honorable?"

"But I don't want you to be!" she cried urgently. "I'd much rather you just went ahead and kissed me."

He stared at her, nearly as astounded by her bold words as she herself was. She half expected him to scold her, to remind her again that she was merely a girl, and a virgin, both of which apparently made her unworthy of his attention. Instead, something in his stance shifted, hardened. His gaze darkened. His restraint snapped.

His lips didn't have far to go. He'd been hovering over her breathlessly for endless seconds, and now his mouth descended on hers with a suddenness that shocked her. His lips were hard against hers, yet in a moment they softened, coaxed, and administered the purest pleasure she'd ever experienced. Her rapid heartbeat pounded in her ears, and for a moment it seemed that there wasn't enough oxygen in the world to fill her lungs.

He drew away from her quickly. "Was that what you had in mind?"

She gripped his shoulders and nodded, biting back a gasp for air. "Only more."

His lips broke out in a grin. "What's made you so brazen all of the sudden?"

You. What other answer was there? Every time she looked at him she felt herself go hollow inside, as if some part of her needed filling, a task only Sam could accomplish. Was that brazen, or could it possibly be love? For all her bravado, in spite of her eleven fiancés, her heart remained untested. She wasn't sure what name to put to her feelings, to the terrible aching need overwhelming her; she only knew that Sam was at the core of this confusing jumble of emotion and desire.

"Please don't tease me," she said.

His eyes fairly glittered. The man held her spellbound. "I thought maybe you were the one teasing. If so, you should be careful, Princess." To show her how dead serious he was, he tugged her full against him; there was no mistaking the power in his frame, the blatant desire he had for her.

It should have frightened her, but instead she felt exhilarated. Every inch of her that touched him felt fully, completely alive. Instead of shrinking away, she met his challenge. "I've never been so serious about anything in my life," she blurted out. "Sam, I think I—"

Before she could finish the statement, he cut her off with a long, devastating kiss. There wasn't a trace of roughness in it this time, just a tenderness that made her crave more— more of the way he coaxed his mouth against hers, tasting and exploring as if they had all the time in the world. More of the way he would draw back just a bit to nibble at her lower lip. More of the way his hands slowly explored her hair, her back, right down to her bottom, which should have shocked her beyond all imagination, but failed to.

She was moving against him blindly—his every touch seemed to light a little brushfire wherever it landed, until so much of her was alight that she feared her whole body would be engulfed in flame.

He broke away from her mouth and started bestowing small kisses on her chin, her neck, up to the soft, sensitive skin of her ear. She shuddered at the sensuality of it and grabbed tightly to his arms to steady herself.

"Oh, Sam..." she moaned. It was too much, yet she wanted so much more. How could words be put to desires she barely understood?

In one swift motion, he lifted her up into his arms. "I know, sweetheart," he said, taking a few steps to the side and bringing them both down to the ground. He laid her out on the top of the blanket and petticoats she'd spread out with the most extreme care and, without missing a beat, leaned down to kiss her again.

This time it was even better, because when he started unleashing firestorms inside her, she could pull herself to him, so that his body was practically lying full against her. His bulk should have crushed her, yet their frames seemed to fit together so perfectly that she craved *more* of his weight against her, not less. He accommodated her every physical demand, withdrawing from her only enough to unbutton the top of her dress, a task he performed with trembling but practiced hands. Her undergarments, too, he made short work of, pushing them aside as necessary so that she hardly noticed the full exposure of her torso to the night air until his mouth descended upon the hard, aching nipple of her breast.

She stiffened, sucking in a breath of utter shock. Never in all her born days had she been led to expect *that!* And yet it felt so right, so natural, so unbearably wonderful.... Nothing in the world would have made her push him away from her, especially not when his tongue began laving the aching bud in tantalizing circles. Instead, her hands moved instinctively to the short hair at his nape, directing his attention to the other breast, which now ached for similar attention.

"Sweet," he murmured. "You're so sweet."

Sweet, sweetheart... Such strange, *sweet* words coming from his mouth only heightened her rising sense of dizzying need. Just when she thought she could stand no more of these shocking new sensations, he surprised her yet again, tracing a finger from her breast, down across her stomach, pale in the moonlight, to the vee between her thighs. She gasped, but no longer in shock. *Yes,* she thought. It seemed as if all their movements, their kisses and caresses, were simply building to the moment when he should touch the flames that he had stoked at her very core.

She understood now how Sam could fulfill this urgent need he had built up inside her. In the darkness, she couldn't see him, but she could certainly feel the evidence of his own need pressing insistently against her thigh.

"Sam," she said again, trying to voice her need.

He drew back. His eyes glittered, his mouth was drawn tight. "I'm not sure I could stop now...."

"I don't want you to," she said, her voice a rasp.

"But if you asked, Millie, I would."

She looked at him then, trying to telegraph every overwhelming feeling in her heart. "I'm not asking, Sam," she forced out, even though her insides were beginning to quiver now at the license she was allowing him.

They were all the words he needed to hear. He shed the rest of his clothes and knelt over her; the shadowy darkness was unable to conceal the impressiveness of his desire. Millie's mouth felt bone dry, and she attempted a gulp as he hesitated, cupping her cheek in one hand.

"I don't want to hurt you," he said.

"You won't," she told him, knowing it was a lie. How could he not? The whole endeavor suddenly seemed so physically improbable, yet she couldn't draw away. In fact, she felt herself pulling him down to meet her, knowing that attempting this folly would be the only thing to quench the fire roaring inside her.

Slowly he entered her, filling her so completely that she felt as though the world might come to an end—which it did a split second later, when white-hot pain tore through her body. She bit her lip against a cry that rose in her throat, and he stopped, his gaze wounded. He stilled his movement, then bent down and kissed her gently, coaxingly. After a moment of hesitation, she gave in to the urge to kiss him back, and relaxed. Answering a need stirring to life inside her again, she moved her hips tentatively.

"That's right, sweetheart," he whispered against her ear, sending a quiver of desire through her that caused her to move against him again. With every stroke, pain subsided, replaced by another, more insistent burning. With heart-breaking gentleness, Sam initiated her in the rite of love-making, holding back only until both of them could stand restraint no more.

Suddenly it seemed as though a full-fledged firestorm were unleashed inside her, utterly gripping in its fury. Feverishly she clung to Sam, seeking an anchor against the furious sensations swirling out of control inside her. She closed her eyes and heard a cry that had to be her own. Yet it was answered in his own voice just as the frenzied movement of their bodies suddenly stilled, and she was filled with the glorious sensation of being completely happy, completely alive, completely in love.

Chapter Twelve

It was hard for Sam to believe he was looking at the same person. Millie's face was sweet and innocent in sleep, her warm upturned lips so different from the ones he remembered kissing passionately the night before. And her body, which had writhed against his with such abandon only hours ago, now was curled chastely, its nakedness covered by the very dress he vividly remembered peeling off her.

With thoughts like that racing through his mind, it was hard to move, hard to think, hard to contemplate leaving her. As he quietly went about saddling the black in the dawning light, every time he caught a glimpse of her dark brown hair, his movements would cease and he would stare transfixed at her, elation making his heart feel close to bursting. Millie. He must have repeated her name to himself a million times, trying to make it all seem a little less unbelievable. The possessive feeling in his heart as he looked down at her was certainly real. So, too, was the way every inch of her exposed skin hit him with a sharp punch of desire. If he didn't stop looking at her soon, he would never be able to get the day's work under way.

And he definitely wanted to get going. The sooner he left, the sooner he would come back to Millie. Strange how she was foremost in his mind now. For weeks he had been consumed by his brother's dilemma, embroiled in the deceit of a murderer and a crooked sheriff. Then he'd run into Millie, and she'd started taking up about as much of his attention as Jesse. Now, instead of just wanting to get Weems so that he could free Jesse, he also wanted to get Weems so that he could clear his own name and be free to take Millie for his wife.

Every muscle in his body went stock-still.

His *what?*

It was all Sam could do to stifle a laugh. He shook his head, marveling at how his desires could leapfrog right over his common sense. But even though he had about a million things to work out before then, he knew that his ultimate goal now would be to marry the incredible woman he'd made love to last night. And *woman* was precisely the word for her. He would never call her a girl again. Spoiled, maybe...

That was the only thing that worried him still. She was used to having everything she wanted, yet what he had to offer her—in the event that he ever got out of jail or, better yet, managed to escape this escapade with his neck free of a noose—was considerably less than she was used to with her daddy. Horace P. Lively was another problem Sam just didn't even have the heart to consider at this precise moment.

Right now, he had enough trouble just wondering how he was going to handle Darnell Weems. One way, of course, was to catch him early, while he was still in his long underwear. He prayed that the man didn't have any hands on his place. From what he could tell of the decrepit little ranch in the pitch darkness, that didn't seem likely. Darnell Weems's homestead gave the term *hardscrabble* new meaning. Sam didn't quite understand how even one man could subsist there.

All his hopes were pinned on having the element of surprise on his side. Not that he expected Darnell to confess... without a little persuasion. He instinctively reached for his gun, and felt his jaw clench tight. In all his years, he'd never been one to rely on violence to solve his problems. There had never been the need. His farm had been blessedly free from strife with his neighbors, and he stayed out of town enough to avoid getting in trouble there. But in the past month he had learned how a man could get caught up in a cycle of violence, forced to defend himself any way possible when his back was against the wall. Maybe so much violence had hardened him a little, but not as much as being unfairly stripped of his liberty had.

He wasn't looking for retribution, he thought as he walked the black away from their little campsite. He simply wanted justice, wanted the same judge who had condemned his brother to death to clap eyes on Weems and hear about the ring and Jesse's having sighted his old partner. And if he had to capture Darnell Weems at gunpoint and hog-tie him on the back of his horse, he was determined to take the man bodily back to Chariton.

He stopped when he was far enough away to ensure that his mounting the black wouldn't cause Millie to stir. He could just make out her pink cheeks poking out from the top of the blanket, crowned by her tumble of long dark hair. He remembered its softness with piercing clarity, so much so that he froze in midmotion, one arm looped over the saddle and his left foot reaching for the stirrup, as he took in his fill of her.

But of course that was impossible. He doubted a whole lifetime would afford him the necessary leisure to look all he wanted at Millie Lively. What a pleasurable experiment it would be to find out. He definitely intended to try it.

If he got back from Weems's ranch in one piece. Or even alive.

The thought of Millie out here waiting for him sent cold determination through him. He couldn't abandon her here. He had to live, to come out of this whole mess a free man. So much depended on it. Jesse's future. His future.

And Millie's?

The possibility buoyed his spirits. Feeling foolish but strangely compelled, he finished mounting up and then blew Millie a kiss.

"See you soon, Princess," he promised, then quickly rode away.

A soft breeze swept across the plain and kissed Millie's cheek as she slept, causing her to twitch involuntarily in response. She tried to burrow farther under her cover, but there wasn't much material there to work with. As she moved, she felt a strange aching between her legs and immediately awoke, her eyes popping open. She had to see Sam, to make sure the wonderful sensations she remembered from the night hadn't merely been a dream.

She propped herself on her elbows and squinted into the dawn light. Next to her there was only bare ground where Sam's body had been. It *had* been there, she was sure of that now. Nothing else could account for the vision of him gloriously naked that played in her mind, or for the many aches and twinges she felt in the oddest places, or for the warm sense of completeness deep inside her.

No, the question wasn't whether that had been Sam last night—more aptly, she wondered, had that been *her?* Had she, sheltered, pampered Millicent Lively, actually behaved in such an outrageously brazen fashion? Well-bred young ladies just didn't give themselves over to the pursuit of carnal satisfaction. And to think she had had to *connive* her way into Sam's arms, had actually begged him to have his way with her.

Well, no. She'd merely asked him to kiss her, but she'd had little doubt at the time that it would lead to more.

More than she'd ever imagined, as it turned out. Never in her life had she expected the secret activity that went on between men and women to be so... *pleasurable.* She took a moment to try to relive each sensation, her cheeks flaming pink as she remembered how it had felt when Sam touched each private part of her, the noises she'd made....

Oh, dear. She and Sally Hall had quite a few unappealing appellations for women of easy virtue, and that, painful though it might be, was precisely what she'd become. Why, she was no better than Laurette Jackson, who had been a sweet, pretty thing once upon a time. Then, one year, Laurette had suddenly up and married the town blacksmith—a stoop-shouldered old codger who was sixty if he was a day, and on top of that had absolutely no teeth. None, except for a set of false wooden ones. And half the time he didn't bother to put them in.

Poor Laurette. The whole town couldn't think what had come over the girl. Then, five months after she wedded her wooden-toothed groom, she bore him a strapping, robust son who bore a striking resemblance to a dashing lumbago-tonic salesman who'd come through Chariton just that spring.

Now Millie's transgression would probably make the town gossips forget all about Laurette and her lumbago baby. Overnight, a lifetime of solid moral living—at least when it came to relations with men—had gone up in smoke. Or, more correctly, it had been consumed in the fires Sam had created inside her.

And the terrible thing was, she didn't feel the remorse she knew she should. Right now, she only wanted to see Sam again, to be in his arms again.

But where in the blazes was he?

She shot to her feet, not even bothering to step into her dress; instead, she covered her nakedness by slinging the garment over her shoulder as if it were a Roman's toga. It didn't take her long to realize that Sam's black horse was missing. Millie strained to see in what direction he had ridden off, but, though she couldn't catch sight of him in the still dark morning, it didn't require a genius to know that he'd already set off to meet Weems.

She felt her heart pound heavily. He hadn't even waited, or said goodbye to her! She wondered if he'd even spared her a thought when he rode off to meet heaven only knew what fate.

She had hoped that they would have time together this morning—precious time that she had intended to use trying to persuade Sam to let her accompany him to the Weems ranch, to watch out for him in case there was someone else there besides Darnell. Not that she believed she would actually have been successful in persuading him. Since when did Sam see reason?

Then again, since when did she allow him to decide whether she would go along with him or not?

Nary a soul was stirring at the Weems homestead. Sam peered around the house cautiously, not trusting the eerie stillness around him. It was just morning, but there was no rooster to crow; in fact, not even a stray sickly hen scratched around the bare dirt surrounding the house. There were no farm animals at all, or even a songbird chirping a hello to the new day. No stores in the little outbuilding that he supposed Weems used as a barn. There was no life here.

But, still, he didn't quite trust the deserted appearance. Something seemed wrong. He couldn't put his finger on it exactly, but there was an uneasiness in the air, despite the silence. That uneasiness made his hair stand on end, and kept his gun positioned stiffly in his right hand as he approached the front entrance of the odd-looking soddie, to which an extra room had been tacked on in back. And all the time he kept looking behind him, peering out onto the barren, sloping grassy plain around the tiny house, trying to detect an invisible presence he sensed but couldn't see.

Crazy. Ever since he'd started off the morning blowing kisses at Millie like a lovestruck schoolboy, things had been off-balance. Millie. The very name made him pause, distracted. He pictured her again, sleeping, and tried to hold at bay memories of how she felt beneath him, the sound of their mingled breathing as he made love to her.

He shook his head sharply. No time for that line of thinking. What if Darnell was just on the other side of the wooden door, waiting for him?

The thought brought Sam back into focus. Deciding the best way to get it over with was simply to go on in, he gently shoved the wooden door with the heel of his boot, praying the hinges wouldn't squeak. But, of course, they did. The rusty metal sent out a warning that sounded to Sam's sensitized ears as if it could be heard in California. He winced, then took the only course of action he thought available to him—he cocked his pistol and barged right into the little house.

The first room was spare, and obviously empty. The next—a hastily added-on kitchen—was only half-visible from where he stood, his gun trained on the bare bed, his eyes darting from one corner to another. He even glanced up at the rafter beam to make sure Weems wasn't perched up there like a vulture about to swoop down on him. Then, carefully, he crept toward the kitchen, relaxing his grip on the revolver only when he discovered that it was as empty as the other room had been.

His first instinct was to sigh in relief, but on second thought, the sigh came out as one of frustration. Where the hell was Weems? He felt like stomping his foot in frustration the way he'd seen Millie do. If he couldn't find Darnell Weems, then he doubted he would ever be able to get Jesse free. Maybe the man was just out hunting, or some such thing. That would make sense, seeing as how nothing appeared to be growing here. Sam stood in the middle of the tidy kitchen, wondering.

The tidy kitchen . . .

The *too*-tidy kitchen. He'd never met Darnell Weems, but neither had he ever known a man able to keep a dirty little hovel like this one so squeaky-clean. Every piece of mismatched, chipped china was in its rightful place. The floors, half dirt and half wood, were swept, and the table, chairs and small cupboard were freshly dusted and oiled. Then he remembered the living room. It was tidy, too, and there were touches—a needlework pillow, a flowery cover on an old chair—that would indicate a wife. But Jesse had never mentioned a woman.

Darnell had gotten himself hitched?

Something about the idea didn't sit right. Maybe because at that moment he remembered Salina, his brother's wife. She had been beautiful, so full of life. So young. How could Darnell kill a woman like that in cold blood, if he himself was so recently married? The man had to be a monster!

In the next room, a squeak sounded, so gentle that he would have thought it was just the wind blowing the door a little. Except there was no wind outside. The morning had been spookily still.

Sam stiffened and stepped quickly to flatten himself against the wall, out of sight of whoever had entered the next room. Weems? His wife? Someone else he hadn't even figured on?

He stifled a curse under his breath. He'd nearly been caught with his pants down—and even now, hidden, he didn't like the possibility that there were two people in the next room. Or maybe his horse had been spotted and someone else was coming around to the kitchen so that he could be trapped. Once again, Sam could see no alternative to taking the initiative.

Sending up a silent prayer, Sam swung into the doorway, his gun at the end of his outstretched arms, which he held stiffly in front of him. "Don't move!" he growled at the lone figure in the yellow morning light filtering through the few windows of the hut.

It was a woman. The most singularly beautiful and annoying woman the world had yet produced.

"Millie!"

Her eyes were so wide open that he could see the whites completely encircling her dark irises. "Sam, put that thing down!" she cried, pivoting with Lou's rifle at the ready. "Do you want to kill me?"

"Right this minute, I'm tempted. Don't you realize I could have shot you?" he asked sternly.

"That's why I asked you to put your weapon away."

"I left you safely sleeping at our camp so this problem wouldn't come up."

A wounded expression appeared in her eyes. "I'm *not* a problem. I was trying to help."

"I think I've heard that before," he muttered disgustedly. "Did it ever occur to you that I could handle this best my own way?"

"Only because you kept telling me that over and over, but I didn't believe you," she said complacently.

He took a step forward, outraged. She looked so small, so delicate, against the rough, spare surroundings. "How could you just waltz in here that way? You had no idea what was going on inside this house."

"That's why I did come," she answered. "You'd been in here for so long—I thought something had happened to you!"

"So you decided to come on in and get yourself killed, too."

His tone softened a shade as he realized the extent of her loyalty, feeble-brained as she had been in her actions. But Millie apparently didn't detect the softening, only the intimation that she hadn't acted wisely.

"Noooo..." she replied, dragging out the word as if she were speaking to a very small child. "I decided to come on in so I could rescue you."

He nearly hooted. Millie and her ridiculous rifle, so old and heavy he wondered if she could even hold it up long enough to take aim. "This is no place for you. That's why I left you back there."

"By myself, unprotected!"

"Anyone with half a brain would steer clear of you, Princess."

She recoiled, smarting at his sharp words, which he immediately wished he could withdraw. Sam never would know what kept the apology lodged deep in his throat, or what prevented him stepping forward and sweeping her into his arms, taking her back to their private place and making love to her once more. Perhaps it was the fear that still coursed through him, the recollection of Jesse in that jail cell that had spurred his every action from the beginning of this fiasco. He still needed to find Darnell Weems, and Millie, for all her insistence on being helpful, was an impediment to him. A beautiful, distracting impediment.

She gave him plenty of time to apologize, too, but sensing that the desired words weren't coming, she finally rested her rifle butt against the wood floor, leaned against it and narrowed her gaze on him. "A fine thanks I get for trying to save you!"

"Only you would think I need saving from an empty building."

"How was I to know no one was here?"

"There were no signs of life out there. No horses. No animals of any kind." He shrugged his arms in disgust. "This place is deserted."

A wicked little smile tickled her mouth. "Is that why you were sweating bullets before you kicked the door open?"

He felt his face go pale. "How long were you watching me?"

"Long enough."

He didn't want to ask how long *that* was. Long enough to watch him make a fool out of himself, apparently. "You shouldn't have come," he repeated.

"No, I shouldn't have. I suppose I should have just hopped on Mrs. Darwimple and trotted back home. That's what you want, right?"

Sam still found himself tongue-tied. What she said *was* what he wanted, in a way. "Only for your sake," he said.

"My mistake," she told him. "I was silly enough to think that last night might have changed things."

"Millie..."

"And don't tell me that you don't want to talk about it, Sam Winter, because it's been a terrible strain for me to keep my mouth going this long without talking about it."

His lips turned up at the corners. "I figured."

"I'll thank you not to laugh at my expense, just this once."

"I wasn't."

"Well, maybe not laughing, but you certainly don't respect me like you should. You've never given me credit for what I can do for you."

Unbidden came thoughts of the previous night and their wild abandon. He stepped forward, the mere recollection making heat simmer in his gut once again. "Oh, I admit I underestimated you, sweetheart."

She blushed at his newest word for her. "Stop calling me that," she told him, taking a step backward to ward off his approach.

"Sweetheart?" he asked, in a husky, suggestive way that had her dark eyes darting between the bed and the nearest exit.

"Go back to calling me 'Princess,' or just plain 'you.'"

"But you said you wanted to talk about last night, and how it changed things," he said with a grin as her back finally bumped into a wall. He reached up and twirled a long, loose strand of her dark hair around his finger. "One of the things it changed was how I think of you."

Through the corner of her eye, she kept track of what he was doing with his hand, which was now resting on her shoulder and working its way up the side of her neck. Shivering slightly, she said, "You still don't think I should be here with you."

"No, I don't," he said, his flat certain tone in no way detracting from the pleasure he took in teasing the sensitive lobe of her ear. He bent down and nipped it.

"Ooooh!" she squeaked.

"Feel good?" he whispered.

"Sam, this is hardly the place!" she cried.

"A bedroom?" he asked huskily, then chuckled. "I see, you like it wild, out in the great outdoors."

She pushed against his chest and shoved with all her might, sending him back a pace. "I *don't* like it in the broad daylight," she said, "in the home of a murderer!"

He nodded curtly. "Well, as you can see, our murderer's not at home."

She looked as concerned as he felt. "What are you going to do now?"

"Maybe I can find someone in Little Bend who knows where he's gone to. Funny that fellow at the bar didn't mention that Weems wasn't here."

"You're right," Millie said. "In a town that size, it seems everyone would know if someone was away."

He looked down at the gun in his hand and frowned. "Unless that fellow at the bar purposefully omitted the fact that Darnell wasn't here."

Millie's eyes rounded in concern. "Oh, Sam! What if he told Darnell you were looking for him?"

That didn't seem likely. "I didn't let on who I was."

"But what if he knew? What if—?"

She shuddered, and Sam did, too. He'd thought he had the element of surprise working for him, but suddenly he felt incredibly vulnerable. Quickly he grabbed Millie's hand and started tugging her toward the door. "Come on, let's get out of here."

The sight of three people blocking their path stopped them cold.

"Not so fast." Sam's eyes alit on the owner of the commanding yet undeniably feminine voice. She was a tall woman, coming just short of his own height, and she held herself like a queen from a child's fairy-tale book. He took in her blond hair and icy blue eyes. An evil snow queen—for there was something intrinsically bad about this woman. He could sense it in the way those cool eyes of hers stared them both down.

"My dress!" Millie muttered angrily.

A leisurely smile touched the woman's mouth. "No, hon, *my* dress."

Millie's cheeks colored crimson, and Sam squeezed her hand to try to keep her from exploding like a powder keg meeting a lit match. His other hand held the cold, heavy weight of the revolver.

"Drop it, mister," barked a short dark man behind the woman. The man from the bar at Little Bend! "You, too, lady."

There was another man too, strangely familiar, flanking the woman in the yellow dress. He had reddish-brown hair, sunburned skin, and a dazed, almost sheepish expression. He didn't look like he would be much of a help to the other man, which about evened the odds of him and Millie getting out of this in one piece. The only question now was which of the three in front of him was the most crucial to take out of commission. As quietly as possible, he cocked the pistol.

"Darnell!" yelled the woman.

Suddenly, snapping to from his lethargy at the sound of the grating tone, the man on her right was propelled into action. He launched himself at Sam full force, sending him reeling backward in surprise. His gun went off, bringing the wiry, dark man into the fray.

"Sam!" he heard Millie cry in alarm. He looked up just in time to see Her Evil Highness reach out and snatch her by the arm and wrench Lou's rifle away. Twirling both in surprise and from the force of the larger woman's grip, Millie scowled and did what he suspected she'd been wanting to do since she first clapped eyes on the woman—she reached up and grabbed a long blond hank of hair and tugged with all her might.

A mighty shriek went out, but Sam was too busy with a fracas of his own to pay much attention to the ladies. It was two against one in his arena, and he was holding them at bay as best he could, kicking one, then turning his fists to the other while his friend was out of commission. But as the fight wore on into minutes, he began to have the sinking feeling that it was a losing battle—with him as the loser.

So when the final blow was struck—a gun butt to the side of his temple—it was with some comfort that he looked up to see Millie still grappling with her foe. Just before his knees gave out beneath him, he heard her release a banshee yell, then spring upon the woman's back, claws extended, looking for all the world like a fluffy house cat pouncing on a mountain lion.

"What do we do with them now?" asked the man with the rusty-colored hair.

"What do you think?" the woman said with a sneer.

A sharp stab of panic shot straight to Millie's gut, but she tried her best to keep from showing it in her expression. It had taken them almost ten minutes to wrestle her to the ground and tie her hands, and then bind her, legs tied together and extended in front of her, back-to-back with Sam, who was still unconscious. She wasn't going to cower now.

Sam, wake up! Her mind raced furiously, trying to keep panic at bay. She tried nudging him gently with her fist. In the first frightening minutes after they were tied together and pushed to the center of the room, Millie had feared Sam was dead, but after a moment she had felt his back slowly expand and contract as he breathed. Now she tried to pace her own breathing with his, hoping it would calm her out-of-control heartbeat. Somehow, they were going to get out of this.

They even had a sort of ally in the enemy camp, she discovered with surprise. At the very mention of more harm being done to her and Sam, Darnell Weems's face drooped slack.

"I'm not gonna kill 'em," he said, his voice surprisingly stubborn. Damned if Millie could figure out if he was the woman's puppet or his own man. Neither of the other two seemed sure of him, either, much to their annoyance.

The blonde rolled her eyes, but said in the most patient voice she could muster, "Of course we are. We can't just leave them here, honey."

"Why not?"

"For one thing, they'd die."

"But we wouldn't be here," he argued.

The blonde and the other man exchanged knowing glances.

"Tess is right. They'd be found here."

"Well, *I'm* not going to kill them. I'm up to my elbows in blood already."

"Shut up!" the woman cried, her patience at an end. "If you're not man enough, give me a gun and I'll do it!"

Cold fear shot through Millie. How could they be standing there talking about murder in such a callous way? They knew she was listening. *Sam, please wake up.* If she could only buy them some time, until she and Sam could work as a team against the other three. Not that they'd been very successful at that so far, but bound up this way, they didn't even stand a fighting chance. The odds were worse than pathetic.

Sam's gun lay next to a candle holder on a small table, around which the three of them stood. Did the woman named Tess intend on shooting them with Sam's own revolver? The idea made Millie nauseous. She looked up to see if Darnell intended to give his ladylove what she wanted.

Large eyes the color of rum stared back at her, startled to find her making direct contact. Throwing him a glance hadn't been a bad idea. Darnell seemed cowed by her gaze—almost as much as he was by the other woman's. Was Tess his wife? Millie wondered. Somewhere in his black heart, did he have a soft spot for women that made him regret his violent actions?

Licking her dry lips and trying to make her own brown eyes as round and pathetic as she knew they could be—knew because she'd practiced in the mirror that time she was about to ask her father for the sweetest little fox stole, which just happened to be frightfully expensive—Millie took a shallow breath and said, in an authentically tremulous voice, "Please don't kill me."

The simple request seemed to be Darnell's undoing. His gaze still locked with Millie's, he reached over and covered the gun with his hand before Tess could reach it.

"You fool," the woman said scornfully. "Are you going to let some little ninny stop you?"

"No," Darnell said coldly, "I'm going to let her stop *you.*"

There was a chilly silence. "Then what do you suggest we do with them now?" Tess demanded.

No answer was forthcoming. Millie's heart pounded like thunder. "You can let us go," she said, although the idea now sounded outrageous even to her own ears. "We won't tell anybody what happened."

Not even Darnell looked convinced, but his wife fairly cackled. "And just what do you think happened, miss?"

Millie had the good sense not to mention anything about her and Sam coming to catch murderers and getting caught themselves, or the fact that she'd heard Darnell say he was up to his elbows in blood.

"We caught you trespassing on our property, that's what!" Tess answered for her.

"Then you should let us go. We won't harm anybody."

"Then what were you doing with the guns?" the other man asked.

"W-we were looking for Darnell Weems," Millie began, not sure where this would lead. All three of them awaited her coming explanation with bated breath. She focused her gaze straight at Darnell. "Sam here was hoping to talk to you, t-to see if you might come to Chariton to vouch for his brother's character. You see, his brother might hang in a short time."

"*Will* hang," Tess said flatly, unimpressed by Millie's lie.

But Darnell seized on it with great interest. "Is that the truth?"

"I swear it," Millie vowed.

"She's lying! She just wants to use you, Darnell. To pin a murder on you."

Darnell began shaking his head in confusion. "I don't know...."

"Please," Millie begged. "If you won't go to Chariton, just release us. Sam will understand if you don't want to get involved. He's risked his own life to come out to ask you."

Tess didn't wait to hear what her man's reply would be. "So help me, Darnell, if you do what that girl says I'll walk out the door this instant and count myself lucky if I never clap eyes on you again."

Darnell hesitated, torn between the plea and the threat— though Millie could tell he was much more moved by Tess's words than by her own. "Please," she begged again, trying to make her voice sound even more plaintive.

"Darnell..." Tess warned again.

He shook his head frantically. "Stop!" he cried, leaning on his hands against the table. "I don't know what's right anymore."

Suddenly, the third man stepped forward. "Tell you what," he said. "Let's say we follow your advice, Darnell, and ditch these two here for a while and worry about 'em later."

When Darnell looked up, his eyes were hopeful. Millie's heart, too, lifted so fast and so high that she felt dizzy.

But Tess looked at the other man as though he'd lost his mind. *"Later?"*

"Trust me," he said, throwing her a meaningful glance. "They'll keep."

"Yes!" Darnell jumped at the idea with great enthusiasm. He put his gun aside and reached over to take both his wife's hands. "Honey, they'll be okay here for a while. No sense being hasty."

Her jaw clenched. "I suppose," she said reluctantly.

"Fine!" Darnell said, turning to the other man. "Let's be on our way."

The cowboy nodded curtly, watching with a gleam in his eye as Darnell led the woman out of the little cabin. His eye especially seemed to tarry in the vicinity of Tess's slender waist.

Slender for an amazon, that is.

Millie didn't trust those two—especially not when the woman turned and shot the other man another one of those meaningful glances. That the two were in cahoots behind Darnell's back was obvious. But what precisely did those meaningful glances mean?

Chapter Thirteen

It wasn't easy to burn a sod hut. He'd have to aim for the roof.

Jitter stood about a hundred yards' distance away from the Weems place, considering. It didn't matter. Tess could have told him to set fire to an Eskimo's igloo and he would have found a way to do it.

Not that she had actually commanded him to do anything, in so many words. But he'd gotten the idea clear enough. The man and the girl had to be gotten rid of, and since Darnell wouldn't do it, the job was up to him. This place was isolated enough that no one would likely see the smoke, and if they did, they'd probably think it was just a brushfire. He'd go into town, maybe, have a drink, afterward. If the place was charred enough, there'd probably be no need to clean up the evidence. No one would be able to tell Winter and the girl from Adam and Eve.

He wasn't squeamish about things like this. Chances were the two in the house would die from breathing the smoke before they so much as got hot. No, it wasn't the crime that was making his palms sweaty and his gut clench tight. Those discomforts he owed to the prospect of how happy Tess would be when she discovered what he had done for her.

Happy enough to betray her husband to thank him.

Beyond that, he didn't give a damn what happened. His conquest of that woman was so close he could fairly taste her sweet lips beneath his—and he knew she *would* be sweet, and soft, and demanding, all rolled into one. Just thinking about her made him hard as a rock. He wanted her in the worst way. And soon he would have her. Soon.

Only he'd never betrayed a friend this way, stealing his woman.

But when the woman was Tess . . .

His hands began to shake, and he took out a match, scraped it against the heel of his boot and watched it burn. Practice. He didn't want anything to go wrong now.

He forced himself to wait until the flame forged a black trail right down to the tip of his thumb. Then he blew out the fire, tossed the match to the ground, and tapped his horse into an easy walk toward the little house.

"Did someone slam a rock against my head?"

"Oh, Sam!" Millie cried. "You're conscious!"

Unfortunately. If Sam's head felt like a taut drum, then Millie's enthusiastic voice was a drumstick beating against it. Instinctively he tried to reach up to rub his temple, but found that he couldn't move. At all. His legs were stretched out in front of him, bound at the ankles, and his hands were tied behind his back. And if he guessed right, that warm lump on his back was Millie herself.

"This is cozy," he quipped.

"Don't even joke about it!" Millie moaned. "Wait till you've been sitting like this for half an hour—it's torture."

"Is that how long I've been out?"

"You came to a few times, but drifted off again. I've been so worried."

"Well, we don't have time to sit here any longer, Millie. They could come back."

"The thought has occurred to me, thank you very much. Let's just say I was a little limited in what I could do, chained to Sleeping Beauty."

"Have you tried getting your hands free?"

"Just until my wrists were rubbed raw," she said.

That was as he figured. He could tell by the slight numbness in his fingers that the ropes were knotted tight. If he could have reached the penknife in his pocket, he could have easily cut them loose.

"You might want to try it yourself, though," she continued. "Raw skin against hemp is quite a sensation."

"I'll pass. We need to get someplace where we can find something to work us out of these bonds. We need a knife."

In unison, their heads swung in the direction of the kitchen door. It couldn't have been more than six feet away, but from where they were sitting, it might have been six miles.

"I don't see how we're ever going to make it," Millie said with a moan.

"The first thing we need to do is turn so that you're facing the kitchen."

"What?"

"Just do it, Millie."

With a huff whose very familiarity heartened him, Millie started wriggling and rocking. "I don't see how this is going to get us any closer," she said testily. "And you're not helping!"

That was true. But she was moving around so crazily, it was hard to figure out her pattern. When finally Millie was facing the kitchen, he bent his knees and brought them up toward him as far as he could. "I'm going to push back against you, and when I do, try to draw your knees up and pull us toward the kitchen."

There followed a short pause. "*This* is your plan?"

"Do you have a better one?" he asked. "Now, on the count of three . . ."

Their first effort took them two inches, tops. But even that was better than nothing. Millie let out a gasp of joy. "Hey! How did you think of this? We should be to the kitchen sometime by the turn of the century."

But their push-me-pull-me routine got better the more they worked on it, with the result that by the time they heard a horse's approach, they were already to the kitchen door.

At the sound, both of them froze, unsure whether to hurry their progress or make as little noise as possible. "Keep going," he finally ordered in a low whisper. They gave up counting to three aloud, which made their progress clumsier, and after a few minutes, when the horse's footsteps began retreating without their ever having heard anyone dismount, both of them twisted in curiosity.

Where had their visitor gone, and why hadn't he stopped in?

"Maybe we should have yelled, Sam," Millie said worriedly. "It might have been someone who could have helped us."

"It was Weems—or that man with him," Sam guessed. "Maybe it was the woman. What was her name?"

Millie nearly spat out the name. "Tess!"

He chuckled. "I take it you didn't like her any better than I did."

"Not just that," Millie said excitedly, "but Sam, while you were out, so to speak, I was thinking. Tess. *She* would be the other initial on the ring. 'T to D,' remember?"

His eyes narrowed as the logic in her assertion hit him. "It figures that she would have given a ring to Darnell. It's clear she wears the pants in the family."

"Unfortunately, her pants happen to be my yellow dress," Millie grumbled.

"Are you still upset about that damn dress?" Sam asked. "I promise, if we ever get out of this, I'll buy you dozens of yellow dresses."

"Oh, Sam . . ." Millie said, her voice despairing.

"What's the matter?"

"You said *if*, not *when*. You think it's hopeless, don't you?"

"Hell, no," Sam said, and deep in his heart—way, way deep—he didn't consider it too much of a lie. There was always a glimmer of hope while a person was still standing—or, in his case, squatting. "Keep scooting, Millie. We'll get out of here."

"But if we do, I have to warn you, I can't accept gifts of clothes from a man."

"Good grief! Let's worry about that later."

"This is important," she insisted as they continued. "Just because I've allowed you to take...certain liberties... doesn't mean that we can do away with decorum altogether. And you can't expect me to turn into one of those horrible women like that Tess creature, wearing too-tight dresses and going around inscribing jewelry for you. How revolting!"

He could just imagine her expression as she tossed her head imperiously. Her nose was no doubt turned up at a pert, disdainful angle—just the right position to catch a whiff of the acrid smell moving quickly through the little building. Sam felt her tense the very moment he himself caught the scent that could spell their doom.

"Smoke!" Millie cried.

"Move!" he commanded quickly. "Fast!"

Adrenaline pumping, he pushed them faster than he would have thought possible five minutes earlier. He and Millie scooted right through the kitchen, toward the back door of the little house, bumping furniture, cursing under their breath, passing right by several sharp, glistening knives. There was no time to think about that now. Being tied together was a wonderful fate compared to being roasted together.

For that was surely what would happen if they didn't make it out of the cabin. Whoever it was who had set the fire had been very discreet. He'd thrown a flame up on the dry grass-and-mud-thatched roof, which served as well for a conduit of fire as a grassy plain after a long drought. The flames spread quickly above them, raising the temperature in the little house to well above bearable. In several places, the roof gave way, dropping little fiery bombs to the floor.

One of them dropped onto an old woven-backed chair near the bed, which soon began to crackle and burn. Smoke was already everywhere. The inside of the house was a hazy gray color, and he and Millie were helpless even to pull the material of their clothes up to their faces to guard against inhaling the noxious stuff.

"Quickly, Millie," Sam ordered, giving her an especially strong push that brought them precious inches closer to the outdoors.

In response, Millie could only cough, but she was obviously doing her best. They made faster progress the more desperate they became, and finally reached the door. The latched door.

"Sam, we're shut in!"

He heard the hysterical edge in Millie's voice, and could have kicked himself. Why hadn't he thought of this? He was already dizzy from lack of oxygen, but he forced himself to think. "All right, Millie, I'm going to lie back. If you can, lean against me and try to hoist your legs up against the door and work the knob with your feet."

He half expected her to insult this unlikely plan, but instead, she quickly obeyed orders. They rocked and crashed to the ground on their sides. "The air's better down here, anyway," Millie said, taking a gasp of the slightly purer air.

She began the unenviable task of hoisting her bound feet up toward the doorknob. To Sam—and surely to her, too— it seemed to take forever, but finally her little feet, encased in the fine leather boots he had once considered laughably dainty, began to struggle with the glass knob on the door. "I think I've got it!" she said, struggling to turn her hips so that the knob would turn to the left. And then she lost her hold.

"Try again," Sam urged. "You're doing great."

He wished he could turn and see her progress, but he was afraid to move, lest he throw her off-balance. He tried to peer at her feet through the corner of his eyes, but it was the satisfying *click* of the latch that let him know they were nearly free. That, and Millie's cry of triumph.

"Eureka!" she said. "We did it."

After that, it was a snap to push-pull their way out to the porch. They rolled down the two steps to the hard ground, onto which they fell with relief, choking and gulping in air by the lungful.

"We made it!" Millie cried exultantly.

But Sam wasn't so sure. He didn't say anything, but his eyes immediately began to scan the horizon for a sign of the lone rider they had heard. Behind him, Millie did, too.

"You think he might come back?" she asked.

"Maybe."

"Sam, I think it must have been that third man—the dark-haired one. Before they left, he and the woman exchanged an odd glance. I wondered at the time what it meant."

"Now you know," Sam said. "It meant murder."

And the murderer would no doubt be back once the smoke had cleared, to make sure his handiwork had done the trick. He and Millie weren't in the clear yet—any more than the house was free of the flames that had set it ablaze. The fire was finally building to full rage, consuming the little home with a fury. Sam and Millie tried to keep scooting away from its heat and smoke, heeding the stray embers that floated through the dark, churning air.

When the worst was over, Sam began moving back toward the smoldering porch. "Sam, it's no use going back there," Millie said. "We'll never be able to get our hands on one of those knives."

"I know." If only he could reach the knife in his pocket! "I've got to try something else."

"But what?"

He was glad he couldn't see Millie's face when she discovered what he had in mind. Finding a patch of porch with a steady flame burning, he lifted his feet and held them over the fire, charring the rope that bound them together.

"What are you doing?" Millie cried, aghast. "Setting us on fire after all?"

"I'm trying to get us loose." And this was merely experimentation, he thought as the fire made quick work of the rope. Sooner than he had hoped, he was able to snap the charred rope before the flames burned through his boots. He feared that freeing his hands—which didn't have leather covering them and were unfortunately close to Millie's—wouldn't be such a cakewalk.

He spotted a splintery piece of wood burning nearby and tugged Millie toward it. "What now?" she asked.

"Hands."

He could well imagine the saucer-round surprise in those brown eyes of hers. "Oh, no! Sam, you'll burn yourself!"

"Maybe not," he said, trying to strike a confident tone, as he inched his wrists toward the flame. Unfortunately, doing so meant bringing Millie closer to the fire, too. He didn't want to burn her, or risk catching her dress on fire. "Tell me if the fire catches you."

"Of course I will, you lunatic," she said.

Sam didn't take offense. How could he? He was beginning to question his sanity himself.

He gritted his teeth as the heat became more intense, more unbearable. But, unbearable as it seemed, wild horses couldn't have forced him to move his hands away. Too much was riding on this. The smell of the burning rope reached his nostrils—along with the smell of his own singed flesh. Millie was perfectly still behind him, just as he had been when she opened the door for them. He wasn't surprised at her stoicism. She might enjoying sparring with him, but when the chips were down, she knew when it was necessary to work in tandem.

Finally, the bonds at his wrists broke free. But not without a price, he discovered as he reached into his pocket for his knife.

"Oh, Sam!" Millie cried as he worked to free her. "Your wrists are burned to a crisp!"

There was no other way to describe the damage. The flesh around where the rope had gnawed into one side of his wrists was charred black in places, and surrounding that were areas of mottled fiery-red skin. He looked up at Millie and they winced together. It hadn't hurt so bad before he got a good glimpse of it.

"We've got to get you to a doctor."

He could have howled with laughter, but he feared it would come out as a howl of pain. He didn't want Millie to know just how bad this hurt, although by her worried expression he assumed she had a pretty good idea.

"No doctors," he said.

"Why not?"

His mouth twisted wryly. "Who would we tell them we were?"

"The Johnsons."

"I hate to disillusion you, Millie, but that little subterfuge won't last very long. Your Sheriff Tom is bound to come through Little Bend sooner or later, and when he does, he won't have to be a genius to figure out who the Johnsons are."

"All right, we'll make up another name."

"I've got to follow Darnell Weems," he said. "So much time wasted. There's only five days now."

"But, Sam, your hand!"

"I'll wash it and wrap it and it'll be as good as new."

"Then we should head back toward Gus and Lou's place," Millie said. "You said yourself she was a good hand at healing, unbelievable as *I* find that to swallow."

He bit back a laugh. "We'll go there if Darnell's headed that way, too. If not..." He had no answer for that, of course. His hand stung like the very devil had seared him with his fiery pitchfork. If he didn't make it to a doctor, or to Lou, he would just have to take his chances. Time was growing exponentially more precious with each passing minute.

"Come on," he ordered, hating the demanding tone in his voice. He grabbed Millie's arm, then drew back when the contact of rough calico against raw skin caused a sharp pain to shoot through his wrist.

She shot him a questioning glance, but trotted along beside him without comment. For a little while, at least. After about a hundred yards, the sigh he'd been expecting issued from her lips. "I wish I knew what happened to our horses."

"Me, too," Sam agreed. But it wasn't just the slow pace he regretted. He felt a sharp sting of remorse for even having Millie out here in the first place. Sure, it hadn't been his idea, but he should have forced her to stay at that hotel, should have tried to win enough in a poker game to cover the hotel bill before taking her along.

Doing so, he would have been denied the experience of making love to Millie. But even now, in the clear light of day, their night together seemed so far off, like something he was remembering from a wonderful, fleeting dream.

And he had put her in danger. Never mind that he had tried to leave her alone, in relative safety. He should have expected that she would follow him, should have guessed that she couldn't stand the thought of anything of importance happening while she wasn't there to see it, whether it be a dance in her hometown or someone attempting to burn Sam alive in a shack.

He should have anticipated, should have insisted, should have forced her to stay behind. Somehow. And, by God, if he ever got them out of this fix they were in, he swore, he would do his best to see that she never faced this kind of danger again.

Worry of a different sort puckered Millie's dark eyebrows together. "Do you think those horrible people found Mrs. Darwimple?"

He didn't want to cause her any more anguish, but neither did he think she would believe a lie. "Maybe," he admitted.

Her jaw clenched fiercely. "The thought of that terrible witch riding my sweet little horse makes my skin crawl."

"That 'sweet little horse' of yours has the constitution of an ox. She's more than a match for anyone."

Millie took no solace in his words. "I can't stand it anymore," she said. Stopping in her tracks, she took a deep breath and bellowed, *"Mrs. Daaaarwimple!"* After a moment of shock, Sam leapt to her side and clapped his hand over her mouth, ignoring the fierce sting. "Are you mad?" he asked her. "Anyone will be able to hear you for miles!"

"That's the point," Millie said. "I had to try—I just couldn't leave her without calling."

"For God's sake!" Sam scolded gruffly. "Have you forgotten that someone just tried to kill us?"

"I've had that horse since I was fifteen," Millie shot back. "I'm not just going to abandon her to a trio of murderers if I can help it."

"Okay, then," he agreed, a curt bite to his words. "You've given it your best shot, so now let's be on our way."

"All right!" She glared up at him, shaking her arm to release his hold on her. Her expression softened a fraction when she caught another glimpse of his scars. "I just had to try," she muttered.

They shambled on in silence for a while, each absorbed in his own thoughts. He could just imagine what Millie was thinking about. Mrs. Darwimple. The day he met her, Millie had claimed she was noted for two things—her honesty and her horsemanship. He'd since discovered that he had attached himself to one of the world's best fibbers—or omitters of truths—but Millie hadn't been lying about how well she could handle that little horse of hers. She was a natural. And having grown up on a farm himself, he understood how attached to animals people could become.

Millie lifted her head, listening, and Sam stopped walking. A rider. The third man was returning, coming back for them, just as he'd expected. Sam cursed under his breath.

He and Millie were unarmed, as helpless as kittens, and standing out in the middle of the pastureland in plain view.

Millie glanced at him, her expression at first strange, then exultant. Poor thing. She thought the sound of the coming rider was Mrs. Darwimple.

"We've got to take cover, Millie."

"No!" she cried, a look of absolute joy on her face.

They stood in a silent and possibly deadly tug-of-war, while the hoofbeats grew increasingly loud. Finally, spotting a low bush that would provide minimal, maybe laughable, camouflage for them, Sam took Millie's arm and started dragging her to it.

"No, Sam!" she cried.

"Don't be a fool," he urged, tugging her harder.

Suddenly, over a slight rise on the horizon, appeared the source of those hoofbeats. Sam's heart leapt into his throat.

Damned if Millie's horse hadn't come back to her.

Millie ran forward to meet the returning animal, stopping only once, to turn to Sam, who was right behind her, spring up on tiptoe and plant a kiss on his cheek. The smile that spread across her face was infectious, and his chest swelled so with feeling that it nearly hurt to look at her. Not that he could have taken his eyes off of her.

"This is a good sign," she said as the mare walked up to greet her.

"We'll have to do away with the saddle," Sam said.

Millie hesitated, then nodded. "Poor Mrs. Darwimple. I wonder if she would have come back if she'd known she'd be forced to ferry two people."

"I'm glad she wasn't given the choice," Sam said, stowing the saddle behind a bush. He came around and swung up on the little mare, then pulled Millie up in front of him. She landed across his lap.

"This won't work," Millie said, laughing.

Sam wished it could have. He couldn't think of any better way to ride than being able to look into her beautiful brown eyes. Millie flushed and then squirmed to reposition herself to a straddle. He helped by encircling his hand around her tiny waist and hoisting her into place.

"Better?" he asked.

"Mmm . . ." she murmured.

He knew what she meant. Though they had been lashed together for the better part of the morning, there hadn't seemed to be anything erotic in their predicament. Now every part of him that touched Millie seemed to come alive with desire, desire he was determined to do nothing about until their future was more certain. If they had a future.

He could smell smoke mixed with soap and sunshine coming from her hair. Even the whiff of acrid air caused desire to stir inside him.

"Aren't you going to put your arm around me?" she asked in a sweet, seductive voice.

It was true, he should have, just as a matter of anchoring them both in place. Yet he couldn't, wouldn't, if only because he wanted to so much. Now that they were on their way again, he knew what he had to do, and Millie wasn't going to like it one bit. "You've got to be the most forward female I've ever run into," he answered tersely, keeping his hands to himself.

He had meant the answer to take her mind off her question, but instead it only seemed to spawn a new, more troubling line of thought in her mind.

"How many females *have* you run into, Sam?"

"Not many, thank God."

"But last night—"

He interrupted her like an indignant schoolmaster lecturing a wayward pupil. "I don't believe we should think about last night just now."

"But back at the cabin you—"

"Back then you hadn't almost been killed!" he snapped guiltily. "Things are different now. A lot different."

"But we survived," Millie said, twisting to look at him. "I know you're still worried about your brother, Sam, but I'm more confident than ever now that we'll get that terrible Weems person, because after seeing him, I'm certain he's guilty. And if I can see it, surely a judge could. I know we'll get him."

"I hope you're right. But from now on, that needs to be my focus."

From the expression on his face, he could tell his words stung like a sharp slap—as if he didn't want to waste any more time on *her*. "Well." She lifted her head proudly and turned forward again. "Don't let me distract you."

"That's impossible," he said gruffly.

"Then maybe the fault's not with me."

"You bet it is," he said, his voice coming out harsh and soft at the same time. He caught another whiff of her hair and felt himself weaken. "I've never been so fetched by anyone."

Suddenly, she reeled around to look at him again. "Really?" She paused a moment, considering. "Have you ever been in love, Sam?"

"Why are you asking me a thing like that?" he asked suspiciously.

"Maybe because I want to know the symptoms."

"Don't tell me you're feeling them."

"Seeing as how I don't know what they are—and you're obviously not going to tell me—I'm not sure," she answered, a hint of exasperation lacing her tone.

His heart felt like lead. "Don't fall in love with me, Princess."

"Why not?"

"Because you need a man with a future."

"*You* have a future," she said.

He smiled. "Yeah, in jail."

"I don't believe it, and what's more, you don't, either," she said, not letting go of his hand when he tried to take it back. "You're a man of honor. You wouldn't have held me as you did last night if you didn't think we would be together."

He took his less damaged hand and combed it through his thick hair. "You are the damnedest female I've ever met!"

Don't you have any sense of self-protection? You can't just run around saying things like that to men!''

"I don't," she explained. "Just to you."

"Millie, what we did last night...it's not something to be taken lightly."

She nodded vigorously, relieved that he was bringing the subject up. "Believe me, one look at Laurette Jackson's husband could tell you that."

"Who?"

"He doesn't have any teeth—not even a single molar." When Sam looked perplexed, she added, "They're wooden. And she was such a pretty thing, too, before she met up with the lumbago man."

The explanation didn't clear up his confusion any, but he forged ahead anyway. "Well...since you understand that there can be complications..." He stumbled for a moment in a verbal fog before taking a resolute breath. "What I mean is, we can't do that again."

"We can't?"

"It's just not possible."

She turned away, but he could feel her confusion in the tense set of her shoulders. After a moment, she said carefully, "I think you might not have your facts straight, Sam. I've heard Alberta say that some people are like rabbits— not in front of me, of course. But I'm sure she was referring to how often they...you know."

Sam blinked at her in disbelief for a moment. "No, uh..." Oh, hell, why didn't he just put it in plain English? "I can't make love to you because I don't want you to end up in trouble, especially when I might not be in a position to marry you. Do you understand?"

"You mean you're worried about me?"

"Hell, yes! How do you think I felt today, knowing how vulnerable you were? If anything had happened to you, I'm not sure what I would have done. Even now you're still in danger—every minute you stay with me you are. All I care about now is getting you back to your father in one piece, back where you belong."

"But I belong here with you," she said, her voice suddenly becoming panicky.

"Not after today. Today we're going to scoot past Little Bend, but the next town we come to with a sheriff in it, I'm sending you to him."

Her chest rose and fell in a dramatic huff. "I won't go."

"Yes, you will," he said, his voice steely with determination. "If you refuse, I'll tie you up, gag you, and pin a sign that says Millie Lively in large block letters on your chest. Understand?"

"How dare you treat me like a child!" she said. "Besides, you can't intimidate me with your vicious-criminal act anymore, Sam. I know you wouldn't do a thing like that."

"Have you forgotten those two deputies you thought I killed?"

For a moment, she seemed to be trying to remember, just as he was, that long day, over a week past, that seemed like a lifetime ago. Her vision of him as the vicious criminal who'd clunked the deputies over the head was no doubt as far in the past as his memory of her as a vapid little daddy's girl. Yet she remained silent.

Suspiciously silent.

"Tomorrow, we split up," he reiterated.

"Maybe so, Sam," she said enigmatically. "But then again, maybe not."

"I can't imagine what happened to Jitter, can you?"

At her husband's question, Tess looked up and regarded him with wide, innocent eyes. "Lord, how should I know? He probably stopped in Little Bend for a drink. The man does seem to have an unusual taste for liquor."

Darnell took a bite out of a piece of dried beef. He and Tess had stopped to eat under a large live oak tree and to give Jitter the opportunity to catch up to them if he could. Now it was almost dark, and Darnell was beginning to worry. To him it appeared that his friend had simply disappeared, but something in Tess's demeanor seemed to indicate she knew more.

Darnell opened his mouth to probe the subject further, but they were interrupted before he could get one word out.

"All right, Winter, come out with your hands up!"

At the surprising command, both Darnell and Tess turned to look at the speaker. A small man wearing a dusty brown suit held a revolver on them. Darnell panicked. His gun, which he'd laid down near the horses, was too far to reach now. As the short man came into the clearing, he noticed a distinguishing feature on him—glasses as thick as the bottom of a whiskey bottle.

"You got the wrong man," Darnell said warily.

The short fellow smiled. "Sure I do."

"But you do!" Tess protested.

"Stand aside, Miss Lively. I've come to rescue you."

"I am *not* Miss Lively," Tess said adamantly.

"What do you take me for, a fool? Anybody could see that he's the fugitive and you're Miss Millicent Lively. Your daddy sure will be glad to see you."

Tess looked to Darnell in a fit of annoyance. "Do something, honey!" she said, not wanting to give away their names.

The little man's lips twitched distastefully at the roughly spoken endearment. "So that's how it is."

"How what is?"

The man with the glasses shook his head. "I've heard of cases where women fall in love with their captors—a sad business, but the fairer sex is, alas, also a fickle one. I'm afraid I'll have to keep you both in my sights until I can deliver you to the proper authorities."

At the word *authorities,* Darnell's heart started beating in double time. Fast as he could, he shot forward and tried to wrest the gun away, but it exploded just as he was reaching for it. Fiery pain shot through his hand, and he jumped back, recoiling from the sting. Tess screamed and reached for him before he could fall to the ground. She snatched his hand and inspected the damage.

"He only grazed you."

They both looked up at the man.

"I'm to bring you in alive, Colonel Lively said."

Darnell wouldn't have thought that the man could see well enough to know whether a bullet was skimming someone's hand or plugging him right through the heart. He swallowed past the dryness in his throat, feeling a grudging respect for their captor.

"Now, now, Miss Lively," the little man said, "you don't have to worry about this blackguard. You'll be free of his influence soon enough."

"You're a fool and a half, mister, if you think I'm this girl you're searching for," Tess said in her coldest, most scathing tone. "I look nothing like her!"

Her words, unfortunately, only seemed to confirm the opposite for their bespectacled foe. "And how would *you* know what Millie Lively looks like, unless you'd seen her, or you were her?"

"Isn't she supposed to have dark hair? That's what the newspapers said."

"I'm a detective, ma'am. I know all about disguises. I've seen women change their hair color before—red, raven black, blond. But hair aside, you forgot about your dress. That dress is just the shade of yellow your father described, *and* the same design."

"That's the most hare-brained thing I've ever heard. Are you running around pointing guns at every female in a yellow dress?"

He shook his head patiently. "Now, now, Miss Lively. I'm sure you've been through a traumatic experience, but believe you me, your daddy can't wait to have you back. So you just come along real nice-like, and you'll be back in your old home in a matter of days."

With his gun cocked, he stepped forward, handcuffed the two of them together and gave them a nudge. "Hope you like to walk," he said as he led them back to where his own horse was. "It's slow, but I can be certain you won't try any funny stuff. You won't get far if you do."

"I can't believe you're not going to do anything!" Tess scolded Darnell.

But he couldn't quite figure out what action to take. He'd tried to get the man's gun, but that hadn't worked. Now, as far as he could tell, their best chance at escape was to hope Jitter caught up with them. "Don't worry, sweetheart," he said. "Sometimes you just have to accept these things until the *jitters* pass."

Tess didn't seem to appreciate his cleverness like a good wife should. "You'd better be right," she warned. "I should have guessed that I'd have to rely on him to get me out of this mess!"

And just to let Darnell know how deeply disappointed she was with him, she gave the cuffs a firm yank, sending the metal biting into his fresh wound.

Chapter Fourteen

"Here it is."

They didn't know the name of the town below them, and neither of them cared. It was just another little village at the edge of nowhere, glued together by sheer will and the universal human need for liquor, gossip and the law. The only buildings Sam could make out were the hotel and a tiny sheriff's office and jail—but just that suited his needs to a T.

Unfortunately, his need to get rid of Millie seemed to be fading as they huddled together on Mrs. Darwimple, staring at the place.

"Yes," she answered finally, "here it is."

Her sad, resigned tone tugged at him. Ever since yesterday, she hadn't said a word about his leaving her. He almost would have thought it was another trick of hers—except now she actually appeared ready to follow his wishes without a fight. Since when did Millie give up so easily?

Of course, it was good for him that she *had* given up. He didn't have time to deal with a headstrong woman. Maybe once everything was over, and he was free . . .

But that might just be a crazy dream.

"You know what to say?" he asked her.

The crown of her head, just in front of him, bobbed up and down in a nod. "I'm to tell them that I walked from

Little Bend. You rode south. And that Darnell Weems as good as confessed before he tried to burn us alive.''

He tried not to touch her. Touching her was lethal to his willpower, he knew that. But he didn't have to touch her to be swayed by the sweet smell of her hair, or the way her voice seemed to vibrate from her back into his chest when she spoke. Or the way his heart told him not to let her go.

That, especially, he had to ignore. ''I guess that's about it, then.''

She made no comment, aside from ''There sure are a lot of people down there.''

It was true. A whole slew of horses were tethered near the jail. Maybe the circuit judge was in town.

Don't let her go....

He shook his head. The strange thing was that after a week of wanting nothing more than to be traveling solo, he seemed to have a million reasons now for *not* getting rid of her. Yesterday Millie had said that she belonged with him, and damned if it wasn't beginning to seem as if she did. He couldn't imagine riding away on Mrs. Darwimple without her. Or stopping to give the horse water without Millie chattering at him in the background. He couldn't imagine going through another day or week or lifetime without tasting Millie's lips.

All last night he'd tossed and turned on the hard ground, unable to get his mind off the woman who lay just a few feet away. But if she wasn't with him, wouldn't it be worse? Wouldn't he be wondering about her all day long, wondering what she was doing?

And what about that Lloyd Boyd character? He was afraid Millie would actually marry the man. Maybe she would fear she was with child. He could have kicked himself for putting her in that predicament, especially since Millie didn't seem to have a very firm grasp on the birds and the bees. There was no telling whether she would panic and think she was carrying a baby even if she wasn't.

A baby. He tried to imagine it—a little kid toddling around the farm, following him as he did his work, sitting on his knee as he sat in front of the fire on a winter night. Or maybe it would be a girl, dark-haired and adorable like her mother. But that was the clincher. Much as he warmed to the thought of a small child running through his house, imagining Millie there, along with this bundle of joy, was a little more difficult.

Help her off the horse and send her on her way.

He sighed. "It's getting pretty late."

They had ridden all morning before coming to this town, and now noon was beating down on them full force. There was an autumn nip to the air, but the sun's rays were still strong.

The sun made her hair smell like that flowery soap she had. Every time he inhaled he got an intoxicating whiff of it, and could remember vividly how it felt to run his hands through that thick black mane, and to kiss the soft, feathery hair at her temples, and to watch the brown locks spill over her white skin as she slept after they made love.

He tried not to breathe.

"Well." She turned then and looked up into his face. Her eyes were glistening with unshed tears, and her cheeks were flushed. Biting back all the emotion inside her by nibbling at her bottom lip, she finally snaked her hand around and thrust it toward him. "It's been nice knowing you, Sam Winter."

Nice? The word fell so short of his feelings that he nearly laughed as he covered her hand with his own. As soon as he clasped her tiny fingers, he waited to experience that pang of wanting that always seemed like it was going to tear him in two. This time, however, it didn't come.

This time he just felt certainty. Certainty that letting Millie go would be the biggest mistake he could ever make. For so long, he'd been alone. Independent. He'd never known what it was like to be with someone, for better and for worse. He'd naturally taken on Millie as a problem that had to be dealt with, a responsibility, a distraction—but Millie had turned that perception upside down. Who had taken care of whom?

She had nursed *him* when he was sick. She had stuck with him—at great peril to herself—when she could have just as easily turned her horse from Gus's house back to Chariton. She had even risked death for him. And while she complained, she didn't buckle under pressure. She had gotten them out of that burning house alive. *They* had gotten them out of that house alive.

They. It took some getting used to being part of a "we" instead of an independent "I." But, given time, he would probably manage.

"Sam, what are you thinking?" Millie asked.

He shrugged. He didn't want her to get the idea that everything would be roses and lacy hearts from here on out. They still had a murderer to catch. "I was thinking how right you were. It has been nice."

A little dark spark of hope appeared in her eyes, and she swallowed. "And ... ?"

Now he knew what she'd been doing this past day—waiting for him to come to his senses.

"And I suppose it'll just have to keep on being nice for a while longer," he said. Then he looped an arm firmly around Millie's waist, whirled Mrs. Darwimple in the opposite direction of the town and urged the mare into a steady lope.

"Here they are, Colonel."

Horace Lively looked at the sheriff of Templeton, the little town he, the posse and anyone else interested in the capture of Sam Winter had been summoned to by Tibbetts. Then they turned to the detective himself, who was standing proudly beside his charges. Behind him, he could hear Sheriff Tom mutter a curse as he pushed to the front.

"You dunderhead!" Tom railed at Tibbetts. "These aren't the right ones."

"That's what *we* told him," the woman said hotly. She was tall, blond—and as different from Millie in her appearance as a hound from a herring.

"What are your names?" the Templeton sheriff asked, asserting himself for the first time since this mob had taken over his jail.

"Dar—"

"David Smith," the woman said over her husband. "Mr. and Mrs. David Smith."

Horace's heart sank with bitter disappointment. "This is the wrong woman, Tibbetts," he confirmed—as if any confirmation were needed. Every man in the room but Tibbetts and the Templeton sheriff could tell at a glance that the detective had made a key blunder.

The little man's face drained of color. "But I thought—"

"I demand to be released at once!" the woman crowed indignantly. "And moreover, I think this man should be arrested for kidnapping innocent travelers. He shot my husband!"

"Tess..." the man handcuffed to her murmured. He smiled sheepishly at the company gathered around. "No harm done."

"No harm?" the woman cried furiously. "What about your hand?"

His hand, wrapped in a white cloth, did indeed appear to be wounded. "Just a scratch," the man assured them all, not looking at the woman next to him.

Something about the couple struck Horace as a little strange. Maybe the way the woman seemed so completely contemptuous of her husband, or that the man seemed desperate to get away from all these people. Not that Horace could blame him. Getting shot and hauled to a jailhouse was bound to shake a body up.

At any rate, they were both so undeniably the wrong people that there could be no question of detaining them. "Now, now," Horace said, coming forward, his heart heavy. "I think we can let the matter drop now. This man only brought you in because the circumstances are so dire for my young daughter."

"What about my husband's—?" Her question was cut off by the man himself, who dug his elbow sharply into his wife's ribs, a movement that caused her complexion to turn a startling shade of scarlet.

"Now, honey, I think we should be on our way."

"You've heard of Sam Winter, the fugitive, haven't you?" Horace asked them. "I'm offering a considerable reward to anyone who has information that could lead to my daughter being brought back alive."

The woman's honey-colored eyebrows jutted upward sharply. "Reward?"

"Come on, darlin'," her husband said, tugging her away as soon as the handcuffs were unlocked. "We don't want to waste any more of these good people's time." He looked at her pointedly. "They got a killer to catch."

She hesitated, then her lips turned down in annoyance. "A lot of luck to them, when they can't even tell innocent people from vicious criminals!"

At that departing barb, the people inside the crowded sheriff office turned back to Tibbetts. "I still think they're suspicious," he said in his own defense. "Very suspicious indeed."

Horace agreed, but he was helpless to stop Sheriff Tom from launching into a tirade against the maverick investigator. "You fool!" the lawman cried. "You've put us nearly a day behind in our search now. Every single man on the hunt was fetched over here to witness the capture—and instead come to find out that your people didn't even resemble Miss Lively and Winter."

"Disguises," said Tibbetts, who, after an initial understandable embarrassment, was recovering some of his professional pride. "One must always be on the lookout for disguises."

"I'd thank you not to be on the lookout for anything," the sheriff said. "I heard Pinkerton didn't want you meddling in his cases, and frankly, I don't either."

"But I'm employed by Colonel Lively."

Horace shifted uncomfortably. He held a certain admiration for the little man, and indeed for any man who had so much determination to succeed against the odds. And being blind *and* a detective was certainly a challenge most men wouldn't want to face. Nevertheless, he couldn't risk his girl's life for the sake of compassion for this man. The sheriff said they were a day behind now. Who knew what fate could have befallen poor Millie in those twenty-four hours? "I'm sorry, Tibbetts. We'll have to do without you from here on out."

Tibbetts's face turned a mottled pink hue, and he swallowed, his Adam's apple jumping past his tightly buttoned collar. "Colonel, I understand your hesitation concerning my services. Today's events have been disappointing—Some, like Sheriff Tom here, might even call it a fiasco. But I'm willing to press on."

Tom brayed in displeasure. "Let it sink through your skull, son—we don't want you anywhere around us. In plain English, you're gumming up the works, holding up the parade, you're an obstruction, a menace, and a nuisance, a—"

"Now, Tom," Horace began, but he was stopped by Tibbetts, who held up a calming hand to stop him from any remonstration he might give the sheriff.

"That's quite all right, Colonel. The sheriff is correct. I'll just have to press on independently, as before."

"No!" The sheriff took off his hat and slapped it adamantly against his leg. "I don't want you looking for the fugitive, period. I don't even want you in the state!"

Tibbetts smiled. "You say that now, Sheriff McMillan. But I guarantee you, someday you'll be thanking me." He sent the whole assembled company a bow. "Good day, gentleman, Colonel Lively."

Rising up to his full height—five foot five if he was an inch—the detective shoved his glasses up the bridge of his nose and marched outside to resume his search.

After the little man was gone, Horace felt strangely bereft. He would have even been glad for Lloyd Boyd at that moment—anyone who held Millie's best interests as close in his heart as he himself did. He sank onto a bench and buried his head in his hands, and was surprised when Sheriff Tom came over to him, bearing more weaponry. He held in his hands an old carbine rifle.

"Don't lose hope now, Colonel," Tom said.

Realizing these were the kindest words the sheriff had spoken to him since the manhunt began, Horace lifted his head.

The sheriff held up the rifle as the men in back of him started shuffling out the door in preparation to move again. "See this?"

"I'd thought you were more modern than to use one of those old things, Tom."

McMillan laughed. "You bet. But a certain old crone complained of losing one of these three days ago—and guess where this one just happened to turn up? At that burned-out house, not far from where your daughter's saddle was found."

Horace's head lifted hopefully. "You think he was hiding out there?"

The sheriff nodded. "And who knows if he might not again? I heard tell of a posse that chased a man three months once, only to find out he was hiding out in his own barn."

Horace doubted they would be so lucky in this case, but with Millie having been spotted alive and shopping in Little Bend just two days ago, perhaps all was not lost. "What are you going to do now?"

"I'm sending my men backtracking—and I'm going back to that little shack and holding those old folks' feet to the fire until they tell us where Sam Winter is."

It was a hope. Horace nodded. "I'll ride with you. Maybe if I talk to them . . . the kidnapped girl's father, you know."

The sheriff head tilted skeptically. "This old lady didn't look like a mountain of sympathy, but you can give it a try, I guess."

"Ouch!" Sam cried as Lou slapped some of her miracle burn poultice onto his hand. "What's in that stuff, alcohol?"

"Nah," Lou muttered gruffly, "just a little whiskey."

Sam winced, and Millie could almost feel the physical pain he was biting back.

"Buck up," the old lady commanded as she slapped more concoction on his hand. "You'll be going through this a few more times in the days ahead."

His gray eyes looked startled. "I can't stay here. I only came because Millie made me."

"She did?" Lou said, sounding surprised. Obviously she didn't think Millie capable of reasoning out that a sick man needed to get help.

The woman's small eyes peered over at Millie through the darkness of the barn, where Sam insisted on staying. He was nervous. Too nervous, Millie thought. And Gus and Lou hadn't helped matters by chattering on about how the posse had come through here days before, acting high handed and mighty suspicious. Of course, *anyone* might have been suspicious of a couple that not only didn't talk to the authorities, but weren't even on speaking terms with each other, either. Millie's disappearance had caused a rift in that already shaky marital alliance that even her reappearance with Sam in tow—but without that rifle—hadn't healed.

Lord knew, even with his hand red and inflamed and hurting like thunder, it had been hard enough just convincing Sam of the need to come see Lou. After a day and a half on the hunt, no sleep, and no sign of the trio that had nearly killed them, Sam was as low-spirited as she'd ever seen him.

She could hardly blame him, of course. Each day that passed made the outlook for his brother seem more bleak.

And what had happened to Weems and his wife and their silent, malicious friend? It seemed that they had simply disappeared into the countryside like clever foxes. Yet they hadn't looked very clever, or inclined to hide themselves away, even.

Millie's breath suddenly caught.

Sam, stiff with alertness, darted a wary glance up at her. "What is it?"

"Oh, Sam, I just thought of something!" she exclaimed. "I think we've been searching the wrong way."

The two of them looked up at her doubtfully. "How so?" asked Sam.

"Looking for them as if they'd be hiding out, like us," she said, pacing back and forth to avoid their skeptical glances. "But Weems and his wife don't think they have anything to hide, so why should they be roughing it, when they could be going from town to town?"

"'Cause deep down, Weems knows he's a murderer. I could see the guilt in his eye. Anybody could. He's going to try to avoid people if he can."

"But his wife—that Tess woman," Millie said distastefully. "*She* wouldn't put up with sleeping out-of-doors, I'll bet. Don't forget where I first saw Tess, out buying a dress that was apparently beyond her means. She'll want to stay in towns, show herself off."

"She'll do what her man tells her," Lou said with a curt nod.

This woman hasn't spoken to her *man in four days!* Millie noted. Tough old Lou apparently thought that every woman besides herself was a fool. Millie turned to Sam. "Is that what you think?"

"Not necessarily..." Sam said carefully. "But aren't you forgetting something? I can't just sashay into every town between here and Chariton looking for someone, when *everyone* is looking for me."

Lou nodded. "A mouse can't go hunting a rattlesnake far from a hidey-hole."

"Maybe not a mouse, but I can," Millie said.

Sam's mouth dropped open, and even Lou stilled in the middle of the finishing touches on her bandaging job to stare at her.

"What are you saying?" he asked, his tone level.

Millie shrugged, suddenly uncomfortable. She wouldn't have thought that hinting at such a logical suggestion would elicit such hostility. "You know, 'You take the high road and I'll take the low.' You can comb the country while I look in the towns."

When he spoke again, his voice had turned gravelly. "You mean split up?"

"Only for a little while."

He stood suddenly. "Hang it, Millie, of all the women in the world, you must be the most frustrating, the most hare-brained, the most—"

"That's what I been thinkin' for days now," Lou put in.

Millie's chest puffed up in offense. "And pray tell what's wrong with my suggestion?"

"What's right with it?" Sam asked. "For a week you've been sticking to me like glue whether I've wanted you to or not."

"I only tried to convince you I was too helpful to be tossed aside, which is what you were about to do," she pointed out. "But this would be different."

"Only because it would be a thousand times worse," Sam argued. "I was going to leave you in the hands of the law, but you're suggesting going out to search for killers who have already tried murdering you once. Do you think they'll be glad to see you alive and well?"

"It won't matter if I see them first."

Sam shook his head. "I won't let you do it."

Millie's cheeks flamed. "I don't need your permission."

Sam stood and walked over to her slowly. She knew the tactic well. He drew himself up to his full height and squinted those steely gray eyes, thinking he could intimidate her. But she wasn't fooled. She doubted Sam was capable of hurting a hair on her head. The only way he could hurt her now was by being caught and being separated from her by iron prison bars for several years. Or being so grief stricken after being forced to watch his brother hang that he would want to forget all about Millie Lively. *Those* possibilities made her cringe and quiver.

"It's my hide at stake here," he said.

It's my heart, she was tempted to answer. What would he have said to *that?* Sam had certainly never said he loved *her,* and for all she knew, he never would.

Putting aside her fleeting temptation, she answered more practically, "You might not have noticed, but I've now invested quite a bit of time in this escapade myself."

"But not your life."

She bit her lip. "Almost." She watched with some satisfaction as his face paled and a scowl moved across his lips. "Remember that fire?"

Sam said nothing.

The barn was silent for a moment. Then, from the door, came the sound of a low chuckle. "Sounds like the woman's got you licked, son," Gus said. "I'd hang it up if'n I were you."

Millie could have kissed the old man's grizzled face. At least she had one ally in the world!

At the sight of her husband, Lou stiffened up like tough old beef jerky. "Some's advice ain't worth takin'."

"Yeah, and the word of an ol' woman who don't know nothin' about anything is one of them," Lou told Sam.

"Some folks should watch who they call *old.*"

Gus ignored the warning. "Leastwise, some folks oughta know when other folks are best left alone to work things out 'mongst themselves."

"Sure, and some folks oughta know they aren't the only ones who can figure out when other folks need privacy."

Lou turned to Sam. "I was just leavin', but I'll be close by in case you need some help."

She shot Millie a warning look—as if *she* planned to do Sam any physical harm! Millie knew it was cowardly, but she wanted to beg Gus not to leave her alone with Sam. She knew he had ways to make her back down. But Gus followed Lou out the barn door; Millie and Sam could hear the couple arguing for minutes after they had disappeared.

"Well," Sam said finally. "At least they're talking again."

His attempt at levity only made her more anxious to stick to the conflict at hand. "I don't see why you should be so bothered by my wanting to hunt for Weems and his wife on my own. We could cover twice as much territory working in tandem but separately."

"I wasn't thinking about that."

"But what else could be more important?" Millie asked. "We must find Darnell Weems, or we might never free your brother. You said yourself that's what you wanted to focus on."

"That was before."

"Before what?" He looked hesitant to answer her. "Before what?" she insisted.

He kicked a toe into the straw-strewn dirt and shrugged. "Before we came to that town and I realized I didn't want to lose you."

Suddenly, the world slammed to a halt.

His words had come out as little more than a resentful mutter, but they rang loud and clear in Millie's head. Her heart started beating as rapidly as a jackrabbit's. This was the closest he'd ever come to saying that he cared for her even a little bit—aside from lustful mutterings. True, not wanting to lose her wasn't exactly love, but it was a start!

She rushed forward. "Oh, Sam, do you mean it?"

"Mean what?"

"That you care for me and that you maybe see a future for us?"

He slapped his hat on his head and squinted down at her in amazement. "Now how did you glean all that out of what I said?"

"You don't fool me!" Her heart surging with joy, she took one of his hands and skipped once around him as if he were a tall, stern maypole. "You said you didn't want to lose me, and you won't. Not ever."

"Then what the hell are you insisting on running off on your own for, if you're so dead set on hanging around me?"

"But I won't be *far* away," Millie said. "I'll just go into towns while you skirt around them and wait for me."

He shook his head. "I don't like the idea of it."

"But, Sam," she pleaded, "it's the only way. Even Gus agreed."

"Of course he did," Sam barked. "That old man's been in cahoots with you from the very beginning."

She stepped forward and moved her hands up Sam's chest, feeling him shiver a little as her fingers brushed the soft, worn fabric of his shirt. "He just knows there's not a lot I wouldn't do for you. You would have known that before now, too, if you weren't so thickheaded."

He gritted his teeth and looked down into her eyes. "You sure are unpredictable," he said, bringing his hands up to her elbows. Her knees went weak at his gentle touch.

How could a man's nearness have such an instant, devastating effect on her? Every time he came near her, it was as if her body became something totally different from the boring old thing she had known her entire life. Her insides melted, her whole body felt weightless and intolerably heavy all at once, and her hands just couldn't seem to resist reaching up and twining together at the back of his neck. When she did so, her breasts brushed against his chest, wreaking havoc on her senses.

He doesn't love you.... She tried to remind herself of that pertinent fact, in case her more animalistic side was tempted to forget. But even as she gave herself the firm mental lecture, another part of her just didn't care. Her feelings for

Sam were so deep now that she wasn't even looking for him to promise devotion—something she'd always taken for granted from all the men who had courted her before. Yet some of those little romances hadn't even lasted weeks, while she felt instinctively that Sam and she would be together years down the road. Or maybe that was just wishful thinking.

But even if it was, that didn't stop her from being swayed by the feeling of Sam's hands beginning to roam up and down her arms, or his stepping closer to her, so that every inch of her front side seemed to be touching him, warmed by the heat coming off his body. He smelled like saddle leather and hay and the chamomile Lou had used in her poultice, and Millie closed her eyes and reveled in his closeness. She wanted him so much sometimes, she thought she might faint.

But now he seemed to want her, too, only he was better at fighting it than she was. The very fact of his not wanting to give in to his attraction to her, yet being unable to hold out for long, gave Millie a sense of power she'd never known she could have over a man.

Yet she felt as if her own resolve were slipping away at the same time. The hardness of him—his strong hands, his broad, muscular chest, his powerful thighs that just brushed her own—made her instinctively want to yield to him, to say anything he wanted so that he would take her into his arms and show her the glories of love that he had demonstrated to her once before. She knew he wanted to.

She resisted the impulse, whispering instead a diplomatic, "But I'll never go away from you, Sam. Not really."

He leaned down and began nibbling slowly at her sensitive earlobe. "I'll see to that. I'm going to keep an eye on you, sweetheart."

"Mmm..." she said, before she realized that she should definitely *not* be agreeing with that statement. "You worry too much about me. I'm not a girl."

He chuckled, darting a feather-light caress over one of her breasts. "I know."

She blushed and leaned in so that he couldn't see her red face. The closeness also allowed her an excellent opportunity to kiss the dark tanned vee of skin revealed at his collar. She traced the light-haired, salty surface and felt a quivering sensation move through her. Her hands came down and wrapped around his back, bringing them ever closer.

"I've got to try to help you, Sam," she said, gathering up her last shred of willpower.

His expression serious and full of unquenched desire, he answered, "And I've got to try to keep you safe."

She swallowed. *He wanted to protect her....* Her heart should have soared, but her own worries remained. Who would protect Sam? Tagging after him did no good. She needed to help him, not hold him back.

"Well..." She sighed. "I guess we're at an impasse, then."

"I guess so."

They both looked down at their bodies, wedged so close together air couldn't get through. Sam's gaze came up and snagged on her lips, which immediately began to crave contact with his. If only they could come to an agreement about this...if only he would kiss her...

His eyes darkened. "Oh, hell!" he cried, sweeping her up into his arms in one easy movement. "You can do what you want tomorrow. Tonight you're staying right where you belong—with me!"

He crossed the barn in four long steps and lowered her onto a soft bed of fresh hay in the corner. The dizzying speed with which he declared his surrender would have toppled Millie over, let alone the way in which he showed her. His mouth bent quickly to her lips, cutting off comment or protest.

Not that she would have voiced either. Though relatively unschooled in the art of love, her body thrummed like a willing pupil eager to be taught. His hand roamed down to her hip, pulling her close, making her feel the evidence of his desire. Her eyes flew open, and a low chuckle emanated from his lips.

"We'll take it slow," he promised in her ear, "but not too slow."

He was as good as his word. With strained patience, he unhooked the buttons down the front of her dress, revealing the pale swells of her breasts. As he grazed them with his fingertips, Millie felt herself arching toward him, remembering, needing the heavenly feeling of having him lave the sensitive pink flesh with his tongue. Beyond shame and embarrassment, and certainly beyond modesty, all she could consider was the pulsing need within her. She aided his task by wriggling out of her worn camisole.

Sam's eyes sparked with something deeper than desire as he looked at her bared flesh. "You're beautiful," he whispered as he reverently traced one of her nipples with his finger, then followed by gently placing a kiss there.

Sensation so powerful raced through her that Millie thought she would faint. She didn't care how she looked; feeling was all that mattered to her now. As Sam lavished attention on her, her hands began their own exploration, tugging his shirt free and pulling it up so that she could feel the hard plane of his back, and the play of muscles there as he moved. There was so much strength in him, yet he could be so achingly tender.

He bent farther, eliciting a disappointed moan from her as he left her breasts and then a sharp gasp as his tongue made a smooth trail down her stomach. He lifted her skirt, his hand skimming up her leg, tarrying as he reached the more sensitive flesh above her knee. Millie felt all her attention shoot to the insistent throbbing at the juncture of her thighs, which could have been the center of the entire universe just at that moment, especially when Sam gently began exploring the vulnerable, sensitive flesh there.

Her hands worked insistently through his thick, soft hair, and she felt herself moving uncontrollably against his hand. Need so demanding that it was almost painful caused her mind to go blank, so that she was completely unfettered by inhibition. Thus freed, she began to thrash more demandingly against him, and he obliged her every desire. Heat began to build and coil inside her with frightening intensity, and she called out Sam's name. He lifted his lips to hers and covered her mouth. When finally all the energy and heat and desire inside her began to spiral out of control, he held her tightly to him, whispering husky murmurs of encouragement that blended with the intense kaleidoscope of sensations crashing around her until there was only stillness.

When her breathing slowed and she gathered the courage to open her eyes again—sure the world would be unalterably changed—she saw only Sam's face, just as before, looking down at her with something like wonder in his eyes. The fingers of one hand skimmed the hairline above her brow, which was wet with perspiration.

At that strange, unreal moment, Millie remembered Alberta's many admonitions about how a lady should strive *never* to sweat in front of a gentleman, and had the terrible urge to laugh.

But she didn't. She doubted she even had the energy inside her to create much more than the light sigh that escaped her lips, unbidden.

"Millie," he said, seeming to enjoy the sound of her name.

She certainly enjoyed hearing him say it, and tried to respond with a breathy "Sam," but all that came out was another of those little dreamy sighs of hers. She feared she would be sighing the rest of her life away.

Sam lifted up and began unbuttoning his shirt. It was the first time it registered that he was almost fully dressed, while she was . . . a hay-strewn mess. Yet it seemed too late to rearrange her skirts to cover herself, especially when Sam peeled off his shirt, giving her a tantalizing view of his torso, which her fingers itched to touch.

She lifted up, placed a light kiss on his upper arm and began rubbing his shoulders gently. She just seemed to be drawn to him, to crave instinctively the feel of her skin against his. She pressed her breast against his back and smiled as she heard and felt his sharp intake of breath.

He undid his belt and she smiled. "Nice of you to undress. I was beginning to feel awkward being the only one."

His movement stilled for a moment. "I'm not doing this to put you at ease, Millie."

She blinked, craning her head around to look into his eyes. There was a strange glint in them. "Then why...?"

He took her hand and gently led it down to the unflinching evidence of his need for her.

"Oh." Millie gulped. "B-but I thought we were finished!"

He slowly pushed her back down into the soft, fragrant hay. "Not by a long shot, sweetheart," he murmured as he began to kiss her, causing the familiar warm sensations to start building inside her all over again. "Maybe this time we'll take it slow," he said with a husky laugh. "Both of us."

Two pairs of eyes stared up in shock.

"Good Lord, Jitter, you like to scared us half to death!" Darnell cried.

Tess jumped to her feet. "Where have you been?"

"You wouldn't believe what happened to us," Darnell said.

Jitter was glad to hear Darnell summarize the day's surprising events, rather than have to answer Tess's question. Because how could he explain to her—much less Darnell—that he'd spent an entire day on a barstool, half craving and half dreading the moment he saw her again?

She was never more beautiful than when her eyes flashed with anger, which they were doing right this minute. "Can you believe that?'' Tess asked him. ''A reward—and he scurries out of that sheriff's office as if they'd just told him about a plague of locusts!''

''No way y'all could get that reward,'' Jitter told them.

''Why not?''

'' 'Cause you said it's for bringing the Lively girl back alive,'' Jitter explained calmly. ''But she ain't alive.''

A slow smile set across Tess's lips, but Darnell's mouth hung open in shock. ''You mean she's dead?''

''Of course that's what he means,'' Tess snapped. ''What else could 'ain't alive' refer to?''

Darnell blinked. ''She looked okay when we left her.''

''Yeah, but after we left the house caught fire,'' Jitter told him. ''Sorry, Darnell—I was too late to stop it.''

For a long moment, the air was deadly silent, and Jitter felt a small pang of regret for what he'd done. Darnell was staring at him as though he'd killed his own mother, not two strangers. Seeking relief from the uncomfortable feeling, he let his eyes wander over to Tess's pretty face. *She* wasn't looking at him as if he were a criminal. More like a hero.

''I don't believe it!'' Darnell cried. ''I plain don't believe it.''

Jitter turned. ''I'll help you build a new place, Darnell.''

''We won't need one,'' Tess said. ''Not if all our plans work out. We'll live in Chariton, remember?''

Darnell stared from one to the other of them in horror. ''Live in a dead man's house, after I've killed his brother, his wife?''

''Don't be silly. You didn't kill his brother.''

''I might as well have,'' Darnell said. ''I don't think that fire started itself, do you, Tess?''

She stared at him in stone-faced silence for a moment. ''I wouldn't know.'' She turned to Jitter. ''Would you?''

Jitter slowly shook his head, if for no other reason than to see Tess's eyes brighten with pleasure. Oh, he knew she was a curse to men. But she was so damned pretty.

Darnell's jaw worked from side to side. "I don't know what to believe," he said, turning.

"Where are you going?" Tess demanded.

"For a walk," he hollered back. "To think."

Tess watched him go, her wide lips puckering into a frown. Jitter could just imagine tasting those lips, pulling her into his arms....

"He'll be back," Jitter said, surprised his voice came out as anything better than a croak. This was the moment he'd been dreading—and the moment he'd been living for.

Slowly, she turned her head back to look at him, and Jitter felt as if he were standing before a queen, and he was the loyal subject who had just slain a dragon for her. But the wicked smile that slowly replaced her frown was all woman, all for him. His insides felt as if they would bottom out.

"Not too soon, I hope," she purred as she stepped into his arms.

Chapter Fifteen

She felt so warm, so invitingly soft, that he could have slept with her forever—and might have, had not the commotion outside caused him to get bolt upright and take fresh stock of his nakedness and noises around them. Instantly, his heart began to beat in double time.

"Millie, wake up," he whispered fiercely, nudging her as he reached over to snatch his pants. "Horses!"

Prancing hooves and men's voices sounded just outside the barn, mingled with Gus's gruff voice barking at them angrily.

Just as Sam had done moments before, Millie shot up to a sitting position, her beautiful face sleepy and disoriented. "Who is it?" she asked.

He lifted a finger to her lips, warning her to be silent. With his other hand, he placed her dress in her lap. "Better put this on. I think we're about to have company."

Her eyes widened in what could only be described as terror. "Oh, Sam—not the posse!" Looking at her, anyone would have thought that *she* was the criminal the band of men was hunting down.

As they listened through a large crack in the old barn's walls, their tired fingers fumbling quickly with the small buttons and awkward ties of their clothes, the voices and sound of horses they heard confirmed their worst fears. The law had caught up with them. Now what were they going to do?

Sam looked at her. "I'll have to make a run for it."

She put a shaking hand to his forearm. "Sam, no—if they see you running, they might shoot at you!"

"I have to try."

"They might not look in here," she suggested.

In the barn? The idea was preposterous. "This is the first place they'll look. I'm surprised they didn't find us already."

"But listen," Millie said, her voice edgy with desperation, her eyes glistening with fear. "Gus is telling them we've gone, I think."

"And you think they'll believe him? If that were the case, they never would have come back here in the first place."

"But if there's no sign of us around..."

"They probably found your horse, Millie," Sam told her sadly. He had tethered Mrs. Darwimple nearby last night. "But in case they haven't, I'm going to try to reach her."

"Sam, wait," Millie begged, hanging on to his arm so tenaciously that he pulled her up when he stood. "You can't leave me here!"

Something in her eyes tugged at him. Or was that his own heart doing the tugging? He hesitated, torn.

"You'll be fine."

"Not if I don't know whether you are," she told him, her words laced with hysteria now. She tightened her grasp on his arm. "Sam, I love you."

The pronouncement stopped him cold. The growing sounds of footsteps and hoofbeats outside stilled, and all that remained was the reverberation of the four words her soft voice had just spoken. With a squeezing feeling in his chest, Sam realized that it was the first time he could remember hearing someone say those words to him.

She loved him. Or at least she said she did. Even for Millie, the woman who had worked her way through eleven fiancés, that declaration had to mean something.

But what could it mean to him, when he had no time to hold her—no right to, given his circumstances? He was nothing but a fugitive, offering her love on the run, taking when he had nothing to give in return. He felt bitter at having to disappoint her. She was probably used to hearts and flowers and happiness from men—and he was able to give her none of those things.

"Oh, Sam, look!" Millie stooped down to the hay and picked up the inscribed ring. "It must have fallen out of your pocket while we were . . . while . . ."

She blushed and held out the ring.

"You keep it, and be very careful with it," he instructed. He knew she wouldn't think of it that way, but it was the only gift he'd ever given her. The only one he ever would, maybe. "I have to go, Millie."

"But when will I see you again?" she asked, gripping the ring in her fist while her other hand held Sam's arm.

"Promise to come to my hanging?"

She shook her head. "Don't joke about that, Sam."

"Who's joking?"

Millie wasn't about to let him give in to despair, no matter how mirthfully he presented it. "Nothing will happen to you," she said with determination. "I won't let it."

The sounds outside once again broke into his consciousness, making his pulse race. He had to get out of there, fast. But he wasn't going anywhere until he'd held Millie once more. Maybe for the last time.

Taking advantage of her viselike grip, he swung her back to him and enfolded her in his arms for a parting kiss. "Here's hoping you're right, Princess," he murmured, just before bringing his mouth down on hers and taking a quick drink from the honeyed sweetness of her mouth.

Before Millie, he had never known mere kisses could be so intoxicating. But just touching her seemed to send his senses reeling out of control. With a groan of frustration, he pulled her petite body close to his, feeling the length of her down his entire front. It was a torturous feeling—but one that would have to sustain him through the days, months, maybe even years, ahead.

"Oh, Sam..."

Hearing her little moan of pleasure jolted him back to the present, back to his senses. He pulled away from her abruptly. "Goodbye, Millie."

Just then, the rusty hinges of Gus's barn door gave out a deafening squeak, and dawn light poured through the new opening, putting Sam and Millie in silhouette in their private little corner, which was now completely exposed.

"Colonel, we found them!" the man in the doorway called.

Millie breathed in sharply and darted a glance to Sam. In her eyes was all the helplessness he felt but didn't dare express. He wanted to tell her not to worry, but he couldn't, not when he noticed suddenly that her dress front was unevenly buttoned, leaving the top of her cleavage gapingly exposed. Her lips were red, her cheeks were flushed, and her hair, a tangled mess, was liberally peppered with hay.

But most of all, he heard the word *colonel* and knew instantly that the man referred to by that title could only be Horace Lively, Millie's father. The man had been a hero of his own father's, but now he seemed like Sam's worst enemy. The man who would take Millie away from him.

In a second, the old war-horse appeared in the doorway, his slight but proud bearing silhouetted magnificently. His face was in shadow, but Sam knew instinctively that the man was scowling at him.

"Millicent!" the man bellowed in a voice loud and clear enough to rally cavalry troops in midbattle.

Millie's frozen response didn't bode well for a heartfelt reunion. Instead, she held fast to Sam's hand and blew a piece of straw away from her bangs.

"Sir, I demand that you unhand my daughter!" Colonel Lively commanded. As if the ten men behind him with guns drawn weren't command enough.

Sam looked down at his arm. His fingers were practically blue from the tense grip Millie had on him. He cleared his throat. "I think you'd better ask your daughter to unhand me first," Sam suggested.

The old soldier glanced down with not a little surprise to Millie's trembling hand, then lifted his gaze to meet her dark eyes.

"Daddy," she said, the slight quiver in her tone belying her usual bravado, "there's something we need to discuss."

Locked in her room! It was intolerable, insufferable, unbelievable. Until now, her father had always seemed such a reasonable man. What did he think—that he could simply lock her away until she was willing to lie and say that Sam wasn't innocent, that Sam had brutalized her into taking his side, that Sam had mistreated her? Over and over Millie had told her father that Sam had been a perfect gentleman—well, except in the beginning. And she didn't dare reveal some of the more intimate details of her latest exploit. She told him only good things about Sam, as well as a detailed account of what had happened to his brother's wife.

Her father had failed to listen to her side of the story. He seemed incapable of believing that his little girl wasn't a helpless victim. As for believing that Sam was innocent, that this was all a classic case of blatant injustice... Well. Sam had been right about that all along. The very idea caused her to laugh now. Even when she described nearly being burned alive, the old colonel had found a way to blame Sam, since she wouldn't have been there in the first place had it not been for his kidnapping her.

How could she have been so naive? She'd been so sure her daddy would take her at her word!

And now Sam languished in the Chariton jail. Millie felt sick at the very idea. She had never, *never*, considered that she might fail to get Sam out of his predicament. But her father turned a deaf ear to all her arguments—even her well presented and articulated case that Darnell Weems was the real murderer.

Only one thing she had told him so far had impressed him at all, and that was her gut feeling that the esteemed sheriff of Chariton wasn't the good man everyone believed him to be. That gave Millie hope that her father wasn't completely blind when it came to reading people's characters.

After a quick knock, Alberta sidled into the room, careful to close the door quickly behind her, as if Millie were a mouse who might scamper out through the smallest crack while she wasn't looking. The woman frowned in dismay to see Millie up and about. "Young lady, you need to stay in bed with a cold compress on your head, like the doctor suggested!"

"Oh, pooh," Millie said. Her father, after hearing her ranting about how wonderful Sam Winter had been to her, had insisted that she be looked over by a physician.

"That ain't very ladylike language."

What would Alberta have said if Millie had come out with some of the truly salty terms she'd picked up in the past days? She smiled secretively and asked, "Did you tell Daddy I wanted to see him?"

"I did."

"Good."

"I'd be careful around your father, if'n I was you. He don't like you talkin' crazy about the ordeal you went through."

Millie wondered if falling in love counted as an ordeal. It certainly felt like one to her—a traumatic, draining physical ordeal. Her every thought centered around Sam; she worried about him, remembered what it felt like to have him hold her through the night. Just the memory of kissing him caused her heart to beat as rapidly as if she'd run up three flights of stairs. And now thinking about Sam caged up in that horrible jail made her feel clammy and ill.

"Oh, Alberta, I think I have been crazy," Millie said.

The older woman stood with her arms akimbo and nodded curtly. "High time you understood that. Now, when your daddy comes up, you apologize to him for makin' him fret."

"I will," Millie promised. "I see now I haven't done a thing right since I got back."

"That's the truth. You should have been trying to reassure him that you're still his little girl. And talk to that nice Mr. Boyd. He's been all tore up since you left, too."

Millie bit her lip as she plopped down in front of her large mirrored dressing table. She wanted to look her best for her father this time. "That's exactly what I'm going to talk to Daddy about. My marriage."

Alberta clapped her hands together and pressed them to her bosom. "Praise be!" she cried. She ran over, grabbed the bottle of rosewater out of Millie's hand and began applying it for her, dabbing it on her hair, neck and elbows. Millie felt thoroughly pampered. Oh, how she had missed Alberta!

Another light knock sounded at the door, and Millie's father poked his head inside.

Millie painted on her sweetest smile. "Come in, Daddy," she chirped, getting up and crossing to him, her hands clasped demurely before her. "I've so wanted to talk to you!"

The colonel beamed as he took her hands, the worry lines of the past hours giving way to the happier wrinkles of his smile. "You look much improved, much improved!" he said.

"She's talkin' better, too," Alberta told him as she scampered out of the room.

One of her father's bushy gray eyebrows shot up with interest. "What's this?"

Millie turned slightly. Oh, she hated to hurt her father, but she couldn't see any other way. "I was just telling Alberta that I've decided to get married after all." She darted a glance at him.

Surprisingly, his sad, worried frown made an instant reappearance. He cleared his throat, took one of her hands and said gently, "I've wanted to mention that, Millie. These past few days have shown me... Well, let's just say dire times can bring a man's true character to the surface. And I've seen quite enough in the last week to understand if you wanted to break off this engagement."

Millie couldn't believe her ears. "Then you *don't* want me to marry Lloyd?" she asked, amazed.

Tenderly, her father pulled her into a gentle embrace, patting her head lightly, just as he had when she was a little girl. "No, Millicent, I don't. And I apologize for having pressed the matter. Only you can be sure of your own heart. I just want you to marry a man who will make you happy."

A joyous smile spread across Millie's face. "Oh, Daddy, thank you!"

Horace chuckled. "I guess the days of fathers picking mates for their children is gone—and good riddance, eh?"

Millie shook her head with glee. Providence couldn't have put her father in a better frame of mind for what he was about to hear. "I'm so happy you feel that way, Daddy. But I know you'll love the man I've picked just as much as I do."

"Got another one lined up already, have you?" he asked in surprise. "Going for an even dozen?"

"This time it's forever. I'm sure of it," Millie said.

"What's the young fellow's name?"

"Sam Winter."

Her father took a shaky step backward, as if he'd just received a mighty blow. A blow so mighty that he couldn't even speak for a few moments, which made Millie anxious. During that time, her father's face flushed to a bright scarlet.

"I don't think I heard you right," he said, his voice low with warning.

Millie opened her mouth, but at first no sound would come. "I said Sam Winter," she repeated in a hushed voice.

"You're mad!" her father cried. "Where's Alberta? Where's that doctor? What has he been giving you? Narcotics?"

"No, Father. I'm telling you the truth. I've fallen in love with Sam Winter and I intend to marry him."

"That's the craziest notion you've had yet!" he cried.

"I'm sure Sam would agree with you."

At that statement, her father was momentarily dumbfounded. "You mean he hasn't even *asked* you?"

"Of course not," she said. "Sam would never ask a woman to marry him while he was in jail, with no future."

"I should hope not!"

"I told you what an honorable man he was."

The colonel snorted in derision. "Some honor, kidnapping a girl—stealing her away from her home and her loved ones, exposing her to all sorts of danger—and then making her believe that he loves her!"

"He's never said he loves me," Millie said.

"What?"

Millie shook her head. "Not even after I told him that I loved him." She shrugged. "That's just the sort of man he is."

Her father shook his head as if to clear it. "I can see what kind of man he is. What's beginning to confound me now is, what kind of girl are *you?"*

Millie straightened her shoulders. "I'm not a girl, I'm a woman, and I'm going to be Sam's wife."

Any father knew it was a bad sign when his daughter started speaking of being a woman. Horace's wrinkled face drooped slack. "What are you saying, Millicent?"

She swallowed. *Here goes,* she thought anxiously, sending a prayer of hope up to whoever was listening. "I don't just want to marry Sam Winter, father," Millie said, squaring her shoulders. "I *have* to marry him."

Her father's mouth dropped open. Instead of the shouts she expected, he whispered only, "Oh, no," and turned away.

She felt terrible for making him go through this—but, for all she knew, it might not even be a lie. "Please don't grieve, Daddy. I'm not going to shame your good name."

"But that man . . . he . . ."

"He didn't do anything I didn't ask him to."

Her father looked up at her, pure shock in his eyes. "Millicent!"

"Well, it's true," she replied. "I told you I love him."

"But you're not married," the colonel said.

"I know. That's what I call my big dilemma. But if Sam weren't in jail—"

"After all he's done?" Her father shook his head. "Harboring a fugitive? Attacking two deputies? Kidnapping? That man will spend a decade, at least, behind bars!"

Millie debated her next move for only seconds. She held fast to her father's hands and sent him her most beseeching look. "Maybe not," she suggested. "Not if he had someone very powerful behind him."

He started shaking his head even before her words were out. "I can't do a thing, honey."

"Oh, but Daddy, you have to!" she cried. "Otherwise, what will I do?"

He looked stumped, bewildered, desperate for a solution. "I don't rightly know," he muttered. "If you start showing and word gets out who the father was—"

"But everyone would know that already."

Her father's face went pale. He swallowed. "Who have you told?"

Millie blinked. She'd only lied to her father a few hundred times and gotten away with it. Now was *not* the moment for her acting skills to fail her. "Why, no one, really."

"Who?" he demanded, his voice urgent.

"Just Sally Hall," Millie said, her eyes widening innocently. "That's all."

At the name, a shudder went through her father's body, and Millie could well guess why. If Sally knew her shame, the whole town would know it, too, soon enough. Sally was the town's most notorious gossip. Had Sally truly known about Millie's relationship with Sam Winter, the honorable Lively name would already have been made history. It was too late to send her to distant relatives until the crisis had passed, too late to marry her to Lloyd and put the episode behind them. Her father knew this, and measured his next words carefully.

"We cannot act in haste."

"I wouldn't, Daddy. Except there doesn't seem to be any reason to wait, that I can see."

"Darling, he's a prisoner. Isn't that reason enough?"

"But if people find out that I'm carrying a man's child and didn't even trust the man enough to marry him while he was in jail, what would that look like? Even if he did get released eventually, even cleared, he would be forever tainted by my failure to stand at his side when it counted most."

Her father nodded. "You have a point, I suppose."

"And if *you* stood by him . . . well, that would mean a lot in the town's mind, I bet."

"Oh, I don't think I'm as important as all that."

"Of course you are," Millie said. "You're famous all over the state—maybe even the whole country. Why, Sam's farm is a hundred miles away from here, and he knew all about you."

"He did?" Horace straightened up at this tidbit of news.

"Of course! He admires you awfully. I wish you could just meet him again, Daddy. You'd see in an instant that he's just been trapped by circumstance. Normally Sam wouldn't hurt a fly."

"He hurt you," Horace pointed out. "I don't know if I can forgive him for that."

"If we were married, you would have to forgive him. But even more important, you would *want* to—I know it!"

He shook his head. "It would take a lot of talk to convince me of that, Princess."

Millie suppressed a sigh. This was going to be harder than she'd thought. But if he needed convincing, she was willing to gab his ear off. It was not for nothing that talking was one of her finest accomplishments.

"So, you couldn't stay away from your little brother."

At the resident inebriate's observation, Jesse smiled wryly. "If he'd wanted to see me, all he'd have to have done was get himself caught. Seems to me he did an okay job dodging the law."

"I reckon you're right," the drunk said. "Half the town was lookin' for him. Me, too. I looked all over Ed's saloon for him!"

He let out a wheezing, toothless laugh that practically knocked Sam off his feet. The man's foul breath was yet another reason to stay close to the bars, looking out. Though Sam wasn't sure what he expected to see. From his vantage point, he could just make out a little of the area beyond the jail door. During the entire day he had been back in the Chariton jail, he had been staring out, and he'd not once caught a glimpse of Millie.

"It wasn't exactly a hayride," he muttered to his two cellmates. "I found your killer for you, didn't I?"

Jesse's faint smile disappeared. "I can't believe that Darnell would..."

"I can," Sam said. "He tried to burn us alive, didn't he? And it's too much of a coincidence that his wife's name is Tess and the ring says 'T to D.'"

"Maybe so," Jesse admitted.

Sam turned and leaned his back against the bars, staring down his brother huddled in a corner. "I swear I've been surrounded by the orneriest people in the world these past weeks! Why a man wouldn't be happy to discover solid evidence that another man did the crime he was accused of is clear beyond me."

"Darnell can't be all bad."

"If he's not, he certainly doesn't have much backbone. Or smarts, if he can't see straight through that woman of his."

"He can't be too dumb, Sam," Jesse noted. "After all, he's out there and we're in here."

As if he needed a reminder! He felt like a wild animal in a cage. How would he ever get used to the terrible, closed-in feeling? From what he could tell, it didn't look as if he would be getting out anytime soon.

And how would he ever get over the bitterness? It was painfully obvious that Millie's influence had been the fairy story he'd assumed it was all along. Her father had whisked her away from him so fast his head spun. And now he would probably never see her again. She would go on with her life somehow, while he would spend years behind bars, thinking about her when he had no right to.

But he was selfish to be dwelling on his romantic problems when Jesse was facing death. "There has to be a way!" he said heatedly, pounding his fist against a bar. His hands still bore Lou's bandages.

Jesse shook his head. For a man about to hang, he was unbelievably calm. Especially when Sam felt as if the slightest thing could make him jump out of his skin. "No chance, Sam. Even if you could prove that Darnell tried to kill you and showed the jury the ring and laid out your little theory for them, that doesn't mean anyone would be listening. A piece of jewelry, a new wife...it doesn't add up to much."

Maybe not. Sam began to feel that terrible nagging despair again and realized it had been days since he'd felt it. Millie and her cockeyed optimism had kept it at bay. "Somebody should be able to detect the true villains in all this."

"Who, the sheriff?" Jesse asked mockingly. "You know he hates me, and now he hates you by association. Besides, who would believe the word of a man who kidnapped the daughter of the most prominent man in town?"

Sam sighed. His brother was so defeatist it almost made him want to surrender, too.

Suddenly, the clanking of keys sounded out front by the sheriff's desk. A sneering Tom McMillan came around the corner. "Well, Winter, you better get yourself gussied up."

"Me?" Jesse asked.

Sam scowled fiercely. If the sheriff was making jokes about anything so terrible as Jesse's hanging, which was only two days away, he would punch him.

"Not you," the sheriff said. "Your lover-boy brother here."

Sam swung his head to meet the sheriff's contemptuous gaze. "You mean I'm being sent to another prison?"

"Not this time," the sheriff said.

"Then what?"

White teeth slashed across the sheriff's mouth. "It has nothing to do with jail," he said. "Seems you're gettin' hitched, Winter."

Chapter Sixteen

"Sorry, Millie, Sam says he don't want to see you."

Millie looked at Ed Herman in disbelief. "But he's got to see me!" she cried. "We're going to be married."

She attempted to peer around the jailhouse door to the single cell inside, but Sheriff Tom's other deputy, Toby Jenkins, blocked her view. "For that matter, he says he don't want to marry you, either."

"Unhappiest-lookin' groom I ever did see," Ed put in.

Toby laughed. "Seems like all the men in town said they would marry you, and then you went and picked the one who says he won't."

Millie flushed down to her hair roots. How could he do this to her? She had so much to tell him—so many plans to discuss!

"And if I was you," Toby told her, "I wouldn't go spreadin' news of your marriage around none. We been told to keep it strictly on the qt."

"Yup," Ed agreed. "If'n I was you, I wouldn't breathe a solitary word about it."

"But Sam's got to talk to me," Millie insisted.

"I'll talk t' her!" a drunken voice called from the back. Toby and Ed turned, giving Millie a view of a drunken, disheveled mountain of a man. He directed a bleary-eyed wink her way. "D-don' you worry your head none, you purty l-l-little l-l-lady. If'n that no-account won't marry you, this no-account will."

His offer sent hoots of mirth through the jailhouse—especially from the esteemed deputies. "Sorry, ma'am," Toby apologized in a decidedly unapologetic voice. "We can't make prisoners talk to nobody they don't want to."

"Not if'n they don't want to," Ed echoed. "And Sam don't."

"Fine." Millie bit the word out, her patience at an end. Sam might not have to talk to her, but he would listen. She raised her voice so that it would carry to the next county, not to mention the back of the jail cell where she could imagine him sitting and scowling. "You tell Sam he'll talk to me soon enough—*after* we're married!"

She tossed her head and turned on her heel, trying to ignore the peels of laughter that trailed after her from the jailhouse. Very funny! How was she going to engineer all that she had planned without Sam's help?

She stomped all the way home, so preoccupied with her dilemma that she very nearly stumbled over Lloyd Boyd, who was waiting for her on the top step of her front porch. "Millicent!" he cried, overcome with emotion. He very rightly refrained from hugging her and instead clasped her hand between his and brought it to his lips. "Oh, my poor, poor Millicent."

"Hello, Lloyd."

"I've just had a talk with your father. He says... says... Is it true?"

Millie nodded. "I'm sorry, Lloyd."

He raised his head gallantly. "No, it is *I* who should be sorry. I should have rescued you faster."

She didn't bother reminding him that he hadn't rescued her at all. "Oh, don't worry yourself, Lloyd." She patted his arm.

He hesitated, then blurted out, "Millie, I want you know that I will stand by you. You're my oldest and dearest friend, and have been since that moment when you decked

Wilbur Tooey on my behalf. All my life I've been grateful. Believe me, when you've come to rack and ruin, and are shunned by polite society, I will come to your aid.''

Suddenly, an idea occurred to Millie that made Lloyd's appearance on her doorstep seem almost providential. ''Will you really, Lloyd?''

''Of course!'' he promised. ''You know there's nothing I wouldn't do for you.''

''Good,'' Millie said, ''because there's something you can do for me right now.''

He looked taken aback. ''Something *I* could do?''

It seemed a terrible risk—but what choice did she have? She was going to be busy getting herself married. She needed an accomplice—and here was Lloyd, volunteering!

She dug the ring out of her little bag and placed it in Lloyd's palm. ''I'm sending you on a mission, Lloyd. A quest,'' she added, knowing he would fancy himself a medieval knight at the service of his lady. ''I'm searching for some people.''

His eyes widened. ''That's perfect! I've become quite adept at hunting down people in the past days. Or, at least, I became adept at *watching* people hunting.''

''Good, because the three I'm looking for are especially slippery.''

In as much detail as she could pull from memory, Millie described Tess, Darnell and their companion. It seemed a long shot that they would find them this late in the game, but a long shot was all they had. Perhaps Lloyd wasn't the best candidate for detective, but he was loyal and, more important, he was willing.

More than willing, as it turned out. Seeing a chance to redeem himself after being sent home in disgrace during the last manhunt, Lloyd was raring to go. ''I won't let you down,'' he said.

''Just do your best,'' Millie said, trying to give him solid encouragement. ''A man's freedom and my happiness are riding on my faith in you.''

Lloyd nodded then turned and took the few porch steps in one leap so spry that Millie was almost beginning to feel confident in her rash decision to give him the most important piece of evidence they had to clear Jesse. Maybe the situation wasn't hopeless, after all.

Then Lloyd turned back, two bright spots in his pale cheeks. "Oh, Millie, I just have one question."

"What's that?"

"These people I'm supposed to find...where do you think they are?"

Sally Hall just couldn't stop weeping. "Oh, Millie, I *had* to come. I couldn't let you go off and disgrace yourself without saying goodbye. You've been such a dear friend!" She looked up at Millie and her pink lips puckered into a distasteful frown. "Is *that* what you're going to wear?"

Millie twirled around in front of her full-length mirror. The dress, though certainly not what she would have designed, had she the time, was the closest thing to a wedding gown to be found in her closet. The ivory color was appropriate for the ceremony, and the plain design would suit her purposes afterward.

Besides, even though it was only a regular Sunday dress, it was hands-down the prettiest thing Sam would have seen her in.

But, apparently, Sally saw this as just further evidence of her sad societal downfall. "Oh, Millie!" she wailed, fresh tears forming. "To be so rich, and not to even have a specially made wedding dress!"

Millie pursed her lips. "Sally, stop boo-hooing. I'm getting married, not dying."

"Yes, but considering the man you're marrying, the two are practically one and the same."

Millie couldn't help smiling as she remembered all the times she'd imagined coming back to Chariton and telling Sally all about her kidnapping ordeal. She couldn't imagine doing so now. In fact, she found she was very uncomfortable around Sally. "How did you find out about the wedding in the first place? No one's supposed to know."

"Oh, everybody knows," Sally assured her. "Even Laurette Jackson was at the back door today, talking about what a scandal it is."

Millie shrugged. "People will forget eventually."

Sally looked horrified. "I hope not! If the colonel's daughter marrying a convict isn't good for a few decades of gossip, what is?" She tossed her blond curls. "But I do think it's so romantic, in a seedy sort of way—and you're so brave."

"Not brave, Sally. Just in love."

Sally let out a delectable trill. "Ooooooh, I do wish you'd let me know when the ceremony will be!"

"I told you, I can't. Father's made me promise to keep it a secret." She smiled ruefully. "He's trying to protect my reputation even now."

"That'll be an even bigger battle for him than Bull Run," Sally noted.

Millie might have taken offense, had the words had less truth in them. "Maybe so." In fact, if she couldn't manage to clear Sam's and Jesse's names, she was sure Sally would be proved right.

Sally sighed and flung herself across Millie's four-poster bed. "But, oh—to be so headstrong that you're willing to throw away all your respectability to be with the beastly ruffian who kidnapped you. Yes, you were certainly the bravest girl I ever knew!"

Normally Millie would have objected to being spoken of in the past tense, but at that moment, she was busy gauging how much weaponry she could conceal in the modest puffs and flounces of her wedding dress. She would need all the bravery Sally attributed to her and more, if she was going to succeed with the plan she had for her nuptials.

When the hour for the ceremony finally arrived, everyone in town knew that Millie Lively was going to disgrace herself—and what was more, that Horace Lively was going to give the wretched couple his blessing. The old colonel still insisted that the wedding would be held while everyone was asleep. So at two in the morning, a small and sleepy crowd gathered quietly at the little jailhouse.

Horace had pull enough to carry off the secret wedding. The town's minister, Reverend Thomas, had been convinced to officiate by the promise of a new roof for the old church. Sheriff Tom couldn't refuse to let one of his prisoners be married—there was no law against it—and with only a small bribe was convinced to free the remaining prisoners, save for the murderer, naturally. Since Jesse Winter was going to serve as best man, there was no reason why he shouldn't be there anyway. No deputies would be present. Just the minister, the sheriff, the prisoner/groom, the prisoner/best man, Horace, and the bride.

All in all, Horace decided ruefully, he was getting off much cheaper than a real church wedding would have cost him.

And Millie did look pretty, with a bloom in her cheeks he hadn't seen since she'd been home. It was terribly hard to stay mad at her when she seemed so happy, so determined to do this crazy thing. And, he supposed, when it came down to it, family was what mattered in this world, and Millie was his family. Millie and now this kidnapper of hers. And soon she would make him a grandfather. Horace guessed he would like that more than the approval of ten communities like Chariton.

And who could tell what would happen? Perhaps the child's father would be out of jail before the little babe made its way into the world. Or at least before it made its way to Harvard.

Millie looked doubtfully into her father's eyes before they crossed the jailhouse threshold. "Are you all right, Daddy?"

"Of course," he answered. "The more important question should be, are *you?*"

"Never better," she assured him, standing on tiptoe to give him a peck on the cheek. "You're going to be surprised by how well this all works out. I'd be willing to lay money on it."

But as they crossed into the sheriff's office, Sam's outraged shouts met their ears. "I want nothing to do with this marriage, Sheriff! You might as well tell these people to go home!"

At the indignity of being referred to as "these people" by her own fiancé, Millie rushed forward. It pained her to see him handcuffed, but despite the late hour and the circumstances, he did look awfully good; his deeply tanned skin and sandy brown hair made him stand out from the other men in the room. He had shaved his growth of beard away and appeared a dashing groom, even if he didn't want to be one. And the look in his gray eyes—a look that was admiring, though she knew he was trying hard not to be—made her knees weak. It also made her all the more resolute to marry the man.

"You might not have to talk to me, Sam Winter," she told him, "but there's no law that says prisoners have a right not to be forced to marry anyone."

Sheriff Tom scratched his head. "That's a fact, Winter," he agreed. "Not a law on the books that says you can't be forced to get hitched to someone."

"That's the craziest thing I've ever heard!" He turned to Millie beseechingly. "Don't you realize what this means for you?"

"Of course," Millie said. "It means I'll be Mrs. Sam Winter."

"And it means your mister might not be out of jail for years," Sam told her.

"I know that," Millie said, smiling secretively. "I'll bring you lots of goodies while you're behind bars."

"Your reputation will be in shreds."

"You can ask any of these gentlemen," Millie informed him. "It already is."

The sheriff and preacher nodded in confirmation.

"Even Alberta won't talk to me," Millie explained to him, "but I don't care. I just want to be your wife. And what's more, my daddy wants me to be your wife."

The colonel let out his most dour, emphatic grunt.

Sam looked frantically at the faces around him for support, but found none. "Hang it all, you can't expect to catch a man while he's in handcuffs!"

"I not only can," Millie told him. "I *am.*"

At that moment, the colonel stepped forward. "The point is," he said in his most authoritative tone, "I believe you should *want* to marry my daughter, sir."

"Hell, I do!" he cried, then noted the older man's disapproving frown. "I mean, shoot, I would—but I'm in no position to. Surely you understand that, Colonel."

The old gentleman looked at him long and hard, then shot Millie a glance. She nodded. Honorable, just as she'd said. "Like the sheriff says, you're in no position not to. Right now that's good enough for me," the colonel pronounced. "Reverend Thomas, you can go on ahead with the ceremony."

"B-but—"

A man who resembled Sam so much that he had to be Jesse leaned up against the bars. "Looks like you're licked, Sam." The oddly familiar fair-haired stranger sent Millie a smile, so much like Sam's, yet gentler, and infinitely sadder. "Sam never told me I was gonna have such a pretty sister-in-law."

Millie had always had a feeling she would like Jesse, and now her hunch was confirmed. She smiled and stepped forward, holding out her hand. "I'm so glad to meet you," she said. "Sam's told me so much—"

"All right, all right," Sam muttered impatiently. "We're all going to be one big happy incarcerated family soon enough. Let's get this over with."

Millie rounded on him in a huff. "If you were a gentleman, you would have made the introductions yourself."

"If I were a gentleman, we wouldn't be in this predicament— Oh, forget it."

She put her hands on her hips and insisted huffily, "No, I won't. And don't think I'll forget your petulant attitude, either. You could at least be pleasant on our wedding day!"

"Wedding day?" Sam laughed. "Wedding day for a possum or a fruit bat, maybe. We can't even get married in daylight like normal people!"

"If you're trying to insinuate something with that fruit-bat comment—"

Reverend Thomas cleared his throat anxiously, causing Millie to cut off her words. Color rushed to her cheeks as she swung around and noted that her father, the sheriff and the reverend were all gaping at her.

Hadn't they ever heard people argue before?

"They sound married already," the sheriff noted.

"Well!" the reverend said, ignoring the comment and clucking his tongue as he stepped forward. "Are you ready?"

Millie squared her shoulders. "Of course."

"Ready as I'll ever be," Sam muttered.

She sent him an annoyed glance and took his hand. Cold metal from the handcuffs nipped into her own wrist. She looked down, hoping silently that there wouldn't be any trouble with those. Or with Jesse's. For the first time since she'd entered the jail, her heart began to beat nervously.

It's just the prejailbreak jitters, she told herself.

"Dearly beloved," Reverend Thomas began, and from there on out everything sounded perfectly normal to Millie, although Sam guffawed when the good preacher reached the part of the ceremony that said that if anyone could cite just cause why these two should not be joined together.... But Millie cut off any comment he might make by pinching her fingernails into his hand.

"Don't you dare," she whispered fiercely.

He looked into her eyes, and the rest of the world around them drifted away again. He had to want to marry her just a little bit. No one could set off fireworks with just a glance without having *some* feeling.

As if in answer to her unspoken question, he squeezed her hand, smiling down at her as if she were truly the one woman in the world for him, for all his protestations about how different they were, how little he had to offer her. In that moment, Millie was one hundred percent positive that their marriage would be the success she wanted it to be.

If she could just get him out of this darned jail.

"Mr. Winter?"

Sam's gaze broke suddenly away from hers, and he snapped his head around to look at the reverend.

"I asked if you would take this woman to be your wife...." Thomas prodded.

"Yes, certainly," Sam said, adding, "What choice do I have?"

Millie smiled. His reluctant agreement was good enough for her. She answered with the proper words when her time came, and at the end of the ceremony, when Reverend Thomas pronounced them man and wife, she presented her lips for her brand-new husband to kiss.

"Thank God that's over with!" Sam muttered, ignoring her bridelike gesture and turning back to his cell. "Open this cage up, Sheriff, I'm ready for some shut-eye."

"Watch out, Sam," Jesse muttered, gesturing behind Sam with a nod.

Before he could even turn, he found himself being spun around by none other than his new father-in-law. The old man was surprisingly strong. "I believe you're supposed to kiss the bride, son," the colonel informed him. "And if you know what's good for you, you'll do it good and proper."

The two other free men in the room looked sternly at him, and Millie smiled, her lips still in midpucker. Rolling his eyes, Sam bent down to peck Millie on the lips, but Millie would have no chaste kisses on her wedding day. She looped a hand around his neck and pulled his lips down to meet hers, pressing herself provocatively against him.

It was showtime now, but Millie found she didn't have to try hard to work herself up to tears. "Oh, Sam," she sobbed, "I don't want to lose you!"

He pulled back from her a little, surprised, but she launched herself at him. "Kiss me again, darling!" She once again found his lips, then began to smother his face with little kisses, working up to his ear, where she stopped long enough to whisper fervently, "Daddy's gun is beneath the bow at my bustle."

Sam's gray eyes bugged. "What?"

She kissed him once more and stepped back, wiping her eyes. "I love you, Sam!"

One of the men reached for her arm—she supposed to keep her from collapsing into a hysterical heap. She turned, noting that it was the sheriff himself. Good. Swallowing a certain amount of revulsion, she threw herself against his chest.

"Land sakes, girl," the man chided. "You knew he was a jailbird when you decided to marry him."

While he admonished her, Millie took the moment to conveniently reach into his holster and disarm him. She cocked the Colt revolver, took a quick step back, and held it on the three men. "Put your hands up!" she growled. She wiggled her rear toward her new husband. "Arm yourself, Sam."

Her poor father seemed the most wide-eyed and horrified of all. "Millicent, this is madness!" he said. "You'll wind up in jail yourself!"

"Not if I can help it," Millie answered. "All right, Sheriff, open the cell."

"I will not!" he said.

Sam finally appeared at her side. "Open it," he growled, holding the colonel's revolver close to the sheriff. "Just for the record, I think this is insane, too. But now that Millie's involved, I won't let anything stop her."

"I knew I shouldn't have agreed to perform this ceremony! I knew it!" the preacher babbled, literally quaking

in his boots. "If it weren't for that roof... My wife Myra
warned me against it, but I said, 'Myra, think about the
leaks we had last winter....'"

"For God's sake, open the cell!" the colonel shouted.

When Sam moved a step closer, pressing the cold steel
against the sheriff's temple, the lawman finally relented.
Reluctantly. "You two won't get away with this," he warned
as he moved toward the cell door. Millie kept her gun aimed
at her father and the preacher. "The people of this town will
never forgive you for this escapade, Millie Lively."

The door clicked open. "That's Mrs. Winter to you," she
told him, directing her charges to follow the sheriff into the
cell. When the three were safely locked in, and Jesse was finally out, she added, "And they will forgive me when they
realize you were about to hang an innocent man, Sheriff.
And they'll also learn how you stacked the trial against him,
just because he testified once against your reprobate son."

"My son is not a criminal," the sheriff spat back, "which
is more than I can say for you, missy!"

"Hey, now," the colonel said, leaning back against the
cold stone wall.

Her poor father! She felt terrible leaving him in such a
dank place, with such miserable company. "I'm sorry,
Daddy. I'll try to be back soon, okay?"

She half expected him to rail at her angrily—and who
could have blamed him? Of all the repercussions of her
brash actions this evening, she most dreaded sinking further in her father's esteem. He knew now that his daughter
was less than pure—what would he think now that he also
realized she had been deceiving him, making him an un-
knowing accessory to her crime? He had every right to dis-
own her.

But instead, he merely nodded, as if she were off to a
dance, instead of to God knew where with a couple of outlaws. And when she looked into his dear old droopy eyes,
they glistened with tears. Was he sad to see her leave with her

new husband? Frightened for her future? Maybe she would never know.

All she knew was that her heart nearly broke when he said softly, "Be careful, Princess."

"I will," she promised.

By the time she turned around, Sam and Jesse had released themselves from their bonds and seemed to be awaiting her instructions. The first order of business was to get out of earshot of the three men in the jail cell. They went outside and shut the jail door firmly.

"Think they'd wake anybody if they started creating a commotion?" Jesse asked.

Millie shook her head as she looked from one brother to the other in the inky darkness. "I don't think so—there's nothing around here but some stores and the school down the road."

"Good," Sam said. "That'll give us a few hours' head start. Which means I have time for this."

Before Millie could even ask, she found herself enveloped in the tightest embrace she had ever had the pleasure to experience. Sam's warm lips covered hers with a fierce possessiveness she wouldn't have believed him capable of, judging from his performance in the jailhouse. He tasted her thoroughly and expertly, taking her breath away.

When he finally released her, she collapsed against him. "Oh, Sam! Isn't it wonderful that we're married?"

"I don't know how you managed it."

"Easy," she answered. "I told my father I was expecting."

"Of all the— No wonder he was so insistent with that shotgun!" She smiled proudly, even as Sam stared at her disapprovingly. He sighed. "Oh, hell, we'll discuss it later. Right now you'd better lead us to some horses, so we can get out of this town."

She had to admit, he was right. "This way, husband," she said, gesturing grandly down the street. "Three saddled horses await us at my father's stables."

He took her outstretched hand and tugged her along.

"It sure is nice to see you finally settled down, Sam," Jesse said, bringing up the rear.

"*Settled down?*" Sam stopped. "Settled down was what I was for years before I met this crazy woman. Ever since then I've been running in circles."

"You started running before you met me," Millie pointed out.

"And thanks to this latest caper of yours, I might be doomed never to stop."

She sent him a wry warning glance. "I would have thought you'd thank me."

Sam finally relented, shooting her a smile and bending in a low bow from the waist. "My lady, I do thank you." He straightened. "Now where are we headed?"

"Oh," Millie said. She'd forgotten that she had omitted telling him this key piece of information. "Fort Worth."

The two brothers exchanged glances. "Fort Worth?" Sam asked. "What's in Fort Worth?"

Back at the little store in Little Bend, Tess Weems had mentioned Fort Worth as if it were a Mecca for people of fashion. It wasn't much to go on, but Millie was hoping against hope that her hunch about the woman's taste in hiding places was correct.

"A colleague of mine I'm sure you'll be interested to meet."

Chapter Seventeen

Millie took their room keys and led the way across the hotel lobby toward the small staircase.

"It's just like I was telling you about Weems and his cohorts—sometimes if you're going to hide, it's best to do it where no one would be looking for you. And right now no one would look for us right here, in a respectable hotel."

"I'll bet twenty people have seen us in the past two minutes," Sam argued, his gaze darting warily around the building.

"That's right—probably not a single one took any notice of us."

He could have contradicted her. Every man who passed Millie took notice of her. Since they had never exactly meandered around city streets before, or in and out of busy hotels, he hadn't had the opportunity to think about Millie's effect on passersby. Realizing she drew the attention of men's stares made him feel fiercely possessive—and gave him one more thing to feel anxious about.

"The trouble with you is you worry too much," Millie said.

Sam gritted his teeth and followed her. The whole situation was beginning to confound him. Here he was, on the lam, checking into a Fort Worth hotel suite with Millie—his wife!—and with Jesse in an adjoining room. If he closed his eyes, he could almost imagine that he was sane.

But Jesse didn't seem to mind. He was wandering around in a dream state, a free man for the first time in over two months, his eyes feasting on everything they viewed. And Millie, still decked out in her wedding dress, sashayed across the hotel lobby as if nothing in the slightest were wrong with their being there. She had even picked herself a bouquet of posies during their flight from Chariton. "Don't fret," she assured him, apparently noticing the queasy look on his face. "We won't be staying here long. I had a hunch that our quarry would be hiding out in this town, but if I'm wrong, we'll find out soon enough."

"I take it we're still waiting to hear from your 'colleague'?"

Millie nodded. "And don't sound so skeptical, husband of mine. One of these days I just might surprise you."

At that prediction, Sam couldn't help tossing his head back to laugh.

"What is it now?" Millie asked, her lips pursing adorably. Sometimes simply looking at her made his heart hurt. If they weren't standing in a public place, he surely would have swung her into his arms, carried her the rest of the way to their room and shown her exactly how adorable—and always surprising—he found his wife.

He still wasn't reconciled to the idea of having gotten himself married this way. Despite the fact that marriage to her was exactly what he wanted, Millie herself was young, and probably viewed liberating him and Jesse as a new crusade. But they would just have to discuss that later. Right now they had more important things to attend to. Like finding this man she was waiting for.

"He was supposed to meet me here this morning," Millie went on worriedly, her lips puckering into a frown. "And now it's after noon! I hope we haven't missed him."

"For the last time, Millie, who is 'he?'"

"Lloyd Boyd."

The name hit his chest like a sledgehammer. "The man you just threw over? *That's* who you entrusted with Weems's ring?"

Millie shrugged as she opened the door to their rooms. "He seemed happy to do it for me, Sam." She peeked into the small but tastefully decorated little bedroom and clapped her hands together in delight. "Isn't it cute?"

Good Lord. Sam couldn't give a flip about the room. Now they had a spurned lover in on the act! "Are you sure you can trust this person? I mean, he might not be harboring any resentments that would make him head for the hills, would he?"

"Lloyd would never head for the hills, as you put it. He positively hates the country," Millie explained. "It's practically impossible to get him to go on a picnic."

With unflappable calm, Jesse stepped into the room and tested the bed by sitting down on it and getting up several times. Millie seemed especially taken with the bright yellow coverlet, which matched the curtains.

Much aggrieved, Sam combed a hand through his thick hair. "What I meant was—"

Millie rolled her eyes. "I *know* what you meant. You think Lloyd will take off with the ring and reappear sometime after Jesse is gone and you're rotting away in jail, and then take advantage of my loneliness. I'm surprised at you! Only a devious-minded creature would think of such a thing. You certainly don't know Lloyd."

"How will he even know where to find us?"

"I told him to look for the Johnsons registered at this hotel." She smiled. "And just think—now we really are newlyweds!"

He telegraphed a look meant to tamp down her enthusiasm concerning the ceremony she'd cooked up. "And we're still using make-believe names," he said. "Furthermore, I'd say your 'colleague' seems to have cut out on you."

Just then, a firm knock sounded at the door, and when Sam opened it, a strange, well-dressed young man stepped into the room, clapped his eyes on Millie and surged toward her with open arms. And, Sam noted, *his* wife didn't hesitate to step right into them.

"Lloyd!" she cried. "Oh, thank heavens! I was so worried about you."

Watching them embrace caused a sharp pain to pierce right through him. Especially when he noted that this Lloyd Boyd character appeared so respectable and upstanding and earnest. Wearing a pressed brown suit and polished boots and holding a narrow-brimmed hat in his hands, Lloyd Boyd looked like he'd just stepped out of the haberdasher's. He even outshone Millie, who after a night of riding and a morning creeping around Fort Worth was not in top form. They made an attractive couple.

Sam suddenly felt the uncanny urge to put his fist through the man's pristine hat.

Behind them, Jesse smiled mischievously from the bed. "I think you'd better make some introductions, Millie, before Sam explodes."

Millie waited for Sam to close the door before doing the honors. "Lloyd, this is Jesse Winter, and over there—" she gestured toward Sam "—the man with the scowl on his face is my husband, Sam Winter."

Lloyd's eyes widened with excitement. "P-pleased to meet you both," he said, sending abbreviated bows to the men. "Oh, my, Millie. Outlaws!"

"Just think of them as wrongly accused, Lloyd," Millie instructed. "It makes things much easier."

"And now you're one, too, by marriage," Lloyd went on. "Did you have any trouble busting out?"

"No, that went pretty smoothly."

Sam's jaw dropped in astonishment. "You told him what you'd planned to do?"

"Naturally," Millie answered. "I couldn't very well keep him in the dark, could I?"

Sam shook his head at how easily everything could have gone kerblooey on them—had Lloyd Boyd so chosen. But the young man seemed happily in cahoots with them. "I guess we owe you a load of thanks," Sam said.

"Thank *me?*" Lloyd asked in amazement. "I should be thanking you. Millie, I think I'm on to something with this detective work. I do believe I have a genuine knack for it!"

"Then you've found them?" Millie asked.

"Indeed I have." The young man modestly polished his neat nails against his finely tailored suit. "Or in any case, I've found a couple sitting in a hotel barroom by the railroad depot who seemed very interested in paying blackmail money to recover a certain ring."

Millie turned to Sam, her face lit up with excitement. "That's them—it has to be!"

"I just came from there. The woman was just as you described her—tall and blond, with extraordinary blue eyes," Lloyd said. "But I wouldn't have described her as common or ungainly, Millie."

Millie lifted her chin. "You just have a man's skewed perspective, I suppose."

Her ex-beau took offense at her words. "I pride myself on being objective."

Sam stepped forward. "Well, whatever way you look at it, I think we'd better get to that barroom, fast, before they disappear."

Jesse agreed. "We don't want to lose them now."

Millie nodded. "Lead on, Mr. Detective."

Lloyd smiled and turned toward the door with a flourish. He seemed to fancy the title, at that. And as long as the man had found the right people, Sam didn't care what he called himself.

"I should have known that imbecile husband of mine would have done something stupid like drop his ring by the dead woman's bed!" Tess said.

Jitter held up a finger to his mouth and glanced at the only other patron in the place, a lone Mexican wrapped up against the chilly early fall day in a colorful serape that seemed out of place in their dull surroundings. He tried to discern whether the foreigner had heard any of what had happened, but he remained turned away from them, nursing a cheap whiskey. "Better mind that fellow over there."

"Him?" Tess asked with scorn. "He's just a Mex. Doesn't even speak English, by the looks of him." She sighed with frustration. "I can't believe Darnell put us in this position. Why didn't he tell me about the ring?"

"Probably 'cause he didn't want you to know." And Jitter wasn't certain he could blame poor Darnell at that. Having already betrayed his best friend, he well knew how in thrall a man could become to her charms.

"I swear, Bob, I feel sick, positively sick, when I think of what a poor excuse for a man I hooked myself up with."

"Don't recall anybody putting a gun to your head," Jitter told her.

Tess bridled in her seat and watched Jitter down his second whiskey of the day. "Don't you think you're hittin' that stuff a little hard? After all, Bob, I'm relyin' on you."

The way she called him Bob made his skin crawl. Nobody called him that anymore—and she was only doing it because she needed something. She thought she could manipulate him as well as she could her husband. "Maybe you shouldn't," Jitter said harshly, cursing himself for getting involved in all this mess. Yet he couldn't walk away from it, either. Couldn't walk away from her. "Where's Darnell now?"

"Where do you think?" Tess asked scornfully. "Where he's been ever since that dandy come sniffin' around here. Hidin' upstairs in our room!"

"We gotta go talk to him, Tess. You two need to either pony up that money or lay low for a while."

"Lay low!" Tess cried, horrified. "I'd as soon die. I've been layin' low all my life, far as I can tell, stuck out in backwater towns. I want to see something of life, finally—and I mean the good life."

"That ain't gonna be possible if they connect Darnell to that murder and he lands in jail, Tess."

"That's Darnell's business."

Jitter felt as though the wind had been knocked out of him.

"Well, isn't it?" she asked. "He killed the woman, not me. I don't know why I should suffer for it."

"You're his wife."

"But we're not in love, Bob. Haven't been for months." She swept a hand emotionally over her blond hair and looked through those eyes of hers, eyes that could have convinced a rooster to give up his feathers. Suddenly, her hand, cool and dry, plunked down on top of his. "I've got an idea."

"I don't think I want to hear it."

"You're such a gruff old soul!" She let out a tinkling laugh, but held fast to his hand. "Listen up. I've heard there's land to be had down in South America for cheap. Good land. Plenty of Confederates went down there after the war—rich planters. They're living high on the hog, and we could be, too!"

"You, me, and Darnell?"

"Nooooo, silly," Tess said, as if she were addressing an infant, "just you and me. We could run away together, leave this horrid place behind."

"You mean leave Texas? You and me?" Jitter had spent his whole life in "this horrid place," and kind of liked it, in fact. He couldn't imagine living in South America any more than he could imagine living in China.

"Why not?" Tess asked. "I've got the rest of our money—it's enough to get us down there, I know it."

"You can't just abandon Darnell, Tess."

"Sure I can!" she crowed. "What's he ever done for me?"

She would do it, he could see that. She had a feverish gleam in her eye—and such enthusiasm for this scheme that she was fairly quaking with it. Her grip was like a tourni-

quet on his hand. The plan was crazy, wrong. She would just
be using him to get away. Yet as he looked into those eyes,
he found something seductive in the idea of chucking everything and heading out. Maybe not to South America . . .
California would do.

"But even if'n we had money enough to get us there, then
what? A couple can't start with nothin'."

Tess bit her lip thoughtfully, but there was no doubt in
Jitter's mind that she knew the answer to his question. He
knew what she was going to say before she even opened her
mouth.

"I know!" she cried. "We forget the ring. And then we
can take the money we would've had to pay, and leave. Today. Now!"

And leave Darnell to pick up the pieces. What would become of him?

"Maybe somebody would even give us more money for
tellin' where Darnell was," Tess said.

"Like who, for instance?"

"That man down in the jail—his ex-partner. I bet we
could squeeze him good, with his hangin' date set for tomorrow."

Jitter shuddered. "You'd do that—send your own man to
the gallows?"

"He killed the woman, didn't he?" Tess asked. "All I'd
be doin' would be savin' an innocent man."

"But you wanted Darnell to do the murder," Jitter said.

She narrowed her eyes on him. "As you're so fond of
saying, nobody was holdin' a gun to his head."

Jitter thought about the folks he'd burned back at the
house. How long before Tess turned on him and used that
against him? He didn't trust her for anything. And when it
came down to it, he couldn't betray his own friend's life like
that, a man who'd taken him in and given him work. He'd
done some rotten things for Tess's sake, but he wouldn't do
this. He just couldn't.

Slowly, he shook his head, and with each shake Tess's expression transformed from bright-eyed optimism to gut-deep resentment. "You're just like him!"

"And you're just like Eve, holdin' out the evil apple for any man to take a hunk out of."

"Amen, brother."

At the sound of the voice coming from the doorway, both Jitter and Tess turned in unison. Tess gasped, and Jitter very nearly did himself. It was like seeing a man rise up from the grave, a ghost come back to haunt him. The man he'd thought he'd killed.

Unfortunately, Sam Winter looked very much alive.

"Barely a scorch," Sam joked as the man and woman in front of him stared in horror. As she appeared beside him, Millie had to admire his bravado. Sam faced down the two creatures looking positively cool, almost breezy, especially when he nodded in greeting to each. "Afternoon, ma'am, sir."

The man was the first to stand, but Tess wasn't far behind. She grabbed hold of the whiskey bottle on the table, as though it might be handy as a weapon, but Sam appeared more concerned about the gun her companion had holstered.

"That's not Darnell," Jesse muttered, coming forward, his hand as ready on his gun as Sam's was.

"That's not the man I spoke to a while back, either," Lloyd said, also stepping into the barroom, albeit slightly behind the other two. Which was just as well, since he carried no weapon.

"No," Millie said, moving between them so that the four formed an effective barricade in front of the door. She didn't want these two getting away from them now. "But that's Darnell's woman, and that's the man who tried to burn us alive."

"You have no proof of anything," Tess said acerbically.

To her surprise, Lloyd laughed bravely. "The lady protests too much, methinks. I happen to have received a promise of quite a bit of cash for a certain ring."

"Well, I ain't payin' it. Jitter here can attest to that. I didn't have nothin' to do with any murder."

Jesse's face froze. "Who mentioned a murder?"

The woman bit her red lower lip nervously. "Tell them, Jitter. Tell them I didn't have nothin' to do with anything."

The man named Jitter looked at her long and hard, his eyes cool and distant.

"Why, you traitor!" Tess cried. "You know I didn't."

"Seems like there's a lot here to sort out," Sam said. "But this time I think we'd best tend to it in a sheriff's office."

"That's fine by me," Tess said, answering his challenge. "I bet any sheriff would be glad to clap eyes on you. You're Sam Winter—there's a price on your head."

Sam smiled. "And this is my brother, Jesse, the reputed murderer. There's an even bigger price on his head, I guess. But even so, I expect a judge would take our word against yours any day, lady."

"You call that a lady?" Millie asked. "She doesn't even know enough to buy a dress that doesn't come up to her knees!"

The woman's face colored even more than it had when they accused her of burning people alive. "What do you know about anything?" she asked. "You're nothing but a pea-brained rich girl."

Millie blinked. "How dare you—you, you murderess!"

"Stop calling me that!"

"As the saying goes, if the shoe fits..." Millie jeered. "And in this case, it fits a lot better than that dress you've got on."

Sam shot Millie a warning look. "Will you lay off about the damn dress? We've got more important business here."

Millie felt herself flush. It might be petty, but she hated this woman. And she wasn't a bit afraid of Miss High-and-Mighty, either. "You might," she said, walking straight up to the Amazon herself, "but I'm still pretty steamed about the 'damn dress,' as you call it." Taking hold of a hunk of lace, she gave it a firm yank, ripping the lace clear down to Tess's waist, where it hung limply.

The woman's face drained to a chalky white. Her gray eyes glittered frighteningly, and then a long-nailed finger reached out and grabbed Millie's collar. Before Millie could so much as let out a grunt, Tess gave a tug that sent her reeling. Suddenly, Millie was more than angry, she was fighting mad. This woman might have gotten the best of her once, but she'd had help then. Millie was more than up to a rematch. She reached up and grabbed a hank of blond hair and pulled with all her might. Letting out a screech, Tess grabbed her arm and twisted, sending a searing pain shooting up her arm.

"Ouch!" Millie cried. She glanced up to see Sam, stupefied, staring at the spectacle of her scrapping with their enemy. "Are you going to do something?" she demanded hotly.

An evil little grin spread across his face. "You seem to be doing all right."

At that moment, Tess took advantage of her preoccupation with her husband to elbow Millie in the stomach. Letting out a grunt of pain, Millie recovered quickly and hurled herself onto her quarry's back, locking her arm around the woman's neck. From this vantage point, she was able to see the man named Jitter reaching surreptitiously for his gun.

"Sam, watch out!"

In that split second, a piercing explosion rang out in the room. Millie froze, her eyes closed. *Sam!* She'd warned him too late! She was almost afraid to open her eyes, terrified that she would find her groom sprawled out on the dusty, sticky floor.

Instead, when she could resist no longer, she found herself staring at Jitter, hunched over, clutching his arm. Standing over him was Sam, revolver still drawn. "Hand it over."

Jitter didn't respond, but to give the man his due, he hardly looked to be in a position to "hand" anything. Blood dripped down to the floor, mixing with other stains from spilled alcohol. The gun dropped to the floor, and Sam kicked it over to Jesse.

"Now get up," he said. "First we're going to round up your boss, and then we're going to take a visit to the jail-house."

"Not yet we aren't, Winter," a voice said from behind them. Jitter looked up, and at the same time, Tess, Millie and Sam swung their heads around.

Darnell Weems stood in the doorway where Sam had recently been standing himself. In his shaking hand was a gun aimed straight at Millie, but he was looking at Jesse. Looking at him like Tess and Jitter had been staring at Millie and Sam moments before, as though he'd never expected to see him again. As though he'd thought he was as good as dead.

"Hello, partner," Jesse said evenly.

Darnell didn't move, except for that twitching hand. The temperature was nowhere close to hot, but tiny beads of sweat appeared on his brow. "Jesse . . ."

Sam couldn't stop looking from the gun in the man's unstable hand to Millie, who it was still pointed at. "Why don't you put the gun down, Weems?"

Darnell didn't hear. He swallowed deeply. "I didn't expect to see you again, Jesse."

Everything about Jesse was still—his gaze on Darnell, his motionless body, his breathing. He, too, seemed aware that the gun was pointed at Millie. "I never expected to walk free again, Darnell. You set things up pretty good."

The gun quivered dangerously—and Millie wasn't the only one frighteningly aware of where it was pointed. Lloyd was gesturing for her to move away, but Tess, who was also in the sights of the gun, was even more disturbed.

"For God's sake, Darnell—point that gun at somebody else!" she cried.

Darnell kept staring at Jesse as if he hadn't even heard her. "I didn't mean to, Jesse." He bit his lip. "I didn't know...."

"Did you think you were killing *me?*" Jesse asked.

"Yes!" An anguished sob erupted from the man's throat. "But I didn't know what I was doing! I just—"

Quick as lightning, Jesse kicked the gun out of Darnell's hand, then reached out and whipped his hand behind his back. At the sudden movement, the room exploded into action. Tess came back to life underneath Millie, spinning until Millie fell off and found herself falling to the floor. When she hit, she found her fall padded by Jitter, whom Sam had felled in a single blow. Grabbing hold of Jitter both for balance and to make sure the wounded man didn't crawl out of the barroom, she watched Sam drag Tess away from her—though he couldn't keep her from landing a swift kick against Millie's hip, resulting in a clear footprint against the white of her wedding dress.

Millie clutched her side and shifted her seating on Jitter. "What do we do now?" she asked, looking at the two brothers and Lloyd, holding the husband and wife at bay. "How can we get all these people to the sheriff?"

"I'll fetch the law," Lloyd offered, running out the door.

At that moment, Sam looked down at Millie, concern written all over his face. Her heart flopped over in her chest.

"Are you all right, Princess?"

She got up, mindful of Jitter, and slapped the dust off her dress. "I'm fine," she replied, "but my wedding dress has seen better days."

At first Sam stared at her as if she'd gone loco, but then, as a muffled sound was heard from behind them, he turned. For the first time since she'd met him, and maybe for the first time in months, Jesse was smiling. Laughing, in fact. Millie giggled and then finally laughed, too, and when she looked back at Sam, he threw back his head and let out a joyful whoop.

Staring up into Sam's dancing gray eyes, Millie was certain she was the luckiest woman in the world. What other female from Chariton had ever gotten married, arranged a jailbreak and captured three vicious criminals, all in the course of twelve hours?

Chapter Eighteen

Fortunately, the jail in Fort Worth was much more spacious than the one in Chariton. Otherwise, it would have been a tight squeeze.

Of course, Sam and Jesse were locked in one cell, since they were known escapees. Darnell and Jitter had been put in another cell, with Darnell sweating and mumbling to himself so much that his cellmate looked as though he'd like to punch him. Which had left Tess and Millie segregated by themselves, until so many scuffles ensued that the local sheriff ordered Tess to join her friends and Millie to be left in a small isolated cell across the room from the others.

Lloyd—the one free man in the group—had protested bitterly when the local sheriff put Millie behind bars.

"Seems to me she done a goodly amount of damage," the sheriff said, taking in Tess's disheveled appearance.

Millie swelled with pride. "There!" she cried across the room to Sam. "The next time you accuse me of not being able to take care of myself, I'll remind you of this man's words."

"You won't be hearing that from me," Sam assured her. After today, he wouldn't think Millie incapable of anything.

"In fact," she boasted to the sheriff, "I masterminded the whole plan."

The sheriff laughed. "So I've got you to thank for my full house, do I?"

"Indeed you do."

Sam motioned across the room for her to be quiet. "There's such a thing as incriminating oneself, sweetheart."

The room remained tense and quiet for another hour, at which time Sheriff Tom McMillan, Ed, Toby and Colonel Lively walked into the jailhouse.

"Daddy!" Millie cried joyfully. "I was hoping you'd come."

"After this morning?" he asked. "I couldn't wait to see what you'd do next."

She straightened her shoulders proudly. "I caught the killers, that's what!"

The Fort Worth lawman took exception to her assertion. "Whoa, now, little lady. We don't know yet—"

"I didn't do a single thing!" Tess cried.

Suddenly, Horace looked over at the woman and at least one of her cellmates, his thick gray eyebrows crinkling in confusion. "Mr. and Mrs....Smith, isn't it?"

The room went quiet. For the first time, Tess Weems seemed to appear at a loss for words. Two red splotches appeared in her cheeks.

"Smith?" Millie asked, confused. "This is Tess Weems, Daddy—you know, the woman who tried to kill me that I was telling you about?"

"But I saw this woman just two days ago." He turned a more suspicious eye on Darnell, who had stepped back from the bars. "She and her husband. They called themselves Mr. and Mrs. David Smith!"

Sheriff Tom stepped forward, his jaw clenched. "I think you've got some explaining to do, mister. Whoever you are."

Darnell glanced from Tess to the two sheriffs and back at his wife again. Ever since being dragged to the jail, he'd looked like he was about to crack, and at that moment, it happened. "I didn't do it!" Darnell cried. "I never tried to kill anybody. Me and my wife, we're innocent."

"He's lying!" Jesse called out from the next cell.

"He confessed," Sam confirmed. "Every person here heard him confess."

Sheriff Tom raised his eyebrow skeptically, showing Sam exactly what he thought of the word of a kidnapper. "*I'll* get down to the bottom of this, Winter, don't worry."

His high-handed tone made Sam want to throttle the man—and Millie didn't seem too pleased, either. "Sheriff, Sam's right! Use your common sense!"

The sheriff shot Millie a seething glance. Clearly he hadn't forgotten her treachery of that morning, or the humiliation of being locked in his own jail cell.

Horace stepped forward, coming to within a foot of Darnell. "Son, you say you didn't kill anybody. Who did?"

Darnell bit his lip anxiously, hesitating.

"You can tell me," the colonel said in his kindliest voice.

After a moment's more hesitation, Darnell said quickly, "It was Bob Jitter what done the murder. And he tried to burn those other two."

The man seated behind him let out an angry sound and ran forward. "That's a lie!"

"It's true," Darnell went on, nodding toward but not turning to face his old employee. "He killed Salina Winter, and when those two come after us, he snuck back and tried to kill them, too, without even telling me."

"You're a coward, Darnell. A rat!"

"Just ask my wife," Darnell said. "He's crazy. We was tryin' to get away from him that day—that's why we used those names. We didn't want him to find us."

Horace and the two sheriffs turned back to Tess. The woman was looking placidly ahead of her, her gaze locked with her husband's. A tight smile tugged at her lips. "That's right," she said. "I told Darnell that if he couldn't fire that

Bob Jitter, then I wasn't going to stay on that farm another minute.''

"They're both lyin'," Jitter said, "tryin' to set me up. I'll admit to tryin' to burn the house down out yonder—but she wanted me to. 'Sides, nobody actually died there. I didn't kill nobody, and I never have. Leastwise, not in a good long spell.''

"Whose word are you going to take, Sheriff?" Tess asked. "A ranch hand's?"

Everyone but Millie, Jesse and Sam turned cold, appraising eyes on Jitter. It was looking bad for him. Out of all of them, he *did* look like a criminal. He had the dark, scarred, weather-beaten and inscrutable face of a man whose conscience forbade very little in this life. His narrow eyes grew wider as it became clearer that the tide was against him.

"Darnell killed the woman!" he cried. "Darnell did— because Tess told him she'd leave him if'n he didn't.''

Sam shook his head, unable to believe how the trio turned on each other.

"It's their word against yours," the sheriff said.

"His and mine," another man said.

All the occupants of the jail turned to stare at the newcomer, who stood just behind Horace and the sheriff with a bundle in his hand. The small, bespectacled man smiled affably, even as Sheriff Tom groaned.

"Tibbetts!" the sheriff said in exasperation. "What now?"

The man named Tibbetts bowed neatly to all gathered, then stepped forward. "*I* was also a witness to Mr. Weems's confession to the crime of killing Jesse Winter's wife. Furthermore, I also took notes during two prior conversations between Mrs. Weems and these two men—including one in which she and her husband agreed to pay a blackmailer money for a ring that was found at the scene of the crime.''

"You weren't there—nobody was in that saloon before those people came bustin' in!" Tess yelled.

Someone needed to give *her* advice on self-incrimination, Sam thought happily.

Tibbetts smiled secretively at the woman. "No one except 'a Mex,' I believe you called him." He unfolded the bundle in his arm, revealing a serape and sombrero. "I hid behind the bar when the pistols were brought out, but believe me, *señora,* I heard every single word spoken. And I have notes to prove it."

Millie smiled and clapped her hands together. "Show them the ring, Lloyd!"

Lloyd stepped forward and handed the ring to the sheriff.

"Look familiar?" Sam asked, feeling a surge of triumph move through him. Finally, this terrible nightmare would be over! He turned to Horace. "During my brother's trial, I tried to bring forward the ring as evidence that Darnell Weems might have committed the crime. The sheriff was having none of it."

Horace looked at the sheriff with raised brows. "Is that true?"

The sheriff's face reddened indignantly. "Absolutely not! I merely thought... Well, it was highly circumstantial. Highly."

"And highly important to my brother's defense," Sam muttered through gritted teeth.

The sheriff took a handkerchief out of his pocket and wiped his brow. "Naturally, now that someone can corroborate..."

"Naturally," Horace said, a stern, disapproving frown for the sheriff on his face. "I expect there'll be a new trial in Chariton soon. Very soon, if I have my say."

Millie looked at Sam and beamed him such a smile of happiness that it lit up the entire dreary room. "There!" she cried, jailbird to jailbird. "I told you my father had influence!"

"A toast," Horace said, raising his glass to the gathered company in the Livelys' dining room. The table was set with the finest plates, silver and crystal in honor of his daughter's marriage and the release of the bridal couple from jail. "To homecomings."

Millie smiled. "And to your new son-in-law?"

Horace nodded at Sam. "That, too."

"Then I want to add one," Sam said. "To women with gumption."

"To freedom," Jesse added.

"And detectives," Lloyd said, finishing the set. The company clinked their glasses and drank the best red wine in the colonel's cupboard.

Thanks to Horace's twisting the arm of the judge who had tried Jesse, he and his brother had been released on Horace's bond. Millie's father had also had some harsh words of criticism for the good sheriff, who would either have to mend his ways, fast, or find himself another line of work. Millie hoped it would be the latter. Too many people had suffered because of his prejudiced way of dispensing justice.

But after an entire evening of discussing everything from a detailed account of her and Sam's travels across Texas to Lloyd's agreement to form the Boyd and Tibbetts Investigation Agency, Millie was tired of thinking about the past. From now on out, she wanted to think about the future.

To that end, she rose, sending the men into action as each shot up out of his chair. "I suggest the men retire for brandy and cigars." She beamed a smile Sam's way. "I feel like taking a stroll."

"What a coincidence," Sam said. "I was beginning to feel a little restless myself."

The couple made a stately exit, passed through the kitchen to tell Alberta and Sonya what a success dinner had been at such short notice, then hit the back door running, and kept running until they were out of sight and earshot of anyone else.

In the darkness under the branches of a large elm tree, Sam suddenly stopped and swung Millie into his arms. "I've been waiting forever to kiss you."

She tossed her head. "And I've been waiting forever for you to mention how clever I was to get you out of jail and myself a husband all at the same time."

He sent her a quelling glance. "Millie, this business about our marriage . . ."

Her eyes widened in dismay. "It's perfectly legal."

"I know—but we never talked about it."

She looked him in the eye challengingly. "Don't you *want* to be married to me?"

"Of course!" he said, folding his arms around her. Millie took the opportunity to snuggle up against his broad chest—something she'd sorely missed doing these past few days. "It's you who I'm worried about. Would you want to be married to someone like me?"

"What do you mean?" she asked.

She could feel his heart thumping irregularly during his slight hesitation. "Well, you know. I'm not rich."

"That's all right," Millie said. "Daddy is."

"But we won't be living with your daddy. We'll be living on a farm, where there's always too much work to do and not enough people to do it."

Millie pulled back and frowned up at him. "Don't think you can frighten me away now, Sam. I'm in love with you. I don't care if you live in a one-room shack like Gus and Lou."

Sam looked down at her with a suspiciously bright smile. "Really?"

Suddenly, Millie became anxious. "W-well," she sputtered, "you don't, do you? You even said once that your house had four bedrooms."

Sam laughed. "I love you, Millie. And tomorrow I'm taking my wife home to a house with more room than we could ever use. And if you don't like it, I'll build you another one. I'll build you a house fit for..."

"A queen?"

"A princess," he said with a laugh. "The Princess Winter."

Millie threw her arms around him and squeezed tight. She was so choked with emotion she feared she couldn't speak. But, naturally, that didn't happen. "Oh, Sam. I think I'm the happiest woman alive." She looked up into his gray eyes, so full of love. "And don't you worry about all that work at the farm. Just think, now there will be two more people to help out."

"*Two* more?" Sam cupped her face in his strong hands, his eyes full of wonder. "Millie, you're not saying... You don't mean... I thought that was just a fib...."

"A fib?" She blinked in confusion. People just didn't lie about things like this! "Of course not! I could never live without Alberta."

"Alberta?" The poor man looked as if he were about to collapse. "Lord, Millie, when you said two, I thought..." He frowned. "We don't have money for a maid."

"But Alberta is like one of the family!" Millie protested. "She's *got* to come with me."

"If you're not the stubbornest—"

"Wife you ever had," Millie finished for him, laughing. "And didn't you say you'd been waiting forever to kiss me?"

Sam raised his arms in surrender. "Oh, hell, Millie, I love you so much," he said, pulling her to him again and lifting her so that their lips were inches apart. "We're together, that's all I care about. We'll work out the details later."

And the kiss he finally gave her made her think that maybe those little details wouldn't matter…so long as they had a calm, uneventful, thoroughly law-abiding future as man and wife stretching before them.

* * * * * *

Harlequin® Historical

Bestselling author **RUTH LANGAN** brings you nonstop
adventure and romance with her new Western series
from Harlequin Historicals

The Jewels of Texas

DIAMOND	February 1996
PEARL	August 1996
JADE	February 1997
RUBY	June 1997

Don't miss these exciting stories of four sisters as wild
and vibrant as the untamed land they're fighting to protect!

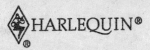

HARLEQUIN®

You are cordially invited to a
HOMETOWN REUNION

September 1996—August 1997

Where can you find romance and adventure,
bad boys, cowboys, feuding families, and babies,
arson, mistaken identity, a mom on the run...?
Tyler, Wisconsin, that's where!

So join us in this not-so-sleepy little town and
experience the love, the laughter and the
tears of those who call it home.

WELCOME TO A
HOMETOWN REUNION

Twelve unforgettable stories, written for you by
some of Harlequin's finest authors. This fall,
begin a yearlong affair with America's favorite
hometown as **Marisa Carroll** brings you
Unexpected Son.

Available in September at your
favorite retail store.

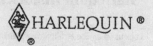HARLEQUIN ®

Look us up on-line at: http://www.romance.net

Harlequin® Historical

Back by popular demand!

National bestselling award-winning
author of **THE BARGAIN**

VERONICA SATTLER

presents

Where a dashing guardian and his fiery ward
discover a forbidden passion....

Don't miss this *sizzling* romance novel
available in September wherever
Harlequin Historicals are sold!

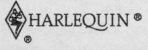

HARLEQUIN®

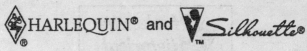
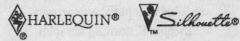 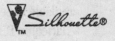